Røyken

By M.K. McGowan

Registered with the IP Rights Office
Copyright Registration Service
Ref: 26081666670

I

A warm breeze carried from the Gulf of Mexico moved the lifeless stalks and stringy tendrils of the once fruitful corn plants in a rhythmic swaying motion. The moon, full and proud, reflected the sun in a brilliance that bathed the field in a melancholic white hue. The night was still.

The moonlight revealed a lone figure amidst a small clearing of decaying plants, lying face down. The man lay as still as a corpse. A bundle of dead plants lay to the edges of the clearing in the large field.

A howl in the distance stirred the man. His eyes snapped open, and he turned his head on the ground, scraping his unshaven cheeks on the abrasive sun-scorched earth. It took several moments before he began to regain some of his senses and his brain to tune into the surroundings.

He looked at the soil. The moonlight revealed an orange, almost brown earth. The man muttered something incoherent; his voice was soft and lethargic. He could feel his forty-something body ache and moan as if he had been lying here for some time, in the same position flat on the hard earth.

Forty-something? Decades of smoking, drinking, and getting into weekly fisticuffs with local residents over misplaced eye contact or something more neanderthal, had left his skin scared and wrinkly.

Forty going on sixty.

His muscles were sore and tender like he had been running. A flash of memory zipped passed his mind's eye. Something had made him run, scared him. But he could not remember why or what it had ran from. For a man that spent most of his time in the bar or sitting in front of the TV watching soccer, he knew his body had been subject to some additional physical activity. He tried to think but his mind was missing the required files. It just clouded over, like a dull day blocking the sun.

He moved his hand to ready himself to sit up and felt something hard and cold by his side. Dulled in the moonlight was a worn-out machete. The long blade, once proud and sharp, was rusted and blunt. The blade had been clumsily secured to a splintered wooden handle with a single bolt that was inadequate to hold it on. This left the blade wonky and loose in its holder. He felt the edge but couldn't comprehend what it was. With his other hand pulled in, he slowly began to push himself up into a sitting position.

He heard a howl in the distance but ignored it. Instead, he snuffed at it and rubbed his eyes, smearing abrasive grains of dirt into them forcing him to blink. The man, now sitting up, his legs in front, looked around to get his bearings.

Where the hell was he? His mind was blank to allow any kind of panic of being lost to set in. He turned his head hearing and feeling his neck crack.

The wind blew his thin string-like hair across his face. The putrid smell of decaying plants helped to jog his memory. He looked down and examined his hands. Small blisters and broken angry skin helped his mind comprehend more of what he was doing here. He had been cutting down these old plants, long after the harvest had finished. One of the few workers kept on the farm to tidy up ready for the next season. He looked down at the machete. The old thing was about as useful as a chocolate fire guard. He remembered trying to hack away at the stalks earlier in the day. The machete was useless at chopping the stalks and took a lot more energy to accomplish.

Then there was that flash, like someone had crept up on him and flashed a powerful a torch into his eyes. Even though he remembered it being early afternoon, and the sun was high, the flash had been extreme. He remembered a burning sensation that made him raise a hand to his cheek to inspect the damage. No burns or injuries could be felt now, but he could still feel the heat of the light. After that he could not remember anything, he tried but all his mind's eye could show him was white. All he could feel was the shortness of breath, as if he had just recovered from a case of the flu; or a heavy night smoking illicit cigarettes bought from a local merchant.

The man pondered a while longer but a strange sensation on his neck blocked his reminiscence and he felt the area. A warm deep red liquid, almost black in the moonlight, coated his fingers. He felt it again and brought his hand close to his face to inspect the dampness.

His neck was wet with blood, and he could smell something potent in their air, or maybe it was something lingering in his nose? Jesus, had he fallen or been severely cut by the corn blades? No, it was probably that damn owner's dog. That bastard beast always chased him, and whenever it had the chance would bite when his back was turned. Sure, he had given it reasons to over the last few weeks when the owner was not looking; a good smack or a kick when no one was looking. He knew it was that damn dog, must have been.

The howl came again in the distance. This time he

acknowledged it as that dog. Oh, he would give it to him now. His train of thoughts were interrupted when he heard a rustling behind him. He snapped his head around and strained his eyes to improve his vision.

The corn was less dense now it was either dead or dying, but still he could only see as far as the moonlight would allow, after that the darkness consumed the rest of the field.

Something in the darkness disturbed the plants, too hard to be the breeze coming from the Gulf of Mexico. Like someone had stepped and crushed the stalks under their weight. Clumsily getting to his feet he raised the machete and slowly walked towards the darkness.

'Fuckin' dog. You gonna get more than a boot now,' he said aloud and firmly gripped the handle. 'C'mon out, you little fuck. Yer head's gonna make a nice trophy.'

The man tried to clear his head by shaking it, which did nothing but make him slightly dizzy. Pressing his dry lips together he whistled to try to attract the mutt to his location so he could have a good swipe at the animal. One swipe? No, two or three at least to put it down, then he could carve away at the bastard's neck and send it to the owner's front door. It was a tough animal. His previous attempts at kicking always resulted with the dog snapping at his legs.

Three steps in he began to feel something ring in his head: a migraine, a hangover? It was most likely the latter as he was partial to a drink upon waking and then any he could get away with when no one was looking. He tried to ignore the pain as a hangover was nothing new to him, but this was slightly different. The pain was more like a severe ringing sensation that began to double his vision. He attempted to stop the pain by shaking and banging his head with his palm but to no avail. Shit! This was bad and it came like a freight train.

His eyes began to close, the blunt machete fell from his grip, and he clasped his hands to his eyes in pain. Jesus, this was the mother of all headaches. The pain grew exponentially, and he fell to his knees; the thought of the dog now beaten out by the throbbing pain. His head felt like it was breaking apart, like something was burrowing deep through his skull trying to get into his brain. His ears felt like they were bleeding. The pressure forced his skull to expand, or at least this was the sensation he was experiencing. He screamed out and placed his head between his legs. His feet kicked at the floor; his mouth foamed with saliva that began to drip in long threads. Pressure forced blood vessels to expand and protrude from his temples so that his flesh resembled more like a leaf than human skin.

Blood began to seep from his nose and clear yellow liquid ran from his ears as the pain grew and his vision blurred. The ringing grew louder, and louder until his ears were deaf to the world around.

This was it; he was about to die here, here on this farm, doing hard work for some ungrateful penny-pinching bastard.

To keep his eyes open was too painful; the moonlight was bright enough to burn deep into the blackness of his brain and rattle whatever matter he had used over the course of his life. The rustling in the field seemed to come from all directions but he was unable to hear or acknowledge them. The ringing in his ears sounded like a fire bell. His stomach cramped and he vomited green bile and half-digested food washed down with tequila onto the ground below. The taste of stomach contents and the drilling in his head combined and made him regurgitate even more until there was nothing left to come up. His stomach continued to spasm forcing him to take deep breaths whenever his body allowed. This was it. His head was about to explode in any moment.

And then —

And then —

The pain just stopped. It stopped as quickly as it had started. The ringing stopped and he once again heard the wind through the stalks. The drilling in his head ceased. He no longer had tunnel vision. He began to regain his senses. He was about to question what the hell had just happened but then another sensation came over him, flooding his mind and body. This sensation was pure anger. Pure heated aggression. He looked at the ground, now soaking up his stomach contents into the dry soil and saw the machete. In one swift movement he snatched it from the ground and leapt to his feet.

He looked around, scanning the surroundings like Arnold Schwarzenegger in those old Terminator movies. Blood mixed with mucus dripped from his nose and mouth. A dog barked in the distance making him snap around to face the direction of the noise. Raising the machete like a Red Indian warrior he launched himself into a sprint ripping through the corn plants.

Leaves and fibres slapped at his face and legs as he dragged his aching body through the field like an unstoppable juggernaut. The dog barked like it was calling out to him for a one-on-one dual, a show down. The man attempted to call back but instead the outburst was a high-pitched scream. Corn broke free from their stalks as the animal acknowledged the man's scream of aggression and sprinted towards him.

The dog broke out of the darkness like a demon from hell. Its coat black and slick like oil in the moonlight, its eyes reflected in the ambient light which looked like two burning lamps. Yet the teeth were white, which were easy to see as it launched its large body straight towards the man's neck. The animal was quick, too quick for the man to respond. The dog launched itself; jaws open wide with large canines poised forward aiming for the man's neck as a primal instinct.

The man twisted his body quickly and threw the animal away with his elbow. He swung the machete aimlessly in the direction the animal was thrown without looking. The machete missed the animal and hit the top of a corn stalk snapping off the dying head.

The beast landed clumsily and rolled on the ground but quickly got up and turned, resetting itself for another attack. Snarling and foaming at the mouth it bared its teeth and made another attempt at its victim. A miscalculated move as it went for the man's ankle.

The animal sank its teeth deep into the skin and clamped down hard connecting with the bone. The animal began to pull and twist, grinding its teeth on the bone trying to free the foot away. Its grip was strong; the dog's powerful jaw and strong teeth easily splintered the bone. The man did not scream, nor did he winch at the pain; he did not respond as a normal person would. The animals ferocious shaking, as if it was playing with a toy, severed the muscles and nerves of the foot. The man buckled to the ground and screamed. Alas, his screams were not of pain, which he barely felt, but of hatred and rage for the beast.

The dog was still holding onto his ankle, twisting its head to break the foot away. The man lifted the machete high above his head and brought the blade down hard against the animal's skull. The blade bounced off the dog's head splitting the thin skin and flicking blood into the air. The man repeated the move three more times before the animal let go.

The dog backed off but did not whimper. Dark blood ran free around the dog's black fur that looked like slick oil. The demon dog reasserted itself, pulling in its front legs and bending the rear. The man, blinded by rage, did not read the situation, and brought the machete back up ready to finish-off the animal. His kneeling position had put him right at the dog's height. He tried to pull in his leg and stand but the foot just dragged along the ground like a useless appendage that no longer responded to his demands.

The dog was fast, too fast for the man. Even in his rage, his body was still only able to react slowly. The animal launched, snatching the man by the neck. It bit hard into the flesh, hitting both major arteries and squeezing the windpipe. The man gurgled and tried to scream that sounded like a high-pitched rasp as the windpipe was constricted.

Blood gushed three feet from the dog's mouth as the man's heart pushed the fluid through the open veins. The restricted flow of oxygenated blood to the brain caused the man's vision to become impaired and his movements lethargic. The dog shook its head violently, tearing out his windpipe. It briefly let go and then snatched the rigid trachea for a better grip. Air wheezed through the severed hole from his throat and the man was unable to breathe.

His head was pulled forward as the dog yanked on the windpipe tearing it from his neck. With his final act of anger, the man drove his blunt old machete hard into the dog's neck. Twisting and pushing with the little energy he had left until the blade came out the other side. Meat and cartilage squelched against the blade.

The dog did not let go, even when both major veins were severed. The man held the dog's head with his free hand and pushed as hard as he could, air wheezing from his exposed neck and torn windpipe. He tried to remain upright, but his brain had had enough from the lack of oxygen, and he began to fall backwards; still holding onto the dog's head with one hand and the machete with the other. The animal's grip loosened, and the dog fell with the man landing on his chest.

The man's eyes remained wide open as he lay on his back looking up at the black sky; his grip on the machete beginning to loosen. Both the man's and the beast's blood ran free from their open wounds and mixed in a pool besides them. Man, and man's best friend lay twitching in the cornfield as their lives drained away with their blood.

Slowly he let go of the machete and his hand fell to the side, while the other fell limp on the dog's back. The last of the air in his lungs wheezed from his open windpipe with blood trickling from the empty veins.

The dog finally let go and slumped into a ball besides the man. The beast huffed its last breath and then stopped. The man's head fell to the side. With his vision fading, and the blackness closing in, his final view of the world was of two long and grey arms reaching out of the darkness for him.

2

The sun crept through a small gap between the bedroom curtains that woke Rachael before her alarm had chance to activate. The sun was pleasantly warm despite being mid-winter. The golden brilliance of the morning sun highlighted her messy blonde hair that rested on her face and pillow, in beautiful autumn yellows. Even in her late thirties she remained stunning, without the need for make-up.

Winter in Norway could range from mild and wet, to heavy snowfall and arctic conditions. The western parts of Norway mostly get rain that comes from all angles; "liquid sunshine," as the locals would call it. So far, this winter seemed to be somewhere in the middle. It was early January, and the snow was just beginning to settle in thin white layers after a very wet and icy period over December.

Rachael moved the strands of blonde hair away from her face and rubbed her eyes. Her movements began to rouse the man lying next to her from his not-so-silent slumber with a groan.

'Are you making coffee?' he asked, keeping his eyes closed and smiling in anticipation his fiancée would be willing to leave the warmth of the bed first.

'Give me ten more minutes then I might have a think about it,' she replied and closed her eyes again.

It was only a minute before the alarm on her phone played a summery tune with birds and waterfalls. The outside could not be further from a summer garden.

Røyken is situated south of Oslo, running down west of the Oslo fjord. The name Røyken translated to *The Smoke* on account that every spring and autumn the sea temperature is different to the air bringing creeping fog to the region.

The sun gave a false sense of warmth to anyone indoors until they went outside. Cyclists, brave enough to venture out in this weather dressed in their best skin-tight outfits resembling something from *Tron*, would quickly realise their errors and find their testis somewhere inside their stomachs, like whimpering puppies form an icy glare.

Rachael opened her eyes once again to the world. At the back of the house were farmlands. The morning did not officially begin until she heard the tractor coming back from ploughing the roads, or the deep reverberating *moos* from the cows staying warm in the large sheds. Rachael did not even need to look at the clock anymore. This was routine, and in the short time of living in Røyken they adapted their morning routine to the daily running of the Olsen farm.

'Okay, okay, I will make the coffee. Don't be sleeping when I get back,' she dug her elbow into the man's back to stop him going back off to sleep. 'Do you hear me, Adrian?'

Adrian grunted, 'Huh, what? Yes, yes. I'm awake,' Adrian sat up. Stubble darkened his face that felt like sandpaper as he rubbed the dried spittle away from his mouth.

His dark hair was spiky with product that hadn't washed out from the previous day. His dark brown eyes met the sunlight that turned them hazel. He squinted, wrinkling up his face. For man in his late thirties his face wrinkled to that of someone much older first thing in the morning.

He checked the clock, 'Bloody hell,' he said forgetting to tone down the Yorkshire dialect for a favourable posh English one. 'I need a job where I don't have to get up this early; role on the weekend.'

Rachael came back downstairs to the bedroom with two cups of coffee. The house was built with the kitchen and living room on the top floor and the bedrooms on the first, as is standard for most Norwegian homes that are built on hard granite with a slight incline.

They sat in bed drinking coffee and flicking through their phones. Rachael was already answering emails while Adrian looked at videos or read the UK news websites. Both being native from the UK meant they liked to have one foot in Norway and the other in the UK. They both spoke Norwegian, but only Adrian was fluent; he needed to be as one of the town's respected general practitioners.

'How did you sleep?' Rachael asked.

Adrian's eyes lowered, 'Okay I guess.'

Rachael turned to face him. She knew he was holding back the truth. Adrian was not a very good liar.

'I don't mean to intrude when I ask, but you were talking a lot in your sleep and at one stage you caught me with your elbow.'

'Sorry, I hope I didn't hurt you,' he said without looking.

'No, but you seemed to be having nightmares again. Was it…?' she stopped herself from saying anymore. To say more would bring the nightmares flooding back.

'I don't remember. What did I say?'

She smiled, 'It was nothing; mostly incoherent gibberish.'

It was Adrian's turn to see his fiancée was lying, 'Please tell me the truth. What did I say?'

Rachael took a deep breath; she didn't want to say anything, but Adrian was insistent, 'I think you were back there again. You said something about an inbound Chinook then some medical jargon. It has been a long time; have you been thinking about those days again?'

Adrian held back. He felt uneasy and a little angry. But that anger was quickly quenched and replaced by shame, 'No. It must have been nothing more than a bad dream. It happens.'

Rachael took his hand, 'It's okay,' she said softly. 'What you went through, what you saw and did will always be with you. But you have moved on, you got away. You are good at your job, you help people. You should focus on the positives. You will never have to relive those times ever again,' she leaned over and kissed his cheek. 'I am always here to listen to you. Never feel ashamed to tell me your feelings. You are not a robot, you are the most kind, caring man I have ever met. That's why I tricked you into proposing.'

Adrian's remorse turned into delight. He knew how fortunate he was to have such a clever, strong, and passionate woman. He quickly changed the subject, feeling uneasy talking about *this* subject, 'Are you going into the lab today?'

'I shall, although I think I will be home around two today. I have one subject in at ten and then I am free to write on the article. So, we can do a bit of shopping. What time will you finish in the clinic?'

Adrian opened his phone's calendar, 'Last patient today will be around two. I can probably be home around three unless we have an emergency,' he said scratching the back of his head. 'Surely as a Ph.D. you can work from home now? I thought that's what technicians were for; to do all the work for you guys?'

'Cheeky bugger, we work just as hard as the techies,' Rachael poked her fiancé in the ribs.

His phone vibrated with a message from the clinic. He huffed displeasingly, 'Oh for God's sake.'

Rachael brought the cup away from her mouth, 'Something wrong?'

'Mrs. Johansen has requested a house call before I go into work.'

'Really? How many times over the last week has she had you out to her? And isn't it someone else's turn for being on call?'

'She is my patient I have to go out to her. It won't be anything important. She's been lonely since her husband died a few years ago. I suppose she just needs the company. I will get the regional care nurse to go round after I leave and just make sure she's okay.'

Rachael smiled, 'Just as long as she isn't trying to steal you away from me then I don't mind how many times you go round to another woman's house, Doctor Hope.'

Adrian laughed and brushed his matted dark hair like a photo modal, 'You know you are the only woman for me. Besides, where else will I find a clever blonde bombshell?'

Mrs. Johansen reached out and shook Adrian's hand. Her grip was weak reminding Adrian of just how old Mrs. Johansen was. She went to stand but Adrian declined.

'No, please stay seated,' Adrian knelt beside the old lady. 'Now, how are you today? Are you still taking your supplements and medication?'

Mrs. Johansen's voice quivered as she replied, 'I am, doctor. But I keep getting these awful pains from my hips and down my legs.'

'And the medication isn't relieving these symptoms?'

The old lady rubbed the backs of her liver-spotted hands before correcting her glasses. She sat hunched in the chair, her shoulders leaned forward showing the progression of osteoporosis. But then at her age of eighty-nine this was to be expected.

She reminded Adrian of the *Simpson's* character *Hans Moleman*, with her large thick glasses and almost toad-like face.

'I take the medication, like you told me, but the pain won't go away. I wonder if it is because of this awful weather we're getting now,' she let her hands relax by the sides of the chair and eased herself back.

'Yes, it is getting very cold now. The nurse comes around daily, doesn't she?'

Mrs. Johansen squinted and leaned towards him, 'Eh? Say that again. David? I don't know anyone called David.'

Adrian smiled, 'No, not David,' he raised his voice and exaggerated his words so she could understand. 'The nurse… she comes and visits you every day?'

The old lady sat back smiling, 'Oh, yes, yes. She comes and helps me with cooking and helps me do my washing. But after she leaves it gets hard. My hands hurt in the evenings, and I can't move around so quickly anymore.'

Adrian already knew this. A walking stick besides the old lady's chair, and the wheelchair in the kitchen he had ordered for her a few months ago when her legs became weak, highlighted her decline in abilities to do most things for herself. He couldn't help but feel sadness for her.

She had lost her husband two years ago to a heart attack that had left her empty inside. She was a woman who had always been strong. But after her husband's death her health began to decline and was continuing to worsen by the month. And to cap it all off, no family.

Her only son wanted nothing to do with her since he was not mentioned in the will of his father. And why should he be? He had spent most of his adult life travelling around the Mediterranean, collecting sexually transmitted diseases and hospital bills he couldn't afford; expecting his parents to bail him out every time.

Adrian rubbed his mouth to try and stop the words coming out, but he needed to put his emotions away and do what was best for Mrs. Johansen, 'You're not going to like what I have to suggest, but I think it is time to consider a home, Mrs. Johansen.'

The old lady just looked at her doctor and smiled, 'But I have a home, Doctor Hope.'

Adrian reached out and took her hand, 'I mean a home where people can take care of you, you will be around people you can talk to and play games with,' he cringed at his last comment, like he was talking to a five-year old. 'I mean, you will have things to do. Mostly I want to make sure you are kept warm, especially in this cold. We are in for a very cold winter, Mrs. Johansen.'

Her face turned from a smiling toad to a cringe. She repeated herself, 'But, this is *my* home. My husband and I bought this house in 1953; we raised our son here, spent Christmas here. My husband died here. I am not leaving my house; I am not leaving my husband, Doctor Hope.'

Adrian felt his throat stiffen at Mrs. Johansen's words. This house had been hers and her husband's life. To leave this place would be to leave the memory of her husband and sixty years of marriage. All those Christmases, all of those birthdays, all were celebrated and shared under this roof. Adrian was not yet married and thus could not relate to the notion of sharing such a life. Hell, in today's world, all couples do is wake up, go to work in different places (sometimes different countries) come home late, eat, sleep, and maybe find time to make love. They probably spend less time with one another and more time at work.

And here was Mrs. Johansen, beginning to smile at all the memories this house had seen. She tried to explain to this fairly young doctor that a building can also be a living entity that one could not live without.

'I only wish, Mrs. Johansen, that mine and Rachael's life would be even a fraction of you and your husbands,' he cleared his throat. 'But a house is just bricks and mortar. I completely understand your attachment here, and I really wish we could do more. But as your GP I have to put your health and safety first. I am more than just a signature on a prescription, I am here for you. But in this case, I think that your hip pain is worsening and the fact the medication is not working as well as it once did makes me think that round the clock assistance is a better way forward than a nurse call once a day,' he stood and looked towards the kitchen adjacent to the living room.

He saw coffee grinds on the counter and some on the floor. A spoon lay decadently on the side with brown stains running off the counter and down the cupboard door, 'May I ask you how long your hands have been giving you trouble?'

Mrs. Johansen quickly held her hands as if to hide them from the doctor, 'Oh these old things? No, I don't have any trouble with them. Just the cold, that's all,' her voice was of little convincing to Adrian.

'Now, Mrs. Johansen, I know you are having problems.'

'No, no, please I don't have any troubles with my hands.'

Adrian saw her rubbing them frantically trying to warm them up. It was clear the arthritis was progressing to other areas. He had seen her knuckles and fingers beginning to misshapen when he shook her hand today. She had never taken his hand before and may have been trying to gain some warmth from him. Now he was thinking about heat, he had felt the icy chill inside the house when he came in. His patient was in more pain than she let on, and it seemed she couldn't even make a coffee or light a fire anymore.

'Mrs. Johansen, I understand that leaving your home is going to be a choice only you can make. However, as your doctor and as someone who is genuinely concerned for you, please just have a long think.'

A car pulled up outside that caught Mrs. Johansen's attention, 'Oh, it's Agnes,' the old lady's eyes widened in excitement.

Agnes was the regional nurse that had been coming to see Mrs. Johansen for the past seven months. Sometimes she even brought her dog to cheer the old lady up.

Mrs. Johnson heard the German shepherd bark at some birds, 'Oh wonderful, she brought Dolphus,' she clapped her hands together in excitement.

Adrian took the opportunity to bid Mrs. Johansen a good day so he could talk to the nurse about the possibility to move his patient from this icy tomb and into a warm home. He went outside and felt the Nordic winter bite at his cheeks. The dry icy air made him cough large clouds of steam into the crisp atmosphere.

'Morning Adrian,' Agnes said leaving her car.

'Morning, Agnes. Before you go in, I think it is a good idea that we try to get Mrs. Johansen into a home. Her health is getting worse, and I really doubt she is capable of doing things for herself. I looked into the kitchen and found coffee all over the counter. She is really in a bad shape. Just make sure she gets a warm breakfast and some heat into the room.'

'Don't you worry I will have a word with her. We'll get her to rethink. Tell you what, I'll plan a trip up to the homes over the weekend and get her to meet some of the inmates,' Agnes laughed.

Adrian smiled and understood Agnes was only joking, 'That sounds wonderful. I will write her a stronger prescription of corticosteroids, if you could collect them for her after midday that would be wonderful,' he patted the dog. 'Hello boy. Your winter coat is looking majestic.'

The dog slurped at his hand and tried to paw him.

Agnes smiled, 'No problems, Adrian. I have a few more patients to visit and will do the prescriptions around one.'

Adrian walked to his car and opened the door. He felt something at the back of his neck and turned to look back at the small house nestled between two others that ran up onto a rocky hill near the woods. The place now felt like it was alive; that he could feel the disapproving eyes of Mr. Johansen's ghost glaring at him from the bedroom window. The thought gave him the shivers and he quickly started the engine.

Adrian finished with his last patient for the day, this time a young woman requesting to see a specialist for a nose operation. This was easy enough to do. A quick email to the hospital and the young woman left smiling. He closed his computer and decided to leave ahead of his planned time. He got into his Ford Punto and drove to the train station to collect Rachael.

Adrian saw a purple stain on Rachael's white blouse, 'Were you at an office party or something?'

'Oh God, we had this ten-year old boy in for testing today and he decided it was a good idea to throw his drink over me.'

Adrian quipped, 'Perhaps you should have him in for further examination?'

Rachael failed to see the humour, 'Perhaps we need to enforce parents to be a little stricter with their kids.'

'Now, you know the law; you cannot take a hand to kids anymore,' Adrian's tone was like an adult speaking to a child.

'No, I don't believe in that. But these parents need to stop looking for excuses and start taking responsibility for their kid's actions. Still, he was not the worst I have had in. Remember that day I had to be picked up from work because that girl went on a rampage throughout the waiting room? All because her mother decided it was a wonderful treat to feed her sugar for breakfast and then bring her in?'

'Oh yes. At least those bite marks have faded now.'

Rachael turned her head towards him, 'But, we are making some progress. Preliminary statistics are showing a changed diet reduces glutamine levels in the brain that eliminates the need for medication. That is what we are aiming to do, and it is actually working for the test subjects with ADHD,' she waited for a response that never came. 'Sorry, did you want to get technical?'

'You want to put me out of a job?' Adrian replied.

The road curved and wound around farmland and hills with dense forests leading all the way to Sweden some one hundred and fifty kilometres east. A large school for five- to twelve-year-olds spanned most of the lower part of the hill to the left. Most of the town's meetings took place in the school's gym since it was big enough to accommodate people. If they were to turn left up the hill they would venture into a small community of houses, instead they continued on this road going down under a bridge and bending to the left. Adrian flicked on his indicator and waited for the car to pass before turning right. This road was next to farmland surrounded by more forests. Adrian pulled the car to the left off the road and onto their driveway without indicating.

The house wasn't grand, but in these parts, property was much cheaper than their city counterparts. The house was mostly wood as opposed to the orange brick construction the UK chooses. It had been painted white before they bought it that made it look glamorous. The small balcony at the front was more for decoration than usable. The balcony at the back, however, was used. The sun would rise to the right of the house and set to the left, which gave them the best light in the summer. But now it was winter, and they didn't venture out much; maybe to shovel snow, but there was little need for that at the moment. Adrian parked the car on the drive and saw an elderly man wave to them from the next house to their left.

'Oh look, it's your best friend,' Adrian said to Rachael.

Rachael looked to her left and saw their neighbour. He had seen the car and was already making his way to the hedge fence to greet them.

'Oh God, no I don't want to get into a conversation today. I am just so bloody tired,' she rubbed her eyes hoping their neighbour would see her tiredness.

Rachael unclipped her seat belt and ran out, just making the front door before the neighbour got to the fence. It was now up to Adrian to greet the man.

Harold Klaus was a retired cell biologist and by the looks of things and his constant talkative nature he was not enjoying retirement that much. Often, he would speak of just finding a small lab and going in one or two days a week to keep his hand in. Harold was very good at keeping people's attention to his ramblings. But because his neighbours were of the scientific nature, he felt the desire to engage in long and deep discussions about medicines and clinical trials. Last time he had caught Rachael and had her talking for over an hour when she was trying to get shopping inside and into the freezer. Now Adrian had to keep him entertained.

'Hi Adrian, good day?' the elderly man said from behind the fence. He enjoyed conversing in English, and like many Norwegians, his grasp of the language was impeccable.

'Yeah, was okay. Busy though. I just need to sit down for a while,' he replied

'A lot of patients today? I remember working in a hospital. Researcher of course,' Harold stepped closer to the fence.

Adrian thought he would stride over it but was relieved when he didn't.

'Yes, full clinic again,' Adrian lied. But to him this was a white lie and was necessary to try to stem the conversation quickly.

'Are you having anything nice tonight?' Harold continued.

'Oh, chicken and rice... the usual.'

'Rita and I are having steak; we went to Sweden this morning. Not much else to do in retirement. Does Rachael need a laboratory technician?' Harold chuckled.

Adrian smiled slightly enough to acknowledge his neighbour. The old man adjusted his glasses using a finger to push them back onto his face.

'We should have you both round one evening. Just for some wine. Sweden is much cheaper you know, and we have stocked up some lovely French vintage.'

Adrian knew Harold didn't have vintage wine but said he would need to ask Rachael first in case she had made work plans.

'Well, if you change your mind, doctor, do just pop round. You never need to ring the bell,' Harold looked up at the sky. 'Should be a clear night tonight, forecast says snow early morning and cloudy for a few days. I have a new telescope and fancy myself as a bit of an amateur astronomer. From the back we can see Orion's belt,' Harold's face lit up hoping it would also spark some interest in his physician.

'Actually, that does interest me. Never took up astronomy but I always fancied a telescope. I should have asked Rachael for one last Christmas,' Adrian smiled, this time with genuine interest.

'Ah, just come round tonight if you're not too tired,' Harold waited a moment before getting down to business. 'Also, could you update my prescription for my neck?'

Adrian laughed, 'I can't right now, but sure. I will make a note and sort that out for you tomorrow. I don't think you need to come into the clinic so shouldn't be a problem.'

Adrian went inside and took off his shoes. The warm heated floor was welcoming to his frozen feet. Rachael was upstairs in the living room with her laptop open; answering emails that had been sent on her journey home.

'You should stop working when you're at home you know; not healthy,' Adrian said.

Rachael glanced up, 'A researcher never stops working; we're not physicians,' she smiled and looked back down at her screen.

Adrian sniffed and then replied, 'The benefit of being a GP means I can take some time for myself. A reason I never took the research road.'

Rachael briefly glanced up from her laptop, 'It has its pros and cons. If I want my own group someday, I need papers. The group is fine, but I just don't think they are as clinically orientated as me. Rather than finding a new way to bring treatments to the clinic they just want to boast how much they know about a pathway. Nothing meaningful for the patient comes out of that.'

She was right in a sense, and Adrian knew this. Far too many researchers invest their time and energy into screaming *"hey, look what I know"* rather than being proud and claiming, *"we just found a new way to deal with this disease"*. Sometimes even scientists forget their purpose for the job.

3

Harold and his wife Rita had recently moved back to Norway from Sweden after almost twenty years. It was a good choice as they wanted to be closer to their children and now grandchildren. Taking retirement just over a year ago from his lecturing position at Gothenburg University was a simple decision to make for Harold. All he ever wanted to do after finishing his Ph.D. - now a distant memory - was to work in the lab and aspire to become a group leader. This he achieved very early in his career. But when the only work he could get were contracts for one or three years with several months of unemployment in-between, it soon became a difficult choice of leaving the lab completely and teaching the next generation of students on a full-time permanent basis; these were and are still very challenging for any scientist in the world.

To change the world as a scientist you need a good idea, good resources, financing, and staff. As a group leader raising funds for research and paying salaries to his staff were beginning to keep him awake at night.

After having their first child it became apparent that he needed a permanent position. Happily, the university offered him a fellowship position, which he held for two years. Four years later he held the position of senior lecturer and a seat at the university board, reading through Ph.D. applications. Before his retirement he had tried in vain to persuade the board to change the rules of entry onto the Ph.D. to be more like the UK; taking on candidates with experience as well as those that have managed to achieve superb grades through hard work, or in rare cases, knowing how to flirt with the lecturers to get what they wanted. Happily, those students were found out very quickly during and after their studies.

After the kids moved back to Norway, he took retirement; although retirement was not as pleasant as it once seemed. He had been a workaholic during those years, from seven-thirty in the morning until six or seven at night. Going from a thousand miles an hour to zero was quite the shock. Sure enough, he enjoyed reading about science in the journals, but without access to the University's library, most journals were restricted to the abstract only.

He had taken up amateur astronomy and had become quite good at recognising constellations and planets from memory rather than having to reach for the book every time. But during the day, he was bored.

Rita had spent most of her life looking after the kids while Harold worked full time. She had worked in the same labs as him but as a technician and not a researcher. She had never aspired for a doctoral degree and instead opting to remain as a lab hand. Both their kids, now in their late thirties, lived and worked in Oslo trying to make ends meet and remain employed. Harold had attempted to steer them away from the unforgiving world of science as a career. Even though science is his passion, it was not a stable job with normal working hours. Instead, the youngest had chosen a career in sales and was doing pretty well. The eldest went to university to study genetics but ended up transferring to the medical school and becoming a physician much to his father's ribbings about how physicians didn't understand the body.

The forecast called for a clear cold night. But the clouds had formed sooner than expected. Harold took the opportunity to gaze through his telescope before the clouds obscured most of the interesting astral bodies.

He used the view finder and some coordinates to point the Dobson telescope into a region and then focused in. Saturn was bright, and its rings could just be made out like a halo. He had often thought about installing a night vision tube into the mechanics for fun and would get round to it one day when he could find something cheap.

During the spring and autumn, he would sit out in the back garden for hours looking at the moon or trying to find celestial bodies using a guidebook and binoculars. But now in winter he simply could not be outside for too long since his cervical vertebrae had succumbed to osteoporosis, leaving him in constant need of strong painkillers. Adrian had prescribed strong medication for the discomfort, which Harold supplemented with plenty of brown cheese to help his bones. The supplements and medication helped ease the pain and Harold always put a brave face on his condition, blaming a flare up to bad weather or winter. But both he and Rita knew his condition was slowly crippling him.

Harold continued to admire the sky, training the telescope onto the middle star of Orion's belt observing the constellation by moving the telescope from left to right.

Something caught his eye in the view finder, passing diagonally in the eye piece. He took his eye away and looked over the top of the telescope. He saw nothing and put it down to a bit of dust in the living room passing the lens. He found his spectacle cloth and gave the eyepiece a quick wipe. Sometimes a fly would zip by the lens giving a similar result.

He returned to the view finder and continued to look at the star. A moment later the object passed again in the same direction.

He pulled back and used the sight mounted to the side to get a distant view of Orion's belt.

He had two of the stars of Orion's belt in view now. The glowing object passed both stars in a figure of eight with very fast and smooth actions around the turns.

Harold called for Rita to come and look at it and to also bring his binoculars from their case in the kitchen drawer where old rusty screwdrivers and lose batteries were kept. Rita came with the binoculars wondering what Harold had seen; probably those deer again or maybe something a little more exciting like a wolf. She asked what was going on. Harold immediately took the old binoculars from her without saying anything, removed his glasses and pressed them against his eyes. He turned the magnification wheel and focused in on the object that was playing around Orion's belt.

Rita asked again what had taken his attention. She trained her eyes on the area of sky Harold was looking at and gasped at the white object darting and dancing, 'What on Earth do you think that is?'

'I have no idea and looking through these it is hard to pinpoint it,' he replied.

The binoculars were old and one of the eye lenses was slightly out of focus, which gave Harold a headache if he spent too long looking through them. It passed so quickly that even trying to follow it was hard work when close up. He removed the binoculars from his face and asked for the living room lights to be switched off completely. He suggested it may be a helicopter or something but wasn't sure.

When all the lights and TV were switched off, he was to just about able to see the object dancing around Orion's belt without the binoculars. Now the dim white light resembled more of a firefly Harold had seen on a visit to Florida after taking retirement.

'Should we contact the police?' his wife asked.

'Oh, I don't think so. Pretty strange though. I wonder if anyone else is seeing this?'

The object began to slow its movements between each star of the belt and Harold used this chance to look back through the binoculars. It took a few attempts, but he managed to get a good focus. The object continued to slow its momentum and eventually came to a halt, remaining motionless in the sky.

'Hmmm, I have no explanation. May have just been a satellite or some space debris caught up in the atmosphere. Though, even with that kind of turbulence, remaining in a fixed pattern of descent,' he began to try and explain the object through science to help his mind grasp the situation. 'It would be impossible to maintain that pattern. Must have been though, nothing else in the sky can do that without breaking up under G-force and killing the pilot,' he concluded it was nothing more than space debris and reassured his wife that they had seen something interesting but nothing to get worried about.

She smiled, but only for a second. Harold saw his wife's face go from relaxed to taut in a flash. The room began to illuminate as lights began to switch themselves back on. A faint buzzing sound as the surge of electricity forced the lights to illuminate beyond their limitations.

The TV switched on and Harold dropped the binoculars, 'What the hell is going on?'

A blank expression had washed over Rita's face at something else happening outside the house. Harold swung around and felt his neck crack. He swore at the pain and grimaced, instinctively rubbing the muscle. He reached into his trouser pocket for a pill as he knew a flare up was on its way now. Swallowing the large oval-shaped medicine tickled his throat, but he was used to taking these painkillers without water. Moving his torso as to prevent any further neck pain he looked back at the window.

The object began to get brighter, and brighter as if the object was moving closer. Closer? That was absurd. How could it be getting closer? Harold moved backwards and took his wife by the hand as the sky lit up a brilliant white.

As the object grew brighter so did the intensity of the lights and buzzing sounds from the TV, as the volume increased to maximum by itself. Harold rushed to flick the light switches off, but they remained on. All Rita could do was to watch as the light in the sky intensified. She could almost feel the heat of the light. The sky had now gone from black to bright white within moments.

She was about to cover her eyes from the brightness but stopped. The sky fell back into darkness. The object and the light just disappeared. It just vanished back into the blackness of the night sky. The object that had been the brightest body in the sky was now extinguished like a flare falling back to Earth.

The lights began to fade, and the TV switched off plunging the room back into darkness.

But they were only in the blackness for a few moments before Harold flicked the lights back on. He found the binoculars and examined the sky for the object.

Nothing.

He checked the ground around the farmland and forests for any indication of a crash.

Nothing.

Whatever it was had just vanished without a trace.

'What on Earth was that?' Rita finally asked, feeling her pulse beginning to ease.

Harold took a moment to respond when he was sure nothing had crashed or set on fire, 'I don't know. That was neither a satellite nor anything I have seen before. It could have been a transformer; that was always a possibility.'

He was about to put the binoculars back into their leather

casing when the lights in the living room began to flicker, and the TV switched itself back on showing the evening news. The volume rose rapidly to maximum making Rita to jump. All the electrical appliances inside the house turned on at exactly the same time.

Adrian was beginning to relax and unwind with his feet stretched out over the glass coffee table, while Rachael was hard at work tapping frantically on her laptop in the kitchen. It was so nice to have the chance to relax after dealing with patients; and what a place to relax. It was very quiet living here in Røyken, no crime and no noise. This was a rare, if not an impossible thing to find in the UK. Noise and high crime meant doors needed to be locked along with security cameras spying on every corner of the house to deter wannabe burglars. This was seldom in Norway. Folks could leave their front doors unlocked, cars parked on the street, and there was little need for security cameras. Røyken was especially quiet though, as was the case for most towns away from the bigger cities.

Rachael had moved to the kitchen table as it provided better light and the high back chair prevented her back from cramping.

'Would you like a glass of something?' she called from the kitchen.

'I still have wine, but… go on, be the Devil on my shoulder,' he mimicked a Robert Palmer song. 'Bring that bottle… over here.'

'Okay one sec, I still have to read through this discussion; there seems to be a few errors in the referencing, which is very disappointing for a post-doc.'

Ah, Adrian thought to himself, *the crafty bugger is offering me a drink and having me get her one in the process.* Adrian rolled off the white leather settee that made obscene noises under his shifting weight and went to the kitchen stroking Rachael's shoulder on the way past.

There were only two glasses left in the bottle. He decided to change up the wine for something a little stronger. Washing the wine glasses, he reached for the whisky and poured two small amounts. He gave a glass to Rachael and walked back into the living room. Looking out of the living room window he called back to Rachael, 'It is certainly a lovely night tonight. Cold, yes but I have never seen the stars so bright.'

Pulling back the sliding glass door to the balcony he stepped out. The sudden temperature drop from a warm living room to minus ten degrees forced him to grit his teeth. Quickly taking a long sip of whiskey he felt his chest warm up. He saw Harold to his left in the living room looking through his telescope. He must have seen an interesting star or maybe plane watching, who knew? Adrian always wanted a telescope, but the UK skies and ambient light pollution made it very difficult to see anything at night.

He watched Harold with interest as he left the telescope and chose binoculars instead. Adrian looked in the vicinity of where his neighbour was observing. He couldn't see anything interesting, just a few stars and some brighter ones, probably planets against the black velvet sky. Adrian really had no idea which were planets, or which were stars.

Now succumbing to the cold and his star gazing satisfied, he went back into the warmth of the living room and shut the balcony door behind him. He heard Rachael talking to herself, scrolling through the Word document, highlighting areas with review balloons, and writing comments like *"Needs to be re-read"* and *"This is not a good reference, please find more up-to-date papers"*.

Adrian peered over her shoulder and smirked, 'My teacher would do the same to my essays at school.'

'I'll just be a few minutes,' Rachael replied.

Just before she was able to read anymore the laptop screen flickered, as did the lights in the ceiling. Rachael cursed out loudly and tried to save her work, frantically pressing the disk icon, 'No you don't, you fucker!' she exclaimed.

Adrian laughed, Rachael rarely swore, reserving it for more intense times of stress. He looked at the lights and saw the TV flicker before going into standby mode, 'Bloody hell, we having a power cut?'

He went to the balcony to see if any of the neighbours were also having trouble with their lights. Harold was still looking up at the sky through his binoculars. They too were having similar electrical problems in their living room. The outside streetlights were also flickering and resembled an eighties disco.

Adrian was able to pinpoint Harold's general field of view and saw what had interested him. Up by Orion's belt was a star that was performing a sort of ballet dance between the constellations. The lights inside their house stopped flickering and began to brighten with a faint humming sound.

Adrian reached back inside and tried to switch the power off, but the lights remained on, 'Shit! We're having a power surge.'

Before he could run downstairs to the breakers the sky began to glow white behind him. Adrian turned and saw the sky become a bright white. Small clouds reflected the light as it intensified so that their silver lining stood out against the blackness.

'Hey, Rachael, come and see this quickly,' he called back into the house turning his head slightly to make his voice clearer.

He beckoned her to look up at the glowing sky. Rachael clasped her hands to her mouth. 'Jesus Christ, what the hell is that?' she asked knowing neither of them had any answer.

Adrian scratched his head, 'I haven't the faintest.'

'Can't be an aircraft,' she added.

They both watched as the sky grew brighter. Their eyes were

fixed, though burning from the brightness; like staring at a full moon for too long. Now the object became the brightest body in the sky.

It began to fall, increasing its brightness as it descended. Rachael shouted she was going to switch off the breakers before the lights popped and the TV was permanently damaged. But before she made the stairs the lights and TV switched off. Rachael immediately reached out for the banister as to prevent herself from falling in the darkness. The object in the sky had now faded. The brilliant white just vanished into black and there was nothing more to see.

Adrian laughed and turned to Rachael, 'Well, that was strange.' He turned to go back into the house, sipping his drink and dusting the snow off his slippers. He was unsure himself of what he had just witnessed, but the manly act of just carrying on regardless began to put Rachael at ease, who was still feeling her way back into the living room.

'Well, that was fun. What shall we do…,' and before Adrian could finish his question all the lights flashed on in the house; even those that had been switched off. The TV woke from standby causing Adrian to spin around, almost dropping the glass from his hands. Rachael was less fortunate as her fingers relaxed and was unable to catch her own glass in time. It shattered into dangerous shards as it hit the hardwood, the amber liquid pooling around her bare feet.

The TV screamed as the volume increased to maximum by itself. Electricity surged through the lights until one by one they began to pop. White-hot shards of glass exploded all around them, burning Rachael's skin, feeling like small pins attacking her from all directions. She fell to her knees and covered her head to protect it from the raining glass. Adrian tried to switch off the TV but to no success. The screen was so hot it was hard to get too close to the off switch.

Thinking quickly, he pulled the cord from the back to save it sharing the same fate as the lights. Rachael's phone burst into flames from the kitchen table that had been left to charge. Sparks flew from the burning battery as the screen began to melt in the heat.

Adrian raced over, stepping on broken glass in the process. He tore out the phone charger from the wall and threw the phone out of the window and onto the snow below. It fizzed and exploded with a loud bang as the chemicals in the battery became volatile.

Rachael hobbled to the sofa, dodging the last of the exploding lights raining down white-hot shards of glass. She felt her foot and screamed when her hand flicked a large piece of glass that had managed to embed itself into the softer under part of her foot. She quickly gripped the shard with her thumb and forefinger. With a slow but forceful pull she freed it from her skin. Luckily for Adrian he still had his slippers on and avoided the glass. The last of the bulbs finally popped and the house fell into darkness.

4

Adrian refuelled the open fire with more wood to get both light and heat into the room. Along with some candles Rachael had found under the sink in the kitchen, the flames were the only light source to the living room. The gentle orange glow from the fire danced around the room matched with the flickering candles sitting in egg cups and small glasses that served as makeshift candleholders.

The lights had blown quite violently during the power surge leaving shards of glass on the floor and hanging filaments from the bulbs. These would prove to be a hazard as soon as the house was reconnected.

'Be careful walking around these floors, I just stepped on some glass,' Adrian warned.

The fuses had blown completely and refused to switch back on. A vacuum cleaner would have been fantastic at this point to clean up the almost invisible splinters of glass, but without power they were forced to find a broom and do it manually. Being laminated wooden floor it was easy enough to the brush dirt away rather than having to vacuum a carpet.

Rachael felt the ball of her foot itch and upon inspection pulled another small shard of glass out of her skin, 'Well, we both have our war wounds now,' she smiled in the glow of the fire doing her best to keep it together. She muttered something under her breath about her work being saved.

Adrian couldn't find any plasters so brought some tape and toilet paper to serve as an improvised bandage and dressed Rachael's wounds.

It didn't take too long to sweep up the shards, though all rooms had to be checked. In the meantime, Rachael limped back outside to see if there were damages to the streetlights since they were bathed in light just before the blackout. The lights were still out and must have taken most of the electrical surge. She wondered how long it would be before.... yep, there it was, blue lights and sirens in the distance.

'Shit,' she said to herself. 'The neighbours!' She called to Adrian to go round and check on the neighbours.

The neighbours had some illumination in their living room, possibly from their fire also. He rang the doorbell forgetting there was no power to it. He cursed aloud and knocked instead, 'Hi, it's Adrian. Is everything okay?'

A voice came back, and Rita answered the door holding some kitchen paper to her head. She had a small cut to her right temple that left a thin trickle of blood down her face, but nothing serious. She smiled at Adrian and invited him inside.

Happily, Harold seemed okay apart from a sore neck from twisting during the indoor firework display. He had a small gash to his cheek but said it was nothing. His wife brought in a towel and pressed it against the cut.

'Our phone doesn't work,' Rita said tapping her mobile.

Adrian turned to see the phone Rita was holding had melted at the back and suggested she put it outside in case the battery leaked on her and caused burns. Adrian could see shards of glass on the floor along with burnt filaments from the bulbs.

'How do you feel, Harold?' Adrian asked kneeling beside the elderly man.

'I've been better. Just came as a bit of a shock,' Harold sounded coherent, which relieved Adrian.

'Do you want me to call an ambulance so we can check your neck at the hospital?' Adrian could see Harold was in pain with his osteoporosis.

Harold rubbed the back of his neck and said, 'Oh no, we don't want to be a nuisance.'

'Are you sure? I don't want you getting a bad neck now,' Adrian persisted.

But Harold was adamant a few painkillers and some rest would soon have him back on his feet. Adrian reluctantly respected Harold's wish. Rita too was happy to be at home and did not need any medical attention.

'All these lights going on and off gave me quite a scare,' Rita said. 'When do you think the power will be back on?'

Adrian stood and said he would check their fuses to see if they were serviceable. He doubted they would be but went to see them anyway.

He descended into the dark basement with a candle. The flickering dim light seemed to make the small basement larger than what it was. Eeriness washed over him, and he believed something was going to leap out and snatch him. A childish feeling but nevertheless in the circumstances made him feel like abandoning his task. Boxes stacked in and around the basement made it difficult to navigate to the fuses in the gloom of the candlelight.

He located the metal box and saw the fuses were completely blown with scorch marks up the sides where the sparks had burnt. There was no way these were going back on without an electrician out to make repairs and didn't want to risk a fire by trying them.

He told them both to keep warm tonight and stay by the fire. He would check on them tomorrow morning and if they needed anything he might be able to get some painkillers from the clinic.

Going back outside the doctor was greeted by an unfamiliar sight. The entire town of Røyken was pitch-black. Never had he seen the small town this dark before.

Far from the usual ambient glow of orange and white from streetlights and houses on the hill, the town looked eerie. A blanket of darkness now engulfed the roads, the houses, and the entire town of Røyken. What were those lights, and how did the power suddenly surge throughout the town? As Adrian would soon discover, this was no mere power surge.

5

Hans Olsen woke around 3 a.m. He pressed his watch and illuminated the blue face. He went to turn on the bedside lamp, but it didn't work. He pulled his aging body up and instinctively felt the other side of the bed. It was cold and empty. He cursed at himself for forgetting. Fighting the urge to go back to sleep he got up. The hardwood floor was cold, and he quickly felt around for his slippers.

The house was black. He tried the hallway light switch, but nothing happened. He huffed and thought the fuses had blown again. This happened a lot over winter when the floor heaters had been left on, or the drying room in the basement had both heaters and washing machine on at the same time. Maybe his son had all his electronics on and triggered the fuses? Most likely this was the case.

He used the walls and banister to feel his way to the stairs. The dark did not bother him. As a farmer he often worked early mornings and late into the night, most times alone. The dark was more a friend to him than a source of evil. He made his way to the foot of the stairs and found a lighter in a bowl with various keys to the many types of machinery he owned.

He flicked the lighter and the small glow of burning gas offered some assistance for him to find his way to the kitchen. He walked into the large kitchen and found the drawer just in time before the lighter began to overheat and burn his thumb. Feeling his way through the drawers he found a large powerful torch; the kind that could produce enough wattage to illuminate a field in the darkest of nights. Putting in some fresh batteries the torch came to life.

He didn't have time to go and check the fuses now, he had work to do. Luckily, he had a gas stove installed in the summer for indoor grilling and fired up one of the hobs to boil some water. The heating was off, but the house was still warm from the basement furnace. After working he could call in his friend to come and check the fuses and make repairs if they had seriously blown like they had a few years ago, when he discovered the wiring dated back to the eighties.

After the farming season had finished and the winter months brought the heavy snow and ice, Hans was able to subsidise his government winter salary by using his tractors to plough and grit the roads for the local community. This did not pay that much but he was part of the village and he found it to be more of a civil duty than a paying job, though the money did come in handy for paying extra bills or buying extra wine and food for the weekend. This morning, he would grit all the roads so that the ice did not catch people unaware. The forecast predicted snow and Hans, being the workaholic he was, had organised the grit to be left at the depot so he could work in peace. There was something satisfying about working this early in the morning.

The snow clouds were beginning to gather but left small patches where the stars could shine through. Oslo was many miles north but could be seen by the glow of the city's white and orange ambient light reflected from the clouds above. The added bonus of having the entire road to himself allowed him to enjoy the quiet night atmosphere; listening to the radio of DJ's rambling on about this and that and playing the oldies from his era took his mind off things at home.

He fired up his tractor and let the engine warm up a little before climbing inside. It wasn't well heated, so he wore a large ski jacket, ski trousers, and floppy Lumberjack's hat. He drove out of his farm down the long narrow dirt track and onto the main road. He turned left and left again without even needing to look and drove up towards the town. In the daytime he would have angry drivers trying to pass him up this bit of road. But in the early morning he had the freedom to cruise at his own speed and leisure.

The small depot was at the bottom of a housing estate on Bjørnstadveien – literally meaning *Bear Road* – and just before the boarding school that was closing down. Nobody was there to greet him, which was fine; he knew what he was doing. Fifty bags of grit had been set aside for him. The only issue he had these days was being able to lift the damn things and empty them into his hopper. Being in his fifties these bags seemed to get heavier and heavier as the years passed by.

His hopper could hold roughly a ton of grit, and these bags held 30 kg each. His age caught up with him after lifting the second bag, so he decided to have five minutes break with a coffee while he regained his strength and his knees less angry.

Last winter the council told him that they were going to do away with the bags and get a large distributer that fed grit straight into the dispenser. But, like the large cracks and potholes that needed repairs in the roads, nothing was ever done about it.

His first route was the small roads on the estate. Usually there were streetlights around these houses but tonight they were all out, in fact the entire place was pitch black. This was unusual.

Coming to the foot of the road he flicked a switch and the hopper growled into life. Usually, he needed to work fast around here since his hopper held just enough to cover all the roads before he needed to refill and go out further to the village and the small satellite houses around.

Other than the occasional cat darting between the cars and negotiating around parked cars this route was very easy. He didn't have time to think but occasionally on the lengthier roads his thoughts of his ill wife caught up with him. He planned to visit her in Drammen hospital later today and bring her flowers and grapes since strawberries were now out of season.

It had all seemed to have been quick, her symptoms, the fall, then the hospital tests revealed the nightmare diagnosis… advanced breast cancer. He often asked "Why to us? Why to her?" She had never hurt a fly and had attended church every Sunday and holidays; often volunteering in the community to help with the schools or cleaning the streets. And this is how she is repaid? Hans had quite given up on the notion that God exists. To allow people to get away with crimes, allowing wars to happen and yet victimise those that just want to help others was completely obscene. And this was the work of a God that we are told loves each and every one of us? Obviously, he has his favourites. To Hans, the Devil made more sense; no favouritism, and everyone is treated the same — just not in a positive manner.

He had stopped going to church a long time ago, but his wife continued to pray in the hospital, only removing the cross from around her neck before radiation therapy. The last doctor's report suggested her cancer had stabilized but they were going to put her onto a combination of drugs to try and shrink the cancer before planning any further treatments.

Hans turned his attention back to the road as he pulled the old tractor onto a narrow street requiring him to focus on both his position and hopper speed so that he did not scratch or damage the parked cars. He flicked a switch next to the ignition that slowed the rate of grit leaving his trailer and reduced the heavy vibrations from the engine to avoid waking up the residents. He got to the end and carefully turned the tractor around close to some garages at the end of a cul-de-sac. He kept the hopper on, making sure he put enough of the small stones down to help the cars grip the road.

After clearing the street, he pulled back into the depot and decided to have few minutes sipping at his flask of black coffee before reloading the hopper. Now he would do the main roads running past the infant school and on the way to Røyken train station. He turned on the hopper again and the machine rumbled into life. He set it to full speed to give a good scatter of stones and straddled both sides of the road.

It wasn't the slowing of his hopper, nor the dimming of his lights that caught his attention, but the distortion coming from the radio. He felt the tractor's engine begin to sputter and struggle. He cursed loudly and pressed the accelerator up and down several times to attempt to pump fuel into the engine to keep it alive.

He was able to see the tank was full before the needle fell to empty and his engine packed up. He cursed aloud and tried to coast the vehicle to the side of the road. The lack of power steering meant it took all his might to control the wheel but ended up losing his breaking efficiency and was unable to turn away before coasting off the road and into a ditch.

Had this been a car or another vehicle this ditch would have been the end. But his tractor was built for this kind of terrain, and he knew he would be able to get out under the vehicle's own power just as soon as he could turn on the engine.

He tried turning the key now he was stationary. The engine turned over once then died with a sputter. He tried again and turned the key, nothing. He rummaged around for the torch under his seat and went to the front to inspect the engine. This was completely unexpected as he always checked the fluid levels and cleaned the air filters at least once a month.

He opened the side hood and shone the torch light inside. Nothing looked unusual. He kept a voltmeter in the cabin in case his battery got wet and had earthed itself. He took it out and hooked the positive and negative and switched on the meter. It read a full battery. Perhaps it had earthed just now? He stuck his head back into the engine and pressed the battery contacts receiving a mild shock that made him jump back.

The voltmeter dropped from his hands and fell behind him. He quickly blew on his hands and shook them to regain feeling. Turning around to find his voltmeter he saw a light coming towards him. *Well, maybe these nice people can give me a hand?* He thought to himself as the lights came closer. He held out his arm and waved to try and get the driver's attention. The lights flashed bright and then disappeared into the darkness, like the driver had just switched them off.

'Shit!' he said aloud.

The driver must have turned off by a side road, Hans thought to himself. But were no side roads, at least not this close to him. Where did the car go? A question he quickly dismissed and turned his attention back to his tractor. Climbing back into his cab he tried the engine again. To his delight it started first time.

He was about to close the door when the lights came back, much brighter than before. The lights flooded his cab in burning white forcing him to shield his eyes. Christ, this was bright, and hot. His mind was scrambled in the light; it had taken him completely by surprise. He reached to pull the door closed but it was stuck.

Stuck? He tugged hard but the door did not move. Something was jamming it. Hans pulled thinking some rust was wedging it open. He pulled again but the door would not budge. He was about to give it another hard pull when the door was yanked all the way open. Hans, still holding onto the handle was hurled out of the cab as the door flung open. The sudden impact hitting the frozen ground below forced the wind out of his lungs.

Large thin grey hands appeared from the white light and

grabbed Hans by the ankle. Before he could comprehend what had just happened, he was being dragged away from the tractor that stood idling by the side of the road; dragged into the burning light. He kicked out and screamed but the grip did not relinquish. It was far too bright to see what was holding him. The grip around his ankle was so tight it felt like his bone would crack under the pressure. He kicked out and tried to free his leg. But his kicks only met air.

Another grey hand with long thin fingers reached out to take his other foot, curling each finger around his thin ankle like an octopus snatching its prey. He tried to twist himself around on the ground and grab onto anything to stop from being pulled further into the light. But there was nothing to grab onto. His hands scraped against the icy road and down into the ditch so fierce the skin began to tear on his palms.

Hans screamed and tried to kick his legs free but to no avail. He was completely engulfed in burning white. He believed he was dying, and something was pulling him into the afterlife. His brain was unable to comprehend what was going on. Fear and adrenalin consumed his thoughts and he found himself in sheer panic clawing at the hard frozen soil.

A blue mist came from the light, and he inhaled making him cough and his screams strenuous. The mist did something to him so quick his brain could not process the information fast enough. He saw the lights begin to fade and his senses dampen. He felt his body tire and weaken. His clawing at the ground began to ease up and he allowed himself to be consumed by the light. His last view was of the lights fading to black and the icy air becoming warmer before losing consciousness.

6

Eric Olsen stirred in his bed, still dressed in the clothes he wore the previous day. The young man of eighteen years clapped his hands to his ears when he heard the cows. Usually at this time of the morning he would still be fast asleep, resting from either a night of binge drinking with his friends, or from playing on his *PlayStation* all night and early morning.

Usually, he could sleep right through the noises from the farm; a tractor pulling a rusty trailer that bounced across the field with metallic ping sounds, or the groans of the cows indicating feeding or milking time.

But today was different, today a different sound forced him to become semi-conscious, many hours earlier than his usual two p.m. wake up call. His eyes were red due to lack of sleep. His evening routine of showering at ten before locking himself in his room to play games online until two or three in the morning before his dad drove out to work gritting the roads was interrupted following a power outage. So, he had decided to acquire some alcohol from the cellar and read comics via candlelight.

Eric Olsen rolled over and tried to go back to sleep only to be disturbed once more by the sounds. It sounded like the noise of an injured animal, a kind of scream or at least the animal was calling expending as much air through its throat as possible. Eric felt no option but to peep through his curtains. Perhaps one of his dad's farm hands was jesting with the cows.

He peeped through the curtain and saw nothing on the ground below. His bedroom window faced towards the side of the house where the courtyard ran to the cattle shelter and out further towards the grazing area.

He waited for his father to come storming out of his bedroom – he slept a few more hours after gritting the roads to regain some energy before tending to the cows – but heard nothing.

In the event of his father's absence, and if the farm hands were busy with other duties, then Eric was tasked with tending to the animals' needs. He managed to roll out of bed and onto the floor. Moaning as he pulled the hood over his head. He opened his bedroom door and angrily shouted to his dad, the way teens often treated their providers of free food and lodgings.

He received no answer, which made him curse and thump the wall. Eighteen and raging with hormones meant he was quick to his anger, but this often fizzled out once his father responded or, like a week ago, a member of public took him by his jacket and made threats to *"mess him up"*, a boy of all talk but no action.

Descending the stairs he heard the cow moan again, this time accompanied by two others in a kind of choir of groans. He donned his wellingtons and went outside.

The air was icy cold, striking the boy's face like fine needles. The noises were much louder out here close to the sheds. The cows had not been let out yet and there was no sign of the additional help his father had hired. They owned cows mainly used for breeding but needed to downsize for the winter.

'God damn lazy fucking foreigners, they'll do anything to get out of work,' he said under his breath, but would never dare say this in front of them. Cursing again the young man kicked opened the shelter door and stepped in ready to start yelling and making idle threats. A spoilt brat that needed working on was his own father's description of the boy.

The smell hit his nose long before his eyes could adjust to what he was seeing, or maybe if he could believe what he was seeing. Two of the cows were stooped over something on the floor, their faces stained red with blood. Eric's mouth opened wide, and adrenalin pumped through his veins tunnelling his vision.

Two cows pulled strips of flesh from another lying on the floor, its hind legs still kicking trying to escape. Entrails and stomach contents lay sprawled all over the barn floor in a tangled steaming mess like sausages on a butcher's table. Another had been torn apart, its legs had been flung aside and half of its face had been torn away leaving its teeth and jaw exposed in a hideous grin; the tongue hanging to one side. The meat from the neck and cheeks were tattered and torn. An eye had been plucked out leaving a dark bloody hole in the head.

Eric's eyes shifted to the left and saw one of the workers his father had hired was stuck.

Stuck?

Yes, stuck to the wall. His chest and abdomen had been crushed against the wall with such impact that his innards had exploded like a water balloon sticking him to the side. His head had become inflamed and puffy as some of the body fluids had been pushed violently in all directions. Another worker was lying face down in the saw dust. The head had been stomped leaving brain matter and shards of skull all over in the crater.

The boy stood there looking at what was happening in front of him. This had to be a dream, had to be. Cows did not kill or eat one another, least of all these ones.

The wooden door slammed behind him as a gust of arctic wind passed the barn in a loud clank that startled one of the cows.

Both man and beast looked into each other's eyes before the

cow groaned in a way Eric had never heard before that seemed to make the room shake. The loud groan was the same noise that had woken him just now, and in the same process had woken him again.

The cow, bloodstains around its once black and white face resembled war paint, began to advance towards him in a clumsy fashion, as cows often seemed to move. Heavy movements by an animal that was not really built for this kind of activity advanced towards the boy.

Eric's instincts kicked in and he turned to run. Only his first attempt was futile as he ran into the closed door, hitting the bridge of his nose that made his eyes water almost immediately. Quickly and clumsily, he pushed it open but did not close it behind him. Instead, he ran for the house. A crash and the sound of breaking wood came from behind him, and he turned his head briefly to see one of the cows using its body weight and thick skull to break through the door and advance towards him in a heavy but sluggish manner. Cows do not run fast, but to Eric this was fast enough.

He made the house, opened the door, and locked it behind him. His heart racing, he ran upstairs. Upstairs so he could put as much distance between him and the deranged animal. He could hear the cow moaning and smashing its head into the house, wanting, needing to get in.

Why? Why were these cows doing this? What the hell had got into them? The boy questioned. The cows were mental and just savaging anything and everything.

The door downstairs smashed open under the cow's weight. It mooed and bashed at the banisters easily breaking them and smearing the blood from its victims over the walls and pictures. The young man knew in some way the cow could not make it upstairs to him. He tried his mobile phone but found it did not power.

Shit! He must have forgotten the charge it. He heard the cow smashing its way into the kitchen followed by another crazed cow. The smell of flesh and blood drifted upstairs. The soft fragrance of lavender from a scented candle was masked by the decomposing musk of entrails and stomach contents.

Both cows were now in the house looking for another meal, or something else to stomp on, like they were driven for revenge. But revenge for what purpose? They had been well taken care of, petted, and loved by everyone that had tended to them.

The gun case!

His father kept a double-barrelled shogun for hunting in the autumn locked in a steel container in his bedroom. The slug pellets, however, were in the kitchen drawer. One was no good without the other. The boy opened the door to his parents' bedroom and went in. The gun cabinet hung on the wall locked by a large padlock. His farther always kept the key with him so there was no legitimate way of opening it. He searched around. He needed something to crack the lock or tear open the cabinet.

The cows moaned and groaned from downstairs as plates and glassware broke under their massive weight, tearing through the kitchen. The boy found something. His father had left a sledgehammer under his bed for the very reason of losing his key in case of emergencies. The boy took it and began to pound at the lock. It dented but did not break. He hit it again, and again, still it did not break.

The boy took some deep breaths and continued to hit it and hit it, now fear had fuelled his system into a frantic state.

Open this or die!

The lock cracked, another two hits and it fell apart. The gun was a long and heavy double-barrelled shotgun. The boy managed to snatch it off its hinges and then looked around the drawers for cartridges. His father would have kept one around just in case — which he would put back in the kitchen drawer before the police inspected for safety measures. He didn't find anything.

Another crash from downstairs; the cows were now bashing the stairs trying to climb them. The commotion of breaking the gun cabinet lock had attracted their attention to him. Breaking wood combined with groans resonated throughout the house.

Pulling out socks and pants from the drawer, Eric found two cartridges. Loading both into the gun – after watching his father all these years on God-awful hunting trips had paid off – he closed the barrels, pulled back the hammer on one and flicked the safety switch to off. He had never actually fired a shotgun, or any gun for that matter before. So, there was some apprehension he would be able to hit his target... and that was if he had loaded the cartridges the correct way.

He ran back out to the landing where one of the cows was trying to push itself up the stairs, scraping and knocking pictures off the wall and leaving a long trail of blood in its wake. The boy aimed the shotgun at the head of the cow and squeezed the trigger.

The power of the gun hit his shoulder hard pushing him back against the wall and cracking a picture that was hanging behind him. The impact almost broke his collarbone, and he felt his right arm weaken from the blast. He was able to relinquish his finger on the trigger as the barrel pointed upwards from the blast, preventing him accidently firing off the second cartridge.

The cow, however, felt the full impact of the shot. All the pellets the cartridge held entered the cows head scrambling the brain and eyes instantly and forced the back of the skull to explode onto the walls behind. The large powerful animal fell to the side, crashing through the stairs and onto the other cow impatiently waiting its turn to get up the stairs. The boy ran down and took aim at the other cow, now pinned down by the dead weight of the first. Its front legs scraped at the hardwood floor as it tried to move itself from under the dead cow and get to its intended target.

Eric was not going to let that happen. He had managed to fire this weapon once and could sure enough do it again. This time he aimed carefully at the animal's head and pulled the butt of the shotgun firmly into his shoulder. He pulled on the trigger hard so that the blast would not be as such a surprise to him this time. A bright yellow flame exited the second barrel along with a small plume of smoke from the ignited gunpowder. The groans stopped.

7

The burring sounds of a helicopter woke Adrian first. He looked through the window and saw the air ambulance descending onto the farm behind the house.

'Shit, something's going off at the Olsen farm,' Adrian said trying to focus his eyes.

Rachael began to stir, 'huh?'

Adrian continued, 'The air ambulance and all services are outside Hans Olsen's farm.'

'You know him?' Rachael sat up and rubbed her eyes.

'I've met him a few times. I saw his wife a few months ago. She was diagnosed with breast cancer, poor woman.'

'Are you going over to see?'

Adrian shook his head, 'What am I supposed to do? Looks like the medics are there. I don't think the local GP will be able to offer any meaningful help that a paramedic can't. Anyway, if it is Hans or his son then the hospital will call me later with the details,' he continued to look outside. 'Looks pretty serious,'

Adrian checked in next door after calling out the electrician. He was relieved to see both Harold and Rita were doing well and even said they quite enjoyed having the power off; the candles made the evening cosy regardless to their superficial injuries. Unfortunately, the loss of power had also affected the fridge and freezer.

Adrian took Rachael out of Røyken for breakfast and much needed coffee. After that they drove around the fjord outside of Røyken. They talked for a while and enjoyed the view of the sea and forests now dusted with white snow. Heavy Snow was forecast for later that day, and the clouds had already accumulated; this would probably be the last clear sky for some weeks.

The winter tyres easily gripped the icy roads making driving in such conditions problem-free. A quick turn to the left brought them back onto a lane with dense fern forests at either side. The road snaked around the forest that prohibited seeing too far ahead. Rachael was enjoying the view of trees coated with white snow reminding her of a Christmas card.

'Bloody strange that power surge last night,' Adrian said breaking the silence. 'I hope the electrician can get everything sorted. I bet that will cost a bomb.'

'It's only money. I just feel for the neighbours. That must have been a hell of a shock to them,' Rachael replied and glanced out of the window. 'It's very cold today. We have to get the fire on when we get home.'

'Yeah, cold enough to freeze the nuts off a squirrel. It's hard to see the road markings now. What are those sticks at the side of the road for?' he asked indicating with his finger at some thin poles standing up at the sides of the road.

'I think they are for drivers to know where the sides are so that they don't veer off into a ditch or something.'

'Ah, clever.'

Adrian eased the car around a tight left bend and accelerated trying to get the tyres to skid a little and see how good they were in these conditions.

At first, his reactions were slow, probably only milliseconds but in the situation seemed longer. A man stepped out into the middle of the road; his clothes torn. Rachael screamed and slammed her hands onto the dashboard as Adrian stepped on the brakes and tried to pull the car to the left to avoid the man. The car skidded; the winter tyres did their best to dig hard into the icy road before biting and coming to halt just short of the tree line, which made them both jolt forward and then back in their seats.

Adrian took Rachael by the head and asked if she was okay? She nodded looking shocked. Her eyes were open, but he knew the force of the car coupled with the jamming of the seatbelt had hurt her.

'Are you hurt? Did something break?' Adrian asked, still holding his fiancée by the back of the head for support.

Rachael shook her head, 'No. I'm fine. What was that?'

Adrian turned to see a man from the rear window just standing there, unaware that he was almost hit by a car. His concern for his fiancée quickly tuned into anger. Ripping off the seatbelt and pushing the car door open he leapt out, 'What the fuck are you doing? You could've been killed, you stupid prick!' he shouted.

Adrian's anger quickly extinguished as he walked over to face the man. The man just stood there motionless in the road looking through Adrian and directly into the forest behind, seemingly unaware that someone was yelling obscenities at him. Saliva had frozen and crystallized around his mouth, and his eyes were red and dry. Adrian recognised him immediately. It was Hans Olsen.

'Mr. Olsen? Hans? What the hell are you doing out here? Come with me to the car. Let's get you sat down,' Adrian said, trying to lead Hans away from the road.

Hans was stubborn to move at first, like he was physically frozen to the ground. Adrian took him by the shoulders and twisted the man, aiming his torso in the direction of the car, and gently pulled him to get moving.

Rachael emerged from the car and stretched her neck, 'Do you know him?' she asked.

'Yes,' Adrian replied. 'It's Hans Olsen. We need to get him in the car.'

Rachael helped Hans into the back seat and aimed the heaters onto him from the front. Taking out a tissue from her pocket she wiped the saliva from his mouth.

Hans sat in silence.

'He is in severe shock. I need you to sit with him in the back and keep him warm. Keep talking to him,' Adrian looked at Hans' lifeless eyes. 'We need to get him to a hospital. He looks dehydrated and frozen.'

'Should we get him to the clinic first?' Rachael asked. 'He looks out of it. See, his eyes aren't even focusing,' Rachael snapped her fingers in front of Hans' face and monitored his eyes.

They never once shifted from looking forward and failed to register Rachael's fingers.

'He's had some mental trauma; his eyes aren't responding to stimuli.'

Adrian valued his fiancée's input, she was, after all a Ph.D. in clinical psychology. Adrian further examined his patient by rolling up his sleeve and pinching the bare skin under his forearm. Hans' face never once twitched, 'No, he is unresponsive to stimuli. Hans, Mr. Olsen, I need you to blink once if you can hear me.'

Hans just stared into the abyss somewhere in his own psyche.

'No, he needs proper medical attention at the hospital,' Adrian went to the drivers' side and got in. The warmth of the heater was very welcoming to his frozen hands, but he didn't have time to get them properly warm.

He was about to put the car into first gear when Hans suddenly bolted to the front of the car. Thrusting his arm towards the windscreen, narrowly missing Adrian's face, he pointed to the distance and screamed so loud it almost burst Rachael's ear drum and made Adrian hit the horn in shock.

Hans screamed, took a deep breath, and screamed again.

Rachael flung off her seatbelt and ran from the car to regain her senses. Adrian spun around and saw the look on Hans' face; a look he had seen before, many years ago. A look of someone who had been to war and had seen things no human should ever have to see.

Hans' eyes were wide, like all the muscles in his face were being stretched beyond their limits. Adrian held the man's head and screamed at him, 'Hans calm down, calm down. What the hell happened?'

Hans continued to scream as Rachael flung open the back door, the heat escaping with the screams into the icy air.

'He is in severe trauma. Christ Adrian, we need to get him to the hospital now.'

Hans' screams began to whimper into a rasp. The farmer began to lose energy, like a device using up the last of the battery. With a final breath he slumped back in the seat and passed out.

8

Rita looked at her watch with exhausted eyes and saw it had gone past twelve in the afternoon. The fridge was not receiving power and therefore the milk had begun to sour, and the rest of the food would soon be too warm to keep. She tried the kettle forgetting this also required electricity to function. This afternoon they could only drink warm orange juice and snack on anything in the fridge that needed to be eaten.

Harold came upstairs shortly after, wearing his usual baggy jeans and a shirt bearing the logo *Dept. Cell Biology* in white hand-stitched writing, 'We're going to have our work cut out for us today with this lot,' he gestured to the glass on the floor.

Rita offered him a glass of orange juice, 'Sorry, dear, we can't boil any water; the power's still off.'

Harold took the glass from his wife and drank the lot in one go, 'Hell, that was warm,' he said squinting his face at the drink's acidity. He handed it back to his wife for a refill and looked back at the floor. Taking a broom and pan from behind the door he began to sweep up the glass. The pain in his neck returned making it difficult for him to bend and turn his head.

'I think they've gone out, next door. I can't see the car in the drive,' Rita said filling her husband's glass with more juice. 'She makes a wonderful wife; doesn't she?'

'Fiancée, dear, Fiancée; they're not married yet,' Harold corrected his wife.

'Oh, silly me, they leave it late these days, don't they?' Rita replied.

'Yes well, not everyone can be as lucky as us finding one another so early in life,' Harold looked up and smiled.

'Oh, you are a Saint, dear,' Rita handed the drink back to him and finished hers. She took out the small hand brush and helped her husband.

Harold objected, 'You can't be down like that. You will hurt yourself. There is a larger brush in the basement.'

Rita put the brush away and pulled herself up using the counter for aid. She let out a small groan and felt her knees crack. It was at times like these she felt her age, 'We're getting old dear,' she said hobbling to the stairs in the living room.

Descending two flights of stairs to reach the basement she found a large broom, with long and hard bristles, used mostly for sweeping up leaves outside. It was dark down here. She was grateful the broom was close by and that she didn't have to search in the darkness for it.

She was about to begin the long ascent back upstairs when she heard a crash from the spare room. Startled at the sudden sound she almost dropped the broom. It sounded like the window had broken. Rita took a step towards the door and listened.

She heard something rummaging around inside, knocking into boxes and being very clumsy in doing so. Her first thought was that it may have been a cat that had somehow found its way in from outside. But the window was locked, and they never opened the back door down here during the winter; only in summer when they were out doing the garden. As she stood close to the door, she felt an icy breeze chill her toes. The window was indeed open.

Another box fell and she began to back away as the room fell silent.

Was there someone in there? She felt the urge to run and hurl her old body up the stairs to Harold. But her knees were sore, and her back ached.

Then the door handle began to move. Shakily at first like the operator on the other side was not sure how the contraption worked. But then slowly, very slowly the handle began to turn downwards.

The broom fell from her hand, and she turned for the stairs screaming for Harold. The door opened with a creek, and something stepped out into the dark basement. She didn't see as she tried to climb the stairs, slipping, and using her hands to pull herself up. Her knees cracked as she made the first step. The pain was sharp, and her leg buckled. Trying hard to use her other leg she pushed herself up onto the second step and screamed out, 'Harold!'

Harold was sweeping glass from the stairs leading to the living room when he had heard the crash. He saw his wife climbing on all fours to get to the top step of the basement. Something caught his eye rising behind her, an arm, long and thin reached out from the gloom and snatched Rita's leg.

Harold tried to let out a warning for his wife to get up but his words were choked and sounded more of a gurgle. Rita's hands reached the top step, and before she could pull herself into the arms of her husband felt something grip her ankle tightly. With a violent tug she was dragged back down the stairs, her ribs and knees smashing into each step.

Harold helplessly watched his wife fall down the stairs screaming as her body thumped against the wooden steps and slide across the floor below. Her screams muffled as the spare room door was slammed shut.

Harold screamed her name and flung his aching body down the

stairs so fast he almost lost his balance missing out some steps.

Blood curdling screams came from the spare room. Boxes were hurled aside, along with shoes and clothes as the occupants within struggled. Rita let out one more scream calling for Harold.

He tried the door pulling hard on the handle and pushing his body against it. It opened a crack before something pushed back slamming the door back into its frame knocking Harold backwards and almost onto the floor. But Harold was able to maintain his balance.

The handle was being held up and Harold was unable to budge it. He tried and tried but someone was holding the handle up so hard he couldn't get it to move in the slightest.

'Rita?' he called and hurled himself at the door trying to break it. The jolt against the door cracked his neck. The pain raced through his shoulders like a bolt of lightning weakening him. He groaned in agony. His knees weakened and his hand fell from the doorknob. He tried in vain to reach out to the door; to his wife struggling inside the room.

His legs buckled from under him, and he began to crumple into a heap. He clapped a hand to his neck. His eyes closed to the pain, he tried, oh God how he tried to stand but just couldn't. The pain was too great and had a firm needle-like grip over his entire body. With his eyes closed he failed to see the door open, and a giant figure step out.

The figure was silhouetted against the daylight from the spare room window. Its immense size blocked most of the daylight entering the basement. Harold managed to open his eyes just long enough to see the giant figure standing over him.

Even though it was silhouetted against the dull daylight, its thin frame easily reached the top of the ceiling. Long and thin arms stretched all the way to the floor. He was about to scream but the figure was quick to stem the screams by placing its hand over Harold's mouth. The giant's fingers easily curling around his face and neck, stemming the scream, and restricted Harold's ability to inhale.

A faint odour reached Harold's nostrils and he gasped as the creature relinquished its abrasive grip. Within moments he began to lose all sensation of pain from his crippling disease. He felt his muscles relax and his thoughts to his wife inside the spare room subside with the dampening of his vision. Daylight creeping in from the spare room window began to dim.

Hans was now being treated for dehydration and severe shock, but the doctors assured Adrian he would be allowed home as soon as all the tests were complete, and they were satisfied he was otherwise in good health. For now, the results of the MRI scan and getting him back to a cognitive state were the most important.

So far none of the doctors had any inclination as to what had caused Hans to lose his memory or wonder off into the woods. It was suspected he had sustained a knock to the head. Something the MRI would clear up. But for now, Hans was placed into a ward and attached to a drip of saline and vitamins to help him regain some strength and rehydrate him.

It would be another two hours before Hans regained some of his memory and was able to speak. The doctors asked but Hans could not remember anything other than filling his hopper with grit and doing the main roads. He said something about a bright light and then waking in hospital. Even though he was fully conscious before, he could not recollect being in the forest or meeting Adrian.

Upon further questioning about the light Hans drew a blank, as if part of his memory tried to delete itself. He was complaining of a shortness of breath and felt like he was getting a cold. The doctors said it was probably because he had been out in the elements and maybe had picked up a virus. It was flu season so having a few patients with severe symptoms was routine here in the winter.

Adrian informed the doctors that something had occurred at the Olsen farm but wasn't sure if he had been present at the time.

Leaving Hans in the capable hands of the hospital staff, both Adrian and Rachael drove home. They listened to the radio for the first few kilometres. The weatherman had insisted that everyone make sure their vehicles were fitted with winter tyres as heavy snow was on its way.

During the drive home Adrian saw police cars waiting in lay-bys; not checking for speeding cars but making sure cars were fitted with proper tyres for the conditions. They stood out in full view with safety jackets allowing motorists plenty of time to see them. The police in Norway gave motorists all the chances they could to slow down by being so visible. In the UK or indeed many other countries, the police would hide behind thickets and walls out of view so that they could intentionally catch drivers. The following one-way conversation and idle threats would ensue along with a fine and points on the offender's license; two punishments for the same crime.

Adrian pulled up to their home and Rachael wondered how the neighbours were doing? Being much older and not in the best health, she decided to go right over and see if they needed some help cleaning? She tried the doorbell, but it didn't ring. She assumed they were still out of power, and no one had been round yet to reconnect them. She knocked and waited.

No answer came.

'Adrian?' she called. 'Can you go round the back and see if anyone is there?'

Adrian was just getting out of the car when Rachael called to him. He did what he was asked to do and made his way around the back of their neighbours' house. Rachael continued to knock on the door, but no answer came. She tried the handle, and the door opened a little. With caution she stepped in and shouted out, 'Harold? Rita? It's Rachael from next door. Is everything alright?' she received no answer.

Adrian looked around the back, walking past the shed at the end of the garden. He saw the basement window was broken. Shards of thick glass littered the ground outside. The window frame was cracked with the wood bent and splintered. Upon glancing in he saw Rita was lying on the floor amidst some boxes.

Adrian shouted for Rachael, but she was out of range and the house blocked all sound to the front. He pulled himself up and into the room, carefully minding the broken glass, and checked Rita immediately, 'Rita? Rita? What happened are you okay?' He saw a small cut to her neck; the blood had clotted suggesting she had been here for a while. He pushed his fingers into her neck and was relieved to feel a pulse. 'Rita, wake up,' he begged.

Slowly Rita's eyes began to open. Her dazed expression made Adrian call for Rachael.

'Rita, what happened? Are you in any pain?' he asked.

Rita groaned as she started to come round. She gazed upon Adrian with a blank expression for a few moments, 'Did I… did I have a fall?' she asked lethargically.

Adrian carefully pulled her up into a sitting position and asked her where Harold was. She said upstairs.

The basement door opened, and Rachael stepped in, 'We need an ambulance, Harold has had a very bad fall and he is semi-conscious.'

The phone lines were dead from the power surge, and Adrian's mobile phone was out of commission since the battery was damaged the previous night. The only thing he could do was to get Rachael to help him move their neighbours into the car and take them to the clinic. From there they could administer first aid and call for an ambulance to take them to the hospital.

9

Concerns over her injuries and partial memory loss meant Rita had to remain in the hospital – at least for now while the doctors could be sure this was an isolated incident. The doctor had given her a brief examination for bone fractures and minor trauma before prescribing her some strong pain killers and allowing her to rest for the evening.

The injury to Harold's neck was of concern. They gave him a strong injection of diclofenac sodium for the inflammation and prescribed some strong painkillers.

The clinicians were beginning to question just what was going on in Røyken, what with this being the second incident of patients suffering from injuries and memory loss today. The doctors had a brief discussion with the nurses and none of them could put together any reason for this. It was strange that this had occurred to three patients, all of whom came from the same area. Eventually, their memories would return, and they could document a plausible reason. But, for now getting the patients to rest and recover was the best medicine they could prescribe.

Harold was taken for an X-ray to assess the damage. Happily, this seemed okay, other than the osteoporosis. They would both require and MRI to assess any brain damage or irregularities. But this would need to wait until the morning.

Hans Olsen had now regained his memory and seemed to be making a fast recovery. Although he could still not recollect how he was in the forest. Instead, he made up something to try and convince the doctors he was better so he could see his wife. He tried his best not to worry his sick wife and just told her he must have had a shock that made him a little forgetful.

Of course, she was more concerned than him and tried to tell him to remain at the hospital. But he was too eager to get back to the farm and to sort things out there. The doctors wanted to keep him in longer, but Hans discharged himself suggesting that they could use the bed for some genuinely sick people. Besides, the events of the day had reached him, and he needed to go back home and sort things out.

The MRI had come back with nothing unusual about his brain. A little inflammation around the frontal lobe was dismissed as nothing more than a bump to the head – although Hans showed no signs of bruising to his forehead.

The ward was quiet this evening with the exception of nurses moving around checking on patients; their rubber soles squeaking against the dull polished floors broke Harold from his sleep. It was hard enough to sleep on hospital beds anyway; a small sound would wake anyone up from a shallow snooze at best. Rita woke up and complained of a severe headache around 4 a.m. Harold tried to find a nurse to bring something for his wife. The ward was functioning on a skeleton crew with only one doctor and a handful of nurses.

The nurse came over to look at Rita before suggesting she may have a slight migraine and would find the doctor to give her something to treat the pain and help her sleep. Harold sat next to his wife and watched her hold her head with the pain.

'Do you want a glass of water?' Harold asked, taking his wife in his hands, and trying his best to comfort her. His neck and shoulders were sore, and he could only offer a very light grip.

She tried to shake her head but felt the movements only exacerbated the pain. It felt like someone was ringing a bell from a distance and advancing towards her. She could feel a slight pressure deep within her skull.

'Oh God, I can't stop this pain,' tears ran down her cheeks as she pulled her arms around her head.

Harold held her in his arms and rubbed her head. He could not stand to see his beloved wife in so much pain. He pulled her close to him and kissed her forehead. He spoke in a soft voice that it was going to be okay, and that the doctor would bring her something to ease the pain so she could get back to sleep.

A young dark-haired female doctor dressed in the usual white coat and trousers came into the room followed by the nurse carrying a trey with a glass of water and two large tablets.

'Rita, can you just sit up for me and take these,' the doctor said with a soothing tone.

'What are they?' Harold asked, knowing the answer before the doctor replied.

'These are co-codamol and this one volterol to reduce the inflammation and stop the pain,' she replied.

Rita needed help taking them but managed to swallow both with the water, spilling most of the liquid down her chin. The nurse said she would come back in twenty minutes to see if they had begun to work. The doctor informed them that she was in the nurses' station so would be on hand should they need her. Harold appreciated their help and sat with his wife for a while longer.

He had been so caught up in his wife that he did not recognise the slight ringing in his own head, which he put it down to his neck pain. It was common for him to get a headache if his osteoporosis was acting up. But, after a few years of the disease he had accustomed himself to the discomfort.

It took half an hour for the medication to work, and Rita was able to lay her head down on the pillow and close her eyes. The ringing in her head began to subside much to her relief. Harold let go of his wife's hand and walked back to his bed. He ignored the small headache that had crept up his back and into the rear of his skull. A good sleep would soon sort that out and hopefully they would be allowed home later in the day.

He lay in bed thinking about how in the world they ended up here. He could not remember what had happened at home. The last memory he had was cleaning up broken glass. The more he tried to think, the more fog and haze concealed the memories. Eventually, all thoughts of the night began to subside, and his eyes began to close.

They both slept a little while longer before Rita bolted upright like a spring, her eyes opened wide, her mouth encrusted with dried saliva. The sudden movement of the bed rattled the stainless-steel springs waking Harold.

'Are you okay my dear?' he asked reaching for his glasses that were on the nightstand next to his bed.

She sat without response to his question or even acknowledged his presence. Instead, she just stared at the wall. Harold sat up and switched on the bedside light, 'Rita? Are you okay? Do you want me to get the nurse?'

Rita gave no response and remained silent. He rolled out of bed and tried to turn her around to face him but was unable to move her. Her body had become rigid, and her muscles taught that she was hard to twist. Instead, he moved himself to face her. A strange look on his wife's face concerned him.

Her eyes were wide open, red, and sore. He took a tissue from the sink and wiped the spittle from the sides of her mouth. She barely moved but remained staring directly at the wall, past her husband as though he wasn't even there. Then she blinked and turned her head away. She stood with some unease due to old bones and tiredness but stood erect none-the-less.

'Rita?' Harold called and placed a hand on her back.

She failed to respond or acknowledge he was even there. Instead, she began to take small steps towards the door, opened it and walked out. Harold stood to go after her, thinking she was either sleepwalking or perhaps something worse had materialised by the trauma yesterday.

He went to go after her but stopped. An excruciating pain surged through the centre of his head. It felt like his brain had begun to throb and expand inside his cranium. Pain tickled nerves and synapses causing him to clasp his hands to his forehead and fall to his knees.

Meanwhile, Rita was slowly making her way towards a cabinet at the end of the hallway close to the nurses' station. She glanced left then right to see doors to rooms containing some very sick patients attached to machines that bleeped every few minutes. She continued to walk towards a cabinet outside of the nurses' station, careful not to be seen by anyone.

Her hands were reluctant to respond at first as though she was trying to fight an urge. But she succumbed to the will and her hands moved freely, rummaging around for a few items. The nurses inside the station were either napping or tapping on their laptops keeping up with their social media. Nights were generally quiet on the ward with most patients resting rather than calling.

Rita rummaged around and found large needles and some smaller instruments. A voice suddenly entered her head. It was her own voice suggesting she look for a cutting implement also; maybe something like a scalpel? She looked but did not see any, though there was a pair of scissors with the ends rounded for cutting bandages. They didn't look sharp but would suffice until something better materialised. She picked up what she could and turned back to the wards.

At no stage did she question her own motives or realise what she was about to do. She did, however, feel an urge… anger! Her thoughts were focused on the times she had visited the hospital for treatment, only to be put onto waiting lists behind people that were responsible for their own ill health. Smokers going in for lung cancer treatments, broken bones by youths doing stupid things on bikes, these people were the reason she could not get treatment for herself or Harold.

She began to bare her teeth like a wolf. She entered the first room she found; she was not meticulous which room she entered. The room was inky black, only small LEDs, blue and red, blinked on and off from various machines offering the only light.

Pushing the door open allowed a slither of light to enter illuminating two patients sleeping within. Both patients were connected to drips containing transparent yellow liquids being fed directly to the veins via a machine that beeped every two minutes. One wore a bandage around her head with a large field dressing at the front. The other just looked terrible. The skin around her eyes was dark and sunken as were her cheeks. Rita moved to the first occupant.

Rita snarled rousing the woman from her sleep.

The patient didn't open her eyes fully until she saw the needles and scissors in Rita's right hand. Then her eyes opened fully when she saw the look on the elderly woman's face. Rita grinned bearing yellow teeth; her eyes were wide and staring at this very ill woman in a psychopathic manner. The woman screamed.

Rita quickly stuffed the bed sheets from around the woman's chest and into her open mouth with such force she broke one off one of the woman's front teeth, knocking it to the back of her mouth. The woman's attempts to free her mouth were futile since the anti-cancer drugs were making her weak and feeble. Blood seeped from her broken tooth and were soaked up by the white bed sheets. She tried to pull the bed sheet from her mouth, but Rita pushed hard stopping her patient from freeing herself.

Rita, not normally a woman of great strength, was able to mount the woman and pin her arms down using her knees. Using bed sheet, she tied one hand to the bed and quickly turned around to secure the other. She pivoted and tried to bind the woman's feet, which were kicking out wildly though without much strength. Rita was able to grab one and secure it. The patient kicked out with her remaining free leg, but Rita was able to wrangle that up without any problems. Now her patient was restrained... now her patient was prepped for surgery.

Rita sat on the woman's chest motionless like she was now evaluating the next step. She shuffled over to the woman's face, her screams, powerful but muffled by the sheets with blood oozing down her throat. The lose tooth rattled at the back of her throat firing her gag reflex. The bed sheets combined with Rita's hand pushing down on her mouth forced the vomit back down her throat. The tooth rattled with the sharp broken end scraping the sides of her throat like a difficult pill to swallow, choking the woman.

The commotion roused the other patient in the next bed and Rita snapped her head around. Seeing this she quickly leapt off like a cat after a bird and rushed to the other bed. The old lady was quick to mount the other patient before she could do anything to defend herself. Using the same procedure as with the cancer patient, she lashed the women to her bed, taking full advantage of the woman's weak state.

She tore off the bandage from around her head exposing a large disfiguring scar running diagonally from above her left eye to the top of her hair line — which had been shaved completely — and forced it into her mouth tying the bandage around her neck to secure it.

She turned her attention back to the cancer patient and mounted her again, sitting on her chest and leaning into her face like a succubus. Rita pulled pull back the eye lid on the woman's left eye and peered in. Pure anger surged through her as she produced a needle from her hospital night dress pocket and learned in. The woman thrashed and screamed but Rita had secured her so well that her movements were restricted to her head only. Rita pushed hard on the woman's head to stop it from squirming.

The needle Rita had chosen was fine and long. She pointed it at the woman's pupil only a few inches away like she was demonstrating how this accessory was to be used. And then she began to lower the needle towards the black pupil.

The needle touched the surface of the eye, scraping the thin translucent tissue. Gently, Rita put some additional impetus onto the needle and pushed it through the pupil. The eye popped immediately; a clear liquid erupted from the wound as Rita pushed the fine needle further in, moving it left and right scrapping the inside of the eye, meeting each nerve, and stimulating them in a horrific manner.

The woman screamed in agony, her eye trying to close as a feeble last defence. But it was no good. The needle had punctured her eye. Rita drew back the needle. A small amount of a viscous liquid gushed from the eye as it collapsed inside the socket. The woman kicked and screamed but to no avail. Rita examined the syringe for a moment then threw it away onto the floor.

Now she produced a pair of scissors and branded them in front of the patient as though taunting her. Her eyes were wide and red from lack of moisture, but Rita could not feel the pain. The urge of anger made her mouth foam, dripping onto the patient's cheeks in a stringy mess. The old lady had gone completely insane.

Taking her hand away from the eye lid she forced her finger

into the surrounding socket, using her nails to pinch onto the flesh of the deflated orb. And with one sharp jerk she pulled the eye from its socket exposing the optic nerve that dangled like a worm at the end of a fishing rod.

The patient bounced around in her bed, shaking the metal frames and springs to try to get someone's attention. Placing the nerve between the blades the old lady began to hack away. The pain was extreme, the cancer and chemotherapy combined was nothing compared to the pain now surging through her body like lightning. This was it; her cancer was not going to be the death of her, and after good progress. Her demise would be at the hands of this insane woman.

Rita examined the nerve before casting it aside like she had with the needle. The cancer patient began to lose consciousness, her one remaining eye began to close but Rita wanted her awake; wanted her to feel all the pain she could before her death. Rita removed the bed sheet to expose the mouth. Reaching into the orifice she pulled out the tongue that was caked in vomit and green bile and stretched it as far as she could.

All the while, the other patient screamed and kicked at her bed to try to rouse a nurse or doctor. But they did not resonate loud enough. She thrashed her body and hips against the bed trying to create as much sound as she could. The metal springs and frame bouncing off the floor was surely enough to wake anyone on the ward?

With the scissors still in hand, Rita sliced through the tongue, clumsily hacking at the spongy meat. Blood splattered from the cuts as nerves were severed causing the stump to twitch violently in its housing. She examined the warm tongue, blood mixed with vomit and saliva seeped down her hand from the severed end. She turned to the other patient and gave her a malevolent grin.

Without hesitation, she bit into the moist spongy meat. Its taste was sour from vomit as she chewed, tasting the blood that seemed to be exquisite to the pallet. The squelch of raw meat like chewing on a blue steak echoed around room. Blood and saliva ran down her chin as she chewed like some deranged cannibal that had not feasted for days. Titling her head back she swallowed the tongue and licked her lips.

The last act before turning her attention to the other patient was to drive the scissors deep into the chest of the cancer patient.

One… two… three.

It took many stabs to break through the sternum and into the heart. Blood poured out like lava from a volcano and pooled around the patient's chest, oozing down the back and soaking Rita's legs in the process. She cackled, like a witch in a child's story before turning to the other patient wriggling in her bed, her eyes never once turning away from this witch. Rita grinned and drew the scissors upwards slicing through the skin, tearing up through the cancer patient's neck and chin in a seemingly effortless glide. Then she turned her attention to the other patient.

Working the night shift was long and could be tedious. Once all paperwork was completed – usually taking just a few hours – then there was little else to do. During these down periods, folks often allowed their emotions about the job or people they disliked to surface into conversation.

'Oh, I don't know, sometimes I wonder,' the doctor said without turning away from her laptop. 'They take him on just because his father is friendly with the senior consultant, and two years later he is on a par with me,' Doctor Kristiansen continued.

'I totally get it,' the nurse replied. 'Fresh out of medical school and boom, running around telling everyone they know nothing and thinks he knows it all.'

The person they were talking about was the fresh-faced physician, Doctor Jans Berg – a charismatic prick whose rat-face reflected his personality of a rodent infestation; though that comparison would be unfair to rats. His father was very friendly with the senior consultant, playing golf in the summer or joining for skiing trips in the mountains during the winter. Doctor Berg had been promised a job at the hospital as soon as he graduated from medical school. Berg would parade around the medical school to his lecturers and classmates taunting them that he was already being set up for life as a physician at Drammen hospital. Suffice to say this had never played well to his popularity. A skill he had continued to exercise ever since he got here.

The senior consultant made sure he was taken off hard labour and moved up to specialist training much sooner than the other interns. Kristiansen was annoyed with this move, sharing her co-workers' opinions about him. He was lazy, snobbish, and never followed up with his patients; always leaving that up to others. He was, however, good at barking incoherent orders to the nurses and senior staff.

'Sometimes I wonder just how this hospital survives,' Kristiansen laughed sarcastically.

An alarm went off in the office turning their attention away from general conversation. All heart monitors were fed into the office and when an alarm rang the computer indicated which room on the ward they needed to tend to.

The nurse looked and said, 'Room 406.'

'Call crash team,' Kristiansen shouted as she raced out of the office and down the hall, pulling the stethoscope from her white coat pocket in preparation.

She got to room 406 and found it was wide open. Switching on the light she saw the bloody mess. What she was seeing simply defied belief. Almost screaming but somehow managing to stifle it, Kristiansen watched an elderly woman sitting like a hunched succubus on top of a patient, scissors smeared with bright red blood and tendrils of flesh hanging from the blades.

Both patients had been tied down with their bed sheet and gagged. It took many moments for Kristiansen to understand what had happened, then her training kicked in. She was quick moving over to the bed and taking hold of Rita's right hand forcing the scissors from her and pulling her off and onto the floor. Due to the urgency of the situation, Kristiansen pulled Rita off so hard that she lost her balance and fell to the hard floor; her right elbow smashing into the machines that had fed the patient vital drugs and fluids.

Rita did not scream or resist and remained motionless on the floor as the doctor put pressure on her, binding her hands behind her back to keep her from harming anyone else. All she did was laugh, laugh at the situation.

Meanwhile, the nurse came rushing in to support the doctor. She stopped at the sight of blood and her peer wrestling the elderly patient on the floor. She felt something squelch under her shoe as she stepped forward. Upon lifting her sole to examine what she has stepped on, she saw the remains of a human tongue; mangled, as though a dog had been chewing on it, with congealed blood oozing from the spongy muscle.

'Tend to the patients, quickly,' Kristiansen ordered the nurse.

She hesitated, looking around only to see other organs thrown onto the floor besides her. She looked up at the patient bound to the bed and saw her entire neck from her chest to her chin had been clumsily sliced open, revealing the rigid throat and arteries gleaming with dark congealed blood in the fluorescent light.

What the hell could she do, but to stand there motionless? How could she deal with this? In her three years as a qualified nurse, she had never seen such trauma. The worst she had seen before this was a severed finger from a chain saw accident. He eyes began to tunnel; adrenalin surged through her veins forcing her heart to race. Her stomach gurgled and she felt her muscles contract. The horror of this was too much. Her body reacted in the only way it knew or could. She screamed so loud that other patients on the ward were woken up by the screech.

'Get the warden, and call the police,' the doctor screamed at the nurse, trying to get her to regain her senses.

The nurse just stood there unable to move or acknowledge the demand.

Kristiansen screamed again, 'Anna, go right now.'

Eventually the nurse was able to regain some senses and turned for the door.

Kristiansen continued to struggle with Rita, who had now begun to fight back, clawing, and snarling at the doctor. Kristiansen was amazed at the raw strength of the elderly woman but didn't have time to acknowledge it. Pushing down Rita's wrists and trying to use as much of her sixty-one kilograms of weight to prevent those teeth and nails from inflicting damage.

Kristiansen glanced to her left to see the nurse turn for the door then stop. An awful gurgling sound came as she stood rigid in the doorway. Kristiansen watched as the nurse stepped backwards, clasping a hand to her throat, and turning towards the doctor.

Rita's husband, Harold, was standing in the doorway, a scalpel in his hand dripping with blood. The nurse fell to her knees clutching at her throat in an attempt to stop the gushing blood from the severed arteries; her eyes wide with confusion and disbelief of what had just happened.

Kristiansen screamed as Harold pushed aside the nurse and advanced onto the doctor, easily overpowering her and using fear to his advantage. He swung the scalpel and Kristiansen reacted by raising her arms to her head to protect it, only to feel the sharp sting of the blade slicing through her coat and skin. The deranged old man recoiled and brought the blade back in a reverse motion slicing once again at her arms.

Kristiansen backed off, not registering the pain due to the adrenalin pumping through her body. She briefly examined her arms and saw the blood staining her sleeves. This was her mistake. Harold had already withdrawn the scalpel and was winding up with another. This time no arms were able to protect the head.

Another effortless swing and the doctor clasped at her throat. Harold reached forward, taking a handful of her long dark hair, and forcefully pulled her head back. Kristiansen's severed neck tore at the edges of the wound. Dark blood poured from the deep slice.

Rita, whom was in a state of frenzy as the doctor's blood spilt over her hands and face, assisted her deranged husband, and held the doctor's arms back preventing her from trying to stem the flow of blood. They both laughed hysterically as the doctor's life drained away. Their laughs were high-pitched squeals like pigs at dinnertime.

Footsteps came towards the door and Harold snapped his neck round to see. The sudden movement cracked the bones in his vertebra, but he did not flinch or even feel the surge of pain that should have crippled him as it had done on many occasions before. He brought up the knife as Rita got to her feet. Screaming in a high-pitched voice Harold charged at the crash team, the scalpel held high and coming down to slice anyone that was too close.

10

Mrs. Johansen rubbed the back of her hands to regain some feeling. The house had been reconnected to the new transformer, as the old one had blown leading to the mass power cut in the region. Alas, many lights in house were in dire need of new bulbs.

Mrs. Johansen did her best to keep warm by the fire, which was beginning to dim and needed more wood to stay alive. The living room was warm, but for some reason she felt cold. Without bulbs in every room, the darkness consumed most of the house. The place now felt empty and cold. She never used to be afraid of the dark, but that was when her husband was still alive. Now she was alone, the darkness felt like an evil presence, restricting her to remain in the ambient safety of the fire.

Happily, the regional care nurse had come by that morning to assist and make sure Mrs. Johansen was keeping warm. Agnes cleaned up as much of the broken glass from burst lighting as possible, so that the old woman didn't get hurt. There were shortages of bulbs in the local stores due to mass buying, and Agnes had to do her best to find bulbs that fit the sockets. She was only able to find two and used them in the living room and downstairs bathroom; the bedroom would have to wait until new stocks arrived.

Mrs. Johansen had asked if Doctor Hope could make a visit earlier in the day as she was not feeling so well after the shock. The nurse said he would probably be busy that day but would send a message to see if he could make a call. She felt disappointed he never showed up. But there was probably a good reason for it.

Mrs. Johansen sat as she usually did at night in her antique maroon chair; the arms were now worn to the white fabric and most of the colour was hidden behind a film of dust. Outside she could hear music being played loudly by the kids from the local boarding school. No doubt drinking and causing a mess as they often did. When she was young, they would never have done that, she would think or say to herself.

The passing of her husband had left a deep hole in her life that could not be filled. It had been a few years since he had died, and Mrs. Johansen just felt lonely. Her body now succumbed to old age, her eyesight was worsening, and her strength simply was not there anymore to do anything other than watch TV at night.

She had stayed up late and into the early morning from fear. She didn't want to be in the dark now. Had all the bulbs in the house been replaced then she could have gone to bed, leaving the lights on all over for extra comfort. But the darkness was frightening, and there were no one else in the house to comfort her.

She clumsily poured herself a glass of water from a jug close by and took some painkillers. Her hands, once proud and strong, were now disfigured and too sore to use. Pouring a glass of water was the only exercise her hands cope with; and then they shook to the point of spilling the cups contents.

She watched and admired the TV as young able-bodied celebrities danced on a game show, much to the delight of the audience. She wasn't too sure what they were dancing for? A trophy perhaps? That was the usual reward for dancing. The reason for the "celebrities" doing this was probably because their careers were skydiving faster than a rocket on re-entry, and this was a valid way to get some media attention.

She remembered when she could dance, move, and even sing like that. Her foot tapped to the music, and in her head, she was there with them on that ball room floor with her husband dancing in his arms. His comforting arms around her waist as they slow danced to a big band. She closed her eyes and could almost feel his hands take hers, his smile, and his cologne scenting the air. How she missed him.

The TV flickered and her foot stopped tapping. The lights began to fade in the room. She pressed the TV remote hoping the random tapping of buttons would somehow stop the fluctuation of both her dancing show and the lights. It did not, and within a minute the TV and lights went off. Now the only light source was from the burning embers of the fire.

Scared, she pulled up the blanket from her knees and up to her chest. She reached for her mobile phone, which Agnes was kind to provide her as the last one was broken and dialled her doctor's phone number. It rang twice before there was an answer.

'Hello? Mrs. Johansen?' Adrian's voice was lethargic like he had just been woken up.

'Doctor, the lights have just gone out again. I'm scared,' her voice quivered.

'Okay, Mrs. Johansen can you just remain calm. I am sure this is just temporary as the workmen are still making repairs to parts of the community. I am sure the lights will be back on in a moment,' Adrian said in his best reassuring voice.

'Oh… Oh… I don't know. I don't like this. What if they never come back on? What if the phone lines go down again and I have an accident?' she said scaring herself with the notion.

Adrian paused then said, 'I don't think that will happen again. Have you got your fire lit? Are you warm enough?'

'Yes, but I am too scared to put any more wood on.'

'Do you want me to call out the nurse for you?'

'No. Can you come over please, I would feel better if you were here,' she pleaded with her doctor.

Adrian paused again, 'I can come over, Mrs. Johansen, but there is not much I can do unless you are in need of medical attention.'

'My hands hurt, and my chest is tight. It is hard to breath with all this going off again,' she said.

'Okay, can you just sit tight, and I will come over in about thirty minutes. I will also call out the nurse and see if she can sit with you until the lights come back on.'

'Yes, please do that. I don't like to be alone,' Mrs. Johansen sounded grateful and sincere.

She hung up the phone and sat back smiling. It was true, she did not like to be alone, and with the power off again she just couldn't help but be terrified of the dark. Power blackouts had never bothered her before, but that was when her husband was alive. Now alone, the darkness was her greatest living nightmare, and no one was around to comfort her.

At first, she thought her mind was playing tricks and that the back door leading into the kitchen had just opened. She turned her head to the kitchen door, which was closed to keep as much heat into the room as possible. She watched the door; her breathing began to shallow. She gripped onto her blanket forgetting about the pains in her hands and watched. The handle twitched. She thought and then remembered that the nurse would sometimes use the back door since the driveway was closest to the kitchen.

'Is that you, Agnes?' Mrs. Johansen called out beginning to feel a little relieved.

No answer came.

She called again, 'Agnes, is that you?'

The door handle shook and then began to turn. The door

opened and a cool stream of winter air entered the room chilling Mrs. Johansen immediately. The fire flickered in the breeze creating shadows that moved around the room. She squinted at the kitchen to a tall figure standing in the doorway.

She called out again, her voice quivering with fear, 'Agnes?'

The figure moved forward, and a strange clattering sound like teeth gnashing resonated throughout the room.

Click-click-click.

The figure moved out of the darkness and into the dimly lit room. Its body thin, its head tilting to one side avoiding the ceiling; it was tall… it was a giant.

This was not Agnes!

The figure moved closer towards her. Its arms, long and thin, reached down from its hunched shoulders to its lean thighs. Long fingers, like those of a bat, elongated the length of the arms further reaching what appeared to be knotted knees. This giant thin figure gnashed its teeth as it drew closer. The light from the fire began to cast shadows over the figure's face. This was not Agnes… this was not human!

The creature's eyes were sunken and black, cheekbones and skeletal features protruded beneath the paper-like skin. The fire reflected orange on the creature's face revealing it pale grey, almost white. A malicious grin stretched across its oblong face. It appeared to have no lips, showing the full length of the creature's broken teeth from root to end.

Mrs. Johansen tried to scream but her chest was too tight to allow a full roar. All she could muster was a high-pitched wheeze.

The creature raised its long thin arms like a bat spreading its wings, with the fingers outstretched. The arms spread several feet wide, almost as long as the creature was tall. Its movements towards the old lady added to its horrific stature. Bare feet slapped at the hardwood floor as the creature waddled towards the frightened woman. Its shoulders hunched; its head tilted to one side to prevent scraping along the ceiling. The mouth opened and closed in frantic movements.

Click-click-click.

Then it lunged at Mrs. Johansen. Its thin hands, surprisingly strong, quickly covered her mouth, stemming her feeble screams. Its other hand took her by the neck lifting her out of her chair in one smooth movement.

Her neck cracked due to the porous bones but did not break. The creature swung around and pulled her onto the floor, mounting her. Its long legs, half the width of her own knelt on her chest to pin her down. It leaned towards her. The fire was able to illuminate its face further. Teeth gnashed together aggressively, exposed due to the lack of lips, chomping up and down like it was trying to cut through an invisible steak. Its hand covered her mouth with fingers that easily reached around her head gripping hard.

Mrs. Johansen's eyes were wide, staring deep into the creatures own sunken black orbs. Her body was rigid with fear; the blood in her veins ran ice cold as the creature turned her head to the side. She was unable to free herself, or even attempt to. She was frozen with fear.

The creature held her down with one hand, while bringing the other hand close to her face. The creature released its grip allowing the old lady to gasp a lung full of air. She was able to scream. She inhaled to scream once more but smelled something slightly odd. Something potent like those old smelling salts she had used in the bath, only stronger.

She coughed as her lungs took in the potent vapour. Her lungs immediately inflamed, and she felt like she was drowning. The vapour was fast, penetrating the alveoli and entering her blood stream. Her eyes began to close, and her screams subsided. The creature relinquished its bodyweight on her and stood up.

It turned its crooked head to face the old lady, seeming to be satisfied that she was now subdued. Mrs. Johnson's fading view was that of her husband sitting in her chair smiling. His thick glasses reflected the light from the fire, that danced in the lenses.

'It's okay, sweetheart,' he said with a gentle voice. 'Time to rest. Close your eyes and rest.'

She smiled as she lost consciousness believing to have been visited by an angel.

If only that were true!

II

The boarding school was due to close at the end of the year. This would have allowed students to finish their high school diplomas. But the property owner decided to bring the closing date forward forcing students to either finish their schooling elsewhere or wait and repeat the entire year. The building was owned by a hotel tycoon that had begun to get tired of late rent payments. Therefore decided - behind closed doors of course - to close the school much sooner and seek to renovate the property for the new occupants who have bigger wallets.

Most of the soon-to-be evicted students found new schools, but a majority could not and were left bitter by the system and the state. Some were forced to drop out of school all together. This had been of great debate at the recent town meeting as to why Norwegian students were being thrown out onto the streets with no formal education certificates to their names.

Well, that was not strictly true as most students had homes in other parts of Norway. Alas, many came from broken homes, homes that were inhabited by alcoholics or abusive parents. Students who were trying to escape home life were now being hurled back into the abuse.

The school's management had failed to properly organise their finances and had floundered on many occasions to pay rent to the building's owners.

Money talks and the little people walk.

Students currently residing at the school did not join the debate. Instead, they went out to the local woods, lit fires, and got shit faced. Some cried while others simply vented their aggression hurling rocks and bottles with made-up chants about Norway. The school had failed them, the government had failed them, their own country had left them out to dry; the future of the children was of no concern to anyone but some two-faced hotel owner that did charity work in the face of the public, and evicted children behind closed doors backed by a government wanting to appease external influences.

The students had gathered again this night for their last party in the woods. They drank away their feelings, played music loudly and smashed bottles to make some sort of anarchist point.

Tomas was just six months away from finishing school and had already begun planning his university applications before the news came. For the last three weeks he had been sick to his stomach, often followed with bouts of cramps and vomiting. He could not eat anymore and his once good looks – much to the admiration of the girls often referring him to a young Orlando Bloom – were now tatted with patchy facial hair and an outbreak of yellow spots. He no longer cared about anything. His clothes were beginning to smell as the building's owners had already begun selling off as much of the old equipment and would install new machines, new kitchens and redo the entire building ready for the new occupants once the students had left.

A friend of Tomas had a great idea of what they should do tomorrow night since the day after they would be kicked out. They would trash the place, mess it up, break the windows, and generally cause as much structural damage as possible so that heartless owner would have to fork out more money for repairs.

Tomas was not at all in the mood for an anarchist redecoration of the place. Instead, he drank alone and contemplated what was going to happen next. His parents had recently divorced leaving his mother in custody.

His mother?

He never called her that. Her alcoholism and late-night rantings on having her life ruined by kids had left their scars on him and his younger sister.

His sister would come and stop over at the school during weekends just to get away from smashed bottles and abusive rants. They never called the police after hearing of previous situations where the children were separated from their parents and from one another, only to be sent to different families around Norway. They dared not risk that.

They had both prayed he would get into a university somewhere far away from their mother. She could apply for a new school and move out having her older brother as legal guardian. And now this was not to be the case. Being only seventeen meant he could not take on a full-time job without finishing school. The only option now was to move back home and do his best to keep his sister safe.

He drank from his small bottle and felt the icy chill of beer run down his throat. A small gathering of students had joined the last night of being together. Their tears and hatred echoed throughout the small, wooded area on top of a large hill that overlooked Røyken.

'You done with that?' a voice came from the darkness behind him. A burning fire somewhere in the woods illuminated the figure as a classmate that Tomas knew but didn't socialise with.

'Err, yeah,' Tomas replied taking a final swig from the bottle.

'Great, give it here,' the boy took the empty bottle and gave him a fresh beer.

Tomas smiled in thanks and saw the boy walk a few steps away, turned his body towards the darkness of the woods, and threw the bottle as hard as he could screaming, 'Fuck you school, fuck you Norway!'

The bottle hit something hard in the void and smashed, much to the delight of the teen. He turned to Tomas again and said, 'Let me know when you want another?'

Tomas smiled, *Yeah, fuck you Norway*, he thought to himself.

Later that night, Tomas lay on his bed looking out at the window. He had turned off the lights so that he could see the stars beginning to fade behind gathering clouds. At least the sky and universe were peaceful, unlike down here on Earth. Most of the students had drunk themselves into states fitting for the youth scorned by adults making decisions on their behalf. Some stayed in the woods but would soon be back as the air temperature fell below minus ten.

His eyes began to close slightly but then opened. The orange streetlights outside the building were erratically flickering on and off. He could hear folks running to the windows to see what was happening along with shouts he could not quite understand.

The lights went out plunging the area into darkness. But the darkness was to be momentary before the entire school was lit up in a white light that bathed all the rooms in a bluish hue. Tomas could feel his face and hands burning from the light's intensity.

Tomas dropped to the floor and shielded his eyes. The light was so powerful that he had to shield them with his hands. He could see the brightness of his own blood through the closed hands and eyelids. He could hear screams resonating from other rooms as the light bathed the school in its brilliance.

Then, the light faded, and the screams stopped. Tomas opened his eyes and found he had been blinded by the light. Stars danced in his vision as he frantically blinked to retrieve his eyesight. At first, he thought the light had caused permanent blindness, but then after a short time his vision returned, and he was able to make out objects around the room. His attention was broken from what had just happened when he heard a window break downstairs.

His room was directly above the school kitchen that enabled him to hear every clang of pans and cutlery the cooks hurled around each morning. He listened as pans and aluminium mixing bowls were thrown around the room directly below. Tomas imagined that some of the students had decided to get the redecoration underway ahead of time. But, had no idea where they managed to get the light from.

Then things fell silent, but only for a brief moment. He heard glass crush as whoever was in the kitchen made their way to the door.

Then came the first scream.

The scream was loud, panicked and almost gurgling like someone had walked in on something horrific. The scream took Tomas by surprise. His heart pounded with fear forcing his lungs to spasm and draw in more breath to fuel the rapid circulation of blood with oxygen. More screams came from other dorms like lights turning on in sequence. Tomas felt around his room for a torch. A small Mag-Lite, no bigger than a large pen, provided a small beam of light, allowing Tomas to navigate around his room. He tried the light switch, but it failed to work.

He listened, trying to control his breathing so his rapidly beating heart did not dominate his hearing. The screams began to fade. It was as though the people screaming were passing out or falling asleep. The screams, powerful at first, then became lazy and lethargic before falling silent.

He heard nothing for the first few moments then some shuffling in the corridor outside his room. Turning the doorknob and opening the door he stepped out, aiming the torch in front to illuminate his field of view. He turned to the left and then to the right. Spray-painted graffiti by some of the students decorated the walls, along with damage to the wallpaper and pictures.

Something stirred in the darkness that his light managed to catch.

His light wasn't that strong, only good to break up the darkness just in front of him, after that it scattered into the blackness. The corridor ran long, and it was though the darkness was curling in from the walls, like it was a living entity trying to blanket the light from the torch. The more he tried to focus his light the more of the darkness he revealed.

Tomas called out, 'Hello? Are you okay?' his voice quivered.

The darkness stirred. Tomas leaned further out of his room and shone the light down the corridor, breaking through the darkness. The light caught something, a foot, or what looked like a foot. As the light met, whomever it belonged to, shuffled it back into the darkness. Tomas' brain did not register the shape or length of the foot since it moved quickly out of the torch light.

Then the foot's owner leaned out from the blackness and into the beam of light.

The young man's eyes opened as he looked in complete disbelief at a grey face leaning into the light. Its face bore a grin with teeth gnashing up and down. The creature was on all fours, its head snapping up from the floor to look at Tomas.

Tomas stood frozen as the creature stared at him through sunken black eyes. Slowly the creature moved a thin lanky arm forward then another and crawled towards Tomas, gnashing its teeth together.

Click-click-click.

Tomas remained frozen to the spot. His thoughts raced through his mind, but his brain could not process what his eyes were trying to show him.

His feet tried to move but failed to respond. His brain was only able to regain control as the creature stopped and then began to stand. Its height easily met the ceiling, and its thin frame and elongated limbs made the thing look like a Daddy Long Legs. Its long body, though thin, easily blocked the hallway. Tomas could only stare as the creature erected its thin frame and gnashed its teeth in preparation… but for what?

A clash of pans came from downstairs made Tomas jolt, breaking his fixation on this thing standing before him.

He dropped the torch and ran back into the room, slamming the door behind him and locking it with one swift movement. Tomas heard the creature race towards the door, arms crashing against the walls and knocking off pictures and paintings.

He felt the door handle move as the creature on the other end jiggled it trying to gain entry; to get to Tomas. The creature slammed itself hard against the door, again and again in fits of anger.

Click-click-click.

The door shook in its frame with each impact. Thomas held the handle for dear life but knew it was only a matter of time before the creature broke down the door. Splinters of wood broke free with each impact and the creature chomped down hard gnashing its teeth together in frenzy.

Click-click-click.

Tomas twisted his body around and looked at the window. Rushing over he tried to open it. But it would only go so far since a safety catch prevented it from opening fully – a school policy to prevent anyone from falling out. He pushed hoping it would break, but his strength was not there. He briefly considered breaking the window, but his room was a good ten or fifteen feet from the ground.

'No… no…no!' Tomas shouted as his attempts of escape through the window diminished.

He had only one other option, but this was like walking into the lion's den. He looked around his room for a weapon but only saw his books and chair. Moving quickly, and with added haste as the creature hurled its weight at the door, he took the chair and turned it upside down. He snapped the leg from its base. The leg broke free with part of the screw breaking off in the process. The broken end of the screw was jagged and looked sharp, sharp enough to break skin. This would at least show whatever it was outside the door that he was not only able to break bones but cause serious injuries by stabbing.

Moving back towards the door he gripped the handle. The door was shaking on its hinges as the creature tried every attempt to break in. Tomas began to count, trying to control his breathing and steady his nerves. His plan was to throw back the door and make straight for the stairs swinging blindly in the dark and make his escape through the kitchen window below. He began to count:

One...

Two...

Three...

Four...

He took a deep breath.

Five...

He closed his eyes and tried to build up the courage to face the creature outside his door.

A scream stopped his hand from pulling down on the handle. The scream was outside the door, somewhere down the corridor. The creature stopped crashing into the door now that someone else had taken its fancy. Tomas heard the creature scurry away with heavy footsteps.

A girl screamed an ear-piercing pitch that made Tomas jerk his hand away from the handle and almost had to cover his ears; a scream that sounded like it came from an old 70's movies when screams penetrated the souls of the viewers.

Tomas then heard the screams fall silent followed by a loud thump as her body hit the floor. Tomas took this opportunity to pull down on the handle hard and fast and yank the door fully open. He didn't yell or scream he just swung the chair leg with the nail out in front wildly into the darkness, hitting both sides of the walls.

Click-click-click.

He heard the gnashing of teeth and the shuffling of feet from behind. He knew he had been spotted. The sounds of chattering teeth, scraping of feet on the floor and thumps against the walls made his heart race with fresh adrenalin fuelling his legs to move as fast as he could.

He ran down the spiralling staircase, missing out most of the steps on the way down that made him reach out to the banister to prevent him slipping in the darkness He pushed open the door leading to the downstairs corridor, which in turn led to the canteen, kitchen, and recreational rooms.

He tried the first door he came to, which was locked so he tried another opposite. It opened but to a small, enclosed room full of mops, brooms, and cleaning materials. He heard a noise behind him and swung the chair leg into the darkness. It didn't meet anything, and he felt a brief moment of relief.

Turning again he ran a bit further down and tried another door that opened up to the kitchen. He took a few steps in before freezing on the spot. The room was dark, if not for some ambient light elsewhere in Røyken that dimly lit the room. Pans were scattered across the floor, plates and bowls lay in shatters as though they had been thrown around like at some Greek party.

He was not alone. Before him was a man, or dog or something on all four legs licking out of a bowl that had spilled out from the fridge next to it. Its face was half illuminated in the ambient light. It was an off shade of white; the skull was partly visible through thin stretched skin. He could not see the rest of the body as it was behind a large stainless-steel table with large pans blocking the view. Tomas looked at this animal, or creature? In truth he did not know or could comprehend what he was looking at. If his brain had been functioning, he would have said: *Demon*. But this wasn't a demon, it couldn't have been. They don't exist… do they?

The creature remained undisturbed, licking, and slurping the cream the way a dog would eat from his bowl. It grunted and slapped the bowl with its tongue slurping the cream down while the bowl made the metallic ping as it moved with every flick of its grotesque black tongue.

Suddenly there came a clicking sound from the corridor behind and Tomas looked back. His breath was held as the bowl stopped moving and the slurping noise ceased.

He turned his attention back to the thing on the floor and felt an icy flow of blood from his head down to his bare feet as the creature turned its head in his direction. Its eyes were sunken and black. Cream surrounded its mouth were a black tongue slipped back inside the dark cavity. He tried to tell his brain to lift the chair leg in a threatening manner, but his body refused to work like he was submitting and hoping this thing was not going to get him, and that it was more interested in the cream than in him.

The head drew back behind the table. The creature pulled in its long, thin limbs and began to stand. Tomas watched in horror as the creature's height was revealed; first to his height with its shoulders hunched, and then much taller. It stood fully erect much taller than anyone Tomas had ever seen. Six feet then seven feet, the creature seemed to grow. The arms reached well below the table and Tomas could only guess they were to its legs; much longer than his arms or anyone else he had seen. Its chest was concaved with each rib protruding under the skin. Its back hunched with the creature's head leaning forwards. It stood watching him, its head tilted to the side as if trying to work him out. Then his muscles reacted as the creature lifted an arm and reached out for him. It stretched right across the table as swung violently for his face.

It miscalculated the distance and missed Tomas' face by inches.

The draft from the clawed hand reconnected his brain to his body.

Tomas' muscles fired into action. With one swing he hit the creature's outstretched arm with the chair leg. The impact was hard, and Tomas heard a crack as the creature screamed a low pitched but immensely loud yell in pain. It sounded almost human, but only if a human could scream at such low decibels. It backed off a few steps and examined its arm, which fell limp to its side.

Tomas took the chance to escape as the door behind him burst open. He didn't need to look back as he now knew what was in the building. He ran around the opposite side of the creature without giving it a glance, leaped onto the table under the window, and threw himself out into the night.

The impact on the hard icy ground and broken glass was painful and knocked the wind right out of his body. He didn't notice the shards of glass had sliced through his clothes and skin, some embedding themselves in his arms and face. The adrenalin and cold blocked all sense of pain. He tried to get up, but the impact was too much. He could only crawl on the broken glass and the icy ground until he could catch his breath.

Ice and glass combined to scrape and tear at his flesh as he dragged his winded body across the hard ground. He tried to take deep breaths, but his body fought back, not quite ready to take in air. Extending his stomach and forcing out his solar plexus he inhaled again. This time his lungs took in more air, and he tried to get back to his feet.

He felt something take his ankle with a grip so rough and hard he thought his ankle was going to snap. He fell onto his stomach. The sudden jolt made him twist his head in an uncontrolled reaction to see an arm reaching out of the window holding his foot, pulling him slowly back to the place he was trying to flee.

The hand had completely engulfed his foot, the fingers long and grey, with long nails dug deep into his flesh, anchoring them like a hook on a fishing line. He tried to free himself, clutching at the ground and digging his fingernails into the frozen earth to try and stop himself being dragged back into the kitchen, back towards that creature.

He yanked his foot and felt the skin tear. Blood ran free warming the flesh before cooling in the icy air. The creature held him while another hand reached out for the other foot.

Quickly he reached for the chair leg and using the nail in a stabbing motion began to attack the hand. Missing at first but connecting with the second jab.

The skin broke and liquid ran from the creature's hand. In the process Tomas managed to puncture through the thin skin of the creature's hand and into the flesh of his own foot; though his foot only sustained a superficial stab, which the icy air provided a local anaesthetic. Unfortunately for the creature the air could not provide such medical care and it drew back with a scream so loud Tomas was sure the village would have heard.

Feeling the grip loosen, Tomas scrambled to his feet, the ice making it difficult to grip the ground at first. He began to move clumsily, slipping on the snow beneath. His bare feet dug hard into a soft patch of earth that provided him with both grip and forward momentum.

He took a few more steps before stopping and looking back to the kitchen window. He was curious, curious as his eyes had shown him something his brain simply could not comprehend. Their skin was far too pale even for a Norwegian. In fact, they did not resemble anything human he had ever seen. His breathing was heavy, the vapours from his breath sent clouds of steam in the icy air slightly obscuring his view. He saw no movement but could hear the *click, click* noises coming from the kitchen.

Then he saw a head peer out from the darkness inside the kitchen. Now he had the chance to really study the face as the creature began to study his. The cheeks were sunken, the skin evidently thin reminding him of malnourished children from

Africa he had seen on the TV. It turned its head to the side in apparent study of Tomas. Studying him and slightly perplexed that this human had fought back and caused injury. Perhaps this creature was judging what he was. Or perhaps it was hungry? That very thought made his stomach clench, his muscles tighten, and his bladder relax allowing a small trickle of urine to seep down his leg.

He saw the creature seem to sniff the air through two large holes that would have been a nose; if it wasn't for the fact this *thing* did not have one. It could smell the urine. It opened its mouth showing broken crooked teeth almost human but not quite as arranged with molars being the dominant type. Then it began to chomp up and down in rapid movement.

The creature turned its attention away from him and seemed to communicate with the others back inside. Soon there was an orchestra of gnashing teeth reverberating from the kitchen.

This moment of pause in his attackers gave Tomas time to get moving, to make his escape

His movements were accelerated, however, as one of his attackers quickly leapt up onto the window. It perched on the window in perfect balance, like a spider on a thin blade of grass. The legs and elbow joints raised high above the creature's head, with that same malevolent grin across its face. Its feet, elongated with sharp nails on each toe that etched into the wooden window frame.

Click – click – click!

The creature prepared itself by bringing in all four limbs under its body, like a spider about to jump on an unsuspecting meal. And with one fluid movement it leapt high into the air using all the momentum its skinny arms and legs could muster. Its intention was to land on Tomas with all of its weight, but Tomas was too quick. Jumping backwards away from where the creature intended to land, he avoided its wrath.

Luckily, the ground's contours declined running downhill and to the main road. Tomas lost his balance dodging the attack and fell backwards. The first impact against the ground was sharp, but he quickly realised he was rolling away from his attacker. He relaxed his body and allowed the decline to guide him to safety by the road.

There were houses to the left of the road, up a slight incline. The road provided better grip on his bare feet, and he could easily get some momentum going on the tarmac surface.

Surely someone would be at home at this time of night?

Tomas ran up the hill, passed the school, taking a momentary glance over his shoulder. To his horror he saw the creature was in full pursuit, running on all fours like a spider sprinting across the floor; its arms bent at angles and its teeth chattering. Tomas' feet were fast, but the creature's speed was greater, using all four of its limbs in sequence it could gain more ground than if it was running on two legs.

His feet, now stone cold, felt as though they would twist on the ankles and break at any time; but he kept moving. The first house was only a stone's throw away and he made for that. There were no lights on but that didn't stop him. He ran, and ran, but his fatigue and energy dropped as the adrenalin began to decrease, his breathing harder and his feet torn and bleeding. He felt his entire body drain of energy with the combination of the Nordic winter and panic consuming his fleeting energy.

The creature was close on him. It leapt again into the air but with less impetus, just enough to gain those last few feet of ground landing just behind Tomas. He turned, now breathless, now out of steam and will power, and confronted the creature.

It was no good; he could not outrun the creature. It was too fast, had so much energy that there only way he was getting away was if this thing was dead. But Tomas' lack of energy, lack of will with his fatigue caused him to just stop running. With each breath his body craved for more. Icy air filled his lungs, and he could now feel the sharp stinging sensation from his cuts. He turned to face the creature.

The creature, now seeing its prey had given up and waited for it to finish him off like the other poor students slumped in the corridors and bedrooms of the school.

The creature stood tall giving it an eerie demon-like prescience. Its tall lanky frame dark against the ambient lights like the Grim Reaper himself was standing before the boy. Tomas closed his eyes to prepare for his fate. The creature leaned forward, fowl-smelling breath exhaling from its ugly grey mouth. It reached out and took Tomas by the head, fingers extending from his skull down to his cheeks.

A fine mist extruded from something the creature was holding and into the boy's face. The last thing Tomas experienced was a scent so strong it reminded him of ammonia from chemistry class. His body began to warm-up and the muscles in his relax.

Soon he was unconscious.

12

Adrian took a little longer to get to Mrs. Johansen's house. It took a while for him to wake up enough to drive. Upon getting to the house, he saw the regional care nurse's car was parked outside. He didn't see any lights on inside the house, but a faint glow from the fire along with the pleasing aroma of burning wood from the chimney reassured him all was okay. He hoped this visit would be brief so he could return to the warmth of his own bed.

He knocked on the back door before going in, 'Mrs. Johansen?' he called from the kitchen, closing the door behind him as to not allow the heat to escape and the cold air to rush in.

No answer came. Adrian stepped in and was immediately greeted by a somewhat familiar smell of copper. Copper? It was a faint smell, but none-the-less potent. Adrian tried the light switch, but the lights failed to illuminate. He reached into his coat pocket for his phone – having purchased a new battery the previous day on his drive out with Rachael - and activated the small LED light. He glanced around the kitchen.

The kitchen was small, an old wooden table complete with etches and purple stains from beetroot juice stood against the wall, while the stove and oven, clean and tidy, was close to the door. As

Adrian aimed his phone, he saw a grey metal box. Happily, the breakers were in the kitchen. Opening the circuit box, the doctor found the main breakers had been triggered. Flicking the main fuse on brought light back into the house along with the burring of the heating pump from outside. He switched off his light and placed the phone back into his pocket.

The smell of copper still poignant in the air must have come from the fuses going, he thought. Opening the door to the living room Adrian called out again, 'Mrs. Johansen, it's Doctor Hope. I…' he stopped midsentence.

The regional nurse on the floor; blood stained the rug at the foot of Mrs. Johansen's chair. Agnes was lying face down, her legs tangled like she had been kicking out. Blood stained the back of her blue coat and had coagulated into thick ooze. He now realised the smell of copper was coming from the blood soaking into the rug.

'My God!' the doctor exclaimed. 'What the hell happened?'

He bent down quickly to the care nurse and felt for a pulse. There was no pulse, no heartbeat, and no breathing. Withdrawing he saw his fingers were slick with thick cold blood. Turning his head, he saw Mrs. Johansen standing by the window with a strange look on her face, her back hunched but stood proud, nonetheless. Her left hand dripped with blood, and in her right was a pair of scissors, stained red.

Adrian stood up in alarm unable to comprehend what he was seeing. He asked again, 'Mrs. Johansen, what the hell has happened?'

She didn't respond.

There was something not quite right here. Usually, Mrs. Johansen had a kind and gentle face; the kind a grandmother would have baking cakes and biscuits for grandchildren. But now she had this strange look. Her eyes were wide and fixed on the doctor. Her face seemed taught, like she was unhappy with something. No, that wasn't it, she was angry. Mrs. Johansen bared her false teeth, which would have fallen from her mouth if she wasn't biting down so hard.

'Give me the scissors, right now,' he demanded and held out his hand in a commanding gesture.

The old lady looked down at the scissors and brought them up to her face. With a flick of her tongue, she licked the blood from the blades and smiled. This action made Adrian almost throw up. He grimaced, leaving his hand out for his patient to hand him the scissors.

The old lady was quick to attack the outstretched hand and brought the scissors down in a slicing motion. Adrian was caught by surprise. The old lady was quick. The scissors, though not sharp, managed to cut the doctor's hand. Adrian yelled out as the scissors hit his palm. A small trickle of blood ran from the cut.

The old lady cackled like witch with excitement and launched forward, raising the scissors above her head, trying to stab the doctor. Adrian stepped backwards in an attempt to put distance between him and the scissors. Mrs. Johansen was fixated on the doctor that she had not seen her first victim on the floor. Her right foot kicked the neck of the regional nurse sending the old lady into the air towards Adrian. Both tumbled to the floor, the old lady falling on top of the doctor.

Even though the fall had broken her fixation, her attempt to stab the doctor resumed. Her cackle was now replaced with snarls of anger like a wolf on the attack.

Adrian grabbed her wrist, holding it with all his strength, and pushing to prevent the scissors from inflicting more damage. He felt the weak bone crack under his grip, but the old lady continued to snarl. Long thin tendrils of saliva and blood dripped from her mouth and onto his chin. The old lady wrestled and tried to bite Adrian. He dodged her mouth. Her false teeth fell from her grinning face and onto the floor next to him. In the confusion of the scuffle, Adrian had let go of her other hand and tried to push her off him using her neck for leverage.

Mrs. Johansen screamed and realising her empty hand was free clawed at Adrian's eyes with jagged fingernails. This caused Adrian to throw the old lady off him, no longer caring that she was frail; he could deal with injuries later. The old lady rolled to the side, dropping the scissors, and crashing into a small coffee table knocking off a cup and spilling the cold contents onto the floor. Adrian was much quicker getting to his feet than the old lady and examined the scratch to his face. It wasn't bad, just a small amount of blood came from the wound, but stung, nonetheless.

He kicked the scissors away before Mrs. Johansen could gather them for another attack. The old lady leapt to her feet, which astonished Adrian. Old Mrs. Johansen, once frail and unable to do much for herself, had now become energetic, aggressive and had managed to overpower and kill her regional nurse. Adrian was amazed at her strength.

She launched herself at him again, hands outstretched with jagged fingernails poised for another strike. Adrian side-stepped to his right to dodge the attack. Acting on impulse, he brought up his guard, twisted his body to the right and swinging his fist that met the old lady's jaw; a move even Mike Tyson would have been proud of. Her jaw broke with an audible crack and Mrs. Johansen crumpled like a boxer in the last round.

Adrian waited a moment to see if his attacker would get back up but she didn't. He bent down and felt her pulse racing. Taking out his mobile he called for an ambulance and the police.

Blue lights from police cars and an ambulance raced to the house. When they arrived, no one could have expected the story Adrian gave.

'Well, I don't know what to make of this or your story, Mr. Hope,' the police sergeant said.

'I have told you; I was called in the early hours by Mrs. Johansen to make a house call. I called the regional nurse to come by first and make sure she was okay before I came round,' Adrian handed the phone to the policeman and showed him the messages and received calls.

The sergeant took the phone and made a note in his book, then asked Adrian to sign his name below the childish scribble.

'I came here, and the lights were off. I switched them back on using the circuit breaker – you will find my fingerprints on them if you don't believe me. I came in here and I found the nurse dead from a stab wound to her neck, and Mrs. Johansen holding the scissors. I tried to see if the nurse was still alive when Johansen,' Adrian had stopped calling her Mrs, 'attacked me. She caused these scratches,' Adrian pointed to the cuts on his face and indicated where the scissors had nicked his hand.

'It is not that I don't believe you, Mr. Hope...,'

'Let me stop you there, it is *Doctor Hope*. And Johansen was, is my patient!' Adrian exclaimed.

'Right, Doctor Hope. I just find it difficult that an elderly lady could overpower and attack a middle-aged man. It simply does not make sense.'

Adrian folded his arms and sighed. Johansen was still unconscious from the haymaker Adrian had landed on her jaw and had been taken to the ambulance. To say the whole situation had put Adrian into question had made him very anxious. He was beginning to wish he hadn't bothered turning up or asking the regional nurse to make the house call. But how was he supposed to know Mrs. Johansen was capable of such things?

'Doctor Hope, we are not arresting you, not at least at this point. But we will need a full statement from you at the station. If

Mrs. Johansen regains consciousness, we will get a statement from her also. So, for now we will need to take you in. We are treating this as suspicious and one of you is responsible for the death of...' he checked his notebook, 'Agnes Poulsen. If you need to call anyone to explain the situation then do it now. Forensics will continue to work throughout the night, and I don't want anyone in the house while they are working,' the sergeant said.

Adrian took out his phone and called Rachael to explain what had happened. As he was dialling the number one of the paramedics came rushing into kitchen holding his neck and gurgling something incomprehensible. Adrian looked in his direction and saw the paramedic was holding his neck trying to stem the flow of blood escaping from a puncture wound. Adrian dropped his phone and went to the man. Adrian screamed at the police sergeant to help, who was just standing there with his mouth wide open.

The doctor quickly examined the wound and stuck his finger into the paramedic's neck. Feeling around inside the warm cavity he found the carotid artery. He pushed his thumb into the wound and together with his forefinger was able to pinch the artery and stem the bleeding.

'For God's sake, get the other paramedic. This man needs to get to the hospital fast!' Adrian screamed at the policeman.

The sergeant picked up his radio and called to the other paramedic. Everything had happened so fast and without warning that no one had questioned how the paramedic got injured. No answer came back from the radio. The sergeant called for his companion to get the paramedic while he radioed for another ambulance.

A scream came from the kitchen as the constable stumbled backwards. The young man was not injured but had been shocked by something. Adrian looked away from his patient along with the sergeant to see Mrs. Johansen walking into the living room. Her jaw was slack from the haymaker and dangled like a zombie out of a horror film. In her hand she held something meaty… an eyeball!

The sergeant pulled out his handcuffs and moved towards the old woman. She snapped her head around and swung for him with her hand open and nails aiming to his face. The sergeant was seasoned to aggression and ducked the attempted blinding. He moved around the old woman so that he was now facing her back. Quickly he grabbed the hand holding the eyeball and slapped a cuff on it.

Alas, he was not quick enough to cuff the other hand. The old lady swung an elbow connecting to the side of his head catching him off-guard, slightly stunning him. The sergeant fell backwards and stumbled into the small coffee table.

'For God's sake, get in there and help him!' Adrian screamed to the young policeman.

The policeman jumped into action and hurled himself onto the old woman, pushing her to the floor and landing with all his weight on her. She snapped and snarled at him; trying to bite his cheek, but the lack of teeth and lose jaw did nothing more than just nip rather than tear at the skin. Adrian felt useless, knowing how strong and determined this old woman was, or rather had become; he was still trying to understand how she had become so aggressive and powerful.

He maintained his grip on the artery, letting go every now and then to keep the brain oxygenated. The paramedic was in a state of shock to realise what was going off around him. The young officer held back for a moment since the lady was old. But soon realised she was hell bent and crazy to kill.

'Fucking hit her you idiot!' Adrian had become so angry no one had realised this old woman was now a maniac.

The officer lifted himself and landed a right hook to the side of her head, followed by another, and then another. Finally, the old lady began to relax long enough for the sergeant to get back to his feet and take her other hand and cuff it. They propped her up against a chair. The sergeant ran outside and found the other paramedic slumped in the back of the ambulance, an eye ripped from his head and his throat torn open.

Returning to the living room the sergeant asked, 'How is he doing?' and pointed to Adrian's patient.

'Critical, the artery is punctured, and we need to get him to the hospital now.'

The sergeant radioed the ambulance and asked how long it would be. They told him another ten minutes.

'Not the right time, I know, but do you believe me now?' Adrian asked.

'I do. But right now, let's get this man to the hospital and we can talk more after.'

The old lady, once the gentle and fragile Mrs. Johansen, now sat in her favourite chair coming back round. Her eyes were glazed and red; she twisted and pulled at her handcuffs like a beast trying to break its chains. The sergeant just looked at her with disbelief. How quickly she regained her strength and how much of a maniac she looked.

<h1 style="text-align:center">13</h1>

It was two a.m. before the police dismissed Adrian. A combination of his statement along with their encounter with Mrs. Johansen had cleared him from any wrongdoing. Still, this event was to be investigated. Adrian said that after he got some sleep he would go into the clinic and check on Mrs. Johansen's medical records to see if she had been prescribed or diagnosed with anything that could have contributed to her state. Though perplexed, he needed to make sure the medications she had taken did not contribute to her aggressive state. Adrian also suggested the hospital perform an MRI of her brain to see if anything looked abnormal.

Mrs. Johansen had been taken to hospital heavily sedated and under restraints fitting for Hannibal Lector, but not quite as extreme as the well-mannered cannibal. A blood toxicology report would be concluded the following day, and when she was in better health was to be moved to a psychiatric unit outside of Drammen for more behavioural observations.

Rachael was still awake when Adrian finally arrived home. The police station was only three minutes away located next to some other local government buildings. She threw her arms around him, but he was too exhausted to hug her back. She cleaned up his scratches and poured two generous amounts of whiskey. They talked for a little while until their glasses were empty. They tried to come up with possible reasons for the behaviour. Rachael suggested an MRI scan to see if any underlying brain trauma had led to the aggression. Adrian agreed and said he had already recommended the hospital does that.

Rachael had no trouble falling asleep now she had her fiancé back home safe and sound. But Adrian had trouble. He kept going over and over the events in his head. How was Mrs. Johansen able to gain such strength in her feeble state? How was she even capable of killing and then attacking him and the paramedics?

And that look, that evil grin, that sheer desire to kill on Mrs. Johansen's face. Did she really know what she was doing? Adrian was having trouble believing that this was spontaneous and that something must have been building up to this event. It was true she was lonely after her husband died. But to generate this much desire to kill and be arrested was damn right ridiculous. There were no real motives for her actions or behaviour.

Eventually, Adrian felt his eyes grow tired and his brain relax. He would receive the toxicology reports sometime in the afternoon and then he would know more; or at least rule out drug interactions.

After a rough night of drifting in and out of sleep, Adrian went back into the clinic to update the patient files and see if any reports had been sent through the internal system. Rachael remained at home replacing light bulbs and trying to do as much work as she could on an article she planned to submit to the scientific journals.

'You're in early,' a head appeared from the office door.

Adrian looked up and saw his colleague wearing a clinical white

V-necked shirt, white trousers with the elasticated waist, 'Yes, well I was involved in a bit of a scuffle last night with one of my patients,' Adrian said without smiling.

'Most of your patients are old. Which one was it?' his colleague chuckled.

'Mrs. Johansen. She went, well… crazy. Killed Nurse Poulsen, a paramedic and severely injured another. I am trying to find some medical history to see if anything could have set that off.'

His colleague closed the door as to not let the patients in the waiting room overhear their conversation, 'Agnes is dead?' he said clearly shocked.

'Yes, I was with the police all morning making statements. It was a grotesque scene and one I cannot comprehend. This along with finding Hans Olsen in the woods unable to even remember his own name yesterday is just strange. I haven't had chance to digest any of it yet,' Adrian huffed and continued to search through the files on the computer.

'Hans Olsen, the farmer? What was wrong with him?'

'We found Olsen miles away from his farm in the middle of the road just staring, and completely unresponsive to me or Rachael. I had to drive him into Drammen. Then we found our neighbours with head injuries and memory loss on the way home. All this right after the power cut. So bloody strange.'

'Hmmm, that is interesting,' his colleague sat on the end of his desk. 'I have had two patients come in today complaining of headaches, memory loss and no recollection of time. Both had woken on the floor and had no idea what had happened to them. One minute they were watching TV and the next they wake up on the floor in the morning. No alcohol or drug use.'

Adrian looked up, 'Where are these patients living?'

'Both are up on the hill, just up from you by that old transmitter tower. Do you think something is going on?'

'I don't know, but four patients all exhibiting similar loss of memory and headaches, does make one wonder. I think we may need to alert the health minister and get someone out. Where are these patients now?'

'I called an ambulance to take them into the hospital for observation. They complained of breathing difficulties. It is flu season, so I don't think that is related.'

Adrian leaned back into his chair, 'How old are these patients?'

His colleague looked up trying to remember, 'Oh, err… one was fifty-six and the other is in her thirties. What about yours?'

'Older. So, we can possibly rule out anything age-related. Mine were in good health. Can't be the water, I have been drinking that; we all have. Maybe something in the soil? I mean the farmer would have contact with the soil,' Adrian said.

'I am not sure. Mine claimed they had been inside all day. This power outage may have caused some photosensitivity though. I was seeing stars when our lights went out the other night,' his colleague said.

'So, you saw it too, the flash in the sky?'

'No, I missed that, I heard some folks had seen something in the sky but could have been a transformer going up somewhere. That has happened before; although a while ago due to old telegraph poles and harsh winters.'

Adrian's phone rang stopping his train of thought. It was Rachael.

'Just a second,' he answered. 'Hi, I won't be much longer.'

'Ade, the police are here. They need to speak with you,' Rachael said.

Adrian took off his shoes by the door and slid his feet into a pair of slippers. Coming upstairs he was greeted by Rachael whom in turn introduced the two officers, 'This is Sergeant Stig and Constable Stolten.'

'You are still on duty?' Adrian said to Sergeant Stig.

Stig took a deep breath, 'We have been filling out paperwork all morning, and then we got a call from Drammen to come and speak with you,' he beckoned Adrian to sit down while the younger constable took out his notebook.

'I am afraid there has been an incident at the hospital. Both Harold Klaus and his wife Rita have been, well how do I put this? They were discovered in the early hours of the morning after an altercation with patients and hospital staff leaving four dead and another severely injured.'

Adrian's mouth fell open, 'Are they okay? Are they hurt?'

'No, I'm afraid it was *your* neighbours that caused the fatalities and injuries.'

'What? Harold and Rita?' Rachael interjected. 'I'm sorry but I find that hard to believe.'

'Yes. I am sorry to have to tell you this. But we need to ask you a few questions as to their state the day they came into the hospital. Have you or your fiancée ever had any conflict with your neighbours?'

'Good God no. Harold was a talkative guy and was always inviting us over for coffee,' Adrian said trying to digest what had been said.

'Have you ever seen them take any illegal substance or have you heard any arguments?' the sergeant continued, looking down at his notebook to remind him of names and small details.

Adrian could not believe what he was being told, 'Illegal substances? These are elderly people. I think if they had dabbled with substances then it was back well before either of us were born. And as for arguments, the only argument we have ever witnessed was between Harold and a thorn bush in the back. Are you absolutely sure we are talking about the same people here?' Adrian asked.

'I am. We have positively identified them,' the sergeant replied, nodding his head to further confirm the answer.

The doctor needed a few moments to gather his thoughts and digest the information before asking some questions of his own, 'Where are they now?'

'They are currently undergoing evaluation at the hospital under police supervision. To be honest something is going off around here; last night with Mrs. Johansen, and now hearing about this. I don't suppose the elderly are getting their own back on the young?' the joke washed over everyone in the room. Stig looked at his constable and suggested he take notes. 'You are their physician?'

'I am. They are my patients. Harold comes in once a month to get a repeat prescription for his osteoporosis; that could have been done over the phone. I don't think I have ever seen Rita in the clinic.'

Stig stood up and looked out of the window, 'So would you say this is out of character for them?'

'Yes, that is what I am telling you. I know for a fact that Harold could not hurt a fly, and even if he did, his neck has given him so much pain the best he could do is to raise his voice,' Adrian continued. 'He was in a lot more pain than he ever admitted.'

'You will have to forgive me, but I can assure you from what the hospital security are saying is that either he has been lying about his neck, or he has been on something much stronger than prescription pain killers. You see he managed to man handle hospital staff much younger than himself. When they were both finally restrained, they were deranged and very aggressive. It took four security guards to restrain Mr. Klaus,' Stig stopped and rubbed his eyes, clearly tired and over-worked. 'I haven't seen them or the CCTV footage myself, but it sounds far too similar to Mrs. Johansen's attack on us last night.'

Rachael leaned into the conversation, 'If I may add, clearly something has happened to these people. Have they been drugged? That could explain random aggressive behaviours. I know methamphetamine in high doses can cause aggressiveness in people.'

'They have been checked for known drug stimulants and nothing has shown up positive,' the sergeant said.

'I would like to see them for myself… as their physician,' Adrian demanded.

'I think we can arrange that. At this stage we have no idea what started them off.'

Rachael intervened, 'I am coming also.'

'I am not sure that is a good idea,' the sergeant said.

'I think it would be good for Rachael to be there. She is a psychologist and has previous experience with clinical behaviour ever since my…,' Adrian stopped himself going further and cleared his throat. 'I would like her to accompany me as a professional.'

'Okay, if that is what you request then that is fine with me. What time, roughly, did you last see your neighbours? Were they displaying any signs of unusual behaviour?' Stig asked.

Rachael answered, 'It must have been late afternoon. We came home and I thought I should go and check up on them. It was quite a blackout we had the night before, and I wanted to know they were okay or if they needed anything? Ade went around the back to see if he could find any signs of them. He was the first to find the back window had been broken and Rita lying on her back unconscious.'

'I think it is a good idea that we take a look around outside and in the house. Please show us where you both were and how you found them,' the sergeant placed his cap onto his head and stood up.

Rachael led the way down the stairs and out onto the front, 'We came home, and I went straight to the front door. I rang the bell while Ade went round the back.'

Adrian took Stolten and led him around the back of the Klaus' house. Adrian pointed to the broken window, 'I saw this and went in. I wasn't sure if Rachael had already gone into the house because there was no answer.'

The young constable looked around the thin wooden window frame, examining it but unsure as to what he was supposed to be looking for. Adrian could have laughed as the splintered wood did not need a close-up examination. But in light of things, he felt more inclined to point out the damage rather than wait for the constable to find it by himself.

'I think you are looking for the damage to the frame here,' Adrian pointed. 'Something has splintered it before smashing the window,' he continued.

The window frame was splintered with deep scratches embedded into its wood. The hinges at the sides of the window had been snapped as if they were forcefully pulled with great strength. The constable looked down at the ground. The snow had covered most of the back, but something caught his eye. A foot had left an impression in the snow that was gradually being covered by fresh flutters. He asked Adrian to stand still while he traced the prints back toward the field.

'These look like footprints, but bare feet,' the officer said.

Adrian followed the officer's eyes and intervened, 'They do. But why would someone walk around in these conditions with bare feet?'

'It could have been Harold or Rita. They were a little deranged and may explain the sudden surge of aggression. It must have taken some force to push this window out enough to snap the hinges,' the constable said, looking back at the window.

Adrian thought for a moment, 'If that were the case, then why do the footprints lead towards the window and not in the other direction?'

The constable looked down at the ground and realised in his examination he had almost stood over one of the prints.

'Do you think you should take a photograph?' Adrian asked.

'Oh… yes of course,' the officer fumbled in his black police coat pocket for his phone and Adrian saw him unlock it, pressing the digits *nine-six-nine-seven*; The constable was as clumsy with his investigation as he were concealing his unlocking code.

'Do you want me to put my hand next to the print for scale?' Adrian asked.

'Good idea, but not too close. We can get your hand measurements later. We may need to get forensics out here to take a plaster cast of the print,' the constable said.

'Can you take plaster casts of snow?' Adrian laughed.

'Good point, but they will need to come out. I don't know what they will do but we should mark this area off,' the constable snapped a few pictures with his phone before taking out some police tape he had secluded away on his utility belt. Adrian pondered if the belt also contained gadgets similar to those used by Batman.

'Just thinking about these prints, I don't think they belonged to either Harold or Rita,' Adrian knelt to get a closer look, small flutters of snow now beginning to speckle his black hair white.

'What makes you so sure?' Stolten rubbed his thin arms through the padded jacket, that made his small frame look bulky and masculine, to warm himself.

'Well, the size for one, I mean look at these. Put your foot next to it.'

Stolten stepped close to the print, careful not to disturb it. He wore a size forty-five boot, and this print was at least ten sizes larger.

'Plus, the toes are elongated. These are either large irregular handprints or some sort of animal,' Adrian looked up at the constable to show he was serious.

The prints did indeed look like irregular hands. The main body of the print resembled a foot, but it was longer than that of a human. And the toes extended out. They could both be forgiven thinking the prints belonged to a gorilla, but in Norway, and in these sub-zero conditions? The words "highly unlikely" should be rephrased to "impossible".

'What is your medical diagnosis?' Stolten began to extend the white and blue police tape and found a part of a recently refurbished shed to connect one end over and the other at the house just to prevent anyone disturbing the prints and window.

Adrian sniffed and smiled, 'I can't diagnose a footprint. Perhaps your sergeant can put an animal to these prints. I have never seen feet like these before.'

Adrian helped put a wooden board over the print and rested the other half against the house wall to prevent more snow covering it. They then finished taking more pictures and went inside, much to the appreciation of the constable. The heating pump was off, but the house felt warm compared to being outside.

The sergeant was in the house along with Rachael going over how she found Harold at the bottom of the basement stairs, stooped over and semi-conscious. Adrian and the young constable found their way down to them. Stolten said something in Norwegian to his superior that Adrian couldn't quite catch. He showed the sergeant his phone pictures. Stig said something back and that was the end of that conversation.

Adrian broke into their conversation, 'Do you have everything you need from us and here?'

Stig turned his head towards Adrian. The dimly lit basement almost hid him amongst the shadows due to his black police jacket. If it hadn't been for his typically pale Norwegian complexion, he would have been hard to see, 'I think we will need to wait until forensics arrive and secure the area. Then I will drive you to Drammen,' he said, handing back the phone to his young companion.

14

The journey to Drammen should have taken around twenty minutes from Røyken. But the overnight flutter of snow combined with the ice underneath the white flakes made people more cautious about driving in these conditions; regardless to their deep-treaded winter tyres' ability to grip into the ice.

Despite the nature of their visit to Drammen, the scenery was very picturesque. Evergreen trees now coated with snow looked very much like an image from a Christmas card. The grey sky above was ready to unleash more snow that was due to continue for many days. And the fjord was beginning to ice at the banks.

They pulled up to the hospital with Sergeant Stig leading the way along with the young Constable Stolten riding shotgun. The building looked old despite the technological advances within the hospital. Upon entering through the automatic sliding doors and passing patients standing just outside smoking in thick jackets over hospital-issued white and blue dotted gowns, the place looked very different to the outside.

Large LCD TV screens offered visitors and patients up-to-date weather forecasts along with various department floors. Stig led Adrian and Rachael to some stairs at the far end of the ground floor, past a kiosk and a seating area. To Adrian's surprise they were going downstairs rather than up to the wards. He had never known wards to be in the basement area of a hospital.

Descending the flight of stairs led them to the basement where hospital beds were prepped along with changing rooms and showers for the staff. Another flight of stairs would lead to the magnetic resonance imagery and X-ray machines, which were in constant use. The corridor was long and had the faint unmistakable odour of dampness and bleach. Walls were left undecorated with just the crumbling plaster to hide the cinder blocks behind. Concrete floors with damp stains offered the only decoration to this part of the hospital.

As they drew closer to a room with an armed policeman standing guard did Adrian begin to understand the severity of what had happened. A room had been quickly cleared out that now served as a ward instead of a bed storage area. A doctor stood outside dressed in a white shirt, white trousers, and a lab coat to distinguish clinicians from other staff dressed in similar attire.

He held out his hand to greet the GP, 'We really couldn't have these two on the ward. Not in the condition they are in. I would advise you don't get too close. Both are deranged and quite strong,' the physician warned.

The armed policeman opened the door and Adrian stepped in. The room was well-lit. large examination lights, the kind that had a large circle of high-powered LEDs around a thick piece of convex glass for up-close observations, illuminated a man lying perfectly still strapped to a hospital bed. His arms and legs were secured to the metal bars used to keep patients from falling out and now used to keep this man held in. Although, it wasn't the straps that caught Adrian's eye, it was the look on Harold's face that sent shivers down his spine.

Harold stared at the ceiling; an unblinking stare gave him the appearance of a corpse that the undertaker hadn't yet closed the eyes of. His face was unshaven, which was very unusual for him. His silver hair was messy with dried dark maroon blood holding together the strands like hair gel.

Adrian approached the bed cautiously, he could sense Harold was like a coiled spring, and the last thing he wanted to do was set him off. Looking at his neighbour he couldn't have imagined what Rita must have looked like today. She had been moved to another room away from her deranged husband.

Adrian spoke in a gentle voice, 'Harold? Hi, I see retirement wasn't keeping you occupied enough,' Adrian shunned at his choice of words.

Harold blinked and turned his head to meet Adrian. The cracking and grinding of brittle bones in Harold's neck echoed through the room. A sadistic grin appeared on Harold's face that seemed to stretch from ear to ear like the Joker from Batman. Adrian half-expected a laugh or cackle to emerge but Harold remained silent.

At first, Adrian thought Harold had recognised him, and the grin was of relief at seeing a friendly face. But that notion was quickly wiped from Adrian's mind. Their eyes met and Adrian stood still. The smile was the same as Mrs. Johansen's this morning. This was a crazy, deranged look that was only seen in psychopaths or the FBI's most wanted images.

Harold grinned and showed his teeth.

No… no!

He wasn't showing his teeth, he was baring them. He began to suck air through his gritted teeth making hissing and grunting sounds. His chest began to rise heavily and his breathing more erratic. The once kind, gentle talkative man he once called a neighbour was now like a caged animal working up the strength to break free from his shackles. Adrian knew if Harold managed to break the straps that he would attack. He backed off.

Rachael entered and clasped her hands to her mouth, 'Jesus

Christ. That isn't Harold.'

'I am afraid it is. I need you to focus. This is as much upsetting for me as it is for you. But I need your opinion here.'

Rachael just stared at those glazed eyes, the grin, the pale face. This was not the Harold she had known. She tried to pull herself back and shook her head, breaking the glare, 'I... I don't know. He's just gone, Adrian. He is just gone,' a tear began to form in her eye and Adrian placed a hand on her shoulder.

'Remember, you are a scientist. I need your opinion,' he hoped those words would at least break her emotions off for a moment to examine the man.

Rachael shook her head in an attempt bring herself back into her profession. She moved a little closer and took a long look at the snarling man. His eyes were now fixated on her. White foam formed around his mouth as his hissed. He jolted his arms and legs trying to break the straps but to no avail. This movement halted Rachael's advance and she decided to remain where she was.

'This is a man with hatred in his eyes. Look at him; he is like a caged animal. I've seen this look before, but in the eyes of football hooligans, arsonists, terrorists; this is a primitive look.'

Harold tried again to reach out and grab Rachael, but the straps held him in place.

'Okay, that's enough. Let's get out of here,' Adrian guided her out of the room by the shoulders.

'What hypothesis have you come up with?' Adrian asked the physician.

The doctor took a deep breath, 'We haven't. It took four of us to get him into that bed. He's already bitten one of the nurses when she got too close. We have tried sedating him, but he must have taken something that has interacted with the drug. We cannot give him a higher dose of ketamine than what is recommended. So, we will just give him a few more hours and try again. We are planning on doing some blood tests to check for toxicities, and then we can proceed for an MRI to rule out brain damage. But for now, none of us have any idea. Our resident psychiatrists cannot find anything meaningful since both patients are unresponsive to the usual stimuli: snapping fingers, voice recognition, that sort of thing. The only response is that snarling. We are keeping them here for further observation and hopefully over time we can gather more results to make a full diagnosis before sending them to prison. It is just strange. The doctors who examined them last night said they were such nice people; and now this. In all honesty I don't think we will ever make a confident diagnosis, and they may end up in a mental asylum for the remainder of their days.'

'I just cannot believe it. This has got to be a dream,' Rachael said. 'I have seen this look before, not on him but in the eyes of psychopaths. Charles Manson was exactly the same.'

'Is that a diagnosis?' The physician asked in a demeaning manner, quite clearly not that happy having a psychologist guessing rather than using biological tests to reach a conclusion.

'Not a diagnosis, I cannot do that. I have lectured in criminology and used the eyes of Charles Manson and many others when educating students. This man, Harold, has those same eyes; that very basic human instinct to inflict harm on others; although, Manson chose his victims. From what we have been told, both Harold and Rita attacked whomever they found. Something has unlocked that basic human instinct. That is my professional opinion.'

'We have contacted next of kin, and they should be here soon. We also have some psychiatrists coming down from Oslo to give us their opinions and diagnosis?' the physician said, not too confident in Rachael's opinions.

Adrian sensing conflict spoke up, 'I think it is best for us to leave now. I cannot offer anything to your investigation that you already haven't checked. Please keep me informed as and when results come in so I can update their records in the clinic.'

'Not a problem, I will call you to let you know.'

'What about Hans Olsen?' Rachael asked.

'Who?' the physician had completely forgotten about the farmer.

'Hans Olsen, the farmer we brought in yesterday?'

'Oh yes, him. I haven't seen him since I got the call to attend to these two. Christ, his wife. Oh God I forgot in all the commotion that his wife was killed. I have to get a nurse up there to see him as soon as possible.'

'Oh my God, Harold killed her?' Rachael almost screamed the response.

'No, it was his wife,' the doctor said.

Adrian didn't say anything but felt something inside him, an awful feeling that he hadn't felt in nearly twenty years. It was a feeling of dread and fear. Even though they were far away from the helicopter landing pad just out in front of the hospital, Adrian could hear the burring sounds from a chopper overhead. But there was no helicopter. A loud clank from a clumsy warden as he dropped a metal bowl used for collecting organs made broke Adrian's thoughts.

Rachael caught this and was immediately aware of his situation. She placed a hand on his shoulder and spoke something softly into his ear. Adrian looked at her and then to the doctor.

Adrian cleared his throat and straightened himself up, 'Wouldn't it be better to wait until he is fully responsive?'

'Oh, he is fully conscious now. He put his memory loss to an electrical shock, though the ECG showed no irregularities with his heart rhythm. I will have to relay the news. In fact, he discharged himself against my advice.'

'He did what?' Adrian exclaimed, clearly surprised that Hans would do that, or even be capable since he was completely out of it earlier. 'Well, if he needs me, please tell him to get in touch. I can't imagine how he must be feeling,' Adrian thanked the doctor and was led away by Sergeant Stig.

15

Tomas opened his eyes and began to stir. The curtains were open allowing day light to enter his room. Although it was overcast and snowing, the brightness nevertheless burnt his eyes. He moved a hand to cover them and found he was lying on his bedroom floor, shivering in the cold air. The window was open enough to allow the winter air to flow into his room and frost the inside of the glass.

His bare feet were numb, and his nose frozen and moist. But they were in no way as painful as his head, or his chest and throat. My God what a headache he had woken up with. This must have been from being exposed to the air for so long. How he had managed to sleep this long into the day being almost frozen was beyond him; perhaps he was just plain exhausted from last night. But that dream, that nightmare was unlike any other he had ever had. He was being chased by... by? He was not sure. He tried to think but his mind clouded and all focus diminished the more he tried to remember.

Slowly he pulled himself to his feet and rubbed his eyes and face. He coughed and felt his rawness of his throat. He coughed again and felt his head almost explode with the pressure. He closed his eyes to try to dull the pain without success. The staff must be in work now and may be able to offer him a paracetamol to help with the headache.

He donned some socks and pulled on a jumper. Before leaving he closed the window and felt the radiator to make sure it was pumping out sufficient heat to warm the room. He was a little uncomfortable walking at first, but the blood soon returned to his feet once out in the corridor. The warmer air also brought feeling back to his cheeks and nose. He could now feel the wetness of snot and sniffed to clear it. His throat was sore like he was coming down with a cold or something. This was great timing since he was about to be made homeless very soon.

Tomas wondered where everyone was. It was very unusual for it to be this quiet. He expected to hear yelling from hung-over students still revelling about the closure but did not. Tomas walked down the corridor and noticed some broken glass on the floor just before the stairs. The grey wallpaper almost stripped from angry teens lay in tatters. Something came to mind, but he could not put his finger on it, like he knew why there was broken glass here. The more he tried to think the greater the headache became so he tried to ignore the glass and scratches and continued down the stairs.

He could hear sounds coming from the main dining hall. He heard cutlery being shuffled and the sounds of steel clattering on plates along with the occasional voice. He didn't pay much attention to the voices but was happy to hear them. Though, as he was about to find out, the pleasure to his ears would not be as welcoming to his eyes.

He opened the door after the kitchen that led into a large dining area with a self-help buffet island in the far end of the room. Usually in the morning he would be greeted with the unmistakable aroma of cooked bacon, sausages, and boiled eggs, but not this morning. This morning there was a different aroma drifting from the dining hall.

His eyes now wide as his brain took many moments to process what they were seeing. The drifting aroma that he had smelled was not coming from the food on the buffet table.

The entire place was peppered in blood, with people squirming around like maggots infesting a carcass. The buffet island, once used to serve meats and salads was now being used as some kind of operating table. One of the kitchen staff, a young female, was spread out with her arms and legs held by two boys, while two others had stripped her completely naked and were hands deep inside her severed stomach cavity; pulling out large handfuls of intestines and ripping it from the connective tissue with loud tearing and squelching sounds as the organs were freed from the body. The girl was dead; the horrors clear on her face that reflected the intense pain before she died.

The flesh around the stomach had been clumsily cut with dining knifes and then torn like wrapping paper by eager children at Christmas. The boys' hands were red and black with blood and faecal matter as they tore viciously into the bowls, spilling fluids onto the floor and themselves in fits of rage. The smell was intense, like a cat trey left for weeks without cleaning, or more fitting, like rotting meat in the sun.

Tomas' gazed in disbelief. More of the staff were being subjected to bizarre surgery while awake, or for some of the luckier ones had either died or passed out.

A female student, about the same age as Tomas had used her underwear to plug the mouth of one of the male cooks, while four others held him to the floor. They laughed with joy as the girl pushed a tooth pick deep inside the pupil of the man's eyes and examining the clear liquid that spilled out. His screams muffled by the pants but were nonetheless loud and painful cries.

Another group of students had completely removed a hand from an older female cook. A meat cleaver splattered with blood and splintered bone was lying down next to her arm indicating this was the instrument of choice. One of the boys was holding the hand to his face, examining the severed end, and looking quite pleased with his prize. He must have noticed something of interest in it as he found a fork and began to poke the severed end, stimulating dying nerves making the fingers twitch.

This amused him and he continued to push the fork inside the hand more aggressively like a child making a toy move faster and faster. Another of his colleagues had seen this and decided to push a fork into the woman's severed wrist. Still awake and in pain all she could do in her incapacitated state was lay there and scream as her body spasmed with pain that surged up her arm and into her neck like an electric shock.

The boy laughed like he had just discovered something new. So, he did it again, and again, hoping for more jumping and perhaps some other type of response.

Tomas wanted to throw up. The smell, the screams, the sight of blood spilling onto his fellow students and adults performing these horrific acts of surgery made his stomach cramp up. He had no idea what they were doing. Sure, they were angry, but angry enough to commit these heinous acts of violence and murder?

The lights flickered inside the room drawing Tomas' attention away from the surgeries and up to the large glass ceiling light. This was because a small boy, possibly twelve or thirteen, had found the power outlet and had driven some bare electrical wires into the sockets. At the other end of the wires was the semi-retired caretaker that was incapable of walking and required the use of a wheelchair to conduct his duties. This was one of the most lovable old men anyone had met. He kept the gardens full of colour in the summer and did the odd electrical work as he once was an engineer.

The boy had wrapped the wires from the outlet around the wheelchair without being impeded by the occupant's thrusts or defences. Some of the plastic coating had been frantically stripped exposing the copper wires to the chair's metal frame. Excitedly, he touched one of the wires to the metal frame connecting the circuit and sending large sparks into the air and two-hundred and sixty volts through the old man making him almost leap out of his chair.

'Let's plug Grandpa in,' came the screams of joy from an eighteen-year-old girl. Her black and purple-striped hair flung from side to side as she clapped with joy and amusement of the old man being tortured by this young boy.

The boy did it again making the lights flicker and the old man shake. The volts were not enough to kill him, but his age and frail health were certainly unable to cope. Soon he would die in his chair while the boy would continue to shock and make his body spasm until the fuses blew and no more power could be forced through.

Tomas could not remain in the room any longer and began to step backwards trying not to be seen. He had to get away from the dining room, the kitchen, the entire building. He needed to call the police.

He didn't care about his fellow students now, he had to move, and he had to get out. But he stopped. His train of thoughts now halted in their tracks for an extremely sharp pain shot through his head followed by a high-pitched sound that made him cover his ears and fall to his knees. He could not help it and vomited what little food was left in his stomach onto the floor. He curled up now no longer worried about the people in the house killing and mutilating others He rolled in agony at the migraine that was playing squash inside his head. A pressure rose from the back of his neck and squeezed fluids into his brain. The pain intensified as his brain inflamed. He could feel his skull crack as the fluids created pressure deep inside the cranium. Tomas balled himself up in agony and finally screamed out.

A student stepped over Tomas without giving him as much as

a glance. His hand was black and smouldering from a serious burn, but he seemed not to notice. The boy just causally ignored Tomas and continued on his journey.

The pain began to subside, and Tomas slowly calmed down. The smell of burning flesh, entrails with faecal matter and blood did not seem as bad as it did before. The screams of the dying did not seem to matter also. Instead, Tomas felt his energy returning, first to his head and eyes then all the way down his spine to his legs and feet. The energy felt good, but it also brought with it a strange sensation. No longer did he feel the pain of the headache or the rawness of his throat and lungs.

He looked around the room and failed to see the animals that were once children, mutilating the school staff. All he could see was the building he was being evicted from, evicted by a tycoon that only cared about money… money and greed.

A surge of pure hatred raced throughout his body as his energy returned.

Burn it, an inner voice spoke to him.

All he could think about was that owner, the staff, the people that had let him down, let his sister down!

Burn it, burn it to the ground.

He leapt up off the floor like a coiled spring. The screams and smells seemed more welcoming to his sensors. Tomas observed the room looking for hints to what he wanted to do next. Thoughts of the school's closure and the way the Government had discarded the students like second-class citizens, and then to his mother the drunk. He bit into his lip so hard it began to bleed. His blood boiled and his fists clenched. He could not form words and instead screamed to show his anger.

He walked around the bodies, missing the body parts now being flung around the room once the amateur surgeons had finished observing them. He walked to the young boy still shocking the old man, now a smouldering husk, looking very disappointed that he was no longer twitching violently. Tomas put out his hand and the boy looked at him. Nothing was said but the boy understood what he now had to do.

He pulled the wires from the wall and handed them to Tomas. The old man slumped in his wheelchair, smouldering with a paralysed face of sheer terror; his false teeth fell partially out of his mouth with dribbles of saliva dripping down his chin that steamed from the heat. Tomas left while the boy sat staring at the wall, now with nothing to do; *idol hands do the Devil's work.*

Tomas walked around the building looking for some missing pieces to his jigsaw. He managed to find batteries and with very limited knowledge hurriedly assembled them in series so that the voltage was increased. For his home project he did not need to worry about too many amps going into the wires; just as long as there were enough volts to set the circuit in motion. He headed outside to the gardening shed, kicked open the wooden door that, and found what he was looking for.

A whole bag of artificial fertilizer the gardener would use in the summer to plant roses and other glorious flowers. Now it would be used to make something worse… *much worse.*

16

Pal took a sip of his black coffee and peered out of the police car window. The snow was beautiful, all be it hazardous to driving. He left the car idling so the heaters would continue to pump out warm air. Despite wearing a thick black police jacket, it was still cold.

As Pal marvelled at the winter wonderland his thoughts of skiing and winter sports took his imagination; he needed to wax his skies and get them ready for some cross-country weekends. His wife did not ski, nor enjoyed being out in the snow. This was okay, he had other women he could exercise with in the snow.

His partner was outside the car finishing a cigarette. It was frowned upon to smoke while on duty, but she had gone behind some trees out of the way so no one could see her. Though this early in the morning there were not many cars or people about to see and report her.

She finished her cigarette exhaling large plumes of smoke and vapours into the air that did nothing to conceal her activity and crushed it out in the snow. She brushed her blonde hair with one hand and tied it back into a ponytail with a band, then placed the black police cap on back her head. She heard the radio buzz and

135

quickly opened the door. The waft of perfume and cigarettes entered the car with her.

'I really shouldn't let you sneak off like that. Not good for public appearance,' the sergeant said.

'Oh well. We uphold the law but nothing saying we can't have a moment to ourselves once in a while; besides no one is around. You should join me next time,' she shot a smile across at her senior.

'I have been smoke-free for five years now. I will never miss them or that damn smell.'

She continued to smile and leaned over to his side of the car, blowing into his face. The sergeant grimaced in disgust at first.

'You don't seem to complain when my tongue is in your mouth,' she laughed.

He began to smile as she placed her hand onto his lap moving her fingers around like she was searching for something.

'Wow, wow, Karen. We can't do that here. We're on duty. What if someone sees us?' he tried to brush her hand away but then held it by the wrist to keep it in place.

'There's no one around. Come on, I know you don't get any at home. You always feel more relaxed with me,' she bent her head down and began to unzip his trousers. She felt around and found what she wanted.

She softened up her lips and embraced him. He let out a long sigh. This was not right, not right at all. He was married with children. And yet this felt so good. For a man of forty-five, having a young beautiful blonde woman give him this kind of attention was overwhelming. He placed his hand onto the back of her head and aided her movements instead of pushing her off.

He was almost there; this quick but he could not help himself. He thrust her down again and she in turn felt the need to move her head in syndicate. She bit into him knowing this would make him scream out in pleasure. She moved faster, and faster scratching his leg with her nails.

'Stop, stop, get off,' he eventually shouted and pulled her off as a car came around the corner.

The radio buzzed from the station. He picked it up trying to push himself back into his trousers, 'This is Pal, over.'

Karen raised herself back into the seat. A look of frustration washed over her beautiful face.

'Pal, we have had calls from residents at Bjørnstadveien about loud noises and screaming from the boarding school. Can you go and have a look?'

'Roger, three minutes out,' he placed the radio back into its holder and looked at his mistress. 'We will continue this after, but next time let me do the work.'

She smiled and ran her tongue around her lips to wipe them.

They had parked just the other side of Røyken village, a secluded spot where they had planned to watch traffic this morning, pulling over cars for random checks. Pal pulled the car onto the main road and accelerated. Neither of them spoke during the drive to the school but both wanted this call out to be over as soon as possible, then they could get back to what they wanted to do.

Pal sped through the village and out just as quickly as they entered. All the trees were now bare apart from the snow coating the branches in beautiful crystals that protruded like icy fingers in every direction.

They pulled up to the school to find a few broken windows and some movements from inside. Pal switched on the blue lights but not the siren in the hope of alerting the occupants to stop what they were doing but not startle the neighbours. He switched off the engine and removed the keys from the ignition. Karen fixed her hat and got out. Immediately she saw a red stain on the broken shards of glass below the large dining room window. Screams coming from within the building resonated out into the Nordic winter. It was if though the students were displaying their anarchism before being hurled out of the building.

Carefully they went to the window and saw someone on the floor motionless in a pool of blood. Parts of their anatomy had been carved out. The smell of burnt flesh wafted out of the window and Karen held her nose, 'Better call this in, Pal.'

A crash followed by cheers and screams stopped Pal from going back to the car. He shouted for Karen to keep close as they were going in. They moved to the kitchen door but found it locked. A firm kick easily broke the lock and the door swung open.

The kitchen was a mess; pans and broken pieces of crockery littered the floor. They heard laughter and some more disturbing noises of gurgling and muffled screams. They followed their ears into the main dining room where they were met with images of pure horror.

Nothing had prepared them for the sight and smells of bodies on the floor, mutilations, and body parts scattered around the room. A man hunched over in a wheelchair sat smouldering in the corner. Plumes of smoke rose from the charred figure in the chair as a young boy poked and prodded the burnt carcass.

One of the students saw the police and carefully pulled out the entrails from the stomach of the cook and threw them at the officers, snarling at them like a dog protecting its meal. The police could not believe their eyes. Neither of them had ever witnessed anything like this before. The smell made Pal clasp a hand to his nose and mouth, while Karen just looked around, realising she had stepped in a pool of blood.

She yanked her foot away and moved backwards. Pal heard footsteps from behind and snapped his body around, drawing his pistol. The last thing he saw was Tomas hurling himself into the room. In his hands was a bag of fertilizer with wires sticking out the sides. The boy snarled at the police and screamed something incomprehensible. Karen took aim at the boy but was unable to get off a shot.

A bright flash, burning heat and the place shook. Windows blew out and the walls crumbled at their foundations.

Adrian was in the basement examining the new fuses the electrician had installed when the house shook. At first, he thought Rachael had dropped something large in the kitchen. Then he felt the ground shake and the windows rattle in their frames, 'Are we having an earthquake?' he shouted upstairs.

'God that was loud. I didn't think we got earthquakes in this part of the world,' Rachael said from the living room.

Adrian read the meter and felt the new fuses. All seemed fine and nothing was running hot. He closed the fuse cabinet and switched off the light. At last, power was fully restored to the house, and they could both unwind in front of the TV.

Rachael screamed from the kitchen upstairs, 'Oh God! Ade, come quick. There's been an explosion!'

Adrian raced up the stairs, using the banister to pull himself up, and joined Rachael in the living room. He followed Rachael out onto the balcony and saw black smoke and flames rising from the boarding school in the distance. Taking out his phone Adrian immediately called the fire brigade and ambulance, 'I should go over, I can give medical help to anyone hurt,' he said.

'Be careful, don't be a hero,' Rachael pleaded and looked frightened.

Adrian pulled up to see the school, now completely engulfed in flames. People had gathered from nearby houses and were looking or filming the scene using their mobile phones – as folks seem to do these days instead of helping. No one had attempted to go inside. The fire was so intense that it began to warp the metal around window frames and the nearby streetlights. The smell of burnt wood and something quite different, like a barbeque but not as alluring billowed out of the shattered windows. Adrian instantly knew what the smell was, and he stood watching, his memory flashing back to a faraway country.

The fire licked the black smoke as it furiously rose into the air, blackening the sky and snowing ash; or what seemed to be ash. Adrian could only stand, as with everyone else and watched the inferno engulf the school with such intensity, he already knew no one could have survived.

The fire brigade pulled up and were fast to get water onto the building that vaporised with a loud hiss as it hit the metal frames and wooden structures. Other engines soon turned up along with paramedics and police. Adrian stood back and watched as firemen, dressed in heavy fireproof clothing with breathing apparatus, beat back the flames. Their companions dowsed them with water from behind to prevent overheating and catching fire. They cut down burning timber with large axes, while others ran up from behind and sprayed the inside of the hallway with water to clear a passage through. The flames burst out forcing the firemen back, but only for a moment. Their skill and training coupled with their heroic nature drove them inside to find any survivors.

A police car came screeching up the main road, turned sharply to the left and stopped by handbrake. Sergeant Stig leapt out of the car with such assertion he forgot to apply his cap showing messy, unkempt greying hair.

Adrian ran over to him. 'Stig, what the hell is going on?'

'Adrian, what are you doing here?' Stig looked shocked to see the GP. But his attention was not focused on the doctor but at the school.

'We heard an explosion and then saw the fire. I came over to see if there were any people in need of medical attention.'

Both men needed to shout as the fire roared, wood splintering and cracked in the heat. People screamed when a window, somewhere in the back of the school blew out. Both Adrian and Stig ducked with the force.

'Did you find any injured?' Stig asked standing back up.

'No, it is impossible to get anywhere near that place.'

Stig looked around and saw the police car used by Pal and Karen. He dismissed himself from Adrian and went to investigate the vehicle. No one was in and the keys had been taken. Stig called to the fire chief, 'We have two missing officers to add to whoever is inside. We need a list of names inside the building. How are your men doing in there?' he pointed to the flaming building.

The fire chief called the team leader inside using a large hand-held radio transmitter and waited for a response. The word that they were pulling back until the fire was under control did not fill Stig with much hope of finding his comrades.

'Is there anything I can do?' Adrian asked.

'Who are you?' asked the fire chief.

'Doctor Hope, the local GP here.' Stig answered for the doctor.

'Doctor Hope, go and assist the paramedics as soon as we start bringing people out,' the fire chief shouted and pointed Adrian to the ambulance crew that were already preparing black body bags and stretchers.

Stig shouted his young constable over and told him to get the crowed back to a safe distance and keep them there. The road would also need to be closed off to traffic. More emergency services were on their way to assist and Stig wanted them to have full access to the school.

One of the fire men came out of the building carrying something small and black in his hands. He stumbled holding the object and had a hard time getting back to his feet.

Something blurred over the radio and the fire chief along with Stig raced over. Adrian watched as Stig turned away and almost vomited at the blackened entity the fireman dropped to the floor.

The fire chief seemed more hardened and shouted to the paramedics.

Adrian was about to go but was stopped by a paramedic, 'No need for you to come, doctor, this one is for the bag,' he said.

Adrian stood partially frozen, taken aback of what he said. *For the bag?* The paramedic meant that this was an incinerated body, and by the look of the small, mangled object was a child. Adrian stood staring at the child, curled into a foetal position that resembled nothing more than charred timber. His memory flashed back again; this time clearer. The hot sun burning down onto a sandy desert, the smell of burning bodies combined with the screams from people all around brought Adrian back to his nightmare.

An explosion turned his attention from the dead child to the side of the building. A gas cylinder had burst resulting in a huge fire ball out the back of the school. The crowed screamed and Stolten used this to push the public back. Adrian saw more police cars turn up to the scene. This must have taken all available manpower of Røyken's police station and then whoever could be called in. Another charred body was pulled from the burning school, and then another.

The blackened bodies were bent and disfigured. Adrian could not distinguish adult or child. He watched as the paramedics cooled the bodies with water before stuffing them into black body bags for forensic identification later. Adrian had a newfound admiration for these paramedics and what they were being put through, not once letting their emotions get in the way of work. But he himself simply could not bring himself to understand what he was seeing. He knew that more of these disfigured black bodies would be coming out and that any hope of finding any survivors would be lost with the school.

'We need some help over here,' shouted one of the paramedics.

Adrian just remained motionless. He could not take his eyes off the bodies that were now mounding up before him. The strong putrid smell of burning corpses, like sweet, tanned leather in the sun, gripped his memory so tight he could no longer hear the screams from the crowed or the call from the paramedic.

Eventually the paramedic finished packing a body into a bag and took hold of Adrian's shoulder, 'I need your help, we need to get these bodies into the ambulance quickly. We can't have people seeing these.'

Adrian turned to see the paramedic; their eyes met. The look in Adrian's eyes halted the paramedic, but only for a moment. Knowing that Adrian was in a state of shock or panic made him regret asking for the doctor's help. But help he needed. He shook Adrian by the shoulders and dragged him off his feet to assist, pushing a body bag into his hands and screaming out so that he could be heard for help.

Adrian slowly came back and looked at the bag in his hands. His brain was able to repress those memories for the time being and he began to follow the paramedic's instructions.

The fire team emerged with more charred bodies, one Stig recognised. The torso of an adult, parts of the police rank of sergeant was burnt but distinguishable by the yellow "P" that was stitched to their jackets. Stig waited until the body was cooled before he took off his hat and placed a hand on the torso's chest. He bowed his head and said something.

Twenty blackened bodies had been pulled from the school before the fire was under control. The fire team had only made it as far as the dining hall and could not go any further until the fire was completely out, and it was safe to venture further in. Severe structural damage and difficulty in distinguishing body parts for burnt wood made things more difficult. They pulled out and helped with dowsing the fire from outside as the fire chief barked his orders and pulled his people to other parts of the building to control the fire.

Adrian's body had been running on adrenalin for thirty minutes and was now on a come down. He slumped to the ground knowing that these events were about to unleash something horrific in his psyche. He was exhausted and tired. He tried to stand but was forced back down by the paramedic who knelt beside him.

'It's okay; I think you should go home. There is nothing you can do here. I doubt we will pull anyone alive from this. This is our job now. You go home and drink a very strong black coffee with some whiskey. Trust me when I say this. Go home, do some cleaning, build something, and keep busy. Don't look out of your window and don't come back,' the paramedic looked Adrian in the eyes. His words were stern like he was speaking to child.

Adrian nodded. He had seen death before. The paramedic helped the doctor to his feet and walked him to his car. Without looking at the school he pulled out passed the police tape and onto the main road. Adrian drove home, pulled the car onto the drive and turned off the engine.

Rachael had seen him pull up and was already making her way outside. She stood and saw the look on his face. He was blank. His hands gripped the wheel of the car so tight his knuckles had gone white. He just stared into the distance, unable to hear the words coming from his fiancée's mouth. The whirring of an ambulance helicopter above, combined with the smoke from the fire that had now turned Røyken into a giant bonfire, began to send his mind to the past.

<h1 style="text-align:center">17</h1>

The Government's decision to invade Iraq back in 2003 was not met with support from either opposing parties or the British people. While the then Prime Minister Tony Blair argued for military intervention, the US had already drawn up battle plans and began mobilising ground troops and aircraft to familiar airbases in Kuwait. The US was much quicker at passing the vote through Congress than the UK Parliament. This was partly due to having a majority of Republican representatives, and the previous year's atrocities on New York helped to fuel support.

Both Governments tried to reason with their respective citizens in different ways. Tony Blair – the same person that had found a resolution to the Northern Ireland peace process – now seemed to hound for war. The need to disarm Saddam Husain, to stop his enrichment of chemical weapons, and prevent the use of "weapons of mass destruction" – a phrase that would be used for decades – were the reasons.

President Bush took another route to get his message across. It was patriotic. Not since Pearl Harbour had the United States ever witnessed an attack on American soil. Simply put, Saddam was a risk – not a potential one or someone that was likely to attack

America and her allies, but an actual risk – and he needed to be both disarmed and removed from power. As it transpired, this would not be the first time the West would remove a nation's leader simply because they didn't agree with their ways of doing things; do as we say, not as we do.

The joint UK, US, and Kuwaiti air base Ali Al Salem would need new aprons and rubber aircraft hangers to accommodate Apache helicopters and transport aircraft. The US airbase, Ahmad al-Jaber, was to expect over 200 fighter and bomber jets from both British and American armed forces.

Adrian Hope was serving as a medical officer in the RAF at the time. He was stationed at RAF Marham and worked as one of the GPs. He missed the war with the Taliban in Afghanistan, but now the eminent conflict with Saddam Husain plagued his mind. Every morning he would have breakfast in the Officers' Mess and overhear the talk from the tornado pilots of just how close they were to being deployed. It was not until Adrian got into the station clinic that his commanding officer called him and his colleague in for the news.

'Right, let's get straight down to it,' the wing commander's tone was blunt, even in his best Etonian-schooled accent. 'We still don't know the situation in Parliament, but Strike Command have been given the orders to ramp up personnel in Kuwait. It is my duty to inform you both have been selected for operational deployment to Ali Al Salem.'

Selected was an interesting word to Adrian. Combined with the grin on the wing commander's wrinkled face it seemed more like he had won a competition. In truth, he was a number that happened to come up on the computer.

The wing commander continued, 'You will brief your staff and get an inventory ready to leave from here in a week. If you need to order any additional medications or field supplies, then have this ready for me by the end of the day. I want things packed and ready mid-week so we can go over anything that is missing or needs replacing. Any questions?'

Adrian raised his hand like he was a pupil at school, 'Sir, who will take responsibilities for the clinic while we are busy orchestrating the inventories?'

The wing commander's grin widened, 'There will be civilian GPs coming in tomorrow to take over outpatients, and I shall be on hand to take some clinical duties. I want you to focus on the task in hand; inventory first, clinic second.'

Adrian and his colleague held a meeting to update and brief their nurses and clinical technicians. Many questions were raised, and opinions voiced on how this was unjustified. Adrian could only reiterate what he was told to say. At no point could he voice his own views. He had to show his leadership and trust in command and the prime minister. It was very difficult to bite his tongue, but this was the way of command and management. Later in the Officers' bar could he speak freely to his friends and voice both his concerns, lack of medical care in the field and how this build up was still strongly opposed by the United Nations.

'Don't worry yourself,' said a ginger-haired squadron leader. 'This will be no different from any of the other times Saddam has messed about with UN investigators. He will just wait until we ramp up and then allow everyone in to inspect his weapons.'

'You see, it isn't like the other times,' Adrian said sipping his pint. 'We have never had this kind of build-up and deployment against Iraq. Have you seen the amount of ammunition coming into the camp? Those jets are ready to deploy within the week. We have a carrier out there, the army is sending everyone they have, and now we are ramping up the medical teams also,' Adrian needed to take a deep breath and find the right words before his frustration got the better of his reasoning. 'No, this is no longer a show of strength. The amount of money going into this would suggest it is only a matter of time before we do something this nation will be paying for years to come.'

A friend laughed, 'Don't worry, doctor, you won't actually have to be doing the fighting. You just make sure those soldiers are patched up so we can all come home much sooner.'

'Patched up? These are men and women with families. You make it sound like everything is a quick fix in medicine. Have you not seen the state of people coming back from Afghanistan? You think a box of anti-inflammatories and a medal will see them through the nightmares? If this goes ahead, we will be seeing the repercussions for decades.' Adrian slammmed his beer down spilling most on the bar. Realising his anger he took another deep breath, 'All I am saying is that nothing ever good comes from war.'

A small green waxy tent had been erected in anticipation of Adrian and his group of medical personnel's arrival at Ali Al Salem. The flight had been long and mundane. Books and magazines served as the only entertainment on the very noisy C-130 Hercules aircraft. Ear plugs were issued to prevent the deafening sounds from the ill-insulated aircraft engines vibrating inside the cold cargo compartment.

The flight was long, very long for the slow-moving aircraft. They made a brief stop at RAF Akrotiri in Cyprus for fuel and a chance for everyone on board to recover from the cold and noisy interior.

Upon landing in Kuwait, Adrian was immediately led away for a briefing on how the situation was at the airbase. Rifles were issued and stored at the armoury. Upon request they were signed out, along with only seven rounds. As it turned out, almost all offensive weapons and body armour were of short supply.

'The current situation depicts all personnel to keep a watchful eye out for suspicious characters. Any bag left unattended will be treated as an explosive device. There will be weekly alarms and your commanding officers will be briefed on your nearest shelter. Respirators and nuclear and chemical warfare suits will be issued after this briefing, and will be carried at all times,' the army sergeant said in a strong and confident manner.

Adrian had been on routine deployments before, and a customary briefing was nothing new to him. But this time it was different. The fact the armed forces had scaled up to this magnitude would surely invite some offensiveness from Iraqi or even Taliban militants. Adrian found himself listening more closely than he had on previous briefings. The location of his nearest shelter brought home the realism of what was happening.

The burring noises from Chinook helicopters came with valuable medical supplies for Adrian and his team a few days later. More troops comprising of US and Royal Marines meant more vaccinations, pain killers and a whole stockpile of anti-nerve agent medications. All the time the loom of war grew closer with each passing day. And yet, still no official word from back home of whether this was going to happen or not.

All seemed routine during the build-up of forces; in between running for the steel shipping container that served as a bunker during mock air raids. Prescribing anti-inflammatories for those folks that had been sent out with injuries and sending home the ones that needed proper medical care; much to the anguish of their commanding officers.

Adrian found himself on the end of one army major. A well-built bullyboy from the Wales that believed injuries were a sign of weakness. Sending one of his boys back to the UK seriously understaffed his platoon. It amused Adrian in a strange way. This brotherhood of servicemen and women were mostly for public appearance. Fights were common and were not service-specific. Adrian was spending most of his time dealing with bruises, cuts and even a broken nose from these inter-services boxing matches.

Those personnel that were being sent home for proper medical care were preyed upon by their own, like a pack of wild animals seeking out the weak. All of this, and the shadow of war, gave Adrian serious thoughts about his career aspirations after this whole mess was over.

Folks were issued with nerve agent pre-treatment tablets (or NAPS) and offered anthrax vaccines. Both medications were not without controversy. The infamous Gulf War Syndrome was thought to be caused by these medications. In truth, pyridostigmine bromide, an anti-nerve agent given to the first Gulf War soldiers correlated to the disease. But this was not found out until over a decade later, or a decade too late! Of course, any medication prescribed is only administered with patient consent. But in the military, folks were ordered to take them. *Wait and see*, Adrian thought to himself, and avoided being vaccinated.

It was hard for Adrian, not knowing what was going on. No one, other than those in High Command back in the UK – the ones that wore many medals and had fancy gold braiding around the rims of their caps – if this invasion was ever going to happen. Every Monday and Friday the entire British forces were mustard to a common area for an update on what Parliament – a fancy name that now meant "what Washington ordered" – was debating.

A high-ranking army officer stood at the front of the large group of British Soldiers and Airmen to give the briefs, 'It is still unclear of whether we will go into Iraq or whether all this build up is just to show Saddam we're through messing around. In that sense there is still debate in Parliament and no further orders have been issued. We are to continue establishing ourselves and keep the jets flying,' the general stood with his hands on his hips to further display his confidence and dominance.

There was something strange about his tone. Adrian thought

he sounded disappointed; like he had waited his entire life to go to war. But the next words that came from his commander made Adrian sick to his stomach.

'I want you all to stay sharp, alert and focused. If the order comes, we will be going into a war zone. Not many of you will be coming back. Therefore, you need to be on the ball. Work together, get the job done.'

Why the hell would he say such a thing? There were young men and women in the audience, most had plans, dreams, and very few wanted to go to war or actually believed was necessary.

Adrian muttered to his friend sitting next to him, 'Is this bloody fool going to be doing any of the fighting?'

His friend smiled and whispered, 'He needs an assistant just to pull his trousers on. Do you think he could actually fire a rifle?'

The looming shadow of war played heavily on Adrian's mind. His body was alert twenty-four hours a day. He slept for around two to three hours before he woke believing a gentle breeze to be a helicopter. He, like many others at home and in Kuwait, didn't know what would happen. Saddam had already allowed UN investigators and was now pleading with the world to not allow any invasion to happen. But as it turned out, the Governments had already decided. And that cold and sunny Thursday morning, on March 19th, the order was finally given.

'Come on, it's kicking off,' a balding army officer Arian had treated for sunburn came rushing into all the tents.

Adrian almost fell off his green canvas stretcher bed. The loudspeakers situated all over the airbase screamed out for all personnel to muster immediately outside the mess hall, Adrian went into robot mode and threw on his uniform. Grabbing his medical kit and respirator he joined in the crowed running to the meeting area. He was still half asleep, but his reflexes had been sharpened due to the constant drills and mock attacks.

The same general stood in front of some very tired and exhausted military personnel, 'Right, we've had the call. We're going in. I want everyone to be packed, and ready to go in one hour. We meet back here on the hour for convoy groupings. No lagging, no eating or time for coffee, get it done,' he gestured with a wave of his hand for everyone to dismiss.

And that was it. In a way it was a relief. Over the last few weeks of knowing nothing, they knew this was it; they were actually going to war — or as Adrian had put it, invading a nation without cause.

Within the hour they had packed up all the medical equipment, made a new inventory of drugs, and managed to get the large green canvas tents packed away. Usually this would have taken much longer, but the ever-vigilant general gave them the motivation to achieve this by constantly screaming. They had no idea where they would be setting up next.

The convoy was comprised of four armoured light vehicles, with infantry manning large 50 calibre guns, and a few old Bedford four-ton trucks packed with troops and equipment. And somewhere in the middle were Flight Lieutenant Doctor Hope and his medical team.

The convoy stuck to the main roads heading north. Kuwaiti police had been assigned to guard the main supply routes and permitted the allied forces to ignore speed restrictions. Most waved and cheered, others just looked at the floor and kicked up a stone.

The Bedford truck's suspension was old and met every small dip with a violent bounce in the back. Everyone in the back held their kit bags between their legs and rifles tight. Adrian looked down at his own rifle.

The SA80 was not regarded as a dependable weapon. He had personally encountered issues when firing these before; often jamming and requiring a range supervisor to assist in clearing the problem. He didn't know if the thing would even fire if something were to happen. He looked around and examined each of the military personnel. Everyone was dressed the same, helmets and green combat attire. He was sure he didn't recognise anyone other than his own team. They could be army or air force for all he knew.

The long drive towards the United Nations boarder was semi-joyful. The conversation inside the Truck was pleasant. Most of men joked or talked about the sports they were missing to keep their spirits high. The joking stopped whenever a Challenger tank raced passed them at high speed, or a fighter jet roared above shaking the truck and its occupants. It was not until they reached the boarder when things began to get real.

Suddenly they were in Iraq.

'Keep your eyes peeled and stay sharp,' said one member of the truck. Adrian didn't know which service he was in, but his tone would depict that of the British Army.

'Where exactly are we heading to?' Adrian called out to the man he believed to be army.

'Basra,' he replied.

Adrian had no idea where that was in relation to the capitol. The journey could have been relatively quick or span over several hours. He was already beginning to feel the heat inside his one piece of body armour, with beads of sweat running down his helmet. He called to his team to have their medical kits ready for whatever they were to encounter on the way to Basra. Close air support Apache helicopters flew overhead to provide protection and observation to the convoy.

An explosion somewhere in the distance gently rattled the vehicles and the order to stop came over the radio. Nerves were on edge; Adrian didn't know whether to clutch his medical kit or his rifle. As it turned out he had a hand on both. They waited for a few minutes while the convoy commander talked with the pilots. The pilots informed the convoy an enemy tank had been engaged and no further threat could be seen. Adrian now felt the realism more than ever. He looked down at his hands. They were shaking. With his nerves on edge and his senses sharpened he didn't realise that his legs were also trembling. Looking around he saw the same reaction in most of the people in the truck.

'Jesus Christ, this is for real,' a young airman said.

'Just stay focused,' Adrian said trying his best to appear calm and in control. 'We do our job, patch up broken soldiers and move on,' he continued. The words coming out his mouth tasted bitter.

Broken soldiers? Jesus Christ, he had to mentally tell himself never to use such a phrase ever again. These were people, not robots he could just simply apply some weld and new wires, and all will be happy and chirpy.

Things quietened down when the convoy began to move again. Some of the strangest things happened as they passed small towns and villages on their way to Basra. Folks ran up towards the convoy. Adrian was alarmed and gripped the SA80 with both hands.

Instead of being insurgents these people were waving and smiling at their invaders. *Why on earth were they happy?* Adrian thought. Did they really like the idea of being occupied by Western Forces? As it turned out most of these people had been oppressed by Saddam's regime; some had lost family members to horrific chemical attacks.

But then there were others that either yelled at the convoy or just remained silent and cared little. Whether the invasion was legitimate, a good idea, and liberating, just ask an Iraqi and he or she will give you the honest answer.

The convoy rolled up to Basra and stopped. Adrian couldn't

see anything out of the front; instead, his only view was the rear of the Bedford. During the journey they passed the smouldering remains of the Iraqi tank and were relieved not to see any bodies. Adrian hoped the tank was either unoccupied or that the soldiers had managed to get out alive. To go up against a battle group of this size and strength was suicidal for the limited Iraqi armed forces.

Everyone was told to disembark the truck and wait for new orders. Most took the opportunity to take pictures next to street signs. The British smiled and threw up peace signs for the pictures and seemed to be happy to be here… or at least have made it here in one piece. Adrian also took the opportunity to have his picture taken. He gathered his team and stood smiling by a sign that read "BASRA" underneath the Arabic name in smaller letters. The camera clicked just before a large explosion close by knocked everyone to their feet. The loud and powerful boom felt like being kicked in the back.

Adrian fell to the ground; the combination of the blast and contact with a rock forced the air out from his lungs. The rifle fell from his grip, and he rolled over onto his back. His ears were buzzing, the sudden impact had jolted his brain and he his mind was now blank. He stared at the blue sky that was becoming dusty in his view. Unable to breath he reached down his body and examined his chest.

He tried to suck air back into his lungs. His body fought to inhale but eventually he was able to swallow a large lungful of sandy air. He was relieved when he moved his arms and legs, and realised he was okay. He shook his head, trying to regain his senses.

He searched the ground for his rifle. Sifting around the hard rocky ground he searched for it. He saw the black butt a few feet away. Twisting his body around, he crawled towards his rifle, loaded a round into the chamber, and took a kneeling position.

People in the city ran for cover and Adrian found himself

training his sight on everyone that moved. It was as though time stood still. The adrenalin was slow to enter his blood stream, and this gave him time to gather himself before sheer fear took over. The adrenalin came when his ears finally stopped ringing from the blast.

He heard someone close by scream, 'CONTACT… LEFT… OF… BUILDING!'

Adrian scrambled to his feet. He looked around and saw his team were all okay, though shocked, and not knowing what to do. It was down to him to gather his people and lead.

What seemed to sound like fireworks going off in the city were in fact gunshots. Two UK soldiers came from behind a building dragging someone behind them. Something was very unusual. This looked like a training exercise Adrian had been on many times in the UK. A poor bugger was made up to look injured and Adrian would go through the motions to make the chap better. But this was different.

The two men were dragging an injured soldier behind them, screaming for cover support and a medic. The man's clothes were torn and black, smouldering around the torso and legs. As they got closer Adrian could see the man's right boot was limp behind the right leg. The man's foot was loose just above the ankle. Burning paint and munitions mixed in an unpleasant aroma of diesel fuel drifted with the breeze that passed Adrian's nose. As the soldier was brought closer a new smell reached Adrian's nose, a smell he would never forget. Adrian reached the men pulling their comrade to safety.

Adrian looked down at the soldier. His face was badly burnt. His cheeks were blistered and turning black. The smell of tanned leather from the soldier's burnt flesh seemed to cling to the hairs inside Adrian's nose; a smell he would never again be able to bear without seeing the horrors before him. Adrian stood looking, not knowing what to treat first. He looked at the man's face, then at the foot. Blood oozed from the injury that trailed from the direction in which he was dragged.

Quickly, Adrian reached into his medical bag and found an elastic strap used for applying to a patient's arm before taking a blood sample. This he used as a tourniquet to stop the bleeding. As he tightened the elastic strap the man's foot flopped to one side. It was now clear the foot was completely severed. Only the tattered remains of the soldier's trousers held the foot.

The soldier, dazed and in shock managed to let out a scream, 'I want to go home!'

Reaching back into his medical bag, Adrian found the morphine pen. Ripping off the safety cap and exposing the long needle, he found the soldier's buttock and pushed the needle deep into the muscle. The drug worked quickly, and Adrian ordered his team to get the soldier further back so he could begin applying bandages while taking cover.

Apache helicopters flew overhead, diving into the city like angels from above. Huge explosions followed by screams of people within the city dampened the orders Adrian was trying to give to his team. Plumes of black smoke helped provide some cover while the medical team worked.

A Chinook had been dropping off supplies to the front line a few miles away and was quick to arrive at Adrian's location. The helicopter landed and loaded the soldier and the medical team. There were no field medical tents erected due to the speed of the crossing. So, the Chinook had to go back to Kuwait.

It wasn't until much later that Adrian was able to digest the events. As he sat in a surgeon's office in Kuwait City could he really reflect. He witnessed three more helicopters bringing injured or dead soldiers back from various areas of Iraq.

His patient was now stable, but the horrific injuries he sustained would leave him disfigured and disabled for life. It wasn't the severed foot that made Adrian reach for the bin and expel nothing but bile. It was that smell; the smell of burnt flesh, the smell of tanned leather. It would be days before the smell could be eradicated from his clothes. But wherever he went, he could always smell it. And when he smelled that same sickly scent, he found himself back in the desert, back in the war.

18

Leaving the desert and the war once things had stabilised and Saddam captured, Adrian was finally on his way home. Although his body was on the way home, his mind, however, was still in the sand. The nights were the worst. The darkness brought both the images and the ghosts of the desert into full view. The screams, the explosions, the sights, and the smells all came with the darkness.

It was common to wake and rush out of his room, believing the dream to be real, and that he was back under attack. The lack of sleep was becoming apparent to his work colleagues. Anger was not uncommon for those affected by conflict. And to Adrian, the anger was a way to hide his emotions. Tiredness also contributed to his new attitude.

He had become twitchy, the roar of a jet taking off would trigger some sort of flashback and he would be reaching for his medical bag and shouting out for people to take cover. Eventually, his symptoms were recognised, and he was diagnosed by his colleague with having post-traumatic stress. He was sent to the military hospital Headley Court for help. It was strange to be there. He had sent many patients to the hospital for injuries or rehabilitation. And now he found himself as a patient.

His rehabilitation plan was simplistic. Exercise twice a day and therapy sessions involving guided meditation and deep discussions. It was here that he met Rachael. She was assigned as his one-to-one psychologist, with a specialty for behavioural rehabilitation and studies. It wasn't love at first sight, far from it. In fact, it took Adrian a couple of weeks to really open up about his problems. Rachael was a kind, beautiful woman. She was patient and spoke softly. Even when Adrian raged and kicked at the furniture, her tone never shifted. Eventually he calmed down and began to talk rather than spit out insults.

'Tell me why you are angry, Adrian?' Rachael asked after Adrian had finished screaming at nothing.

'Angry? Have you seen the patients here? These men and women are the real patients. Most have lost limbs, severe scarring and I met one in a wheelchair with severe brain damage; he slurs his speech and is being taught how to use a fuckin' knife and folk again. Do you see why I am pissed? Why am I here? For some nightmares I should have stopped having when I reached ten,' Adrian needed to take a deep breath.

'I hear what you are saying, Adrian,' Rachael's tone softened. 'I have met with many of these people. Yes, they are badly injured and that's why they are here. But this is a multi-disciplined hospital. We don't just take care of the physically injured, but also to treat the mind. And that's what I am here to help you with. You have all your limbs and are healthy compared to others here. But this is about you now, these sessions and your time here is all about getting you better. In order for me to do that, you need to understand you are here to get better.'

Adrian lifted his head from the floor and looked at her. For the first time he saw her through calm eyes. Her words began to relax him. Now he could see her beauty and wisdom. You could say something inside him was beginning to release the hate and was ready to relinquish the nightmares.

During their sessions, Rachael would have Adrian lie on the long couch and go through some guided meditations. They did this at the start and at the end, with discussions in between. Over the next few weeks, Adrian had really begun to open up. And as the sessions continued, the nightmares and darkness began to fade. They never really went away but were less horrific.

Towards the end of his time at Headley Court, Adrian was able to sleep through the night. But there was something else about these sessions, and it wasn't just the relaxation. Adrian had found himself attracted to Rachael. Her blonde hair, softly spoken words and guidance were just some of the traits he liked. Her mind was sharp, and he could easily converse about mostly anything. He had offered to take her out for a meal, but she declined, using a no dating of patient policy. But Adrian was not going to let this one get away.

After returning to Marham, he picked up the phone and called her office.

'Hi, it's Adrian,' he said with a slight nervousness in his voice. 'Since I am no longer a patient, I would like to make the offer of dinner again.'

Rachael took a deep breath, 'Okay, one dinner date. Are you coming down here to Surry? Marham is quite a distance for one night.'

In truth, she was happy he called. There was something about this man that attracted her. Maybe his looks, but his brain – although scrambled when they first met – was sharp. He complimented her very well. Perhaps dinner would be an interesting setting to talk about things not work-related. As it turned out, that would be the first of many dates.

It was Rachael that brought up Norway first. Adrian could not fully go back to operational duties. To see those horrific injuries and bodies would surely send Adrian back to the Gulf. In truth,

Adrian had already tendered his resignation and relinquished his commission. He had had enough. His skills and training were that of a GP and Adrian liked problem solving as well as helping people.

Rachael was also becoming slightly depressed from listening to horrific stories from injured soldiers, and the bullying most were facing on a daily basis. She decided to get a few books on the Norwegian language and encouraged Adrian to make some applications. It would be a few more years until job openings became available, and Adrian proficient enough with the language that he could take a job as a clinician.

After leaving the RAF, he found temporary jobs as a GP in Surry. A few years later he proposed to Rachael and as they celebrated, a call for an interview at a large surgery in Oslo prompted another bottle of wine. He would spend a few years at the surgery while Rachael took her Ph.D. After which, and when they had saved enough money did they decide to buy and resettle in Røyken.

19

The school fire had made both regional and national news, with social media being a large factor in alerting the networks. The government-owned broadcasting service NRK, along with TV2, was at the school long before the flames were fully extinguished. A reporter, holding a large microphone with an over-sized foam filter bearing the channel's colours and logos, tried to get as many interviews and reports as possible.

It had taken over an hour to get the fire under control. Around forty disfigured bodies had been pulled from the blaze with no survivors, the news reported. All of Røyken was in a state of shock, more so the local police department.

Sergeant Stig had been inundated with phone conversations to his seniors and then to regional commissioners. All had asked for a full report of all events over the past twenty-four hours. The sergeant was unable to give reason or cause to any of the events but was able to give his reports, including that of Doctor Hope's altercation with Mrs. Johansen. A few of his seniors were happy with the report, but most of the higher-ranking officers were unhappy; their voices raised and were almost screaming at the sergeant for allowing such events to happen. It was Røyken, for

God's sake. The worst thing to happen here was over seventy years ago when the German Navy sailed up through the fjord. These things just don't happen here, was the response from the commissioners.

By five p.m. the prime minister had been briefed after a lengthy meeting that caught media attention. Though shocked by the media response they played things down saying it was a meeting to discuss up and coming international affairs. The prime minister agreed to have more police and emergency services drafted to the region to provide additional support. The idea was to have more patrols and emergency services on hand until things calmed down; or at least find the cause of this aggressiveness. But there seemed to be an undertone to the order, like something was known but was not being said. In fact, police were being drafted from the major cities of Oslo, Trondheim and Bergen to regional towns and villages to provide extra manpower. But little was said about that and not many people noticed, other than more police cars on the road than normal.

Sergeant Stig had reported that although these incidents did not seem to be connected, it was highly suspicious that all had occurred within a tight time frame, and that they should be cautious. Medical reports were slow, some suggested narcotics but blood and urine samples all showed negative for drug use. Roadblocks and curfews were suggested to keep people within the area and others out may help with safety. This was opposed and warned against human rights by the coalition government. The idea was shelved and instead more officers were to be placed on duty for the next forty-eight hours.

The TV news reporter had spotted the defence minister making his way to the prime minister's building in Oslo. The politician avoided questions and just smiled and waved as though he was some kind of well-loved celebrity. When asked if this was an isolated incident or was this due to the fact similar incidents had also occurred in some other regional parts of Norway, the defence minister smiled and claimed he had not heard of anything and that he was on his way to discuss Norway's new jet fighter program with the British and Americans. The reporter did her best to push but was moved away by the Government's security. All she could do was to turn to the camera and say, "It is quite clear the Government has called an emergency meeting. Coincidence of recent events in parts of Norway, or they are keeping information away from the public? I would speculate the latter."

Hans Olsen sat in his black leather chair and stared at the open fire. The wood burnt with glorious reds and oranges that danced in his melancholic eyes. The lights were off in the living room, but he hadn't noticed. He was still to hire an electrician to fix the fuses but just didn't feel up to the task right now. His eyes were fixated with the fire, but his mind was on his wife.

He was unable to comprehend what had happened. He had been spared the details of her demise. The police had left this up to the hospital doctors. They had done their best to try and make everything sound peaceful, like his wife had died in her sleep. Nothing could have been further from the truth. They said that the attack on hospital staff had sent her fragile state into cardiac arrest. And the resulting spasms led to a fall to which the hospital staff were unable to tend to. The attack by two deranged patients was the one and true cause of her death.

As Hans sat glaring at the fire, he had begun to feel an occasional fluctuation of hatred; not anger per say but just hate. It was hardly noticeable to begin with; and he wasn't sure himself that hate was the correct word for the emotion. He put it down to mixed emotions; and could be forgiven for thinking this. He was supposed to have seen his wife today and bring her flowers that were now lying on the kitchen table still in their paper wrapper; their petals wilting and in dire need of water. Hans couldn't care about anything else right now; even the incident with the cows didn't really cross his mind.

His son had tried to explain everything, but upon learning the news of his wife, simply pushed his worthless son out of the way and went straight for the drinks' cabinet. He could not care less about the farm right now; that could be dealt with another time. He had lost money; all of his livestock were dead, and his son was just full of excuses as usual.

Hans and his son were never close, often avoiding one another for days. It was only his wife that kept the family together. She cooked meals, laid the table, got everyone's clothes washed and ready for the next week. No one had really realised at that time that it was her that was the glue of the family. Hans couldn't cook, couldn't use the washing machine. His clothes smelled of oil and diesel. He couldn't prepare a proper meal and instead opted for the ready boil-in-a-bag variety. He didn't care what his son ate; bread and water for all he gave a shit for. For now, he was happy his son was out of the house as he wanted to be alone in the dimly lit lounge. The darkness was as welcoming as a warm blanket. Shadows danced around the room like friendly angels bringing some comfort as the fire flickered.

He glanced to his left and saw the dark maroon leather chair his wife would use in the evening. When there was nothing on the TV they would sit quietly in their chairs, reading a book with the fire lit in winter, or the doors open during the summer. Now the chair next to his was empty and was never going to be filled by his beautiful wife ever again.

It was true her cancer was aggressive but the last he had known it was stable… no, no he must not go down that road of thought. But his head was not his own tonight. Questions of *what if* managed to penetrate through the brick wall his psyche had constructed to keep away unwanted thoughts. But once one question broke through so did more. What if she was getting better? What if the treatment was killing her breast cancer? What if those old bastards hadn't been taken there for treatment? Then the real question came: why *they* were allowed to live? The last one made his eyes open. *Yes*, he thought, *why should they be allowed to live? They took my wife from me, the very same woman I had spent thirty-years married to and shared my life with.*

His hand began to grip the glass without him realising. He felt a surge of anger race through him along with the catalyst of hate. He felt his neck gently begin to swell as the hate grew. His grip tightened so much the glass began to crack. Small trickles of amber liquid ran free from the cracks until his grip was too much for the tumbler and it shattered. Glass shards punctured his fingers and palm, and blood began to mix with the scotch creating a dark orange mess as both liquids dripped to the floor.

Usually, a person would notice the stinging sensation as the alcohol seeped into the broken skin and scratched at the nerves. But not Hans, he felt the pain but was somewhat welcoming. The vibrations in his head grew stronger and his neck had swollen so much that it was beginning to bulge. His anger was almost rage now. He gripped the shards in his hand and squeezed them deeper into his flesh. The pain fuelled his anger. The more pain he felt, the angrier he became until an overwhelming desire for death to his enemies suppressed any kind of logical thought.

The vicious cycle was a wonderful feeling. The pain was pleasant, and the anger was fantastic. Soon it was like a drug. The more pain he could feel the angrier he became and the better he felt. No longer were his thoughts trained on his dead wife. His attention was fixed on the couple, he knew where they were, knew what needed to be done. But first there was something he had wanted to do for a very long time…

... Where was his son?

20

Police Constable Stolten sipped black coffee and flicked through his phone. He glanced at various dating websites and grinned at some of the profiles that showed more of the ladies he preferred; a drink in one hand and the phone in the other taking selfies against blue seas and white sands. Flicking the profiles left for the ones he didn't prefer and right for later when he was off duty. Somehow the events of the day had left little impression on the young constable's routine. But deep down he was terrified. He had never seen a dead body before, well… not in person anyway. So, he didn't know how to react, or what was considered acceptable for a young man trying to show strength.

Sergeant Stig was finishing an open sandwich - which was the way sandwiches were eaten in Norway; meat on one slice of thick-cut bread with cheese and a piece of lettuce, never should two slices of bread cover a filling; it could be seen as blasphemous. His newspaper was littered with breadcrumbs somehow missing his mouth with every bite. He occasionally checked in with patrol cars around the area making sure things were quiet. He remembered when Røyken was a quiet town. Nothing ever happened here. But the last twenty-four hours had changed the lives of everyone. *How quickly circumstances can change in such little time*, he thought.

His mind darted to the events earlier that day, those poor kids, and his fellow police officers all dead. He had slept very little after the fire. The images of burnt tiny bodies curled into foetal positions as the heat evaporated every molecule of water their developing bodies held. But that smell that overwhelming stench of death still lined the inside of his nostrils. A smell he would never forget. His eyes drooped with exhaustion, his face, clean shaven as it were, looked old and worn out. He had prayed nothing else was going to happen this evening; he didn't think he could handle any further occurrences.

He straightened up as though realising his posture was giving too much of his feelings away and attempted another bite of his open sandwich. He didn't have much of an appetite but knew he needed to keep going, keep moving forwards. And above all else, he had to lead his young constable and remain professional regardless to his spiralling feelings. And truth be known, both men were physically and emotionally drained but didn't want the other to know.

'Good God, look at the tits on this one, Stig. They're fuckin' massive,' the young constable said pushing his phone into his senior's face.

Stig grunted to clear his throat, which had begun to swell with thoughts back to the fire. He pulled back his shoulders and looked at his younger companion, 'I am a married man, and to be frank it is *sergeant*. I didn't get these stripes from looking at porn all day.'

'Sorry, Sarge,' the young policeman paused. 'But they are massive.'

Stig smiled as his constable shied away. He eventually broke his taught posture and laughed. Stolten looked bemused at first but then began to laugh as well. Stig needed this, needed the humour. Stolten was a new, and had lots to learn, but right now his humorous online dating gave Stig a chuckle.

Stig threw down the newspaper with a loud thump the way a dad would when trying to tell the family he was ready to do something, 'Okay,' he said. 'Let's go do another patrol, you're driving.'

The young officer protested with a huff but got up knowing he had to do something. But it wasn't all bad; it was nice to get out of the station and do something to keep his mind from ascending back into the abyss of the fire. Stig wanted to get out of the office anyway; he had to keep busy and since all the paperwork had been filled out and filed this was a good time to get out and pass the time. He radioed to the other two cars out on patrol that he was going to leave the office and that someone should come in and take over.

'We need to check in with security at the school first and then we will do an hour around the roads,' Stig said walking out of the station and throwing the car keys into the air to see if Stolten could catch them in time.

A police car pulled up and Stig waved to the occupants. He checked his watch: 01:00; another six hours left on duty. He had nothing special planned for the day, perhaps shovel some snow and take the dog for a walk with his wife. His younger companion most probably would be looking at porn or chatting to women online. He laughed at the thought of him dressing up in his police uniform and suggesting he was some sort of special task unit. There were plenty of women out there that would fall for that, but also some that were able to use the internet to find out the truth and expose them as frauds. They did that to many social media profiles that claimed they were military war heroes. An internet search later would confirm photoshopping and exposure, which would be shared amongst other people. He would warn Stolten, but then how is he expected to learn anything without experiencing things first-hand.

Stig had been through the experience and learning phases well into his thirties. He used to be quick to his anger that often ended up with him getting into some small fights. He remembered being in his twenties and winning most fights. It wasn't until he was thirty-five that he realised his mind was able but his body not. Those hard lessons taught him calm down and think before getting into any confrontation. Now in his fifties he was so laid back that his angry days were left way behind him. Although, he did feel anger and sometimes for his younger companion, but he knew to ignore it. There was a big difference between anger and aggression. Anger can be extinguished as quickly as it would come if cognitive thoughts prevailed. Many times, he would go to bars and observe scuffles ending with both parties just wanting to beat the living hell out of one other. And the security often didn't help with their wanting to prove themselves and macho man attitude. But these young men needed to learn as he did.

The outside air was crisp, and the young officer didn't waste time turning on the car heaters as he pressed the accelerator to get the engine warm. The car pulled right onto the small road outside the station and continued to the junction. Stig told his companion to go left and head towards Røyken centre to see if any drunks needed help getting off the last train around twenty past one. After that they would hang around the roads and pick up any drunks wondering down the country lanes that needed to get home. Stig liked to help people. Drinking can lead to accidents on these dark roads. Getting people off the roads and back into their beds was a service Stig liked to enforce. After all, the police in Norway were not just there to arrest people; they made sure everyone was safe.

'Looks like winter has finally taken hold,' Stolten said leaning forward towards the windscreen.

'That it does,' Stig replied.

21

Cleaning the house was one way Adrian could keep his mind busy. He avoided TV or anything that allowed his thoughts from the school to fester and surface. He tried his hand at building a stool from some old scraps of wood in the basement, using a rusty blunt saw to cut the wood. He knew the stool would not support his or anyone else's weight, but using his hands kept his mind occupied.

Rachael had once again been his psychologist and tried to use some soothing words to help prevent her fiancé from going back to the desert. She suggested he just drink water and stay away from the caffeine. Her reasoning was that any flavoured drink he had now could be filed under this atrocity. Whenever he drank that again could send off a flashback.

A rusty old saw with a splintered wooden handle only managed to crack the wood he was trying to cut. The fibres splintered as the blade struggled. It began to smell as the wood heated up. Adrian's mind flashed back to the school, then to the gates of Basra. His grip on the saw loosened. Another flash of memory: the soldier's severed foot, the burnt flesh; he could almost smell the aroma through the wood. He felt his anger grow. Why those kids? Why that young soldier. Realising his grip on the saw's splintered handle had loosened he tightened his hand.

The saw cut into the scrap material, splintering the wood rather than a clean cut. His hand pushed forward while he leaned into the action to add more weight. His hand was still stinging from the cut from Mrs. Johansen that somehow managed to fuel his anger. The saw slipped from his grip and his hand went smashing into the wood. He screamed out in anger and without thinking picked up the leg and smashed it hard onto the bench. The leg snapped in two with the impact sending splinters over the stone floor.

Collapsing to the ground he began to sob. The darkness of his past loomed over him, and he was unable to hold the memories back. Holding his head in his hands he allowed himself a moment to cry.

Rachael was in the basement trying washing Adrian's clothes. His clothes reeked of a bonfire, and she could almost visualise the scene. God knows what Adrian had experienced at ground zero. It was going to take a few more washes but ultimately, she knew the clothes would have to be thrown out. She heard the smash of wood and came running into the workroom. She found Adrian slumped on the floor, his head held in his hands, with tears running down his cheeks.

She felt helpless. Never had she seen him like this. The sessions at Headley Court never prepared her for this. He was relapsing, and very badly. The time to be a professional took a back seat. Instead, she could only do what any caring partner could. She threw her arms around him, 'We're going to get through this, together,' she said softly into his ear.

Rachael got Adrian into the shower, helped wash him and took him back upstairs into the living room. There was little else she could do. The sobbing had stopped and now he was in a sombre almost zombie state. She turned on the TV and streamed some UK TV.

Now it was her mind that began to tick over. She decided to do some research on the events. This was extremely bizarre. Her neighbours going insane, Hans found in the road unable to comprehend where he was or how he had gotten there. And now the school! All these people were exhibiting some form of madness. She firmly believed it wasn't by chance.

She couldn't find anything meaningful in her first internet search, mostly bringing up prisoners and psychopaths. Then a thought flashed through her mind, and she quickly typed them into the search engine: "WHITE LIGHTS, POWER CUT, and MEMORY LOSS."

The results loaded and Rachael scrolled down until she found a page that seemed interesting. It was written in Spanish. She copied over the link and translated it using an online webpage:

"Tres Bocas is on lock down this week following a large massacre in the small farming village. Police were called to nearby farmlands where onlookers claimed a group of farm hands were storming into peoples' homes and bars, armed with weapons, and committing heinous acts of violence.

So far twenty people have been killed and many more injured in what police are describing as unprovoked attacks. The assailants were killed on site by armed police following a violent standoff.

One of the assailants killed by police was described as an honest, hardworking family man. The news of the massacre has shocked many residents here into trying to leave the village following some smaller outbreaks of fresh violence amongst the people of Tres Bocas. Local police have now cordoned off most of the village while investigations are taking place.

Many local residents claim the events took place following a power surge, while some have speculated seeing bright lights in the sky. Police and local authorities are yet to comment on these sightings. Many believe the military are testing new weapons on the village, with many trying to flee to neighbouring towns. These events follow similar incidents a week earlier in Lyon Kansas, USA, and Church Falls in Canada; where residents also witnessed strange lights, power cuts and acts of extreme violence in the area. No explanation of these events has yet been made public."

Rachael searched for Lyons and Church Falls. Reports from both areas overlapped. People had reported strange lights in the sky, power cuts, and also violence. These reports were very similar to the events Røyken had just gone through. *Could lights really cause these acts of violence? She thought to herself, photosensitivity perhaps?* No. Epilepsy following stimulus would render the person incapable of even standing let alone going on a killing spree. She needed data. From her behavioural research she knew damage to the frontal lobe and hypothalamus all contributed to these aggressive behaviours. She wanted to pick up the phone and call the hospital but then realised she would not get anywhere. Had they finished the tests? She had not heard anything, and knew Adrian was also unaware. Sometimes these clinicians would send the results, most other times they would forget due to the demands of their work. She needed Adrian to snap back to his senses. But in his current state he was unable to even dress himself.

She thought for a moment, leaning back on the sofa with her hands behind her head. She needed to trigger Adrian. As awful as that sounded even in her own head, she knew a way to bring him back to reality. From their early dinners in Surry, they had both found a peaceful resolve to the flashbacks. And that was science. Whenever they discussed clinical biology Adrian would forget about his past. Could this still work, and right after being exposed to the horrors again? It was worth a try, at the very least.

She used her soft voice, 'Are their T cells in the brain?' She asked.

Adrian remained stagnant for a moment then finally spoke, 'No, the brain has its own immune system.'

She smiled. 'Hmmm, so how does the brain fight an infection?'

'Usually, the blood brain barrier protects against pathogens. If that fails, and something gets through the central nervous system then antibodies immunoglobulins are secreted. And maybe sometimes T cells can gain access into the cerebrospinal fluid.'

'Can you give me an example of such a pathogen that can gain access to the brain?'

'Borrelia bacteria from a tick bite can gain access to the brain and cause Lyme disease.'

Rachael continued with the questions, 'And the immune system can detect and fight this?'

Adrian shook his head, 'No. we have to treat with antibiotics.'

Finally, he turned his head to Rachael. She could see some life had finally come back into his body.

'Why the sudden interest in immunology?' he asked.

'I cannot lie; I am trying to understand what is causing these people to act this way. You know it isn't just here. It's happened all over, in mostly remote places. So I did a bit of research and found something quite interesting,' she glanced at the clock on the wall: it was way past midnight. She had a second thought and decided that tomorrow morning would be a better time to show him the other incidents, 'On second thoughts, maybe tomorrow is a better time to talk about these.' she closed the laptop.

Adrian leaned forward and stopped her from closing the computer, 'No, let's look at them now. What are they?' he asked sounding genuinely interested.

And that was how Rachael managed to resolve Adrian. His passion for the job and his inquisitive nature could fight back the darkness. Like reading by candlelight, he could only see the book and not the darkness.

'Are you sure you want to read them now? Rachael asked.

He quickly read through pages skipping along the headlines and glancing over the words then turned back to Rachael. 'What does this mean?' his eyes widened.

'It seems what we have been experiencing has been reported in other places of the world,' she pointed to the Spanish page she had translated. 'This one was in Mexico a week ago, and the other in the USA. Although similar, we haven't had riots like these reports have written. But power surges, acts of violence, sound pretty similar to what we have. I don't know, maybe government experiments or sophisticated weapons by terrorists? But these all seem to stem from the same lights and power cut we had the other night. People couldn't remember what had happened, then going on a rampage and causing all these killings,' she took the laptop back. 'Adrian, something is going off here, and I think it is intentional.'

Adrian rubbed his face, 'Well, what we will do is lock the doors tonight, and sleep upstairs in the living room. The police are out in full now so I think this will be the end of all the trouble. Most of the places in the reports are isolated from any cities; Røyken is far too close to Oslo not to go unnoticed. And now with media attention, we should see all these awful things stop.'

'Have you heard anything from the hospital?' Rachael asked.

'Nothing yet. I will call them tomorrow.'

'I have some questions of my own, if I may request to ask?'

'What do you have in mind?'

'I want to know if they have done any brain scans. I need to know if the frontal lobe or the hypothalamus has been damaged in any way. At least that will tell us how these people have turned into raging monsters.'

Rachael left Adrian to go and fetch some bed sheets while he stocked the fire. Deciding that he needed a drink, Adrian went into the kitchen and found the whiskey and two glasses. As he poured, he peered out of the window to the street below. It was quiet. A gentle flurry of snow was falling and reflected the orange streetlight.

His attention was momentarily distracted from pouring the amber liquid when he thought he saw a figure pass the grounds below under a streetlight. He stopped pouring and leaned forwards to get a better look. He was sure something had caught his eye scuttling across the street in the snow, perhaps a deer; they had many around the area. Or perhaps it was just the reflection of light from the glass or from the living room. Sometimes the light from the living room would bounce back if the glass met it at the right angle. He finished pouring and took the glasses back to Rachael, who was laying out the duvet on the large white leather settee.

'I wonder if Hans is okay?' Rachael questioned.

'I doubt it, the state he must have been in when they told him about his wife. If it was me, I would not have discharged him,' Adrian brought the glass to his lips and took a small sip.

'I agree, but then why keep him in the hospital when they need the beds?'

Adrian sat the glass on the table, 'I think they are okay for beds in Drammen, but yes a decision I am happy I don't need to make.'

Rachael looked at his glass and then back at him with a sour face. 'Coaster, Doctor Hope, use a coaster.' Rachael was always cleaning rings left by glasses on the table.

Adrian huffed and pulled a coaster from the middle of the table and rested his glass upon it. 'Why have them in the middle of the table anyway?'

'Because it looks nice for when guests come over,' she said sternly.

'What bloody guests? Only person to visit was your father and I don't recall him using a coaster for his pint glass.'

The TV slightly flickered and Rachael took the remote and

pressed the channel button in an attempt to rescue the signal, 'Bloody thing, must be still woozy from the power surge,' she said.

'Try switching it off and on again; usually does the trick with these things,' Adrian smirked.

Rachael tried but the TV didn't respond. Adrian noticed the lights begin to flicker. 'Ah bugger me, not again. We've just had the breakers fixed.' Adrian began to rise hoping the flickering would stop and the power remained stable.

Suddenly, and without warning, their attentions were directed downstairs. Rachael jumped and almost dropped her glass when a loud crash came from the basement.

'What the hell was that?' Adrian said and looked over the banister.

'We need to call the police and get out of the house,' Rachael said.

Adrian picked up his phone but before he had time to open it the lights inside the house failed and they were engulfed in darkness. Rachael stifled a gasp by placing a hand over her mouth. Adrian reached out using the glow of the fire to find the iron poker leaning against the wall and pulled Rachael behind him.

A small wall Adrian had recently plastered separated the stairs from the living room. Adrian pulled Rachael behind it and knelt. He could feel Rachael's pulse race as he held onto her arm. After the recent events he was still on edge and was taking no chances. Rachael held Adrian's right shoulder and began to pull on him.

Oh God, not now, not today, Adrian thought to himself. His mind was beginning to cast back to the fire; the stress brought back the desert. His hand reached down for a medical bag that was not there. Realising this he brought it back up and held the poker firmly in both hands. He didn't realise it, but he was kneeling in a position as though he was holding a rifle and about to fire.

A strange sound resonated from below. It was a clicking sound, the sort of sound Tribes in Africa made by using the back of the mouth while conversing to one another.

Click-click-click.

The sound echoed from downstairs. A revolver? The flicking of a knife perhaps? Adrian could not identify the sound since his heart was pounding with adrenaline.

Rachael whispered into Adrian's ear, 'We need to get out of the house and call the police.'

'We can't,' Adrian lowered his voice. 'The only way out is down there.'

They could have risked going out onto the balcony and hoped the snow was just deep enough to cushion the fall. But that was out of the question. The risk of severe injury was too great.

The footsteps grew louder as the intruder ascended the basement stairs.

Click... click... click.

Pictures fell from their hooks and broke on the floor. Something sharp scraped at the walls, etching deep into plaster.

Click... click... click.

The intruder breathed deep like a sleeping dog. Adrian listened. The intruder stopped moving. The banister shook as the intruder grasped the end. Then the footsteps began to ascend the stairs to them. Adrian coiled himself. He tried to formulate a plan of attack as soon as he saw the intruder. Should he strike out first or wait in case there were two of them coming up? After the events of the day and then the flashbacks to the desert earlier, Adrian found himself feeling the level of sharpness he had when the bomb had gone off in Basra. The open fire dimly lit the room, but it would be enough to see what was coming, and in turn provide enough darkness for Adrian to spring his attack.

The footsteps came closer, and Adrian could hear clicking sounds coming from the other side of the small wall. He took the chance to glance. His heart fell, his mouth opened wide, but no scream came out. His throat tightened and a surge of adrenalin raced through his veins dimming his vision to an almost tunnel.

Ascending the stairs was a very tall and very slim figure. It was unusually thin, skinny with absolutely no muscle mass whatsoever; it was like looking at an X-ray. Its back was hunched with each vertebra protruding just under the skin.

Rachael now saw what had made her fiancé go stiff and rigid. This was no man. The fire illuminated the intruder's arm. It was a dark grey in the orange and red from the fire. If this wasn't alarming enough the arm itself was elongated more so than that of a man or woman. Rachael gripped Adrian's trapezium muscle as the figure got to the top of the stairs.

It was a giant grey skeleton. The creature had to bend its head to one side to avoid the ceiling. Its back was facing them with bones clearly visible under the skin, like damp tissue paper pulled tight over a sculpture. Its pelvis was concaved. This creature looked to be double-jointed at the hip.

Adrian's grip loosened and his heart pounded so fast he was sure it would burst from his chest. The figure or creature, as it was now clearly not a man… not even human, walked past; its movements were slow like it was hunting its prey. But it's large size, too big for the room, made any attempts of a stealthy attack futile. It stopped at the top of the stairs.

Click…click…click.

The creature turned its head from side to side and an eerie movement, searching for the occupants. Adrian was sure it hadn't seen him. He glanced down and saw a thin leg at the bottom of end of the wall. He felt the urge surge through him. Those legs were thin; those bones must be able to break easily with just one swing. It was now or never. He had to act now. He tightened his grip on the poker. Rachael felt the muscles in Adrian's neck tighten and instinctively knew what was about to happen. She mentally prepared herself to push passed the creature and make for the stairs.

In one fluid motion Adrian jumped to feet and swung at the creature's right shin so hard the vibrations from iron meeting hard bone reverberated through his hand causing the poker to launch from his grip. The bone broke with a loud audible crack. The creature screamed and fell to the right breaking into the coffee table; glass shards helped cause more damage by puncturing the creature's thin grey skin. Adrian took Rachael by the arm and made for the stairs.

As the creature turned its oval head in their direction, Rachael caught a glimpse of its features. She didn't have time to get a full look as Adrian was pulling her so hard, she almost fell down the stairs. Later she would make the connection to those awful Russian sleep studies. The *volunteers* had gone insane, and some had mutilated themselves in such horrific ways that left them disfigured without lips or facial features. This thing looked very much the same. Due to the lack of lips, it would seem to be smiling at them both, if not for the great pain it was in, and screaming like a wild cat trying to scare off an attacker, holding its dangling leg evidently waiting for help.

Adrian had to pull Rachael down the stairs and out of the front door. They heard rapid footsteps behind them as another creature was racing up from the basement to investigate the screams. Adrian ran shoulder first into the front door breaking it off its hinges. The door burst open. Neither of them had coats or shoes. The icy snow dampened their socks before letting in the icy needles to freeze their feet. Regardless they had to run, had to keep moving as far away from the house as they could.

There was one other neighbour across the road but there were no lights on. Their only hope was to flag down a passing car, but at this time of night it was highly unlikely. *God, please let there be car* Adrian prayed. Rachael looked back and was relieved not to see anyone or anything following them. The screams continued from the house so loud and cat-like that Rachael screamed herself.

They ran holding hands; Adrian pulling on Rachael's almost dragging her across the icy snow.

At one moment Rachael saw something emerge from the distant house carrying the wounded creature and laying it down on the ground. She watched as more creatures moved out of the darkness and surrounded the wounded one. Giant thin creatures. Their thin arms dangled right down to their skins. Their backs hunched, and their heads grotesque.

'Keep going. We need to get to the main road and into those streetlights.' Adrian held tight onto Rachael's hand and kept her moving. The snow was slippery under their feet. Wearing only socks the icy water quickly soaked into them numbing their toes and ankles. Their movements and pace were beginning to succumb to the icy grip.

The screams began to fade behind them as the creatures abandoned any notion of venturing after them. Instead, they decided to return with their wounded aggressor back into the darkness.

The sergeant instructed his young subordinate to drive out of the town and to the houses further up from Røyken centre. The last train had come and gone; only one person got off and was picked up by another car. Apart from a wondering deer, Røyken was quiet, perhaps a little too quiet? Stig had kept an eye out for Hans but saw no signs of him or even a plough. The roads should have been gritted by now.

'I don't see Hans anywhere tonight, Sarge,' Stolten said, leaning towards the window to get a better look.

'I know. Maybe he's home tonight. I wouldn't be surprised if we don't see him for a few weeks. A death is hard to deal with. I'll nip round tomorrow and see how he is. Shame really,' Stig continued, 'I was quite looking forward to a cup of his coffee.'

They talked throughout the drive – mostly about police work and a little about the football results and upcoming winter sporting events – occasionally slowing down when the snow became too dense to see clearly. The windscreen wipers did very little to help the view, screeching across the glass as the snow offered little lubrication for the rubber.

They drove a while longer, weaving around the winding road that led up from the train station, passed some farm fields – now encased in snow – and by the junction leading to the police station.

'Shall we head on back?' Stolten asked hopefully.

'No,' replied Stig. 'Let's do a few more rounds.'

Stolten had already turned on the indicator in anticipation of going back to the warmth of the station. Grudgingly he switched it off and pressed down on the accelerator.

'Easy there, Starsky. No need for the speed in these conditions,' Stig said, tapping on the dashboard.

'Whose Starsky?' asked Stolten.

'Jesus Christ, you don't know who he is? What are they teaching the kids these days?' Stig laughed.

Stolten drove further down, under the bridge and switched on the indicator to turn left; even though no one was around to benefit from his intended direction.

'Want some coffee?' Stig asked.

'Can't really drive and drink at the same time, Sarge,' Stolten smiled.

'Pull over when we get to the school. May as well have a look around and make sure the place is not being vandalized or any reporters hanging about.'

As Stolten drove up the small incline two figures came into the car's headlights sitting by the side of the road. One tried to wave at the car, but their movements were sluggish.

'Slow down,' instructed Stig.

'What's their game? Shall I radio this in?' Stolten reached for the radio.

'That's my job, and no we won't. Let's see what's going off. You just be ready with that Taser if they fancy their chances. Put the lights on, make them know we've seen them.'

The young officer flicked on the blue lights but kept the siren on mute. He gradually decreased the car's speed as not to skid on the slippery snow and pulled over.

'They look in a bad way, you get the blanket,' Stig instructed zipping up his thick jacket in preparation to meet the crisp air.

The car stopped and the young officer turned off the engine taking the keys with him as was procedure.

'Okay, what's going on? You drunk or something? Hands where I can see them,' Stig said, walking slowly towards the two.

He saw that the figures were a man and woman; their arms around one another, shielding themselves from the cold. Stig noticed neither were wearing shoes or anything protective against the elements. Then he saw the man's face, 'Adrian? What the hell are you doing out here?' he asked and looked down at his feet.

Adrian tried to speak but his mouth was so cold he could hardly form any words.

'Jesus, never mind the explanation, get into the car quick.' Stig helped Adrian to the back of the car; offering him a blanket and taking his spare set of keys to turn the engine back on and engage the heaters.

Stolten put a blanket around Rachael's shoulders and rubbed her feet, 'Ma'am, can you stand?' he asked.

Rachael was unable to respond. Stolten put his arms around her and stood her up. He placed her by Adrian and got back in the front seat.

Stig closed the doors and turned to Adrian, 'Adrian, do you need an ambulance or hospital?'

Adrian shook his head.

'Okay, back to the station quickly. Let's get these two warmed up. Maybe then we can get some answers.'

Stolten put the car into first and eased up to speed. The snow made traction difficult but not impossible for the winter tyres.

'Can you tell us why you are out here freezing yourselves to death?' Stig asked when he heard some murmuring in the back.

Adrian answered with a slight slur as his lips were frozen, 'W… w… we ha… had a break in,' he looked up at Stig, who was twisted in his seat so he could face the two occupants.

The doctor's next words made Stolten lose focus on the road and almost swerve into a ditch.

'They weren't human; they were giants… de… demons!'

Stig smacked Stolten on the shoulder to get him to pay attention to the road, 'What do you mean not human?'

'They were like demons, t… tall gr… grey demons.' Adrian had the look of fright in his eyes recalling the creature's great size, features and… and those sounds; that clicking and cat-like screams.

Stig glanced at Stolten and indicated for him to get a move on before turning back to the doctor, 'Adrian, we're taking you to the station, get you two warmed up. I need you to calm down. We can talk about this later.'

'Demons?' Stolten exclaimed and had to hold back the laughter.

Stig shot him a look, 'Just drive, constable. I'll ask the questions.'

22

Stig brought two cups of strong black coffee and sat them down on a large table cluttered with magazines and newspapers. The lounge was only for when the police were having a break or lunch. Now it had been made up with blankets and pillows to comfort both Adrian and Rachael. The room was brightly lit from large fluorescent lights. The smell of strong coffee from the percolator at the end of the room scented the room.

Adrian was beginning to warm up now but found it hard to stop the shivering. Stolten had brought a pair of thick socks to keep their feet warm and placed their wet socks on a radiator to dry. The feeling was returning to Rachael's lips as she held the cup with both hands, staring at the floor.

'Okay, so do you want to tell me why you were out in the cold like you were?' Stig pulled up a chair next to Adrian.

Adrian took a sip from his cup that warmed his chest and stomach, 'They were monsters; tall… monsters.'

'What were?'

'The things that broke into the house.'

Stig took out his notebook and began to write down a statement, 'Right, so you had a break in tonight, roughly what time was this?'

Adrian sipped again at his coffee, unable to recognise the question.

Stig tried again, 'Adrian, what time did you have the break in?'

A blank look fell over Adrian's face.

Stig placed a hand on Adrian's shoulder, 'Doctor Hope. Did these men attack you?'

Adrian nodded then said, 'They weren't men, they were monsters!'

Stig sat back in the plastic chair. 'Okay, monsters. Did they attack you?'

Adrian shook his head, 'One tried but I hit it.'

'Fair enough, with everything that you have been through. Where did you hit him?' Stig continued to use the pronoun *him*.

'I… I hit it on the leg. I think I got it just right. I think I broke it.'

'Okay, Stolten, can you radio the hospital and local clinics to keep an eye out for anyone coming in with a broken leg,' Stig asked his constable.

'It wasn't a man, sergeant, it was a monster,' Adrian tried to get the term right.

'Describe the *monster* to me, Adrian,' Stig had given up trying to convince Adrian his attacker was just a man; maybe a tall one, but still only a man.

Adrian looked at the floor, his eyes never blinking once, 'It was tall with grey skin. It was as tall as the ceiling and then some. It wasn't human, damn it. It was like a giant skeleton. And that noise. Click… click… click.' Adrian seemed to go back into himself reliving the moment.

Click-click…click.

Stig turned to Stolten who was asking patrolling paramedics to radio them if anyone with a leg injury was taken in, 'I think we need to get out there and see for ourselves,' he turned back to

Adrian. 'We are going to treat this as a break-in. I think it is best me and my constable go and search your home right away.'

'Take guns. If they are still there you will need guns,' Adrian said now staring Stig deep into his eyes.

This sent shivers up Stolten's back.

Stig placed his hand on the doctor's shoulder, 'Just keep calm and focus on staying warm. Look, we understand you have been through a lot yesterday and a break-in is going to make things worse. We do believe you were broken into, and we are treating this as such. We will pack you some clothes and shoes and bring them here. We have showers and think it is a good idea you use them to warm up. The constable and I will head over to your house now and take a look. I'll get one of the officers here to call in forensics and seal off the house if we find anything. So, I suggest you both remain here. Now, do you need me to call out a paramedic? Your wife looks in a state of shock.'

Adrian turned to Rachael. She didn't say anything but just shook her head. Other than being frozen and the trauma, she was okay.

Another officer came into the lounge and sat down with Rachael.

Stig stood and called to Stolten, 'Right, let's go and check this out.'

'Sarge, should we take firearms?' Stolten seemed pretty shaken by what Adrian had been saying.

Stig thought for a moment. Finally, he said, 'Fine. But you will listen for my orders, okay?'

On the drive out to the house Stig betted that any burglars would be long gone by now and most of the belongings would be stolen.

At best fingerprints could be taken, and if Adrian had caused injury there must be some blood to take a DNA sample. They pulled up to the house and onto the driveway.

Stig zipped up his coat, put on his cap, 'I think it is best we stay together and search the outside first,' Stig said to Stolten. 'Bring that camera also, we may need to take photos.'

They flicked on their torches and saw the front door wide open. Stig told Stolten to leave it for now and check the outside first. Their torch lights sparkled in the powdery snow as they made their way to the rear of the house. Stig shone his light to the basement window, it had been broken inwards. He drew his pistol but did not cock it. After everything that had been going on he was glad he brought his firearm. He placed the pistol over the torch, so they were both aiming in his field of view, and slowly approached the window. He half expected someone to be inside but upon investigation saw the room was empty. He beckoned Stolten to stay still so he could listen if anyone was still inside the house. The snow helped dampen out the sounds of the wind coming in over the farmland to the rear of the house. He couldn't hear anything, which made him nervous.

'Stig look,' Stolten said, aiming his light to the ground.

Stig took his attention away from the broken window and looked down at the snow. On the ground were footprints and some sort of blue stain dotted in the snow that was almost translucent in the white light from the torch. Stig withdrew his pistol back into its holder and indicated for Stolten to snap a picture.

'These look similar to the prints next door. Could be a local burglar, maybe someone working the area.' Stig beckoned Stolten to hand him an evidence bag so he could also take some of this blue liquid. The flash from the Nikon illuminated the snow and reflected off the blue liquid. Satisfied enough pictures had been taken they turned their attention back to the window. Stig told

Stolten to keep his side arm poised ready to cock if someone was to come bursting out. Even though cocking a pistol without immediate threat was against regulations, Stig was not taking any chances.

The sergeant entered through the broken window and into the room. Wearing gloves as to not contaminate any evidence he carefully avoided the shards of glass. He shone his light around and found more of that blue liquid in small puddles around the floor. Stolten followed clumsily and almost dropped his handgun narrowly avoiding the broken edges around the window. Stig scooped up some more of the blue substance into evidence bags using sterile cotton buds.

'What the hell is that stuff, Sarge?' Stolten asked raising the camera to take a few more pictures.

'Shhh, and put that camera away. We'll snap these later.'

They left the room and slowly begun to ascend the stairs to the first floor. Stig found a light switch at the top and flicked on the lights. He could see more of the blue liquid on the floor and heard a dripping from above. He looked up to the second set of stairs leading to the third floor and saw more of the blue liquid dripping in thick oozing droplets from the upper step.

'This is the police,' Stig shouted, almost shocking Stolten with his commanding tone. 'We are coming up; put your hands in the air and backs to the far wall. We are armed.'

He told Stolten to go first and keep his handgun ready. Stig watched their rear. They slowly crept up the stairs pointing their weapons in front. Stolten got to the top and shone his light around the living room, finding the light switch in the process and flicking it on. Stig came up and looked around.

The place was empty. The TV, expensive-looking glassware in glass cabinets were all here. This quick glance suggested that nothing of great value had been stolen. The small glass coffee table by the sofa was now in shatters indicating some kind of altercation that matched Adrian's description.

It was Stolten that saw it first and was unable to get his words out in one go. He choked, 'Fu… fuck is that?'

Stig followed the gaze of his startled constable to a severed foot lying close to the now extinguished fireplace. He bent down and examined it. Blue liquid had congealed around the severed end, which ran down the ankle of the foot. It was large, much larger than any human foot. The skin was grey, and the toes looked more like fingers with jagged yellow toenails at the ends. It looked more like a foot from a chimpanzee or some member of the great ape family, yet the toes were much longer and curved like the nerves had seized up and formed a fist. Stig took out another evidence bag to retrieve this strange-looking foot. The severed end was jagged indicating this had been clumsily removed in a hurry by something blunt. The bone was shattered from the strike Adrian had claimed he made. The foot was surprisingly heavy despite its slimness. Holding it by a toe like it was a dirty tea bag he carefully placed it into a large evidence bag.

'What is it? Is it real?' Stolten asked looking more nervous now than he had been.

Stig examined it for a moment. 'Take a photo quickly. Real or not I don't want to hold onto this thing any longer than I need to.'

It was now becoming apparent that Adrian may have been telling the truth. The poker lying next to the foot indicated he had indeed taken a swipe at whatever this foot had once belonged to. As a result, the broken shin had been so severe that the foot was removed. But where was all the blood? Surely a wound like that would have caused severe bleeding. Realising this Stig smelled the air. The air gave a scent of burnt flesh, unmistakable now that reminded him of the school fire yesterday morning. He forced himself to snap back into the situation and not to the burnt bodies of children. He quickly remembered the film Jaws where Hooper asked Chief Brody to stand between him and the shark to get a size comparison. Laying the foot to the floor once more his placed his hand alongside it and got a picture for scale before being too grossed.

'Here, you hold onto this,' Stig thrust the bag towards Stolten. 'The thing is giving me the creeps.'

'Oh, thank you, sarge.'

After checking the remaining rooms Stig got onto the radio while Stolten went to the master bedroom to gather some clean clothes and necessities for Adrian and Rachael. He sat on the floor and tried to think what the hell was going on? Two days ago, everything just seemed fine. The folks of Røyken were just happy to go about their business, go skiing, make snow forts and take the dogs for long walks. Then all hell breaks loose, old folks killing one another, schools exploding, and now this foot. Stolten came back upstairs with a black bin liner of anything he could find for Adrian and Rachael. He saw his sergeant sitting on the floor with a look of disbelief in his eyes.

'You okay, sarge?' Stolten asked.

'What? Yeah. Yeah. It's just a little overwhelming.'

'If I can say something, sarge, we are in over our heads here. What the hell did we just find, and what did that foot belong to?'

'I don't know,' Stig straightened himself. 'Whatever it belonged to I don't want to meet. Let's talk about this later and start being policemen again. Get onto the radio. I want police presence here until forensics turn up. Keep people away from the house. I need to get back to the office and make a few phone calls. We need some additional help here.'

23

The tractor weaved from side to side as Hans Olsen twisted the wheel. His raw strength fuelled by hatred made turning the wheel easy, regardless to the lack of power steering. He had tried to hit an elk that ventured too far into the road; narrowly missing the large passive animal, causing the old vehicle to come off the road and down a bank. But the large farm vehicle was capable of such punishing terrain and was easily guided back onto the icy tarmac.

Hans' thoughts were erratic, flashes of his wife being murdered, his God-damn lazy son spending all his time in the bedroom tapping on his phone instead helping out when he needed it the most. It was *his* fault the animals went crazy. It was *his* fault that there was death on his land.

God damn, fuck them all!

He pressed hard on the accelerator and pulled on the steering wheel. His teeth clenched; his body taught.

God damn them all!

The vehicle could only do fifty kilometres per hour at best, and that was with plumes of burning diesel and oil spewing from the chimney exhaust like a 1950s coal mine. The cab shook violently at this speed, bouncing Hans around like a rag doll.

His attention diverted from the farm, his wife, and no good excuse for a son when a beam of headlights from a distant vehicle shone over the brow of the incline. Immediately, Hans turned the wheel drifting into the centre of the road. The tractor responded to his wish and straddled both sides of the road; its thick-treaded tyres bit hard into the snow that would have caused any other vehicle to skid out of control.

A large swelling at the back of his neck grew larger until it was a bulge of fluid. This pain he should have felt, but instead it just increased his anger to a blind rage. The other car had not yet seen him, and Hans flicked a switch to his left turning on the overhead flood lights bathing the road in front in a brilliant white – much like the white that had engulfed him. His intention was to blind the driver and make them either veer off the road or better yet stay on course so he could go over the car crushing the occupants inside like a tin of tomatoes.

The oncoming vehicle must have realised the lights were on and began to flash to alert Hans.

Hans did not move, nor did he turn off his light. Still his foot was pressed firmly down, and his aim never shifted. The other vehicle flashed again. Hans did not comply even when the blue lights came on. The car got closer; Hans began to turn the wheel from left to right to confuse the other driver as to which way he intended to go or restrict their options. In his aggression, the farmer veered violently to the right and was unable to correct his position forcing him off the road. The tractor, as forgiving as it were, could not be corrected in time and the bank was so steep that the weight began to shift from the wheels to the top and the vehicle began to roll onto its side.

Hans was thrown to the right, smashing his shoulder and side into the window breaking it with a loud crack. The tractor skidded on its side for a few meters and then came to a grinding halt as snow built up in front. The fuel hose snapped from the engine and began spilling red diesel into the snow. The engine spluttered before dying. The key was still in the ignition allowing the lights of the tractor to remain on.

The police car slowed down and stopped. Hans was shaken, even in his rage-filled state his body and brain shook with the impact. He fought hard not to lose consciousness but found he was clumsy to get to his feet like a stunned boxer after a well-placed hook. But the torrent of rage came flooding back like a tsunami. The rage of the crash fuelled him and gave him the energy to lift himself up and punch through the window as though his hand was made of steel.

Unfortunately for him, his hand was just bone and meat, even though his mind was that of an enraged wild animal. The impact with the glass broke most of his fingers and cracked his forearm. Parts of the jagged window slashed into his forearm, which soon soaked his coat in crimson.

His arm fell at an awkward angle by his side, and he couldn't understand why it he was unable to move it. He looked and saw it was broken, with a small shard of the ulna breaking through the skin. He did not feel any pain and tried to push the bone back in cutting his hand on the jagged edge. It failed to go back in despite all the cracks and snaps coming from the wound.

He peered through the broken window and saw two policemen approaching. Reaching down he felt for the iron crowbar used for prising the wheels off the tractor. His armed cracked as he tried to free it from the passenger side; before his forearm gave in to the pressure and finally snapped clean. The arm was now useless, only attached by loose tissue and some muscle fibres. Propping himself up with his good arm he watched as the two police officers approached.

Wriggling out of the wreckage, still partially stunned he stumbled onto the ground like a maggot free from a corpse; wriggling on the snow and trying to get back to his feet. The two officers saw the farmer was holding something in his hand and immediately made quicker pace to get to him; stopping only when they saw the brace raise above his head in a threatening manner. Hans heard one of the officers shout out to him, but he did not hear the words. He rose to his feet, looked at the two officers with rage in his eyes and sluggishly moved towards them, dragging his feet across the thickening snow.

'Hans, for God's sake is that you?' Stig shouted.

Hans did not respond with words, just grunts as he continued his advance.

'Hans, are you okay? Shall we get an ambulance?' Stig tried again but to no avail.

'Sarge, he's not stopping,' Stolten said, reaching for his pistol.

'Hans, put down the bar and onto your knees,' Stig ordered, but this just enraged the farmer even more.

Hans began to regain full consciousness and picked up pace. His grunts were now screams and he advanced quicker to his targets waving the bar like he was showing how he would massacre them. His broken arms dangling to his side that swung with his movements.

'Hans, this is your last warning,' Stig drew his pistol and took aim. 'Put down the bar, drop to your knees and stay there.'

'I'll kill you all,' Hans screamed and leapt forwards trying to make up for the last few meters between him and the officers.

One shot… then a second followed as Stig cocked his pistol and fired in one smooth, yet reluctant manner. The first shot hit the top of Hans' left thigh followed by the second coming from Stolten whose inexperience with a firearm managed to graze the farmers already injured shoulder. The farmer fell to his left knee feeling an unusual disability to his left leg. He looked down as his winter trousers oozed a dark red liquid. He screamed out and tried to rise using his right leg to support his weight.

'Fuck sake,' Stig screamed at Stolten. 'Put that thing away. I only wanted to stop him not kill him!'

Stolten did as he was commanded and secured his pistol. He suddenly felt naked without the protection at hand and began to fear the worst as they advanced towards the farmer.

'Hans stop right now,' Stig's orders were now pleads to his friend, the memories of losing yet another colleague was too much. 'Please, Hans, please just stop.'

But the farmer did not. He threw the iron bar at Stig narrowly missing him in an attempt to get some retribution for the gun shot to his blood-soaked thigh. Stig could not wait any longer. His orders, his pleads were being unmet. His once good friend did not seem to recognise him. Instead, he was now a lunatic, the same as Mrs. Johansen the other night. That same strange look, the snarls, the anger, all were depicting Hans was out to kill.

Stig steadied his aim to the man's other right leg and pulled on the trigger praying his shot would not be fatal. Hans collapsed face down into the snow as both his legs lost strength with his momentum carrying him forward. All he could do now was watch as the two officers approached him, one taking the farmer's hands and placing them behind his back, while the other went for the handcuffs.

Hans bit wildly into the air trying to snatch Stolten's leg. The young constable pressed his knee against the back of the farmer's neck preventing his head from snapping round. Stig quickly applied the handcuffs and almost vomited when he felt the farmer's broken arm dangle with only the skin and jacket holding it together. He got onto the radio to call for an ambulance.

'Get him onto his back,' Stig commanded.

Hans snarled and gnashed his teeth together as the two officers put more pressure onto his neck, preventing a bite. The farmer squirmed and kicked at the ground trying to free himself. Stolten had to use his entire body weight and a second pair of cuffs to restrain his legs. Now Olsen looked more like a worm wriggling on the floor. Snarls and white foam formed around his gnashing mouth.

'Jesus, Sarge, he's strong. What the hell is going on?' Stolten asked trying his best to hold the farmer's legs down.

No way were they taking any chances after Mrs. Johansen easily overpowered them. Hans had the same deranged look of rage in his eyes as Mrs. Johansen but was younger and stronger. Stig went back to the car and brought out an old blanket to keep the farmer warm. He wriggled and screamed from underneath it. It would be another ten minutes before the ambulance arrived. Stig used his belt as a tourniquet to stop Hans from bleeding out. Not that it would make any difference to the man. His wild look and rage did not subside, even with blood loss.

'What the hell is going on, Stig?' Stolten asked.

Stig slumped onto the ground, kicking away the blood-stained snow. Hans still wriggling trying to escape; a bandage from the first aid kit in the car was stuffed in his mouth and tied around his head to prevent those snapping teeth from doing anyone any damage.

'I don't know, but we need help here. If there are more of these people running about the town then we have no way of finding them until too late,' Stig said.

24

Captain Larsen poured another generous volume of port into his lead crystal tumbler and sat himself down in front of the TV. There wasn't much on at this time of night but that didn't stop him flicking through the channels using his phone as a remote control hoping to find something of interest, or at least occupy his mind. He found using his phone to control the TV somewhat cumbersome. But the remote was lost or was being held hostage by his ex-wife in some evil spite against him. It was probably being used by her new lover now anyway.

She had never admitted to having a secret lover whilst they were married, but he knew… he wasn't stupid. Months away on exercise or operational tours meant she got lonely and had needs he could no longer fulfil, so a younger man was brought in to satisfy those needs that quickly escalated to something more than just sex. For a man of forty with looks that had seen cold shaves, rough dirt, minus thirty temperatures, and sun-scorched deserts he was still pretty good looking to a certain group of ladies: a real man's man. His body had picked up some excess weight when back in Norway from overseas duties. But this could be quickly lost and his muscular physique back on display when his squad was dispatched again.

He took a small sip of port from his glass and let the sweet liquid swirl in his mouth before swallowing it down. There were still some boxes in his new apartment that were unopened, and he had promised himself that he would get round to opening them and finding new places for the contents to live.

He spent longer at work than his colleagues; something that had caught the attention of his commanding officer. Larsen was a good soldier, if not one of the best on the platoon. He commanded respect from his troops, and they gave it to him. Yes, he was a bastard in the field and made everyone under his command work extra hard, but the rewards were there. Occasionally the British Army would come over for winter training that would finish up with some war games. These war games were a bit of fun and usually the British would come out with more kills. But Larsen used this opportunity to show the British that the Norwegians were made of hard stuff; hell, he even had pictures of Vikings on his wall and often quoted them before going into these games. There was no room for friendliness, not until it was over.

He would secretly train his men weeks in advance to love the cold, after all this was their homeland. The British would always complain about the weather during exercise training, "It's fuckin' cold boss," or the more commonly heard phrase, "Think my knackers have frozen and a penguin ran off with 'em."

Larsen knew how to get under the British skin. Occasionally he would meet another officer with the same eagerness as him to win, and the two would play mind games. Larsen, not only being a cunning soldier with excellent abilities on the battlefield to lead and think on his feet but was also wonderful at mind games. Things like putting the British through their paces and keeping them in the cold by telling them to jump into lakes as the water temperature was warmer than the air. This was true but once they got out the air quickly froze them, and they rapidly lost moral.

Also, in the Officers' Mess he would order the British drinks and spike them with vodka or some locally made illegal moonshine, and then put them into the lake with severe hangovers.

His name was infamous with the British and the latter tactic was now carefully monitored on exercise. He liked to win, wanted to win, which he did but only the smaller battles and very few of the overall war games. He demanded the best and his troops gave it to him; but as soon as exercises were over, he made sure his troops spent the night in the bar without ever having to spend their money. A Viking tradition of warriors drinking mead after a battle, he made sure the tradition remained alive, replacing mead with beer.

He took another sip, and the phone rang.

'Hello,' he answered.

'Captain Larsen? This is Colonel Becker. I am sorry to disturb you this late, I trust you weren't sleeping?'

'No, sir, I am always awake,' Larsen replied.

Becker laughed on the other side, 'Are you fit to drive? I need you to come in rather urgently.'

'I am afraid I have had a few drinks, is there a driver available?'

'Of course, I shall send out someone to collect you; no need for uniform just comes as you are.'

'May I ask what this is about, sir?'

'Let's save the explanation for when you arrive,' Becker hung up the phone without as much as a goodbye.

Larsen was a little taken aback by his commanding officer's abruptness, but then Becker was never one for lengthy phone conversations. Larsen sank the remainder of his port in two gulps, ran his fingers through his shaved ginger hair and stood up. No uniform was needed but since he was being called in to see his commanding officer he decided to dress for the occasion. He was glad in a way, the thoughts of his now ex-wife and her new lover were beginning to surface on his mind. Getting into work regardless to the hour was a blessing.

He checked his watch, *call ended two minutes ago, driver takes two minutes to get to car and begin moving, distance six kilometres to base, average speed sixty, time now is twelve-forty-five, car will be here in exactly ten minutes.* Perhaps time for a quick glass before the corporal arrives?

The car took a little longer than Larsen had calculated due to the weather conditions. This was fine with him, as he managed to just finish his port and wash the glass before the driver showed up. The driver was about to get out and open the door for his officer, but Larsen waved him back in and opened it up for himself. This was usual practice only for higher ranks, but this being one of his troops the driver wanted to show respect.

There was little dialogue between officer and rank; just the basic questions of how the weekend was and the weather. Larsen used the time in the car to test his mathematical skills and judge the time to get into the base. He enjoyed keeping his brain ticking, whether doing a crossword or sharpening his mental arithmetic by dividing or multiplying car number plates. He was a firm believer that the mind should be sharp from the moment a man wakes. By not giving it daily exercises, the mind would become lazy and useless, like any other part of the body.

The car pulled up to the main entrance where an armed guard requested his identification. The captain presented his identification, and the guard gave a quick salute and opened the gate. There was an informal rule amongst the men that at night there were no need for headdress, but Larsen always wore his. The car pulled up into a small courtyard outside an orange brick building that looked as though it was built pre-World War Two.

A small fountain, that had now iced over and no longer provided beautiful arching streams water, was just in the middle of the courtyard where official figures could be dropped allowing the cars to swing around in one uniform motion.

He got out, returned a salute from his driver, and walked into the large brick house; most of the other battalions and platoons were stationed in wooden houses and offices. Being one of the senior platoons at the base they had their pick of offices.

Upon entering the building, Larsen always took his time to marvel at the pictures and paintings from the Second World War, and more recently Afghanistan and African conflicts. They were mainly of helicopters with troops leaping out onto the desert floor with plumes of sand and dust being kicked up around them from the rotors. Larsen found his CO's office and knocked on the door. He waited even though it was open.

'Captain, come in, shut the door behind you please,' Colonel Becker said never once looking up from a report tucked inside a manila folder.

Colonel Anders Becker was dressed in his green distorted camouflage uniform. His beret was sitting on his oak desk next to a clean empty ashtray – a symbol of the old days. His thinning silver hair brushed back with Brylcreem resembled a finely ploughed field.

Larsen threw up a salute and remained standing until allowed to sit.

'How many more times, captain, we really do not need salutes this late at night, or early morning. Good God, we both need to have more things to do in our spare time,' Becker laughed. 'Okay, well let's get things started. I was called about thirty minutes before I called you by our beloved defence minister. You may need some time to take in what I am about to say.'

'Okay, sir, I am sure I will be able to digest this,' Larsen said with confidence.

'We have been having reports of… well how do I put this? I don't think there is any other way, reports of strange activities around Norway.'

Larsen looked perplexed, 'Strange things, sir?'

'Isolated incidents involving members of the public committing strange acts of violence, murders and everything in between,' Becker said.

'Excuse me, sir, but isn't this for the police to handle?' Larsen said with a respectful tone.

'Yes absolutely. This is exactly what I said to our defence minister. But as you know, he never calls… not unless it is a matter of defence,' Becker leaned back in his chair and took a deep breath. 'You see, these acts of violence have followed from power cuts and power surges. No explanation other than a very powerful electromagnetic pulse could have cause such an outage. In fact, there have been a few in a small village called Røyken. Have you heard of this place?'

Larsen shook his head

'A small village between Asker and Drammen, I will show you on the map. Well to make things even stranger we have had some reports of strange lights in the sky. Normally we would never act upon such reports since they have always been proven to be something explainable. However, the air force picked up something a few days ago for a fraction of a second before disappearing over that area. Since then, there have been reports of strange activities in the area following blackouts. There have been police reports of aggressive people with no previous records of anti-social behaviour. More to the point we have had an eyewitness report of, again this was very hard for me to understand and equally hard for me to tell you, unknown entities.'

'Unknown entities?' Larsen questioned.

'Yes, a British couple were fleeing from these *entities* after they were broken into. One of the occupants managed to sever a foot of the assailant, which was recovered by the police and quickly forwarded to his superiors, which in turn was quickly forwarded to our government,' Becker handed a brown folder to Larsen which included maps, reports and a large A4 colour photo of the severed foot in a clear plastic evidence bag.

'Is this a human foot? It looks like an Ape's foot, but the toes are much longer… and white?' Larsen studied the photo unable to fully understand what he was seeing.

'Our defence minister is quite concerned with these reports along with our PM. Usually this sort of thing would be dismissed at the police level, but to get all the way to the PM, and then from the defence minister, well something doesn't sit right with me. I don't know what is going on in Røyken or around Norway, but we need boots on the ground. There are local platoons making searchers of other areas of Norway and the defence minister wants eyes and ears in Røyken. That's why you are here, captain,' the colonel sat up in his chair, realising his fatigue and needed to straighten himself up.

'I see, sir, and what does our defence minister want from us?'

'He wants us to setup a forward observation post, surveillance only at this time. Under no circumstances must the people or the police know we are there. My orders are to keep a very low profile in the area. I have been in contact with my air force counterpart and asked to have reports of any unusual activity over Norwegian airspace. Of course, all of this is on a need-to-know basis,' Becker leaned forward to show his seriousness and continued, 'I don't believe a word of the report about lights in the sky or damn entities. But these are orders, captain; we do what we are told. I don't know if this is a hoax or more likely a novel weaponry system by terrorists or the Russians, but something has certainly got out government's backs up. The quicker we quash these nonsense reports, the faster we move back onto real matters of national security, also known as our job.'

'What is it you want us to do, sir?'

'Your task will be to observe and patrol the surrounding areas. The police have the town monitored but will have no idea we will be there. The order is for the operation to last two weeks,' Becker produced a large A1 sized map from under his desk with various coloured circles in different areas. 'Now, the incidents have been occurring here,' he pointed to the circles, which highlighted the school, farm, and some street areas. 'The green crosses here are where the first eyewitness reports of lights were seen, with this red circle being where the entities were contacted. Blue circles are areas of disturbances filed by the police. We want you to take your platoon and cover these areas during the night and early morning. We just want observations. We do believe in the disturbances, and we have all seen the school fire on the news. So that part we are taking seriously.'

'Observe only, sir? And what of these disturbances you mentioned?'

The colonel glanced back up from the map, 'Radom killings, and people going insane, that sort of thing.' Becker's eyes opened despite being early morning and the lack of sleep evident.

Larsen smiled, 'And what if we meet these entities?'

Anders leaned back, the smile wiped from his face, 'Chances are whomever is responsible has now got all the data they require and packed up. But, if you find them, we need them bringing in for interrogation. We need to know what they are using and why.'

'How many men do I have?'

'You will take eleven for now; set up divisions to relay your commands, sergeants, corporals and privates. You will be the only officer there. This is not a training exercise but there is nothing to say you can't run a few drills to keep their minds turning. I want all operations late afternoon to first light. Keep in contact with the command centre hourly and more importantly report to me if you do witness anything.'

Larsen thought for a moment and then asked, 'Do we know why these people have gone insane?'

Becker shook his head this time, 'Authorities are performing toxicology and psychological tests as we speak. We hope to identify the substance responsible for all this. To me this sounds like a military operation. I am treating it as such. That's why I want to send my best. Identify the nation, and maybe we might get a little more money in our budget,' Becker said with a smile. But the smile had a serious undertone.

Larsen collected the files and stood to leave, but not without giving a salute first.

25

Dark, deep sunken eyes watched him from the shadows. A malicious grin spread wide across the creature's elliptical-shaped head. A finger, long and thin, extended towards his face and pressed hard against the skull. The jagged nail, like an old bread knife, etched deep into the thin flesh. He screamed and felt the warm trickle of blood run down his face from the wound. Like a disciple to a religious leader, the man knelt at the creature's feet; unable to move like he was glued to that position.

The creature, knowing the man was at its mercy, began to laugh. Or what seemed to be a laugh. The teeth chomped up and down franticly, but the noise was a cat-like growl. The growl grew louder and louder as the nail dug in deeper, and deeper.

Adrian bolted up from the sofa like a coiled spring finally released. The creature's face, burnt into his vision from the nightmare, seemed to be wherever he turned his head. It took a few moments for Adrian to realise where he was and remember why he was at the police station. Laying back down he felt his forehead. He felt the dampness on his fingertips. Bringing his hand back in front of his face he was relieved to see only sweat and not blood. But the area felt sore and tender.

Adrian leaned to one side to see another sofa adjacent to the one he was lying on. Rachael was fast asleep. A large white clock on the wall showed it was very early morning. He was supposed to be in work today but felt like the events of the last twenty-four hours were too much to face patients. Eventually he summoned enough energy to get off the sofa. With only a few hours' sleep, Adrian was woozy and lacked energy. He poured himself a cup of black coffee that had been sitting on the heater for over an hour. It tasted bitter and awful but gave him the kick he needed. Turning back to his fiancée he saw she was also beginning to stir. He handed her a coffee.

'What time is it?' Rachael asked. Her eyes were red indicating she also didn't get much sleep either.

'Just gone five. How are you feeling?' Adrian asked already knowing the answer.

'Jesus Christ, all I dreamt about were those things coming out of the basement. Oh God Adrian, what were those things?' she began to tremble, and her voice panicked.

Adrian quickly threw his arms around her shoulders. 'It's okay, they're gone now. They are all gone.' His words were long to emphasise that they were now safe. In truth he had no idea if they had gone, but he had to sound convincing.

'What are we going to do?' Rachael tried to drink her coffee but found the cup difficult to hold.

Adrian took the cup from her before she spilt the hot contents over herself, 'We are going to get out, go to the city and spend a few nights away. I'll call in work and take these as sick days. They won't believe me about those creatures. But the break in should be enough. And besides, I think being ill is justified.'

A police officer came into the lounge. Adrian did not recognise him, 'Where is Stig?' he asked.

'Stig is out at Drammen hospital with another incident last night. Poor bastard is being worked overtime again. Anyway, how are you two feeling this morning? Is there anything I can get for you?' the officer sounded chirpy despite everything that was going off.

Adrian shook his head, 'I think just coffee for now. I have to call the clinic up when someone comes in.'

The lights began to flicker directing everyone's attention to the ceiling.

The officer frowned. 'Yeah, that's been happening a lot recently. Guess the Russian's have finally found a useful weapon.'

'Russians?' Adrian asked with complete disbelief.

'Well, it's not official, but if you asked me I would say it were the Russians testing out something new. Mind control, electromagnetic pulses, they have all the tricks.'

'You really believe the Russians are behind all this?' Adrian's voice grew angry. 'We were attacked last night by giant creatures. Did you read my report? Giant... fucking... CREATURES!' Adrian's fists clenched.

Rachael quickly put a hand on his lap, 'Adrian, take a moment. The officer has his theories, wrong but he wasn't there last night.'

Her words would take a few moments to calm Adrian down.

'I'm sorry, officer, my fiancé has been dealing with a lot over the years. I can assure you, those things last night were not Russian, not Chinese, not terrorists. They were not even human. Has there been any news back from the hospital?'

Adrian was amazed how Rachael could go from traumatised to professional with a soothing voice in a flash of an instance. Later he would ask how she was able to do this.

'Not yet, well actually some results have come back to us showing the toxicology reports. I haven't had chance to type them up yet.'

Adrian stood, 'Show me those results.'

'I... I don't think I can. These are official documents,' the officer was unsure.

'God damn it, I am their physician. I have a duty to see those results.' Adrian snapped once again.

The officer looked slightly taken aback and was wondering whether he was allowed to show the reports or put Adrian into a cell to calm down.

'Hang on,' he said finally. 'I'll radio Stig, see what he says. Is that okay I just call my supervisor?'

'Yes, yes please do. Sorry, I am just having a hard time with the lack of sleep and everything else.'

The officer smiled, 'I understand. Just wait a moment.'

The officer radioed Stig and asked if Adrian was allowed to see the reports. Stig's response was loud like he was under a lot of stress and didn't want to be called unless it was an emergency. After the tirade of abuse towards the officer he finally agreed that Adrian could see the results. Maybe Adrian could offer some medical opinions also.

Adrian was led into a small office just outside the lounge. It appeared this officer was the only one occupying the station.

'We're running on a skeleton crew in Røyken. But I think we are getting some more help in later,' the officer said and shifted around his unkempt desk to find the medical report.

Adrian snatched it from the officer's hands and read down the test results, 'White cell count high, immunoglobulin G high in cerebrospinal fluid, erythrocyte normal, leukocytes high. So, an infection of some kind? Doesn't say which leukocytes are high just all of them. That doesn't help me with a diagnosis. Toxicology reports negative for narcotics, cannabis, heroin, and cocaine. Like my neighbours would have used such drugs.'

'So, you think this is an infection?' the officer had a look of surprise on his face.

'Well, this report indicates an immune response.'

'Hang on, I have another report here.' the officer fumbled around to find the file. 'Yes, this one is an autopsy report.'

'Autopsy? My god, did something happen to Harold and Rita?'
''No, this is Johansen. It seemed she died last night.'
'Jesus Christ. How?'
'Maybe this report will explain it.'

Adrian sat down and read through the report. It stated Mrs. Johansen had died from unknown courses and as such an autopsy was carried out. The liver was slightly underweight and no signs of fibrosis or necrosis. Most of her internal organs appeared fine. There were, however, inflammation of the airways and lungs. The report read that they were waiting on bacterial and viral results from the laboratory. The brain had been removed and weighed with indication of damage to the frontal lobe and an enlarged hypothalamus. Again, samples had been taken for toxicology and pathogen assessment. Adrian called for Rachael to come in. The officer was reluctant to allow her to see the reports, but Adrian gave him a stern look.

'What is it?' she asked holding her coffee.

'Take a look at these autopsy reports from Mrs. Johansen,' Adrian handed her the report.

She read down the medical jargon to the part about the brain. She paused to digest the information, 'Frontal lobe damage and an enlarged hypothalamus? This is what we would expect the brain of a serial killer to look like. No wonder she felt no pain, her receptors didn't register this. Now we have causality to her behaviour, Adrian. Do we know anything else like infection or severe trauma?'

'Look at these reports also,' Adrian pointed to the part referencing the airways. 'Infection of the lung.'

The officer stood up. 'I need to radio Stig again. We need to get this information to our regional commissionaire. If there is a virus going round that is causing this behaviour, then we need to act.'

'Hang on, I didn't say that. I just said she had an infection. That could have nothing to do with the brain damage. We need more data. We have to wait and see what the lab comes back with. I think I have to go into the clinic and get the files on my patients. See if I have treated her for the flu or pneumonia in the past. That will at least help out the lab staff narrow things down.'

Hans Olsen struggled in his restraints. His good arm tied down to the bed, while his broken arm had been strapped to his chest.

'Not another one?' the doctor said wondering how this man was not responding to sedation. 'How many lunatics have you sent us now?'

Stig, not being in the mood for comedic smart-arses, remained silent. He watched carefully over his friend in case he tried to bite anyone that came within reach. Hans could not be sedated; he struggled in his restraints and bit out wildly at anyone that came too close. The nurses could not understand it, they had given the man morphine, but it had very little effect.

Medical staff tried their best to sedate the farmer. All of them now wearing face shields face masks and gloves. That was a little strange, Stig thought, but said nothing. His attention was on his friend screaming at the hospital staff.

'What are the injuries?' the doctor asked while his nurses attempted to secure a drip to Hans' vein.

'Clean broken radius and ulna in the right arm, and gunshots to the thighs. We cannot sedate the patient. We advise great caution; he's just like the others.' the nurse said.

'Others?' Stig questioned.

'A few more have come in with injuries all exhibiting the same behaviour,' the nurse replied. She took a look at Stig then asked, 'Have you experienced any shortness of breath, headaches or coughing fits over the last twenty-four hours?' her eyes never blinked showing she was both deadly serious and exhausted.

'Err... no... no. why?'

'We've been told to assess anyone that comes into the hospital whether they have had any of these symptoms. It seems like there is something going round that may be related to this behaviour. Although, this is precautionary, we ask that you wear a facemask while around others and watch out for symptoms of breathing difficulties, headaches and sore throat.'

Stig was handed a sterile bag of facemasks and told to wear them while on duty. Stig covered his mouth and nose with the mask, 'You really think all this is due to a virus or bacteria?'

'As I said, we have no idea right now, but the lab is coming out with updates every hour. Soon we shall know more, health officials have stated an hour ago that everyone is to wear these. It seems like all of these patients have been exposed to something that has set off an immune reaction. This is purely cautionary.'

Hans was removed and taken to somewhere quieter until the clinicians could figure out a way to anaesthetise the man for surgery.

Stig was dismissed by the doctors and informed he would be updated as soon as they could do a report.

'Facemasks, Sarge? We doing surgery now?' Stolten said when Stig handed him a mask.

Stig looked down at the bag of masks and then to Stolten, 'New working regulations. Masks are to be worn when on duty. Word is there is something going round. And we don't want to end up like these poor bastards.'

It was now five a.m., and he was due off shift as soon as his replacement showed up.

'Is this some sort of military experiment?' Stolten continued.

'Why would you say that?'

'Well, haven't they tried mind control before? This could be part of a biological weapon.'

'Right? And how did they manage to sneak into Norway and deliver this?'

Stolten paused for a moment, 'Those lights. Could have flown over and dropped something.'

Stig laughed at his young constable, 'I very much doubt that without the military knowing. And if they did just *drop something*, then it would have affected us all.'

Stolten nodded his head, 'Oh yeah.'

'You need to stop reading about military things, Stolten. You are a policeman, not a soldier.'

'Well, what do you think it is?'

Stig glanced at his constable before replying, 'I don't know what is going off. But we need to keep an eye on our GP and his fiancée. Chances are they could have been exposed to something.'

'Do you think the killings and the school are connected?' Stolten was hesitant about the school but felt he needed ask the big question.

Stig rubbed his eyes, which had reddened from exhaustion, 'Perhaps,' was all he could say.

Back at the station Stig examined a map trying to link all the places where the incidents had happened. It all started with the lights in the sky and blackouts followed by the power surge. The word from the hospital was that Hans had been taken into surgery for the gunshot and broken arm. Nothing life-threatening and it was expected he would make a complete recovery; his mental recovery, however, was highly questionable. The Klaus were still hell bent on attacking hospital staff and were now subjected to brain scans and psychological assessments. They were no longer being treated like patients but like mice in a laboratory. They were both regularly sedated followed with spinal taps and blood draws for pathogen assessments.

Results from the laboratory were perplexing the staff. Nothing was growing on the regular agar dishes under different conditions that ruled out known bacterial infections. Genetic screening of genes brought back nothing about viral infection either. Samples were being sent to larger government and industrial laboratories for electron microscopy, deep sequencing of genes, and virologists with expertise in exotic pathogens. Early data pointed to an infection of the airways, lungs and brain, although a pathogen could not be linked to the inflammation.

The regional health director was informed of the findings and decided to alert his superiors, mostly as a preventative measure. If there was a bug going round or something in the water supply, food, or household chemicals, then they needed to address this.

Adrian was still at the station. He had left the keys to the clinic at home and needed to wait until staff arrived. He tried to talk to Stig but was informed the sergeant needed to do some work before he was able to talk to anyone. In the meantime, Adrian was given an update on how healthcare workers should now wear masks. Adrian accepted that this would probably help slow down the virus or bacteria – in truth no one knew what was causing these problems. Rachael, on the other hand, was a little sceptical as to how folks would react to doctors, nurses and the emergency services wearing these masks. Her comment was that it would cause unrest and only raise more questions. It would probably be better to wait for an official word from parliament.

Stig looked up from the map and beckoned the doctor to sit down. 'Right, Adrian,' the sergeant said in a stern manner. 'We went to your house last night and found there to be a break in. We examined all the rooms and can't tell if anything has been stolen. But from our observations all the expensive items: electronics, dining plates and glassware, all have been left untouched. The forensic team are still working,' he checked his watch. 'We should be hearing from them soon. We can get you back home in a while.'

Adrian shook his head, 'Rachael will not want to go back there.'

'I understand. I would suggest you get a hotel in Oslo or something until things settle down here.'

Adrian agreed, 'We will need to get some things from the house. I will need to get the car. When can we go home and pack?'

The phone rang and Stig answered. He turned to Adrian upon finishing the call and said, 'Well, forensics have finished. I guess we can drive you home now if you like? I am about to finish on duty until tonight so we can drop you off on the way.'

Rachael wanted to come home also, even though she was scared to hell of the house now, she just couldn't leave Adrian there alone. What if he smelled the clothes or a sound triggered him? She was not going to let that happen. She had calmed down a lot since last night. She had even noticed how quickly he had calmed down from everything. But there was one more question Adrian had, and he had to ask, 'Did you find anything of those creatures?'

Stig took a deep breath. His mind was exhausted, overworked, and unable to make decisions. He was going to say he and Stolten found nothing unusual, but he just couldn't be bothered lying and have to fabricate a story just to keep Adrian calm. He also believed by not telling the truth would be the worst decision he could make, 'Yes, yes we did. We found a blue liquid all over the house. And we found a foot that meets your description.'

It would have been inappropriate to smile at that time in acknowledgment that his story was correct, but Adrian decided against it, 'So now what do we do?'

'I have to make some calls and speak to my superiors. We should draft in some additional help and find out more about these health risks. We have to contain this. You said you are going into the clinic? Well then, I need you to do something for me. Explain the situation, explain the findings from the hospital and get your clinicians to screen anyone that has symptoms of a cough, chest pains and signs of abnormal behaviour. God forbid, we have more of these crazies running about the village.' Stig stood up and grabbed his car keys, 'I really can't deal with any more of these people, Adrian. I'm tired,' Stig bowed his head.

The car arrived at the house. Stig and Stolten made sure forensics had left before allowing the occupants to go back inside. Once they were happy all the blue liquid had been cleaned up and glass removed then they let them in.

'I think you will need to get that window replaced as soon as possible,' Stolten said. 'Have you got any wood you can board it up with until then?'

Adrian said he had a lot of scrap wood in the work room and could nail up a few boards to keep the winter out. He could also lock the basement doors and isolate the upper two levels of the house. The policemen said they would wait until he had boarded up the broken window and then get home to rest before the night shift.

Stig reassured them both that an increase of police would mean more patrols. The police presence would also scare off any would-be burglars and deter anyone looking for trouble. But Rachael expressed her fears of staying in the house too long and could not get that creature's face out of her mind. Those deep sunken black eyes, the bone structure, its height, and elongation of the thin limbs. It was a monster pure and simple, and Rachael did not want to spend any more time in this place. Adrian said he intended them to stay in Oslo for a few nights while things settled down in Røyken.

'Just get some things packed for two or three days. I will go to the clinic shortly and arrange some sick leave, I am sure they have enough doctors to cover appointments,' he said as Rachael came up the stairs.

She slowly stepped to the top and stared at the coffee table and to then the floor. The nightmare of last night relived in her mind's eye and she began to tremble. She twisted her body around as she heard footsteps from behind. Adrian brought her a coffee and beckoned her to relax on the sofa. Dawn was breaking and the daylight would offer them both a safe haven while they got cleaned up and organised a hotel in the city.

Rachael looked exhausted. Adrian could see her eyes opening and closing as she sat with her feet up on the sofa. He looked at his watch and decided it may be a good idea to have a little snooze also. He was in no fit state to drive at the moment. He pulled up a chair and sat next to her. Soon his eyes succumbed to the tiredness, and he drifted off to sleep, dreaming almost immediately.

26

Larsen tried his best to stay alert and awake. Having spent the entire morning in the office going over the files and reports, he was quickly feeling the lack of sleep was affecting his judgement. He rubbed his red eyes and took another long sip of black coffee. Neither helped much but gave his brain some stimulant. Carefully he arranged the small meeting room and activated the overhead projector.

Larsen's platoon entered the room yawning; the younger soldiers dragging their feet on the carpet. Larsen gestured with a wave of his hand for the small eleven-man platoon to take a seat. The captain tried to hide his tiredness by covering a yawn with a cough or by turning his head so his team could not see any weakness in their leader.

There was random chatter amongst the team. Some didn't like the idea of having to come into work early. The more senior ranks were keener on getting this over with so they could sneak off to the mess hall and fill their stomachs.

Colonel Becker entered through a door at the rear of the small briefing room along with his assistant; a very striking young blonde lady with her hair tied neatly back in a ponytail.

'That will be all, Melissa, thank you,' Becker dismissed the young female private.

The younger privates heard the name and tried to get a look at Melissa before she left. Becker placed his cap onto a small desk at the front that looked more at home in a school than a briefing room. His grey hair, normally neatly brushed back with Brylcreem, was messy and unkempt. The strands fell onto his face, and he quickly brushed them back. He too was not going to show any weakness of being tired to the lower ranks.

'Room, *uh-ten-shuhn!*' Larsen elongated the command to assure its importance. His words broke through the room that startled some of the younger ranks as well as his commanding officer.

Everyone rose to their feet with the sounds of chairs scraping at the carpet. The captain threw up a salute and moved out of the way so the colonel could take his position at the small wooden lecturers' post.

Becker straightened himself, 'Right, I don't know how many of you have been following the news lately, but there have been some unusual disturbances around Norway in the last few days,' Becker paused to look at the soldiers' faces. 'Trondheim has seen mass brawlings and inexplicable acts of violence in surrounding towns and villages. Unexplained power outages in the north followed by assaults and murders. A few days earlier the air force picked up some radar blips coming over from the Russian and Swedish boarder that quickly disappeared and reappeared around various villages and towns that saw these behaviours. It is unknown as to what or why these are occurring. The minister of defence has instructed the heads of staff to begin investigations,' he paused again to either catch his breath or think about how to phrase the next part. 'At one a.m. this morning police in the small village of Røyken intercepted a young couple while out on patrol. They were spotted fleeing from their home following a break in. Later they arrested a deranged farmer veering into them that required two gunshots to subdue the assailant. Before this we had some smaller incidents, the Drammen hospital killings, the explosion at the school, and some outbreaks of fighting. Put it simply something is going on in my territory,' the colonel opened the first PowerPoint slide and beckoned for the blinds to be closed and the lights dimmed.

The screen displayed various police photos. Some pictures of the deranged patients at Drammen hospital, pictures of the school fire and bodies, and one of a blue stain on the floor of someone's house.

'Forensic experts could not identify this blue liquid on site,' Becker continued. 'They have sent this to other laboratories for further investigation and we hope to have some results back later today. Early guesses are that this liquid could be linked to the violent behaviour,' he flicked through more slides each showing different areas of Røyken where the attacks and incidents had taken place. Neat red lines tried to connect rings circled around the incident areas in a poor attempt to find a pattern.

The dim lighting was beginning to subdue all the occupants in the briefing room. Even with his strong voice, the colonel could not keep his audience focused without a yawn breaking through the pauses.

'Now, this is interesting,' the presentation went to the next slide displaying what seemed to be an Ape's foot. The grey skin hanging off a thin bone with the same blue liquid as in the previous slides all encased in a see-through sterile evidence bag. 'A foot, or at least that is what experts are calling it, was recovered from the house. No known animal has been matched to this appendage but from what we have been told it is biological. That means that whatever this belonged to was alive.'

The room seemed to wake up at the image.

One private mused, 'Are we hunting Yetis? I should bring my

camera and a net.'

The room laughed before seeing the unamused look on the face their captain.

'Quiet, Higgs,' the captain said.

Becker, clearly unamused continued, 'Since the violence appears to be on-going across Norway, the police will be charged with enforcing a curfew after twenty-one hundred hours today. After lengthy discussion about this blue liquid and some preliminary reports from autopsies, it appears our attackers have been using some kind of biological weapon. Although, at this time it is not known what is being use. With that there is also a mandatory request that all civilians wear face masks and refrain from contact until the eggheads get this under control. Now, I don't have an explanation at this time, and nothing has been made official, so this is a secret operation. If I was to guess, however, I believe this to be a foreign invasion of Norway. I believe they are testing some kind of weapon on small areas. Therefore, respirators will be carried at all times during patrol, and face masks issued during working hours. These are to be worn at all times, understand?'

The room went quiet. An actual biological or chemical weapon had been used in Norway was unheard of.

'We are also informed to monitor ourselves and others for the following conditions: coughing, headaches, shortness of breath and basic cold or flu-like symptoms. These are attributed to the weapon's early signs. If this is observed, then you must seek medical attention right away. Captain Larsen will be CO in the field so all further questions can be put to him. That is all.'

The room stood to attention as Becker left, the door opening as he came close. Heads turned to have one final glimpse of his lovely assistant before being closed.

The room sat back down, and Larsen took over before his team began to chatter, 'I couldn't agree more. A terrorist attack on Norwegian soil has, and probably still is, occurring. But be that as it may we are now on operations in our own country. This has not happened since World War two and I expect each and every one of you to do your job. Our task is to observe and not be seen, plain and simple. So, the plan will be easy for this evening's operation. We are eleven men, twelve with me, so I want four teams of three with myself rotating between teams,' he pulled up a slide on the computer showing a map of the area with red circles around various points. 'Now I didn't have time to come up with some fancy names for the teams, I shall leave that up to you, but for radio reasons we need to have codes. My team will be Alpha, Sergeant Olsen will head team Bravo, Charlie will be Corporal Evans, and Delta will be Corporal Baxter. These are your superiors and will relay orders from myself. We are armed because we are soldiers, but we will not under any circumstances fire until you request from me directly, is that understood?'

The room nodded in agreement.

Larsen continued, 'We are there to observe only. Are there any questions so far?'

Corporal Baxter raised his hand, 'Yes, sir, how long are we to remain on operations?'

'Until we get orders to terminate. My feelings are that we will be there for two weeks. Any more questions?'

The room went quiet for a moment before one ginger-haired private decided to ask a question that was on everyone's mind. 'Sir, what was that foot?'

Larsen shot the private a long stare. 'Nothing. Probably something placed to make us believe a diseased monkey escaped or something. A stupid notion that I want you to forget about. Any more questions?'

The room fell silent again, trying to take in what was happening around them and probably how things would turn out. For many of the soldiers, actual conflict was never on their agenda when they were conscripted. They just wanted to do their one-year service and get back to playing their Xbox and PlayStations.

'Good, your equipment lists are in front of you, you can pick up the night vision scopes and goggles from the armoury; make sure you check them before we all head back to our beds to rest up before tonight,' Larsen said, believing this to be the end of the brief.

'Sir?' Another young private put up his hand, 'Sir, it doesn't mention torches.'

'No, there will be no lights, no signs that we are there. That also includes toilets. You will find that they left dog bags off the list. I have brought them, and you will have to make do using them. Operations will begin at six tonight and the driver will drop all teams off at their grid references. Your patrols will start at seven tonight and finish at six tomorrow morning, before daybreak. You will be pushing this for a while. The colonel gave me the pleasure to name this operation, and after thinking for a while I have come up with Operation Mole. This is because by the time we end this, we will all have faces like moles, be digging in the dark like moles and sleep during the day… like moles.'

Lethargic laughter met the poor attempt at a joke. Humour was most certainly not Larsen's strong point. It was believed the captain had an upper-class sense of humour. The kind of man who would think a knock-knock joke was topical and humorous.

'Okay, team leaders synchronise watches at local time, coming up to six-thirty in three… two… one… now,' Larsen closely monitored the hands on his watch as he counted down the seconds.

A single beep came from the room as all watches synchronised precisely. Larsen collected his notes into manila folders and beckoned Sergeant Olsen to join him for a further briefing. The room waited for the door to close behind them.

'Ah shit, I was hoping we would have a relaxing week.' Private Higgs was always the first to pipe up.

'Dibbs on observation duties,' Corporal Baxter interjected raising his hand to further show his enthusiasm for volunteering.

'Not a chance,' said Corporal Evans. 'Observers do fuck all. I have some seniority over you so it will be me and my team that will be doing the observation duties.'

'I volunteer for that team,' said Higgs.

'Seniority? You're the same rank as me,' Baxter replied to Evans and looked slightly unhappy.

Evans had been a corporal for many years and wasn't about to see a promotion for a few more. Most of the men didn't like him that much. He wasn't ready to get his hands dirty with the boys like everyone else. He took at least a week off every two months on sick because of a common cold or stomach virus he claimed he had. If there was a daunting difficult task set, he was always happy to pass the hard work onto his men. After all, isn't that a privilege of rank?

'No fucking way, Evans. It's about time you dug in with your boys. If Larsen gets dirty, then so should you. Or will you be trying to pull another sickie and get out of duties?' Baxter smiled at his comment.

'My leg hurts, Evans,' Higgs spoke up and pretended to limp.

'I'll be there.' Evans said. The rat-faced man, with an unusually pointed nose that made him look like the Vampire from Sesame Street, backed away. He did not want to engage the well-built corporal. Instead, he shuffled some files and pretended to be invested in the operation.

'Higgs, stop fucking about or I will give you a limp,' Baxter shouted at Higgs, who was wobbling about as though his leg was broken.

Evans waited for Baxter to leave the room before pulling up a chair and ordering Private Forberg, one of the newest recruits that still had the basic training short haircut made famous by US Marines, to make some coffee. *I'm not going to freeze my balls off when I have the ranks to do that,* Evans thought.

27

Johnson prepared himself this morning as he had done for the past thirty years; waking at six a.m. and taking a quick shower to wash away the previous night's decadence of binging on brand beer and that awful Swedish fermented fish – the famous fish "*Surströmming*" that must be opened outside in a bucket of water to hide the rotting smell.

His wife prepared a typical breakfast of scrambled eggs, thick hand-cut slices of bread and some Norwegian smoked Salmon – the best salmon in the word, Johnson claimed.

He liked to take his morning slow allowing time to come round and shake off the hangover. Part of the morning ritual was to take his dog, Lucky, out for a morning stroll in the woods close by. Lucky was a good-sized mix Boarder Colley with Rottweiler thrown in. The phenotypic results were a black coat with a white patchy belly and unusually large paws, which most people found adorable. Lucky would lie under the table during meals, catching anything tasty or what looked to be edible falling his way. Today was no exception; he lay by his master's feet keeping them warm on this cold morning waiting for some sort of reward for his efforts.

Johnson read the news to his wife saying it was good now that these monsters from Røyken were being put away and that this curfew the police were going to enforce would keep those rowdy kids off the streets at night. His wife smiled and just agreed as she had been doing during their long marriage. It wasn't worth questioning his far-right political views unless she wanted to be told she was stupid and idiotic for thinking loony left politics. It was much easier to just agree and keep her views to herself.

Johnson was a train driver for the national railway company. Not one to hide his opinions, he had been arguing with his superiors about faulty lines and broken signals. He claimed these were the reasons delays were occurring on his route. Truth be told, he wasn't one for keeping time. If he wanted a leisurely ride, he would slow the train down. If he was in a rush, he could get the carriages to ride on one side. Usually, a text message would alert him as to the state of the tracks before he began his shift. The snow had been falling heavy overnight and no doubt would have created some problems with the tracks. But this didn't bother him that much. Did he feel for the commuters? Not really, if he was late so what, if someone was running for the train and he decided to leave, the doors were locked, and he would not batter an eyelid about pulling away with or without his passengers.

He never considered this a form of bullying – though many of his co-workers would beg to differ – he had always stood his ground. Not one for education, he was always quick to settle a dispute using his fists rather than simply walk away. Even now at fifty, he was no different to when he was eighteen; though his body was not as bulky with muscle as it once was. His once proud washboard stomach now hidden behind too many cakes and sugary delights that his health was also in decline and diabetes was knocking at the door. But why should that matter? He is who he is.

'What time does your shift end?' his wife asked before taking a small nibble from the single slice of bread and cheese in front of her.

Johnson didn't bother to wait to swallow his food before answering, 'About four,' he spat bits of egg onto the table and floor, to which Lucky was quick to claim the prize. 'But I am going to meet friends in Oslo after work so will be home around seven or eight; I haven't decided yet.'

An hour after eating, and an hour before work, he put the lead on Lucky and took him for his woodland walk. The sun was now coming up through thick clouds and provided some light around his walk. Heavy snow had been predicted to last a few days. Johnson didn't mind the snow. It was nice to walk in. He preferred the snow and ice to the roasting temperatures of summer. The thick jacket and trousers helped hide his overhanging stomach. He never admitted it, but he had grown to be slightly ashamed of his body.

The local news reported the killings and school fires, trying to find links and cause without offering anything concrete. Johnson had read and re-read the stories but wasn't fazed. The school burnt because kids fucked about and needed a good hand taking to them. Old bastards went on killing sprees because they hadn't saved enough for their pension and were looking for some free jail time. No, this was the reason because he deemed it so. He felt perfectly safe walking Lucky. Should he meet any idiot then he could deal out his own form of justice: *pow-pow,* left then right and goodnight.

His house was close to the woods being on the highest point of the estate that overlooked much of the village. In the summer he would avoid the woods because of ticks, and he was fed up having to pluck their fat bodies off his dog… or himself. He had heard of some guy that was infected by Lyme disease following a tick bite, which he wanted to avoid. Winter was a better time; the air was cold and that was the way he liked it.

The snow was soft, almost a powder on the woodland floor. Lucky ran around sniffing for other dogs and urinating every few meters to mark his territory in bright yellow puddles on the white snow. Only when he found a place where other dogs had defecated did he do the same. By law you are supposed to pick up after your dog, but Johnson didn't seem to think he needed to do that in the snow. A confident kick of snow to bury it followed by a good padding down ensured the dog mess was well hidden until spring was good enough.

He walked in front of the dog and whistled for him to follow his master. He wasn't looking forward to work, but then this was all he was good at. At least he no longer had the late shift. Driving the last train at one a.m. with drunks and rowdy teens often left him angrier than usual. He knew where the security cameras were and if he ever needed to discipline someone it was always away from others and well away from cameras. Many complaints were put against him, but none could be verified or proven. His managers suspected him of things but did not have any evidence to make a formal investigation. Even his ticket masters were afraid of his wrath should they testify against him. He was good at getting away with things. Fear of what he could do kept his train on the right tracks.

The trees grew dense down a small valley as Johnson followed the path trodden by other walkers. Silver birch, now shed of leaves, stood tall and thin. The snow complimented their silver look and it was quite soothing for Johnson here. He loved the woods and forests, especially when it had snowed. There was a quiet that he liked and only after the snow had fallen and began to colonise the area did the sounds dampen significantly. When he stood still and held his breath could he really enjoy the tranquillity? He did this now, sitting on a log. Closing his eyes, he enjoyed a few moments of silence. Lucky had run ahead but not too far from his master. Work, home, and life in general were subdued in this environment and it was almost like he belonged here.

Lucky barked in the distance that broke Johnson's moment of being one with nature. Johnson opened his eyes and was brought back to reality once more. He looked but could not see his dog. Leaping to his feet in anger that his tranquillity was interrupted, he shouted and whistled for Lucky to come back. The dog did not. Lucky continued to bark somewhere in the distance, passed the trees and bushes thick with snow. Johnson thought there was another dog or maybe someone else in the area that had made Lucky protective. This was unusual for Lucky; he barked, yes, but never really stood his ground, always running away and barking over his shoulder.

Johnson whistled again and shouted for his dog to return. Lucky continued to bark loudly and then growl. It was hard to see him at a distance, but when close enough the dog's black coat stood out from the white background. Johnson shouted and the dog turned his head to see his master, 'Get back here,' he commanded.

Johnson saw the hair on Lucky's back was stood on end; he had never before witnessed this. He suddenly had a fearful thought run through his mind and he quickly searched the ground for a large stick. If one of those fucking nutcases were hiding in the forest waiting to have a go then he would unleash hell, reassess then go in with the fists for some personal attention. He found one but it was rotten with moisture. Maybe that would be enough to stun someone long enough for the fists of fury.

Lucky began to walk backwards never keeping his eyes from a heavily wooded area close to a rocky wall. The Ever-Green trees and ferns heavily coated with snow blocked whatever it was the dog was watching. Johnson was much closer now and he reached out and grabbed Lucky by the collar. The dog didn't even acknowledge his master. He looked down and saw the dog's teeth were bare; the hair on his back on end and the tail was down.

Lucky crouched to the likes his master had never seen before. The domestic dog now looked and acted like a wolf ready to attack, or defend?

Slightly concerned he quickly hooked the lead around the dog's collar and looked in the direction Lucky was guarding. There was nothing there. It was deadly silent but for the growling from Lucky. Johnson placed his hand onto the dog's head and tried his best to hush him. Usually, a smack would be a good enough way to shush the dog. But his posture and defensiveness made Johnson think twice to dealing out corporal punishment. The dog began to snarl, white foaming saliva dripping from large canine teeth.

Johnson gave up and decided that this was enough, and it was time for home. He began to pull on the lead for his dog to follow. Lucky did as he was requested but insisted on walking backwards so that he could face the trees. He was completely fixated on those trees. Johnson hated to admit to himself that he was a little uneasy… hell he was frightened. Nonetheless he picked up his pace and pulled his dog with him.

Lucky never stopped snarling at something behind them. The dog's insistence one walking backwards slowed their pace. Johnson had a brief thought of picking him up but thought it may be a bad idea as the dog was on edge. He looked back to see why Lucky was still guarding, then he saw something. Not clearly, but he saw something move amidst the ferns. Powdery snow fell from the pine needles and Johnson stood still.

Lucky hunched up looking like he was ready to pounce on whoever or whatever came close. The trees settled and Johnson strained his eyes. There was something there. It could have been a deer, they were very common around these parts, and sometimes they would wonder into people's gardens and eat the roses. Shuffling branches from left of him, much closer, caused him to swing around.

He yanked on Lucky's lead and began to pick up pace; almost

dragging the spooked dog. Lucky turned to face forward aware of what his master was doing and quickly pushed in front, almost knocking his master off the path and into the denser snow that had formed small hills at the sides.

Johnson heard movements behind him. He turned his head and caught a glimpse of his pursuer. Something grey was hiding in the woods darting between trees, trying to hide its presence but had clumsily given itself away. Now he knew someone else was in the woods, hiding.

Johnson faced forwards again and began to pick up the pace, but for only a moment. Another noise now attracted his attention. A strange noise; like twigs breaking in rhythm.

Click-click-click.

He turned around again, only this time he saw two figures standing tall on the path behind him: bare trees standing either side of them. Johnson stopped and stared.

Was he really seeing this? Was he really seeing these two tall grey stick men in the woods? He was staring at two six or maybe seven-foot thin grey men with sunken faces and deep dark sunken eyes. He shook his head in disbelief. Surely it was the silver birch he was seeing. They were completely naked. Johnson could not make out any features that would distinguish gender. Their skinny arms drooped low to the ground, extending way past the hips and to the knees, their faces seemed to be smiling at him. The figures stood in full view, almost mocking him, now they no longer felt the need to hide.

They looked at one another with a slow turn of their heads and then back at him. Standing like trees, and just as tall, these white, tall, and thin figures' features began to take form.

Click-click-click.

As Johnson's eyes adjusted to the brilliance of the white snow, he could make out the features of these darker grey men. But these were not men. They resembled elongated disfigured skeletons wrapped in paper-like skin.

Lucky broke Johnson's fixation by barking and tugging on his lead in an aim to get him and his master moving. Johnson jumped and looked down to see the dog facing behind him. Twisting his body, he looked. Lucky stood his ground growling and baring his teeth to protect his master from something blocking their path.

Another creature emerged from behind some trees, though this one was different to the tall stick men now behind Johnson. This was a much smaller creature standing around four feet maybe? Its height was not the only thing that was different; its physical appearance also differed. It too had thin arms and was grey in colour, but the legs were stumpy, its head much larger than its body and the eyes bigger, almost like two large black avocados on a marzipan cake.

Johnson could easily overpower this thing; in fact, he could simply push it or set Lucky on it. But fear and shock held him in place. Fear and disbelief of what he was seeing his brain could not understand. The small creature raised its grey hand revealing something that resembled a gun but looked smaller. A small thin barrel aimed at Johnson with the creature's thin stumpy fingers curled around a trigger just above a black canister that bubbled with something inside.

Lucky barked viciously and pulled hard on the lead. The two larger creatures dropped to the ground on all fours. Their heads bent back and hips downwards. They scurried across the woodland floor at great pace with rapid leg and arm movements that matched an arachnid about to strike. Johnson now knew what he was seeing was real. He tried to move his feet, but they didn't respond at first. Lucky launched himself towards the smaller creature pulling Johnson off balance.

The small creature backed away, probably realising that Lucky was hell bent on tearing out its throat. Johnson's feet began to move in the direction lucky was pulling him. The small creature blinked, briefly turning its large oval black eyes silver, and tilted its head sideways as if understanding or planning something. Johnson finally let out a scream and the creature jolted. It seemed to have been expecting the man to be passive like many other victims before, but this man had a protector, and both seemed capable of inflicting severe harm.

By this time Johnson was now running towards it but had no intention of confronting or fighting the thing. The small creature leapt out of the way just in time before the dog was able to tear into its thin flesh.

Lucky pulled himself and his master away from danger. Johnson responded and tried to pick up the pace, his legs tiring having to carry his weight and unhealthy diet of cakes and fatty foods struggling to keep the pace. The deepening snow made it hard to run. Behind him the creatures were making ground, eager to catch their prey. The deep snow and ice did nothing to hinder their pace. Their thin legs and large feet were the perfect size and shape to glide through the snow.

Suddenly, his momentum was halted after one of the creatures lurched up from its spider-like posture and took hold of his shoulders. A hard tug and Johnson was forced backwards. A strong kick to the back of his right knee buckled his leg and he fell to the ground. Before he knew it, both taller creatures were now kneeling on him and holding him down, pinning him to the ground. He screamed and let go of the lead. Lucky, now free, launched at the one of the taller creatures, successfully sinking his teeth deep into the thin tissue. The creature let out a high-pitched howl, like a cat would scream at another in its territory.

Lucky shook his head the same way he would a toy, tearing at the creature's thin arm; his jaws clamping down hard splintering the bone with blue blood seeping out of broken skin. Screams from both Johnson and the creature echoed throughout the forest. Johnson did not see but heard the commotion. He was close enough to the houses now and someone must be able to hear him. The creature let go of Johnson and swung to hit the beast. Lucky yelped and briefly let go only to re-establish himself and try again.

Johnson watched as the tall creature left him and turned its attention onto his dog. Lucky reset itself and hunched its back. He leapt at the creature's leg and managed to take hold of the ankle in its vice-like jaws. The creature did not scream this time. It bent down to the animal's head and extended its fingers to wrap around the dog's skull that reached down under its neck. Johnson heard the growl slowly subside as Lucky began to lose consciousness.

Johnson screamed out, 'You fuckin' bastards, I'm gonna kill you!' his anger replaced fear and he was him again; the same man that would happily fight a drunk twice his size.

Both taller creatures relinquished their attention long enough for him to wriggle away. Raising his arms and balling his fist he swung and hit one of the larger creatures square in the face. He reset and swung again, and again, and again until the creature had no option to lean over and stop that hand from hitting it. His right hand, his Saturday night right was still free. He balled up a fist and landed it against the creature's floating rib. It was a beauty of a hook, the creature's ribs cracked under the impact as Johnson brought back his fist for another body punch. The creature let go of his left arm and now his fists had come together again; left and right goodnight, *pow-pow*.

The smaller one was standing at his feet with the gun held ready for use. It didn't join in the fight, knowing that its small frame would be useless against such a volatile specimen. It sidestepped a kick Johnson tried to land but missed. He tried to get to his feet, to unleash hell on his attackers. The second creature, which no longer needed to deal with an aggressive dog, leapt on him to push him back down onto the icy snow. Johnson tried to move but was now completely helpless. The most he could muster was a slight shuffle in a feeble attempt to free himself. Both taller creatures were applying as much body weight onto Johnson that all he could now do was watch in terror as the smaller creature knelt beside him, the gun-like device held out in front with the canister of black bubbling liquid poised by the man's face.

Those large black eyes squinted silver that now looked like the eyes of a snake or octopus. Its small grey fingers squeezed on the trigger releasing an aerosol of black, almost dark grey mist into the face of Johnson.

Johnson coughed as the vile gas burned his throat and lungs. The unmistakable aroma of ammonia coated the inside of his nose. He tried to hold his breath. Unfortunately, a lifetime of unhealthy living meant he could only hold it for so long before gasping for air and breathing in even more of the noxious vapour.

The small creature backed away and tapped the shoulder of one of the taller ones to step back. Johnson was now free but was unable to move from coughing. Each gasp of air resulted in another coughing spasm, like he had taken a huge punch to his solar plexus. The tall creature to his left bent back its left wrist revealing a dark vein which grew darker as this skin around inflamed. Veins running the entire length of the arm darkened before a small protrusion broke the skin followed by a blue mist engulfing Johnson's face. Within seconds of inhaling the vapour his coughing began to subside. He began to relax, his muscles weaken. Slowly his eyes began to close. He tried to fight it but the vapour had already flooded his blood. The snow, the tress and the creatures began to fade away into a dark haze.

28

Johnson opened his eyes. He felt cold and wet. He raised a hand to his lips to moisten them a little with the melted snow on his fingers. Something furry tapped his hand and he turned his head. Lucky was resting with his eyes open looking at his master. When he realised his master was awake, he began to sit up and wag his tail. Johnson petted him lethargically and tried to sit up. It was hard at first and his head felt like it had been pounded with a hammer. He supported himself by placing his left hand behind him and used his right to rub his head then eyes.

Shit, what just happened? He looked around and tried to figure out why he was in the forest. He tried to think but his mind drew a blank between breakfast and here. He looked around hoping something would jolt his memory. He could only remember walking the dog after breakfast. Thankfully his daily routine had embedded itself deep in his mind that no amount of amnesia could wash over. He saw the sky was getting brighter and the snow descending much heavier with larger flakes.

He checked his watch: seven-thirty a.m. He cursed at the time. He didn't know why or how he had fallen asleep on the snow but right now he didn't care; he was running late for work. He stood and felt the full impact of a massive headache along with a sore throat and heavy lungs He should call in work sick since this could possibly be a bad case of a hangover or possibly getting a cold.

He contemplated a sick day. As a train driver he needed to be one hundred per cent when operating these large juggernauts. But his personal pride got in the way of sound judgement. He had never taken a day off sick… ever! And to hell and high water he was not going to start now. They had toilets on the train, and he was sure throwing a couple of aspirins down his throat with some strong black coffee would ease everything up. Strapping the dog to the leash he made quick time walking back home; his vision blurry due to the immense pain in his head that worsened with each cough of vile green phlegm.

His wife questioned where he had been. A wave of his hand put an end to the question. He said he was going to work and that he would go to a bar later and see if he can dowse the pain with something strong. He got dressed in his uniform of white shirt with company emblem, black trousers and cheap shoes with the soles buckling under fallen archers. He cleaned his face, walked downstairs, and slammed the door shut to further emphasise his anger of being hung-over after very little to drink.

He reached for his throat and tried to ease the rawness by rubbing it. Getting into the car he saw a blue Mazda parked on the opposite side, 'Cheeky fucker,' he said and got out.

Taking out a piece of paper and a pen from his top pocket he wrote a note and slapped it hard under the windscreen wiper.

'Don't fucking park here again, otherwise accidents *will* happen,' he read the note out loud and felt slightly satisfied venting some of his frustration.

He knew all the cars on the road and made sure everyone parked accordingly. None of his neighbours liked him for these actions. He didn't care one bit. One time the neighbour across the street challenged him over a parking space that he had rightfully taken —

a big mistake. Johnson had taken the younger man by the collar and made a gesture that if he saw the car again both vehicle and owner were going to get their headlights put out. He was in charge of this street, and if he wanted to park elsewhere who would stop *him*? Nobody would dare to argue with him.

He got back in the car, turned the key, and drove off with a wheel screech to prove a point to himself. He didn't bother with the seat belt, hell, he didn't need it. Fuck the police, fuck the law, and fuck this place. He really hoped someone would piss him off today as he really wanted a fight; that always made him feel better. Ignoring the speed restriction and constant reminders for drivers to slow down as children played here, he sped up.

Pulling into Røyken train station he yanked the car into a free spot, stopping it by tugging hard on the handbrake almost ripping it from its gears. He was indeed in a foul mood today and his nagging headache wasn't helping. He waited impatiently for the train to arrive. God help the driver if he was late again. Luckily for the driver he turned up on time. He waved to Johnson but got no gesture back. Some night workers were getting off shift, but Johnson barged right past them; *his* train, *he* was the boss here now. Storming into the cab he put in his time sheet and took out his phone to read the news while passengers seated themselves. The signal came from his ticket master that everyone was on board, and he pressed a series of buttons and pushed the throttle forward to get the train moving.

'Fucking hang over,' he said out loud and smacked his fist onto the control panel.

29

The phone rang, abruptly waking Adrian from a deep sleep. His eyes took a moment to adjust to the phone's display. There were several missed calls and a few text messages waiting for his attention.

'Hi, Adrian,' he answered not fully awake and rubbing his eyes trying to regain some awareness.

'Adrian, where are you?' came the voice on the other end. 'You're late and we have had to push some of your patients onto other doctors.' The man's voice was stressed, like he had been running around trying to fix several problems at once.

Adrian looked at his watch: nine-thirty a.m., 'Oh shit, damn sorry. It has been a hell of a night,' he said beginning to sit up.

'Are you coming in?' the voice said.

'Yeah sure, sure. I'll be right in,' Adrian closed the phone and gently woke Rachael, 'I have to go into work. Get some things together and I will come get you when I sort out patients and some time off.'

Rachael stirred on the sofa and looked up at Adrian. The makeup around her eyes had smeared leaving some on the pillows and duvet she was curled up in, 'Huh, what time is it?' She asked slowly coming round but showed no indication that she was ready to get up.

'Gone past nine,' Adrian said. 'I have to go in. I will speak with other doctors and see if I can get my patients moved so we can get away.'

'Just come and get me when you're done,' she said and with that she closed her eyes again.

Adrian was amazed how she could sleep with everything that had happened. But then she needed the rest, and it was daytime so hopefully nothing will happen while he was away. He said he had his phone and will be back shortly. What he meant was if anything happens to call him right away. But he wanted to let her mind rest and not to excite her senses. She needed the rest. He didn't bother to change. He grabbed his coat and keys and went to the clinic.

Johnson's mid ticked over. He tried to think how he ended up asleep in the woods. The headache he had put down to overindulging the night before. But he had a good tolerance to alcohol. He had taken a couple more aspirins while driving but nothing could take the pain away.

Reaching the back of his neck he felt a large swelling. He thought that maybe he had hit his head on a low branch. His face felt like it was boiling, his thoughts and judgement were beginning to lapse, and his vision was becoming impaired. It was hard to see the tracks and the various lights and instrument readouts from his panel.

He noticed the computer screen warn him of an upcoming stop and he was able to apply the brakes and slow the train down to a halt. He looked at his watch but was unable to define what the time was. The longer he looked at the hands ticking the more perplexed he felt. It was as though the large numbers were written in a strange alien language. He could not tell what those numbers meant, then why there were hands ticking clockwise around the small white face of the watch. Then like a child unable to understand a mathematical problem, he ripped off the watch and threw it against the wall of the cab.

The face cracked but the watch did not break. He snarled at the object, mocking him, cleverer than him. Lying in the corner, its face turned towards him, ticking away a mathematical problem that was easy for anyone but Johnson to understand.

His mind flashed to a school classroom. He was sitting at the back in a line of five chairs. His arms rested on an old wooden desk with carvings of names and obscenities, and splintered edges. A female teacher he recognised stood at the front, pointing to Johnson with a long bony finger. Her face stern with large circular spectacles slipping down to the edge of her pointed nose.

'My God, it is such a simple question. What is nine multiplied by four?' she asked, smirking at the most loathed child in the classroom.

Johnson simply did not know. He felt the sweat run down his forehead as the other kids giggled.

'Come on, Johnson, answer the question,' the old teacher repeated the question, this time with more force in her voice like she was demanding he answer right now.

'Eighteen?' Johnson knew he was wrong. The pressure of the question coupled to the long stare from his teacher pressed heavily on his shoulders that seemed to push him down into his seat.

The classroom erupted into laughter. The teacher's soul-piercing glare did not turn from Johnson. The class were allowed to laugh, mock and poke fun at Johnson's inability to use his brain.

'You are stupid, Johnson, stupid as they come,' the teacher began to walk slowly over to Johnson. Her back began to bend, her arms dropped to the side, and her eyes... her eyes turned a dark black.

As she walked over her frame began to extend. He arms stretched and reached the floor in an unnatural way. The fingers reached out, her hair began to turn white and recede. The mouth, once stern and menacing, now formed an evil grin that extended the full width of the face. And the face… the face became oblong. As the teacher reached his desk, she was no longer the same person that was asking the questions. Her skin was grey, her eyes deep and black, and the grin on her face made Johnson scream out.

Click-click-click.

The once old woman now looked like a demon. It was when she opened her mouth to speak that her demonic appearance was real. 'Time to go, Johnson… TIME… TO… GO!'

Johnson screamed and slapped his hands over his eyes to shield them from the demon scolding him.

Another voice came through the darkness. This one was from a man and not a demon, 'Johnson, we have to go now. Get the train moving, we're running late.'

Johnson removed his hands from his eyes and looked around. The demon teacher was gone, the laughter of the class subsided, and the sounds of his train returned. It took a moment for him to realise what he was doing.

'Come on, we have to go now,' the conductor said from behind.

Johnson swung in his chair and caught his conductor with a menacing stare, 'Get the fuck out of here. I will go when I am good and ready.'

His screams were heard from the passengers; some knew this man and were already thinking of getting off at the next stop and walking the rest of their journey.

Johnson reached for the accelerator and pushed it hard from idle to full with such force he bent the aluminium neck. The train jerked into motion throwing some of the passengers backwards. His anger and the vision melted together in a furnace that roared with hate. He remembered that teacher, he remembered those kids – some of whom still lived in the area… perhaps some of them were on his train?

Once again, he pushed the throttle leaver, bending the neck with such force that the neck reached a ninety-degree angle. The lever was already at the full position and would not go any further. He pushed again regardless; his rage increased when the laughter of the classroom echoed in his mind. His teeth bare, he began to snarl. He let go of the leaver and smashed at the panel bruising the knuckles that turned purple immediately. Though the pain was severe, he failed to register it. Even the headache and pains in his chest began to subside. It was though the rage itself was the best medicine for pain.

Realising his hands were no good, he turned to find the small emergency axe in a glass case on the wall. That was a much better choice. He left his seat and was able to put his fist through the glass without as much as a winch of pain. Snatching the red handle, he yanked the axe from its holder. Although small, it would be enough to do the job. He turned back to the control panel, and without any thought to his actions he brought the sharp blade down hard against the controls.

Sparks and metal flew from the broken circuits and metal dashboard as he swung the axe down again, and again, and again. In his mind he was not looking at the metal control panel. Instead of sparks and fragments of circuits, he was seeing splintered wood from that old school desk. Laughter echoed throughout the cab that further fuelled his rage.

The warning of an upcoming stop was severely damaged that that only a single letter was visible through the cracked screen. Not that this would have received any action on Johnson's part if it were intact. The train sped towards the station and the emergency brakes used for this exact purpose when the driver failed to slow the juggernaut down, clamped onto the steel wheels. Travelling from a hundred and twenty miles per hour to zero in seconds caused all the carriages to push hard against one another. The old train simply could not cope with the stress and some carriages broke loose and began to free themselves of their iron masters. Johnson was thrown headfirst into the window, snapping his neck and killing him instantly.

Passengers were flung from their seats into other occupants, windows and walls as the carriages derailed. The wheels sparked as the emergency break gripped tight onto the steel wheels that began to glow red hot. The metal beams began to bend with the stress. The Plexiglas windows cracked and broke in large, pointed shards leaving jagged edges. Some passengers were forced onto the edges, slicing their arms and faces leaving long trails of blood in their wake.

The train began to lean to the left as it approached a corner. The brake lines, now melting due to the heat, snapped off. The train was now free from restrictions. Passengers fell to the left as the cabs tilted and fell smashing hard into the trees and snow. Branches tore through the weakened walls like a knife through tin foil. Some passengers were fortunate to have their falls cushioned by others and were spared the icy fingers of penetrating branches and rocks. For the unfortunate, death either came quickly with decapitation or a crushed skull, or a few moments later with severe blood loss from a punctured artery.

30

Colonel Becker flicked through various internet news pages. He only read the titles, which never really gave an indication of what was in the report. The killings in Røyken were now generally forgotten in the media. Now the front pages and headlines wrote *"Private school explosion still a mystery"* and variations amongst different news sources.

Colonel Anders Becker sat back in his brown leather chair, a symbol of a high-ranking officer. He glanced down to a brown folder marked with the words "FOR AUTHORISED EYES ONLY". He had never thought about those words before until now. Who would know if an unauthorised person was to read the contents? A brown folder can be opened by a child if they chose to do so. He pressed his intercom by the telephone to buzz his personal assistant and requested a strong black coffee and perhaps a couple of biscuits, should there be some left in the communal room. Unlike many of the other officers in the building he didn't need to chug down coffee all day to stay alert. But the last twenty-four hours reminded him that as a fifty-something year old man, his ability to focus while in a sleep-deprived state were well in the past.

The phone on his desk was one of those large, advanced phones complete with various lights from green to amber to red depending on who was calling and how high up the food chain they were. Green was, of course, for those below him. The amber lights and quick dial buttons were for those on a par with him; perhaps a little further up or down but generally people he needed favours from and vice versa. And then there were the red lights.

Only three were on his speed dial. Those were for top brass, high officials in the military and government. At times of conflict where one of his platoons were out on operational duties abroad then the only button he pressed was to his superiors. The other two speed dials were to the Norwegian Intelligence Service (or NIS), and the other to the defence minister. Contacting either NIS or the defence minister would only occur by direct request only. As high a rank he was, calling either of those two without request was frowned upon. And now the second red light flashed.

Becker averted his attention from the folder and quickly picked up the phone, 'Colonel Becker.'

The voice from the other end was loud and draconian, 'Is this Anders?' The man down the other end of the line asked.

'Yes, sir, this is Colonel Anders Becker. I'm sorry who is this?'

'Becker? That sounds like a German surname.'

'Yes, my grandfather was German.'

'Interesting, during the war?'

'I'm sorry,' Becker felt uneasy having his German ancestry – and being an ancestor from the war to add – brought into a conversation, 'who is this?'

'Sorry, where are my manners, this is Agent Daniel Karlsson from NIS. I'm calling regarding your platoon that will be conducting operations in Røyken this evening.'

'Karlsson?' Anders said smiling to himself. 'Isn't that a Swedish surname?'

Karlsson laughed down the line, 'A good memory for surnames, yes, it is. My mother kept her last name after splitting up with my father.'

'So, Mr. Karlsson, how may I help you?'

'There has been another incident just outside of Røyken, I don't expect the news media have had the chance to catch up with these events, but social media is going nuts. A train derailed at around nine-thirty a.m. this morning; a lot of casualties and many fatalities. With regards to the events in Røyken we are acting upon this and would like your team to include the area of the wreckage during their patrol this evening.'

Becker paused before asking, 'Why would this be of interest to what has been going on?'

'We are treating this as suspicious and think it is connected to the, ahem,' he cleared his throat, 'disturbances in the area.'

Becker was a little perplexed as the NIS employee seemed to sidestep the question, 'Sir, with respect, but why is this our issue? It is outside of Røyken and surely a police matter. I need to know if this has anything to do with the reports, we got from the defence minister?'

'This is on a need-to-know basis, colonel.'

'Yes, I believe it to be so, but if I am sending my men into an area where the likelihood of contacts will be made then I need to know.'

The line went silent for a moment, 'We are involved as we believe these incidents to be terrorist-related.'

'Is my team in any threat while on operation?' he asked again.

'No,' came the reply. 'But you will be happy to know your team has been granted additional funds while on operation. We are sending in some personnel that will equip your team with cameras and thermal TVs linked to helicopters that will patrol the skies.'

Now this did sound like something was happening in the area and Becker was becoming reluctant to send his men out into an area he had no prior intelligence on, 'Just what is it you are hoping we find?'

Again, the line went quiet, 'If you can just do what we request we'd appreciate your efforts. Some of our counterintelligence will be over later today to set up equipment. We greatly appreciate your commitment to the operation and our team looks forward to working with you.'

It was now Becker that needed a pause to collect his thoughts, 'Sir, the intelligence I have had is pretty thin to go on. My men and I are now beginning to wonder just who is behind all of these killings, this madness? If you have anything you can add to just help us have some focal area of just who is conducting these killings and sending people insane then for the love of God, tell me.'

Whispering came from the other side of the line, like the NIS agent was getting clearance for information. Karlsson returned, 'Okay colonel, we have some new information we can share. Firstly, let's put your mind at ease... as such. We don't believe these acts are Russian, or Chinese.'

'How can you be so sure?' Becker asked.

'Because we are not the only ones seeing these incidents; these events are being seen across the globe. China has had over a hundred incidents recorded. Russia has reported several hundred incidents and inexplicable riots not politically motivated. The USA, UK, and well... everywhere have reported the same kind of incidents we have seen in Norway,' Karlsson took a deep breath. 'And to add, we have had both lab and clinical reports back. It is now believed the source of this insanity seen in these people is due to a biological weapon, a virus. Although, and this is confidential as we do not want to start a panic here, scientists have been unable to define what kind of virus it is. It seems like a new strain.'

'Manmade?' Becker asked.

'The lab boys think not, though they still haven't managed to classify the strain. The reports suggest no lab in the world is capable of creating such a virus.'

Becker was having a difficult time believing this not to be the work of the Russians. How many times they had used poisons, mind control, and drugs on people? Either they had managed to cover their tracks this time or were trying to invade detection.

'And what of the blips on radar over our skies a few days ago? Were they not Russian aircraft?' Becker changed the conversation back to a military bearing.

'Becker, I just told you this was not Russian. We don't know enough about those blips to give any information out. But for now, our prime minister has enforced a curfew around the nation. Movements between towns and cities are to cease, and mandatory face masks are to be worn when outside. I need not tell you how this will impact our way of life and economy, but we all need to stop the spread of this virus before we see a major pandemic in our cities. We also need to minimize exposure. God help us if this virus gets to the major cities.'

'I can warn you of the revolt this will cause. Not since the war did we have any such curfews. People are not ready for this, and questions will be asked.'

'We are well aware of that. We have something in place for the prime minister's state address later today. Just do the operations and we will share all we know when we arrive later.'

Becker couldn't quite understand what was happening. This was a lot of information to share, but then most of this would be presented to the public later. But surely, they had some knowledge of where this virus had come from?

'Good luck with your preparations and we will see you later.' Karlsson cut the line.

Becker looked at the phone receiver and replaced it. A knock on the door and he beckoned his assistant in with his coffee and a few biscuits carefully placed on the side of the blue and white saucer.

'Everything okay, sir? You look like you've seen a ghost,' she smiled knowing this would ease him somewhat.

He didn't look at her and instead moved the folder out of the way so she could place the cup and saucer on his desk. Sensing something was wrong she asked if she could do anything for him, but he shook his head. She left after giving him a salute and closed the door.

Becker paced the room, taking small sips from his coffee. Just what was all this about? Counterterrorism is now involved. Blips on radar and they think this is terrorism? No, it had to be the Russians or Chinese, had to be. Something just did not add up. Just what did they know that they didn't want him to know? He had a right, damn it, to know if his team was in danger going out there tonight. One thing was for certain, NIS would not be calling him up directly unless something had them spooked. If this was indeed a terrorist act, then their fears of biological weapon use were being revealed. But who was behind this, Taliban, Pro-Islamic parties, far left or even far right activists? There were many overseas and home-based groups that could be responsible. But to orchestrate such an attack required finance and expert guidance. No, Becker was sure it was the Russians regardless to what Karlsson said.

Becker felt uneasy about the situation. He placed the coffee mug back down on his desk and picked up his phone hitting one of the amber keys. The phone pulse came in long beeps before someone answered.

'Radar, Colonel Haugan?'

'Haugan, Becker. Long story short, do you have any information regarding that blip over the south of Oslo the other night?'

'Ah Anders, I think we have just finished with some reports. Funny, before you called, I was on the phone to NIS about the same thing.'

NIS? Just what were they after?

'Me too. Did they ask for anything specific?'

'Not really, just what we had seen along with details of dimensions, speed, ascent rate. They weren't really in any mood for a chit chat just the brass tax as the British would say.'

'They said nothing at all?'

'Not really, I think the guy was new. He seemed to try and keep quiet when I asked questions, but he was obviously a bit shit. He did say something about MI6 and the CIA interested in our data but then tried to tell me it was for counterterrorism. Guess our skies are not only watched by us these days. I have some satellite images coming over from NASA shortly that might help us with aircraft recognition. Look at us, NASA are sharing information with little old Norway. Guess they are a little concerned about something. I can get a man on a bike to send them over if it helps with your operations tonight?'

'That would be great. Also, I think we need to keep our dialogues off the phone. Something isn't sitting too well with me and these NIS chaps. It would be better if you came in person. We need to talk,' Becker replaced the receiver.

More people and more equipment with live feeds, he thought to himself He had never heard of any platoon or brigade that required such devices; least of all in the Norwegian military. It was quite obvious by now that the government knew more than they were letting on, and Becker hated being left out of the loop.

31

Adrian was presented with a face mask and a disposable apron when he arrived at the clinic. He was briefed on the new procedures when dealing with patients. Facemasks were to be worn at all times, aprons disposed of after seeing a patient, and hands were to be washed regularly and sprayed with ethanol for extra sanitary precautions.

The waiting room was full of people. Some were stifling a cough using their sleeve to prevent fragments of their lungs reaching others. Others were coming in with scratches and abrasions to their faces and arms. Adrian had no time, at the moment, to organise his sick leave. Patients were beginning to get upset they hadn't been seen and were becoming vocal about it.

Mentally and physically exhausted, with constant worry about Rachael being left alone, Adrian could not focus on his patient's needs. All he could think about was that creature; the tall slender figure, with those deep menacing black eyes that stared deep into his soul. No one had any answers, and no one believed him.

He was unable to leave right away due to the surge of patients calling in today. He almost snapped at one for coming into the clinic smelling like a bonfire. The old man had been lighting some sticks and branches from clearing up the garden. The smoke had clung to his clothes that took Adrian back to the fire, back to the school and back to the Gulf.

Usually, this time of year brought in cases of flu or arthritis flare ups due to the cold weather. But today the injuries and complaints were very different, yet similar. People were treated for scratches from wild animal attacks. Some needed rabies or tetanus shot following a bite by wild deer and even small rodents. Some kids that had been playing out in the snow had been attacked by a tiding of magpies. Adrian had never heard of magpies attacking a human; cats yes, they loved to tease the cats. This was highly unusual behaviour. A couple of stitches or blue skin glue to close the wounds and he sent them on their way. All the time his mind was firmly on getting out of here.

He was allowed a few minutes to gather his thoughts before the next patient came in from the waiting area. But even this was interrupted by a fellow physician. A tall lanky and unkempt man came through the office door.

'Have you heard the news?' the doctor asked but didn't give Adrian a chance to reply. 'They have found all these incidents are due to a virus. So now we all have to wear face masks when at work and outside. I've had to send four patients off to Drammen to be checked as per the new procedure.'

'What? So, it is a virus? Well what kind is it? I haven't heard anything back from the clinic personally, but saw the police report this morning.'

'That's just it, they have no idea. They tried to genotype it but nothing showed up on the PCR. They ended up having to do mass spectrometry and electron microscopy just to identify it was a virus. Those results were weird, and I mean absolutely weird.'

'What did they find?'

'It is small enough to pass through the blood brain barrier and was identified in the airways and cerebral fluid. Its genetic makeup is the strangest of all. The lab is saying it has DNA, but nothing like what they have seen before. No carbon atoms. Seems this virus is silicon-based, which has completely messed up the gene and accounts for the virus being classed as a new strain. So, with that… no treatment. We've had the health minister relay to all medical staff across the country to start issuing out masks, and take extra steps to protect ourselves.'

'Jesus! But probably for the best. I heard this morning that Mrs. Johansen died. At the post-mortem they found inflammation of the airways and parts of the brain. I had Rachael take a look, and she suggested that the enlargement of the frontal lobe and hypothalamus could be responsible for the behaviour.' Adrian paused for a moment to make sure his next few words came out right. 'I know what is behind this.'

The other physician closed his office door and sat on the end of his table, eager to hear the news.

'Last night we had a break in.'

'Good God, are you both okay? No wonder you need some time off. What did they take?'

Adrian stared deep into his colleague's eyes. '*They* didn't take anything. *They* were not even human.'

Adrian's colleague didn't know whether to laugh or think what Adrian meant was they did not behave like normal people.

'*They* were creatures, giant thin grey creatures. I know exactly what is going on here, and around the world. We're not being tested on by a foreign nation. We're being attacked by something… not human!'

This time his colleague burst into laughter, 'You can't be serious, Adrian. You are suggesting we have monsters running about the place?'

Adrian's stare never flinched, 'You remember that power surge? Those folks reporting strange objects in the sky? And suddenly we have demented people running around killing one another; that have been infected by an unknown pathogen. I know this to be true. I… we saw them first-hand.'

Adrian's colleague tried to laugh but then began to think. He had also seen something unusual in the sky. His TV had blown, and electrics fail when that power surge came through the other night. And to add, he had sent some patients off to the hospital today complaining of chest pains and headaches – although this being flu season may account for those symptoms.

'The police have our reports, I don't know if they believe me, but I am telling them the truth. There was enough evidence from my house to convince them something was unusual. I just wish I got a photo or something. I am going to leave now; it isn't safe here. They will be back. If I were you, I would get out of the village and head to Oslo. We're heading out of the village before something else happens.'

'You should leave right now. I hear they have enforced a curfew now so no leaving the house from six at night until six in the morning.'

Adrian nodded. His gut told him that the government would be treating this like a severe pandemic. God knows what they could enforce. Face masks were one thing, and a curfew would just make people sitting targets for these things. Poor Mrs. Johansen was just that. If anything happened to Rachael, he would never forgive himself.

Adrian picked up his car keys and a small medical bag of bandages and surgical skin glue. Leaving patients untreated was not what Adrian wanted. But most needed vaccinations or sending off to the hospital. But this wasn't about them it was about him; him and Rachael. As they said in the military, and something he said to other people, "Take care of number one, because no one else will." A selfish phrase but absolutely true in all aspects of life.

Rachael was waiting by the front door with two suitcases as Adrian pulled up the car. Her blonde hair was messy and her eyes sunken and dark. The poor woman was exhausted and looked to be in the same state as Adrian.

'We should go now. We'll just head into Oslo and find a hotel. I have a feeling they will be getting booked up very soon,' Adrian looked at Rachael as she applied her seat belt. 'I hate the fact I left you here alone.'

Rachael gave him slight smile that showed her forgiveness, 'I assumed that if they did come back, a fire poker would be their worst nightmare. I kept it with me at all times… and the big knife from the kitchen,' Rachael said.

Adrian reversed the car back onto the road and headed towards the school where he met the main road out of Røyken. He pressed hard on the accelerator and saw the school disappear in his rear-view mirror. Never once did he look at the twisted remains of metal and blackened wood. Rachael felt a load fall from her shoulders as the town began to disappear behind them. She felt happy to be getting out of this place. Adrian pressed the accelerator down further pushing the car passed the designated speed limit. A police car was by the side of the road a little further up tending to a tractor that had rolled down a ditch. Neither he nor Rachael said anything, but their thoughts were the same. Those things had infected someone else.

Adrian didn't care he was speeding passed a police car; no doubt the local police were now dealing with much bigger problems to care about a speeding car. The sooner they were away from this forested area and to the city the better. The road snaked to the left and then a little further to the right. Adrian sharply applied the brakes after seeing an obstruction ahead and Rachael shunted in her seat.

'What the hell is this?' Adrian said looking ahead.

A policeman was standing in front of a red and white concrete barrier. Two yellow flashing beacons at either side alerting drivers to stop, as if the concrete roadblocks weren't enough. Two other policemen stood by blocking off both sides of the road wearing face masks, blue latex gloves, bullet proof jackets and handguns by their sides in holsters.

Adrian brought the car to a halt and wound down his window, 'Has there been an accident?' he asked.

'I'm sorry, sir, no one is to leave the village until further notice. We ask that you return to Røyken and keep the radio and TV on for updates,' the officer must have said this hundreds of times already today that his voice sounded robotic.

'Until further what? We just want to get to Oslo,' Rachael leaned over to Adrian's side.

'A lot of people do ma'am, but we have been told to close off Røyken. You must remain in the town until further notice,' the officer repeated himself.

'Are you suggesting you are locking down the entire town now?' Adrian said almost shouting in disbelief.

'Sir, turn your vehicle back and return to your home. The government has passed emergency laws to secure off small towns and villages around the country,' the policeman tapped a pair of handcuffs attached to his waist belt.

Adrian looked at the officer's fingers tapping on the handcuffs and got the general understanding, 'So, you're going to arrest people trying to leave? Hey, a better idea, why not just shoot us and save us the trouble of being cooped up.'

Rachael quickly tried to calm her fiancé down by placing a hand on his leg, 'I'm sorry, officer. Me and my fiancé have been through a lot in the last few days. We had a break in last night and we just need to stay away from here and our home. Just for a few nights while things calm down,' her sweet voice fell on deaf ears.

'No ma'am. Now I am going to instruct you once again, turn your car around and return home,' this time it was the policeman's turn to display some anger in his voice.

Adrian managed to regain his composure and stared into the

officer's eyes. Feeling some uncertainty of whether the man was getting tired of people arguing or maybe something else had got into his system, Adrian decided to back down. He put the car into reverse, performed a three-point turn and drove back to Røyken; much slower than he did trying to get out of there.

'A fucking lockdown! With all that's going on, they are locking us in?' Rachael pounded the dashboard with her fist.

'This is just bloody ridiculous; they can't do that. It's against human rights. There must be another way out of here,' Adrian said thinking of the road to Drammen.

Unfortunately for them, this road had also been closed and guarded by policemen that informed them to remain in their own homes. It would be only a matter of time before word got out and the people of Røyken begin to protest.

'We'd better get home. I will call Stig and see what he knows,' Adrian said.

Stig had been called back into work. He was briefed that all officers are now to remain at the station until further notice. Beds were made up and the station was beginning to look like a refugee centre.

'My hands are tied,' he said angrily down the phone to Adrian. 'This came from the top, Adrian. Only emergency vehicles can pass in and out of Røyken while civilians are to remain in their homes. We hope this will pass soon.'

'But those things, those people. They tried to kill us,' Adrian exclaimed down the phone.

'I am very sorry; the station is full of officers, and we have been handed a regional commander also. I am no longer heading the station. Look, if it helps, I can come round with Stolten later and we can talk this through. God knows I need to get out of here for a while,' Stig said.

Stig arrived with Stolten, and Rachael let them both in.

'Now just what the hell is going on, Stig?' Adrian blurred out allowing his anger to get the better of him, or was it fear?

'Adrian sit down and listen,' Stig made them both sit. 'Earlier today we had another incident, this time a train derailed. Now I wasn't there but my officers informed me that as soon as news got out the station was flooded with more policemen, senior officers and even a forensic team. Don't ask me why as no one is being told anything other than a total lock down of Røyken has been enforced. And it's not just here, they are isolating the cities from the smaller towns and villages that have reported violence. I agree, Adrian, people should be allowed to leave. But this is not going to be the case. My advice is for you to remain in your home here and just keep that fire lit and lights on at all times, so we know you are okay. More instructions will go out on the radio and internet later,' Stig said.

Rachael flicked on the kettle and brought in three cups of coffee. There was no point getting upset with Stig or the police. It seemed they had been caught up in something bigger and were not being told anything. Rachael handed the coffee to the policemen who hadn't asked or been asked if they wanted one. Stig wondered if his tired appearance was a giveaway of his reduced mental capacity.

'You said we need to keep lights on at all times, why?' Rachael asked sitting on the arm rest by Adrian.

Stig thanked her for the coffee and took a large gulp, 'I don't know. This was an order from our new station commander, and that order came from further up and so on. No one knows anymore, just all homes that are occupied will keep lights on in all rooms during hours of darkness. I assume this is to help our patrols at night to see which houses to keep an eye on.'

'Is that because if something was to happen you would see the lights go off?' she asked.

Stig looked at her with questioning eyes, 'What do you mean?'

'Well, every incident that has been reported, including ours, began with power cuts. I think the two are related, don't you?' Rachael stood up to fetch the laptop from the kitchen table.

'I am sorry, but I don't quite follow. I just assumed this was to let us know houses were being occupied,' Stig said.

'No, I think someone knows something higher up and is keeping this from you and us. This has been happening all over the world. Take a look,' Rachael handed him the laptop with the webpages she had been looking at yesterday.

Stig and Stolten looked though them with interest. Twice Stig was about to laugh it off then something in the text caught his eye.

Stolten chimed in, 'Are you telling us that the events happening here have also been happening in other places?'

'Yes, and from looking today the UK, Spain and areas of Russia are also having similar reports,' Rachael took her cup and drank the coffee.

'These places, they are in the middle of nowhere. I have never heard of *Tres Bocas*. I assume it is not unusual for these small towns to have power cuts and the odd fight,' Stig tried to reassure Rachael.

'Other than the Mexican one, all others have been satellite towns around large cities. These reports all state the same things, power cuts, power surges and violence. A few, as you have probably read looking at your eyes raising just now, have even gone on to talk about strange lights in the sky and unknown entities being seen hiding in woods or nearby hills,' Rachael stood and began to pace the room like she was giving a presentation at the University. 'Do you see what is going on here? And with each day more and more countries are reporting the same story. The only other country that has enforced these lockdowns is America.

Thankfully, the press are still getting reports out. Stig, you have to let people out of Røyken,' Rachael pleaded.

Stig rubbed his eyes to relieve some of the tiredness, 'Rachael, I agree. But let's look at this from the other side of the coin. There is a virus, a very potent one that is infecting these people and driving them insane. We already know this is airborne and infects the airways and brain. There's no way of knowing whether this is transmittable. That's why you, me and everyone is to maintain social distancing from one another and wear the proper facemasks issued by the clinic and hospitals. We cannot afford to let this virus spread to the major cities. Our priority is to control this until we have zero incidents. Now, as for those creatures,' Stig straightened himself. 'Forensics has identified it as biological, but no known species has been attributed to the foot.'

Adrian, now in a much calmer state was able to realise what was happening, 'I think this is the right course of action. Contain and manage the virus. But we still have those things out there. Just what is being done about *them*?'

'I don't know. I'm not sure anyone knows about *them*, as you put it. I explained everything to my superiors and presented the foot. Nothing more was said about that. I think their main concern is containment. Just shit that we are all contained with it,' Stig finished his coffee in one gulp and checked his watch. 'I am sorry I didn't tell you earlier. I had no idea this was going to happen. We only found out about the virus a few hours ago and then things moved so quickly no one had time to take it all in. Look, I want you to get a fire on here now. The very least we can do is to keep you safe. We will personally do patrols every thirty minutes by the house all evening. I wish we could do more, but our commander has final word on all patrols and policing. We will just do our best.'

Rachael lit the fire and brought up clean clothes and bedding to make a small apartment out of the living room for them both.

They would sleep and live in the living room now until everything calmed down and the curfews lifted – whenever that would be. After the break-ins by those creatures, and the attacks by virus-infected people, Røyken was no longer the sleepy haven it was once.

32

The ascending darkness drifted over Norway like a large blanket covering the once tranquil Nordic country in deep blackness. The main roads were ploughed regularly under police guidance to maintain clear paths for emergency vehicles. The woodlands and forests were thick with snow, in some places up to the knee.

The people of Røyken had not taken the isolation too well. Angry neighbours vented their frustration at the police station but were quickly dispersed and sent home. The same could not be said about other areas of the nation, where some small riots broke out. People refused to wear masks or remain out of reach of friends and family; most were worried about their relatives while others just wanted to be anarchists. Police were sent to break up small gatherings. Violence, fear, and madness now engulfed the country.

Larsen zipped up his white overalls and donned his hood and white balaclava. The only time he had worn such a specific camouflage outfit was in the North with UK and US forces during war game exercises – the kind that was supposed to put fear into the Russians. As he donned his outfit and saw his men doing the same, he thought back to the times he was on these exercises. A Russian invasion was never going to happen. In fact, and while on exercise close to the Russian boarder, he and the Russian soldiers would wave to one another across the large open area between boarders. In some cases, and without either higher command knowing, they would even exchange alcohol to one another if the exercises were in December. There was nothing sinister about the Russians, regardless to what the tabloids and films may say. But those days were in the past. Now he was wearing the same outfit but on an actual operational assignment; how quickly things can change.

The teams were dropped off just outside Røyken where no one would see; and far away from the police barricades. From there they would walk, or as the British army would say "Tab" uphill through the woods and to the train wreckage. There they would get as much visual information as possible and send over the helicopter for a thermal reading. If satisfied, then Larsen would radio check again with teams and continue to where the blip on radar vanished. They hoped to find some indication of an aircraft landing or a camp. Images from both satellite and drone aircraft would provide additional intelligence for both Colonel Becker and the newly assembled team of NIS employees.

Becker had spoken with his air force counterpart. They had a long and detailed discussion about the satellite images and recordings by air traffic control. To say Becker felt uneasy was an understatement. He did not like this one bit. NIS had set up equipment that made his department look more like a NASA mission control. His phone constantly rang. The government wanted to be kept updated at all times. Just what the hell was going on? No one was telling him just exactly what his team were walking into. And whenever he tried to ask, he was cut down and reminded where his place was.

Streetlights offered a little help to their vision — having spent the last thirty minutes in a truck illuminated only by a red bulb to adjust their eyes to the darkness. When they got far enough into

the forest then they would switch on their night vision goggles –
to which many of his team couldn't wait to use.

Larsen instructed all his teams to keep the chatter down to a
minimum while on patrol. Instead, using hand signals or tapping
on the shoulder to whisper was the correct way to communicate.
He took point and had his men flank his position in a V shape.

The snow was dense here, coming up to the thighs in some
parts making it hard to walk through with all the weight they were
carrying. More snow was beginning to fall, which would both
mask their tracks and make walking even harder.

Eventually, they arrived at the train wreckage just outside
Røyken. Larsen gestured with a shake of his hand for his men to
spread out and go to ground. Here they would wait until the
helicopter flew overhead using the darkness to cover its identity to
locals. The rotors would be enough to encourage someone to have
a look skywards. But they would pass this off as a police or medical
helicopter; just as long as the aircraft maintained a high altitude
and make short passes every now and then.

Larsen used the night vision scope on his rifle to zoom into the
train wreckage and gazed into the cab of the train. He found it
strange that the train was not removed and instead remained on
its side tangled and twisted in a horrific mess that was displayed
in green through his image intensifier.

Forensic blankets did their best to cloak the mess inside the
train from both pesky reporters and inquisitive townspeople.
Police waited in their car minding the wreck and keeping a
watchful eye out for anyone not adhering to the curfew. Their
faces were covered in surgical masks issued earlier that day that
displayed a dark green in Larsen's night vision.

Larsen wanted to get closer and have a good look but knew
better to go against orders or compromise their position. If there
were idiots out tonight, then the two policemen sitting in a car
would be compromised and probably wouldn't be able to put up

much of a fight.

As Larsen brought the scope away from his eye and replaced his goggles, he noticed something in the snow. It was difficult to see clearly through the night vision, displaying dark green with some distortion on the screen. He was tempted to use his torch with a red filter, but decided against it, what with the police around and possibly giving away his position. He could make out a footprint close to some evergreens that were hiding their position. He shuffled over in the snow, careful not to disturb the print. It looked fresh, a little snow had begun to hide it, but for now it looked easy to identify.

'Sergeant Olsen,' Larsen whispered. 'Do these look familiar to you?'

Olsen followed his commanding officer's gaze and saw large footprints in the snow, 'They look like bare feet, but the prints are all wrong. Look...,' Olsen put his hand in the snow next to it to compare, 'the toes are too long.'

The prints looked like it was made by the foot they had been shown earlier. This was making the men feel uneasy, with some of the more inexperienced privates shifting their heads around.

'Okay, head cameras on this,' Larsen asked the sergeant to put his hand next to the print for scale. He radioed into his superior, 'Alpha to Ulysses, are you getting this?'

'Ulysses-one, yes, stand-by,' the radio went quiet for a moment then came further commands. 'Scrub-clean, move to point Bravo, out.'

'Copy, Alpha out.'

Larsen's team looked around for more prints and quickly distorted them by brushing the snow with their boots or hands. There were probably more, but the falling snow would take care of the rest. Larsen checked his small hand-held TV monitor that beamed a live thermal image from the helicopter.

He could make out his team displayed in white against a grey and black background that seemed fitting for the low temperature tonight. He needed to be sure no one else was in the area before his team began to move to the next point. In a strange way, he was enjoying this. It had been a long time since his last operational deployment. And while at work he never gave his ex-wife and her secret toy boy lover as much as a flashing thought.

The lynx helicopter made a few passes around each team and pre-designated grid references in and just outside of Røyken but did not find anything unusual on the thermal camera. People were in their homes; the streets were empty, and the police were doing their patrols. Larsen thought, as his team marched to the next grid reference, about those prints. The army wouldn't have been drafted in this soon without the defence minister knowing something he wasn't supposed to know. No. This was a hunt. An aircraft suddenly going off radar meant it had gone below detection… landing? What else were they hiding and what else were they going to find tonight?

In light of their find today, Larsen was now thinking why they were put here. Having his small platoon of soldiers performing observation expeditions was a clever way to keep Norway in control of the situation without having NATO or God forbid the Americans coming over to take control. But how long could they keep this quiet?

He checked the positions of his teams by radio. He then checked his map and compass to determine his position. They were now coming up steep incline towards the woods. This was probably a good enough time to have a ten-minute rest and take in some water and food. Even though his men were hardened to the cold, it was still not nice to have to eat cold rations.

After eating and having a little rest, Larsen once again signalled for complete silence. He wanted single file marching to hide their numbers this time, and complete three-sixty visual. He placed Olsen at the rear and the four privates in the middle.

Private Higgs quipped, 'Bet it is a naked guy running about the place making those tracks. Bet the Sarge would be happy to wrestle him to the ground.'

'Shut the fuck up, Higgs. Otherwise, it will be you I knock to the ground,' Olsen replied and was quickly hushed by his captain.

Unease crept through each of the soldiers as the trees grew dense. Even in the density they felt open and vulnerable. The night vision worked okay, but without light sources from the moon or stars, due to the thick clouds, the night vision was only able to pick up little ambient light. The snow illuminated green through their goggles, with flakes of snow sparkling in their phosphorus displays. Any other time this may have been something to smile at and enjoy. But now the flakes were annoying and often made the men jumpy thinking each flake was something hiding in the woods.

The helicopter flew a few miles away and beamed back a live TV feed to Larsen's monitor. The display showed grey fields and trees with only Larsen's men showing up as white figures on the screen. Higgs waved to indicate that this was indeed them on the TV.

Corporal Baxter's Delta team were observing from a large hill towards the south of Røyken. From here they could see the entire village. Baxter and his men were happy that Evans didn't get this assignment. Knowing that Evans had to tread through dense snow, carry all that equipment made for merriment to the team.

This was by far the easiest yet most boring job of all. They had to remain here in the snow for the next twelve hours keeping an eye on the small town.

Luckily, the town had left the streetlights on that helped pick up buildings and features. Using the night vision to observe the village was problematic. The streetlights could burn the intensifier tubes and render the viewer's own ability to see in the dark distorted.

Nothing much was happening, apart from a few patrolling police cars going by. Baxter could sense his team getting sleepy with boredom, so to keep everyone awake he made some small talk, which had been strictly forbidden by Sergeant Olsen; but he wasn't around.

The radio crackled and Larsen came over the other end, 'Alpha to Delta, Cat sees squirrels four clicks north-east. Please advise, over.'

Baxter used the zoom function on his night vision scope and scanned the vicinity of where Larsen had instructed, 'Delta to Alpha, negative for squirrels.'

Cat and *Squirrels* were code names for the lynx helicopter and possible thermal signatures. Baxter checked the area to see if he could see anyone around that vicinity. The streetlights in that area made it difficult to see with the night vision, almost blinding him in the intensity, but saw no one. He listened over the radio as Larsen called for team Charlie to investigate since they were close by. Baxter's team laughed.

'Evans will be pissed tomorrow,' a private laughed.

'Fuck him. He'll be tabbing for a few weeks now. This is exactly what that gobshite needs,' Baxter was enjoying this.

Corporal Evans kicked at the ground in annoyance. He had been hoping nothing would happen tonight. He had found a nice spot out of view they could kick back and relax. Larsen's orders broke Evans' hopes of an easy night.

Evans gathered everyone's attention by tapping on shoulders and indicated to the right with his hand. That was all he needed to do, if there was any question as to why they were suddenly changing direction his next radio call answered it.

'Alpha to Charlie, vector change to five-niner-seven, ten-four-four, wait on Ghost call.'

'Copy, out,' Evans replied.

Ghost call was the code they had come up with on briefing today, which signified a potential contact; the code name for a visual contact would be *Raven*.

The snow thickened as they left the main trial close to the Olsen farm. Happily, they had all worn appropriate socks that prevented their feet from freezing up; there was nothing worse than frozen toes while on field duties with no possible way of warming them until the morning.

Evans felt his legs moisten as he pushed through the snow on point. He decided it was enough and tapped the private behind him to take lead while he went to the back allowing his thighs to rest. This was not a completely cowardly act but more a chance for the lactic acid to drain from his muscles. He knew Captain Larsen would always remain on point regardless to the conditions or how tired he felt, but Evans was not made of such manly material; he was a corporal after all, and his two companions were of lower rank. Why not let them do the hard work?

Larsen came over the radio after having new information from the lynx helicopter, 'Alpha to Charlie, ghost call thirty meters north. Wait out.'

The lynx has spotted some white objects in the woods close to where Evans and his team were. It was probably a bunch of deer or elk in the area, but Larsen needed to be sure. He also wanted Evans to dig in a bit with his team. It was no secret Larsen had a dislike for Evans, and Evans knew this. Rather than step up to his captain's expectations, Evans just shrunk away. Whenever possible, he would take sick days or have an allergy flare up.

Evans signalled for everyone to go to ground. A quick check to make sure everyone's night vision was working, and then opened his hand to indicate a triangle position so that their surroundings were monitored.

The team fell silent and listened as best as they could. The wind blew gently in the trees. The sounds of snow crunching under their stomachs as the heat from their bodies melted the ice. They watched the dark woods through green displays.

'Alpha to Charlie, ghost call has disappeared from thermal camera, remain in position, out,' Larsen said over the radio.

Evans could feel the icy wind through his balaclava. His rifle was also equipped with a night vision scope, which he now used by lifting one of the goggles from his right eye. He turned the rifle from left to right looking for any movement. His two privates had gone quiet but kept in contact by touching feet together. They could hear the lynx in the distance keeping an eye on their location. He waited patiently for any word back from Larsen.

He felt a foot tap his right and he turned back.

'What's happening?' the private whispered.

'Shhh, ghost call,' Evans replied.

The lynx circled above the clouds in the distance. The team's heat signature was clear against the grey background in the thermal camera display. Captain Larsen was also watching his monitor, having now left point for third place next to Olsen. The screen just showed grey trees with hot white bodies of team Charlie lying perfectly still. He felt a sense of pride of his team being so professional. Perhaps Evans did have the makings of a fine soldier? But that sense of pride quickly turned to alarm.

A white glow appeared on Larsen's monitor from behind Evans' and his two privates. This was followed by another to the right, and then another to the left. Slowly, white heat signatures began to pop up around team Charlie. The lynx radioed to Larsen, but he had already seen the white objects appear on his monitor.

'Alpha to Charlie, Ghost Call is Raven...,' the radio crackled, and Larsen tried again. 'Alpha to Charlie, contact Raven, repeat, Raven,' the radio fizzed.

Evans heard something on his radio, but he couldn't make out what was being said due to the distortion. He banged the side of his receiver box and tapped his earpiece thinking that was faulty. He tapped the foot of one of his privates to check his radio. The private tested and gave a faulty hand signal in return.

Larsen radioed base command, 'Alpha to Ulysses, do you have camera visual with team Charlie, over?'

The radio was silent for a moment then came back, 'Ulysses to Alpha, we have limited feed, too much static. Radios are down; send Bravo to Charlie's location, keep Delta observing and Alpha to next check point.'

'Copy, out,' Larsen didn't need to worry about being too silent now. He faced Olsen, 'Take Bravo to team Charlie and assist. Their communications are down, and Raven has been identified.'

Olsen glanced over at the monitor and saw several white bodies surrounding team Charlie. They were not moving but clearly had seen the soldiers since they were keeping a good distance. He told his team to pick up the pace if they were to reach Evans' in time.

Larsen radioed to team Delta; currently observing Røyken, to see if they had eyes on Charlie. Baxter said Evans was too far away to see, and the streetlights were obstructing their night vision. Larsen thought for a moment, tempted to send that team to assist Charlie but then realising they were at the advantage point of observation. He told them to wait and keep in touch should anything be seen.

Scanning from left to right Evans caught a glimpse of something through his night vision in the trees. Something had popped its head out from behind a fern and looked directly at him before ducking back down. Evans kicked his two privates hard.

Their breathing now hard and fast, their nerves on end and their fingers ready to pull the trigger and engage at any moment. They knew they couldn't fire without direct orders from their captain. But something had made them all nervous. Whether it was being out in the dark forest or the notion of insane people roaming the village, something had made the men twitchy.

'Charlie to Alpha, contact Raven,' the line fizzed and crackled as Evans screamed upon seeing the same head pop out of hiding again.

One of his privates was the second to see something emerge from some evergreens about twenty yards away. A head and shoulders ran from his right to left disturbing snow.

He shouted, 'Contact!' his finger instinctively pulling on the trigger resulting in a loud boom as the five point five-six bullet left the Koch HK416N rifle.

This caused a chain of events for the other private to move from his position to join in. He took aim and fired a few rounds aimlessly splintering branches and bark from the trees, with every fifth round being a tracer that whizzed with red phosphorus like a laser beam through the dark.

Evans tried to pull the private back to his position but couldn't get him to respond. The private was rigid with adrenalin. They had seen something and were now engaging without orders. Evans looked back to his direction and saw three heads rise from the snow like serpents from a swamp. The figures were grinning, tall and thin. Evans could not believe what he was seeing. Fear took hold in an icy grip, and he froze staring down the scope.

He felt his nerves trigger and blood rush to his feet, trying to pull him in that direction away from these demons he was seeing.

He screamed and fired at the figure in the center, hitting it hard and seeing bright green shards explode with the impact.

The other two creatures ducked for cover and Evans fired two more shots in their direction. Reaching into to his pocket he found a flare. Pulling off the trigger catch he threw it into the darkness in front. It fizzed and ignited in a brilliant display of white that cast shadows all around.

The burning phosphorus revealed more of those demons hiding in the bushes. They knew they had been seen, and like caged animals they broke cover and headed straight for Evans and his team.

Click-click-click.

Evans fired again and again. His two privates were already on their second and third magazines, emptying them at speed, mostly hitting trees and branches. They were surrounded but did not know it.

Evans screamed for them to fall back but they could not hear over the gun fire. He picked up his rifle and ran from the team never looking back. He was too scared to remain where he was. Fear drove his legs through the deep snow as branches attacked his torso and face. He took out another flare and threw it in front. His path was illuminated in bright white that was almost pink in the snow. He saw large shadows grow to the sides cast by the burning flare.

The gunshots behind fell silent and were replaced with screams. Evans, never once looking behind kept running as fast as he could, throwing off his equipment bag and night vision to reduce the weight. He kept running, taking shallow breaths of icy air into his lungs. Long and thin branches smacked at his face and shoulders. He felt his thighs tire, but he kept on moving. In a strange way he was hoping the creatures had taken more of an interest in his two privates that would allow for his escape.

<h1 style="text-align:center">33</h1>

Adrian made the rounds around the house, checking on windows, doors, and the basement. His attempts at boarding up the broken window were nothing shy of a lousy attempt. But the boards were thick, and it would take a hard attempt to break them down. To be extra secure he placed a few boards on the outside just to give anyone or anything an extra challenge at breaking in.

Adrian decided to leave all the outside lights on as instructed by Stig. He closed the door to the spare room in the basement, locked it and used some boxes filled with anything he could lay his hands on to barricade the door. The work room was also locked and barricaded. It was surreal being a prisoner in his own home. Not that he wanted to venture outside now, but also knowing that it was against the law to do so. The police had enforced a curfew and a lockdown to prevent the spread of the virus. Adrian cursed aloud. Stig should have got everyone out of Røyken as soon as they found the foot. Twice Adrian had to stop himself thinking of if he had just left earlier, or last night. Those thoughts were of little use now.

He left the lights on in the basement and went back upstairs to meet Rachael. She had made a cosy arrangement in the living room. In any other circumstances this could have passed for a romantic slumber party. She took a sip of whisky from her glass and handed Adrian one.

'How are you feeling?' she asked.

'I've been better… I've been worse. Locked in our own home and in the town. I keep thinking we are being watched. I heard a helicopter overhead a few times tonight but cannot see anything. No doubt the police are keeping an eye on us.'

A barrage of loud gunshots resonated from the forest close by that shook the large window in its frame. Adrian instinctively ducked for cover, recognising both the sound and frequency of each shot fired. Rachael, on the other hand had never heard such sounds. Unlike the shotgun Hans used during the hunting season, these shots were much louder and far more powerful.

They both looked out of the window and tried to pinpoint where the shots were coming from. Rachael decided to open the balcony door to get a better look. Gunshots came from a nearby area that reverberated around the woods and fields. It was too difficult to place a location. Then a white light followed by another illuminated a small area of woodland far passed the Olsen farm.

'Oh God, do you think this has anything to do with *them*?' Rachael asked not looking away and gripping onto Adrian's arm.

'Those are flares. And those sounds are from military rifles,' Adrian's body began to tense up. He knew those sounds; he knew those flares. The only thing he could see was the icy snow turn from white to a light yellow.

Rachael saw her fiancé reach down to his side, like he was looking for something that wasn't there. She realised he was going back to the desert. Quickly she turned him by the shoulders and looked deep into his eyes, 'Adrian, I need you to take some calm breaths. We're not in Iraq, we're in Norway. You are not in the RAF now; you are not part of this problem. You are at home with me.'

Even though Adrian was now looking at Rachael, he did not see her. All he could see was yellow sand, green military camouflage and a young soldier dying on the ground. The smells, the sounds, the desert had returned once again. Only this time it was going to take more than Rachael's psychological methods to bring him back.

A faint buzzing of a helicopter broke their gaze from one another. They couldn't see anything as the cloud base was too low and had begun to sprinkle snow onto the land below. Adrian half expected the helicopter to land and a battalion of soldiers to come racing out all heroic with guns blazing like in the movies. Instead, the helicopter remained above the clouds, circling. The gun fire stopped, and the flares began to run out of phosphorus and die out.

Everything went quiet apart from the helicopter above. Eventually, it also decided to leave. Blue lights flashed by the main road as two police cars sped towards the Olsen farm. It was evident that the police had just heard the gunshots and were now on their way to investigate.

Adrian hoped the army or whoever was firing those guns had killed those things. Then another thought raced through his mind, a thought that send chills down his spine. What if those gunshots were not for those demons? What if some loonies had found weapons and were going on a mass killing spree? With this thought Adrian began to back into the house pulling Rachael with him.

'What should we do?' Rachael said, not looking away from the window.

'I… I don't know what we should do. Stig said to leave them on. If we turn them off, they won't know people are here and keep visual with us,' Adrian reasoned.

'God damn them, God damn the police for keeping us locked

up here like some dictatorship regime,' Rachael hit the wall with her fist. Her anger replaced the fear, and she was almost ready to get the car and drive passed the police control points and to hell with the consequences.

'I don't know what to do? I can't handle this anymore.' Adrian's eyes were wide; the blank look on his face said more than he could.

Rachael did not know how to pull Adrian out of his flash back. The only thing she could do, and it came with much reluctance, but she needed him back with a sharp mind, was to open her hand and strike hard across his face. Her hand met Adrian's unshaven face much harder than Rachael had anticipated. The sudden impact jolted his nerves and Adrian reached for his cheek.

'Now you listen to me, you are a Doctor of Medicine, a brilliant physician. What happened in the past is in the past and not our future. You need to use your skills and knowledge and keep us safe. We keep the lights on, we keep those things out. We survive however we can.'

Larsen had watched as Evans became surrounded before losing the TV signal. He tried Delta who informed him that gunshots were fired, and the police were now mobilizing to investigate. Larsen radioed back to his base command, 'Alpha to Ulysses, Raven contact, radios are down, please advise?' he waited for a reply.

'Ulysses to Alpha, authorised to make ready. Raven confirmed hostile,' the radio began to fizz with static breaking up the voice at the other end.

Larsen looked at his team through the night vision, their faces bright green in the displays all showed the same expression of disbelief, 'Alpha to Ulysses, come in, over,' the radio crackled a moment longer.

Then the colonel came back, 'Communications have been compromised; Charlie is down, sending Thor.'

Thor was a sea king helicopter carrying extra troops. It was now, at this very instance, that Larsen understood that they were up against a sophisticated enemy. Whoever was behind all of this had firmly set up and established themselves. He now needed to outsmart his enemy, think ahead, and gain the upper hand. Just how he would do this was something he needed to think about. He looked at his watch and made a quick calculation of ETA. Communications were compromised meaning that someone had tapped into their conversation and probably knew their positions. This had happened once before while in Africa. Back then Larsen had a much larger team and was on routine interception. What he did then he was going to do now.

Radio silence until Becker got back to him with details of the extra troops. He decided that moving to Charlie's location was almost certainly suicidal. It would be a better option to gather everyone together and go find Evans and his team. He called team Delta and requested they begin to move close to Charlie's grid reference and stand by for everyone's arrival — power in numbers.

'We are now on a rescue mission now?' Private Higgs asked.

'Shhh, and yes. So, get your war faces on, we're going to show these bastards we are not here to mess around.'

Larsen dropped his Bergen rucksack and fumbled around inside. He produced a large hunting knife and attached it into his webbing harness around his chest. He then found a pistol and loaded a magazine into it, cocking it as he had done his rifle. He then handed some flash grenades to his privates and attached two to his chest.

'Right, when we make contact, we're going to be ready. We dig in, we fight, we win,' Larsen smiled to his men.

His men were both worried and yet they felt manly. This was the first time his two privates had seen combat. They were nervous, but Larsen had strength and very much resembled his Viking ancestors rallying up his men and getting them to believe they would be invincible to the enemy. He led from the front with large confident strides showing his men he was ready, confident, and relentless in winning this fight.

Adrian followed the blue lights from the police cars towards the Olsen farm. The lights came to a stop. Adrian and Rachael waited. They waited because deep down they had a feeling something was going to happen. Immediately he knew things had taken a turn for the worst and his fears had been realised when a bright white flash bathed the fields in a bright hue.

The lights in the house flickered but this time they survived and remained on. Then something else caught Rachael's eye in the distance. The clouds were thick, and the snow was beginning to fall in larger flakes, but she saw something break free from the tree line and spill onto the field. The bright flash from the farm created a shadow of the figure running towards the house. The figure was white and stumbling around in the snow, trying to get to the house.

'Shit, I think it's one of those things,' Rachael said and looked around for a weapon.

Adrian, who was fighting back the memories, was also standing close by, unable to take his eyes away from the window. He saw the figure and started to back away, 'Oh God, not now.'

He reached around and found the bent fire poker. If this was one of those things or deranged psychos then he would not think twice at giving him, her or even it a good thrashing. He began to feel his blood boil, and uncontrolled rage began to brew deep inside. If he was going back to the desert now, then he was going to make sure whoever or whatever wanted to brake in here would feel the full impact of the rage.

Rachael felt her pulse increase as the surge of adrenalin pumped through her veins. She had never fought before, but now she felt this was going to be the only option tonight. They should have been in the car as soon as those gunshots were fired. But now they realised those things were all around. Remaining in the house was safer than being in the car outside. What if they had a puncture or the car battery failed like the electrics had? They would be out in the darkness and would be prey for whatever evil was out there.

Adrian reached for his glass of whiskey and took a long swallow draining the glass. Rachael seeing this did the same. The alcohol helped ease her adrenalin and her thinking became clearer, 'This is what the Vikings did,' she said handing the glass to Adrian indicating a refill.

'No, this is what the British do,' now his words were the voice of strength. He had straightened up, his accent changed from Yorkshire to that of a military officer. He was not going to let anything happen to his fiancée, and she in turn was not going to let anything happen to him.

A moment passed and the figure came into the illumination from the streetlights. Adrian squinted trying to improve his vision. The figure was falling over in the snow and constantly looking backwards. As the figure got closer Adrian could clearly see it was a man, a man dressed in white overalls. It was clear he was running from something and was probably a reason for all those gunshots and flares in the woods. Rachael opened the balcony door much to Adrian's protest.

'No, don't open it,' he said trying to hold her back.

'No, he is obviously running from something. We need to get him inside,' she persisted and stepped outside. She shouted to the man.

The man looked up and shouted back, 'Help me!'

'Adrian, go downstairs and get him inside quickly,' she said.

Adrian did as he was told and ran downstairs and out the front door, still clutching the poker for protection.

Rachael waved to the man, who was evidently tired from running through the dense snow. She screamed for him to keep moving as he was only thirty meters or so away. Adrian appeared at the back and was clearly feeling vulnerable being outside. He kept twisting his head in all directions to make sure nothing else was there waiting to ambush him. The man stumbled and fell, and Adrian reluctantly moved towards him.

Rachael glanced into the distance, the ambient streetlights helping to illuminate the field to a degree. She saw more figures emerge from the darkness looking like spiders running from a dark crevice between rocks. They raced across the snow at great speed, sprinting on all fours towards the man and Adrian. She saw their bodies were slender, their heads bent backwards and their arms and legs resembling a four-legged arachnid. She instantly knew these were the same creatures that broke into the house. She cried down below in a high-pitched voice, 'Adrian, they're coming!'

Adrian reached the man and looked up to see these creatures moving towards them. Their nimbleness moving across the deep snow made him yank the soldier up onto his feet and back towards the house. The soldier's eyes were glazed but not through some deranged psychotic malevolence, through fear and the cold air. Grabbing the soldier's webbing he pulled him around the house and back in the front door, shouting for Rachael to get back inside and close the balcony.

The creatures were almost upon the house. Rachael counted four of them and could hear their movements through the snow as their limbs punched through the icy water. She heard the door slam shut and locked. She couldn't help them; she needed to stay here and watch what these creatures would do next.

She saw them spill onto the lawn and stand upright, pushing

their heads back to a forward position. Their great heights were alarming now they had no ceiling to obscure their heads. They looked up and began to gnash their teeth together.

Click-click-click.

One pointed with a slender finger towards the balcony indicating new targets for their malevolent plans. Rachael stepped back.

Adrian left the soldier and ran upstairs to Rachael, 'Where are they?' He said, almost screaming the words.

She pointed downwards and Adrian looked. Sure, enough there were four creatures looking back up at him, chattering their teeth and seemingly signalling to one another with gestures. Adrian raised his poker as a warning that the same fate would happen to them as it did their friend the last time they came here. One instinctively knew he was holding something that could cause pain and opened its mouth.

The creature was clumsy and seemed to hobble. Limping as it moved backwards it almost falling to its left. Then Adrian saw it was missing a foot. The other three began to back away also that made Adrian smirk at the side of his mouth. He felt he had an advantage here. He had the high ground, and if Anakin Skywalker wanted to try it, he would take another leg. The creature with the missing foot may have been the same that he had encountered the last night. It may have remembered him, the poker, and the act of aggression towards it. Adrian swung the poker to show them he meant business. With this gesture the creatures fell to the ground and scuttled off into and back the darkness.

Rachael was shaking uncontrollably, 'Will… will they be back?' she managed to say.

'Probably,' Adriane replied. 'Keep an eye out here; I need to talk to that soldier.'

The man's face was frozen, his eyes blood-shot from the icy wind; he stood lazily as all of his energy was zapped. Never before had he run so fast or been as afraid. Adrian put his arms around the soldier's torso and helped lift him into a standing position.

The man's breathing was hard, his body starved of oxygen, and he could not inhale enough of the life-giving gas. He coughed inhibiting his body from absorbing more oxygen. Adrian got the man upstairs to the living room and sat him down. He slumped breathing more heavily now the air was warm from the fire.

'Watch him; I will put the kettle on,' Adrian left the room knowing that if this man was infected by that virus, he was simply too exhausted to do anything about it… at least for now.

Rachael watched the man slump on the sofa and bent down to meet him at eye level, 'What's your name?' she asked.

The soldier could not answer for trying to catch his breath. Instead, he just raised a hand. Rachael instinctively backed away then realised he wasn't trying to harm her; he put a hand on her shoulder in gratitude. She took his hand and began to rub it. She smiled at him, and he did the same, but not in a malevolent way, this seemed more genuinely kind. He began to control his breathing and finally spoke as Adrian brought in a black coffee, 'My name is Evans, Corporal Evans.'

'Corporal, what are you doing here?' Adrian asked handing him the mug.

Evans took it and warmed both hands, 'They took my team, they're all dead!'

Rachael saw the man beginning to relive the events. His eyes were wide and alarming, 'Calm down, corporal,' she thought by using his rank he would regain some military posture.

'They're all dead. Those things ambushed us and killed my men,' Evans was almost screaming with fear.

It was Adrian's turn to try and calm the man using a reassuring voice that was reserved for a frightened child about to be given a vaccine, 'Evans, is it? Mr. Evans, I understand you are scared, we all are. I need you to relax. You are safe here. Those things have run off,' Adrian guided Evans' eyes to the poker by the window. 'You see that? They are scared too. They hurt easily and they don't want to come here anymore. Now what happened?'

Evans slowed his breathing and looked at the floor, 'I left them. After we were ambushed, I just left my men.'

'Those things ambushed you?'

Evans nodded.

'I see. Were you out here to find them?'

'No. We were sent to observe. None of us knew about those things.'

'You will need to forgive me, but the army doesn't send troops out to watch a small town without good reason. You do know we are under lock down and curfew because of the virus and violence?' Adrian's voice became stern.

Evans took a deep breath, 'Our commander wanted us to look for more of those psychotic killers. We didn't know these things were here. They didn't tell us anything. We all thought, as did our colonel, that this was a Russian experiment or something. We knew about the virus, that's why we are all carrying masks.'

Experiment was an interesting word. Rachael was thinking about that, 'If this was an experiment then why not just leave it here and return wherever they came from?' she wasn't really asking anyone in particular with that question.

Evans replied, 'I don't know what they are doing or why. I didn't believe the reports until tonight.'

Rachael came closer, 'Listen to me, corporal. This has been going off all over; Mexico, the US, Canada, and as far as we can guess many other places also. I understand you probably weren't told this. But this is happening all over. Not the big cities, but just outside. Can you think why they are doing this? Why they have unleashed a virus upon us?'

Evans shook his head and Rachael decided to let the man rest for now. They could think of some more questions when he regained some strength. She helped him take off his jacket and boots and placed a blanket over him. Meanwhile Adrian went back to the window and was relieved to see the last of those things scuttling back into the forest.

Adrian took out his mobile phone and called Stig.

'Adrian? What's happening?' Stig asked, the sounds of the car engine in the background indicated he was mobile.

'We have a member of the army in the house. It seems his team was just attacked by those creatures. They rushed over but have gone back to the woods. We saw some of your cars go over to the Olsen farm, but I think they have been attacked too.'

'Fuck. Okay, stay inside, looks like things are kicking off again out here. Keep everything locked. We'll swing by you when we can,' Stig went back to driving.

Some small fights had broken out, isolated and nothing the police couldn't handle. And then there were some other strange complaints made to the police, complaints about giant grey men stalking the outside of people's homes.

34

Larsen kicked the snow and had to stifle a scream of obscenities. One of his men, no, one of his team leaders had deserted his men after being ambushed. Olsen had informed his captain on the radio after reaching the area. He was sure as bags were recovered from team. Evans' belongings were found further away. Olsen said he could see tracks leading away, and that those must have belonged to Evans. There was little doubt in Olsen's head that Evans, being the rodent he was, would have bolted at the first sign of trouble.

When asked about the two privates, Olsen said they were no bodies and must have been taken. Larsen ordered the lynx to circle above Olsen's team and provide aerial thermal images and as much intelligence as possible. Olsen was told to collect the bags and any munitions he could find. The rifles, along with the two privates were also missing.

Larsen radioed back to the colonel asking if he had seen the video footage of Evan's team.

Colonel Becker replied that he had seen something before the video link went down. The agents from NIS were going back over the footage and trying to get a clear look at the aggressors. So far, they could only make out a head in the distance and something blurry before the video distorted and died.

'Sir, what did they look like? Do we have any idea if they were civilians or military?' Larsen asked.

'At this point we have no idea. The NIS guys are going back over the footage.'

'Sir, I request to set up an outpost here until we find Charlie. I request additional light armoured support and drones overhead. They are hiding and may have the numbers to ambush our teams. I want to find them quickly.'

'Granted,' came the quick reply.

Larsen wasn't really asking he wanted to know something. He wanted to know if his colonel knew more than he was letting on. By granting him light armoured vehicles and additional air reconnaissance confirmed that Becker knew his platoon was in immediate threat. Usually on operational tours in the Middle East or Africa, if the troops were going to an area of conflict, they always had either light or heavy armoured support. Larsen had always trusted his colonel; he had no reason to not trust him now. Becker would never say over the radio, or within the ears of other officers, but Becker needed to get information to his boys. Were NIS and the government holding back on them?

'God damn it,' Larsen said under his breath. He turned to his team who were showing the signs of exhaustion from ploughing through the dense snow. Usually, he would read these signs and call for a break, but while his team was missing, he commanded they picked up the pace. Frozen, fatigued, and frightened, Larsen had to push his team; he simply had no other choice. Never a good call to push your men harder at the point of exhaustion, but he knew they could do this.

They reached the area team Charlie had been ambushed and met up with the Olsen. Larsen called for silence, pointing to various places for his team to investigate. The woods were dense and through his night vision saw the snow disturbed with empty bullet cases lying around. It looked as though they were firing in all directions and now Larsen had walked into the same arena.

He ordered his men to fan out and form a large circle. Everyone was responsible for keeping their field of view free from attackers. Their weapons were primed ready to fire, but only when given orders. All they had to do was pull the trigger and their weapons would fire. Larsen felt for his large hunting knife to make sure it was still attached and ready to be yanked free if someone managed to get close enough.

All of team Charlie's belongings, apart from their rifles, had been collected and anything useful poached. A few phosphorus flares, some extra batteries for the night vision, and one magazine of ammunition.

Larsen had seen two police cars by the road on his way to the location. The cars were empty and the keys still in the ignition. It was clear the attackers had numbers to deal with both police and small military groups. Larsen's senses were sharp. He listened and watched the woods through his night vision. Never once did his finger fall from the rifle's trigger.

A noise came from the woods to the left of Larsen, and he turned his head leaving his rifle aiming forwards. He saw a disturbance of snow from a tree a good fifteen meters from his position. There was another shuffle of snow from his right and then some disturbance from behind. He signalled for his team to take cover behind trees and throw their Bergen's to the ground in front. By doing this provided additional support when aiming their rifles.

The captain recognised what was going on and was able to read both the situation and possible outcomes. If this was an ambush, he knew what they were trying to do. This was a trick he had learnt in Afghanistan to confuse the enemy and make them lose focus. He had trained his men to never look away from their position, to maintain cover in that area.

Movement came from his left field of view and then to his right. Whatever was out there knew the aim of his rifle and were moving away from it. Noises came from behind and a sort of clicking sound began to emerge. The sounds then came from all around. Larsen knew they were surrounded. The clicking and feet moving through the snow hitting branches were all traits of trying to confuse Larsen. But Larsen was cunning. He knew instantly what was going on and could even predict the next move of attack. Whoever was out there did have the numbers and were running around the teams in circles. At some point one of them had to break cover and then the fighting would begin.

'Alpha to Ulysses contact Raven at team Charlie location, engaging hostiles. And for God's sake get this on video this time,' Larsen said in a clear voice that resonated confidence and authority to his commander.

He could not see anything but knew whatever was out there could see him. He heard the faint sounds of the lynx coming back to their location and he took that chance to shout for flares to go out. Within seconds white phosphorous flares were thrown in all directions illuminating the area around them. The light casting shadows and for the first time Larsen saw what he believed didn't exist.

The creatures broke cover, and Larsen shouted in a single dominant command, 'Engage!'

One, two, then three creatures began to reveal themselves now that their positions and tactics had been compromised. Larsen's plan worked. He had read the situation and managed to take away their advantage. Oval heads appeared in the dense forest. Large sunken black eyes and bare teeth absent of lips grinned back at him.

Now Larsen had a clear shot. His rifle fired first. The snow flew from the trees and a crunch came from the distance. He saw an eye explode with a precise shot through his green night vision scope. Other creatures ducked for cover, but Larsen was too quick and could easily predict their movements. He fired two more shots into the bushes, hitting both creatures with satisfying screams.

Firing came from his behind as one of his men shouted, 'Contact rear.' Larsen did not stop to care about the creatures' size or appearance; he was a soldier and engaged these as he would any insurgent; he wouldn't have believed his own eyes anyway. His training, his pride, his ancestry kept his mind focused on the task in hand. When this was all over, then he could take the time to think about what he was seeing.

The flares continued to expose their aggressors and each shot was carefully aimed, only throwing out another when the phosphorus began to fade. The soldiers had to keep the area illuminated, keep the idea of confusing the enemy and restricting their options of going to ground. The rifles fired single shots, no automatic firing like in Hollywood, spraying the woods with bullets.

But as one creature fell another propped up and took its place. They stood showing their oblong head, bare teeth, and long thin limbs. Larsen fired again hitting one in the stomach. It fell while another from behind leapt over and charged at their position. Clicking sounds came from all around, resembling the beating of clubs on shields of the Zulu warriors charging the British ranks at Rourke's Drift.

Larsen knew they could not reload fast enough as one creature fell two more leapt over. They were almost committing suicide exhausting their bullets. Larsen recognised this but had never actually seen it happen. His unique ability to calm his mind enough for it to be able to think and assess was one of his many great attributes. They must have the numbers sufficient for this attack. He continued to fire single rounds dropping the creatures one by one, but others crawled or leapt over the bodies into full view. He had counted six attackers, with even more revealing themselves from the dark edges of the white flares.

'There's too many of them!'

Larsen heard one of his men shout over the booming of the rifles but didn't know who from.

He too agreed but they were surrounded. They were completely outnumbered in all directions. But then a thought occurred to him, firing all around would exhaust their resources quickly. However, firing in one direction would only require one person, and have another from behind. If he could get these creatures to attack in a single direction, then that would both ease their escape and save ammunition. That was his escape plan, cover and retreat to a better position out of these woods.

He ripped a flash grenade from his webbing and pulled the pin, 'Move!' he shouted and hurled the grenade into the distance. He turned his back to the bang that almost disorientated him as the non-lethal weapon exploded with such forced the vibrations punched through his back. The forest was bathed in a brilliant white. The heat was felt on everyone's faces against the icy wind and snow. Larsen looked up and saw the creatures were bent over shielding their eyes. The air fell silent to gun shots and Larsen screamed, 'Move to the rear. Go-go!'

Larsen pulled his knife and charged the ranks of the creatures in full Viking spirit. He did not fear these things; they fell like any other enemy he had encountered. They were blinded by the flash but would soon regain their sight. Larsen launched at one plunging his knife deep into the creature's thin neck. It screamed and gurgled as he pushed it aside. He would not use bullets on these things and needed to save in case their escape was futile. He swung his knife again slicing through the thin skin of another creature's face, pushing its gigantic body aside.

A gun shot came from behind as one of his men shot a rear attacker. Larsen knew which way to go. He had memorised the area and knew they needed to get out in the open, head to the open field. If these things wanted to pursue then his team being the first to get to the field first would have command of who entered it.

They broke through the woods, two firing at the rear, while the rest ran past. Two more would drop and supply fire and so on until all of the team were on the field.

Larsen ordered another flash grenade and his private was quick to respond. The private hurled the grenade into the tree line. Howls of cat-like screams came from the forest as the grenade exploded stunning the creatures in their pursuit. Larsen did not allow his team to think of what they had just encountered; they were still out in the open though now in control of the field. He turned around in a dizzy three-sixty and saw houses to the end of the field. *Screw the silence*, he thought and ordered a fall back to the houses.

His team fell into the classic fire and fall-back manoeuvre where the first man leading the retreat would fall and cover. The creatures never fell back. Angered by the act of aggression towards them, they sprinted out of the woods, some on all fours, some leaping high into the air.

Like before, as one creature was hit, another appeared and took its place. Just how many of them were out here? Larsen didn't have time to think about that. He knew he was outnumbered, outgunned and his team in extreme danger. He had to get his men away.

Larsen was now directing his troops to the houses on the street. They could make a stand there. His mission was his men, keeping them safe and trying to establish what happened to team Charlie. Larsen pulled the pin on another flash grenade and threw it towards the wood line as more creatures emerged.

He shouted, 'Fire in the hole!'

The soldiers heard the command and turned their backs to the blast. The creatures were once again taken by surprise. The blast and bright flash disorientated them long enough for Larsen and his teams to increase the distance between them and their attackers.

'Come on, move, move! Get to that house,' Larsen screamed even though no one was going to lag behind.

Evans' tracks led the way to the house. Larsen looked over his shoulder and saw the creatures were now retreating into the forest. He ordered his men to keep going while he watched for any lose attacks. Larsen did not want to be lulled into a false sense of security. The fall back of those creatures could have been a ruse to attack from another angle.

Then it came. A loud boom and a blinding white flash sent Larsen to the ground. It felt like his entire body had been shaken and organs rearranged. Larsen hit the ground from the blast and ended up face down in the snow. The blast had momentarily deafened him. His vision was distorted and all he could see were stars dancing against a black background. He looked up to see strange men running towards him. It took a few moments for Larsen to regain his senses. He began to stagger to his feet and picked up his rifle that was knocked from his hands. He was slow to get into a firing position but luckily nothing was in pursuit. One of the creatures must have found a lose stun grenade and had figured out how to use it.

The captain looked behind and saw another creature holding a grenade in the wood line. It must have picked it off someone's webbing and now understood what it was used for. It threw the grenade too short. Larsen's team had time to react and take cover. The creature that had thrown the grenade was not as fortunate and was blinded by the explosion. Its large hands holding its grotesque face from the blasts impact.

They knew how to use the grenades; they understood Larsen's tactics and were taking advantage of that. These creatures were learning fast. The next grenade could land closer, and its impact most certainly would disable Larsen's team long enough for the creatures to get on top of them.

Larsen used all his strength to get back onto his feet before those creatures found more grenades or maybe something tastier like a rifle. He had no plans to be made game for these sportsmen. Picking up two privates who were stunned by the attack they made for the houses. His plan was to break down the door and tell the occupants this was now under military jurisdiction until further notice, or something to that nature. If the occupants wanted a fight, he was sure as hell going to give it to them.

35

Evans felt his strength returning, but his ability to form meaningful words took longer to recover. At first, he was incoherent and neither Adrian nor Rachael could understand a word he was saying. Rachael asked the soldier to speak slowly and think about his words. She handed him more black coffee. He took a long sip to warm his throat. The heat from the liquid eased the muscles around his cheeks and jaw, allowing his words to form.

A loud boom shook the windows in their frames followed by another. Everyone hit the floor half expecting the glass to bend inwards and shatter all over the occupants. Thankfully, the glass remained in place. Adrian managed to scramble to his feet and went to the window to investigate. Rachael was covering her head and Evans was curled up on the chair in a ball. Adrian saw several figures running from the field. Two dropped and fired back into the tree line while the rest bee-lined for the house.

'I think there are more of your team coming over,' Adrian said making sure the window frame hadn't cracked with the explosion.

Evans leapt out of the chair and came to the window, 'Alpha, it's Captain Larsen. We need to let them in.'

Adrian and Evans wasted no time getting to the front door,

with Adrian taking the poker again for protection. Larsen moved as fast as he could, slightly dazed from the stun grenade attack but otherwise uninjured. His men were slowing down but Larsen managed drive them with every last ounce of energy he had.

Adrian beckoned them from the side of the house and got them in. The privates fell to the floor exhausted and weighted down with wet clothes and heavy equipment. Olsen tried to remain standing but found his legs were beginning to buckle. Larsen slumped against the wall and tried to control his breathing.

Adrian quickly got to work pulling off boots and getting the soldiers to sit upright. Larsen tapped Adrian on the shoulder to thank him while he too caught his breath but refused to succumb to fatigue. Adrian said his men were fine but needed to rest. The fire was lit, and they should get out of the wet clothes right away.

Larsen was taken aback by Adrian's warm welcome, and then he saw Evans. Larsen ignored his fatigue and launched at the corporal grabbing him by his collar and pressing him hard up against the wall, knocking off pictures.

Adrian took Larsen by the shoulder, 'Hey-Hey! That's enough,' he shouted.

'Why in God's name, did you leave your team behind?' Larsen was almost spitting at his corporal.

Evans was in shock, 'They came out of nowhere and just took them all. I tried to fall back into a better position, but they were too quick,' Evans stumbled with his words, trying to make up a story as spoke.

'Bull shit, you failed to do what any soldier would have done. You stay with your team even if that means dying with them. When we get back you will be charged and I will personally see to it that you will never forget this,' Larsen relinquished his grip and shrugged off Adrian's hand.

Picking up his rifle he turned to his team, anger at his corporal energising his body, 'Secure these windows and door. I want overlapping arcs of fire. Change this house into a fort while I try to organise communications.'

The privates did what they were told and helped one another to get back on their feet.

Adrian asked Larsen, 'I assume you are the man in charge? Just what the hell is happening out there?'

'Captain Larsen. English?' he questioned. 'These are my men, and I don't have time to shoot the shit with you. Boys get this place locked down. Olsen, get onto coms and get those lights off,' he barked out his orders and pushed past Adrian to climb the stairs.

Adrian shouted up the stairs, 'Hey, captain. This is my house. You can't come in here screaming the place down until you tell me what the hell is going off.'

The captain looked back and gave Adrian a stare that sent chills through his spine, 'I don't need to tell you anything. Who are you anyway?' he asked.

Adrian tried to find his voice but instead found a rage brewing up inside him, 'My name is Doctor Adrian Hope, my fiancée Rachael is upstairs. Can I get you something to warm up?' he felt like he was showing his belly to the captain but knew showing any aggression would not be the wisest move right now. He needed to save that for those creatures should they manage to get inside.

There was an odd familiarity about the captain. Adrian had seen men like him before in the military. Bullies were the word. Men with rank and power spoke to anyone how they damn well pleased. Well not now, not to Adrian.

'You're a doctor? Good, see to it my men are looked after,' there was no kindness in Larsen's commands. His men came first; the occupants came second.

Adrian had to bite hard on his tongue, 'I shall make sure they are okay. You, I will happily tend to last.'

Larsen, fatigued but still in a battle mode, took a step down to

Adrian. 'Watch yourself, doctor. I'm not in the mood for pleasantries.' Larsen never once blinked and stared Adrian directly in the eyes to show he meant business. He then turned his attention to Olsen, 'Have you got coms up yet?'

Sergeant Olsen was sitting close to one of the bedrooms frantically trying to reach command, frantically pressing a series of numbers and twisting the long bendy receiver, 'Signal's shit but I think we have comms up again. That blast damaged our radios a bit. But I think it is repairable.'

Adrian interrupted, 'Captain, with respect, you are welcome to use my house to establish whatever you need. I am a medical doctor, and I can assist your men if they require it. But you have to understand, there is to be no fighting amongst us this evening. Whatever beef you have with your corporal and me can wait for a more appropriate time. Right now, I am interested in what you have seen?' this time it was Adrian's turn to give the captain a long unblinking stare.

'I cannot, and will not, speak about our presence here. I have already lost two of my men tonight and need to get in touch with another team. I want them to meet us here. If this is okay with you?' Larsen wasn't really asking.

Adrian nodded and felt the anger of this officer grow with every opening and closing of his mouth. It was as though this man liked to ask the questions but could not abide by being questioned.

Rachael came down the stairs after the argument and saw the military personnel moving around and checking the windows, 'Well, if I had known we were having more guests today I would have picked the place up a bit,' she used humour as a defence to what was happening around her.

Private Higgs put down his radio and descended the stairs to the basement before shouting up, 'All clear down here, Sir.'

The other privates also found their feet and pushed past everyone to check the upstairs window.

'No sign of those things, Sir. I think they fell back,' one said.

'So, you have seen those creatures?' Rachael looked Larsen in the eye after following him upstairs.

Larsen understood her gaze and felt she was trying to work him out. She never broke the gaze or relinquished her smile, 'What do *you* know about them?' Larsen asked.

'Probably less than you. We had one break in here the other night before the lock down?' she said, maintaining eye contact.

Larsen began to feel uneasy. He was hoping for something to break her gaze away and stop the questions for a moment while he collected himself. That came right after his wish. The lights in the house began to flicker, then surge with power getting brighter and hotter. Adrian saw this and ran to the fuse room switching off as many breakers as he could. The house fell into darkness.

'What the hell was that?' Larsen asked glancing up at the ceiling.

'That, my dear captain was them,' Adrian said ascending the stairs holding a torch out in front.

'They did this a few nights ago before all the trouble began. A power surge and then the lights popped,' Rachael added.

'Happily, we had the breakers changed and I have just saved our bulbs and TV,' Adrian sounded smug but then knew what was coming next.

Larsen looked around, 'Okay, we are compromised, and they are looking for a way in. Evans, go to the basement with the doctor here and establish an arc of fire and cover all entrances. Private Forberg, you guard the front doors and bedrooms. Private Higgs you stay here with,' he looked at Rachael and then asked. 'Who are you?'

'Doctor Rachael Taylor,' she said holding out her hand for him to shake it.

Larsen avoided the hand and continued his orders, 'Keep the other doctor with you and keep her out of the way. I will try and make contact with Delta.'

The *other doctor*, Rachael thought, cheeky bastard. But there was no time to fester on the captain's rudeness. She had to understand they were under stress. It was better for now that they did their job and secure the house without adding to the frustration. She began to think they were hoping the house was deserted. Then her thoughts returned to Adrian. Adrian is ex-military and has post-traumatic stress.

After experiencing the bodies, blasts and those creatures having the army turn up on their doorstep could trigger more of his experiences. And those experiences always brought back anger. Rachael knew it would just take the wrong word from this captain to set Adrian off. Right now, was not the time to have an internal fight, especially when these men were armed. They were all trapped here now, and they needed the army to get rid of these things before more people were killed.

Adrian tried the breakers to get the lights back on but they but failed. Larsen called from upstairs that all streetlights had been extinguished and Røyken was as dark as the sky. Larsen tried his radio, 'Alpha to Delta, give me your location, over.'

The radio crackled.

'Alpha to Delta, your location, over.'

No answer came from the radio.

'Alpha to Delta, give me your location, over,' Larsen continued.

'Delta to Alpha, currently mobile. Give me your location, over.'

Larsen sighed with some relief. He provided a grid reference and told them to exercise extreme caution as contact had been made and were hostile. His train of thought was momentarily disturbed when Rachael shouted from the window with Private Forberg. Larsen raced over to the kitchen window to investigate, his boots clunking hard against the wooden floor leaving wet footprints in his wake.

Flashes of white light were illuminating the sky around Røyken.

One at first then another and another until Røyken resembled more of a disco than a town. Police cars drove out of the station in the distance and stopped. They all watched through the window as a bright yellow flame rose into the air followed by a loud bang that shook the house. Larsen got onto the radio again, 'Alpha to Delta, do you see any fires, over?'

'Delta to Alpha, confirm police station on fire. Multiple targets on site. Finding a way round.'

Larsen called to base command, 'Alpha to Ulysses, check cameras on Delta. We are holding up at a local residential house. Request immediate evacuation and additional troops. Tell Thor to hurry the hell up.'

'Ulysses to On-Alpha, Thor inbound, ETA thirty minutes. Extra personnel and light brigade one hour. Out.'

'Okay, so what is going on?' Rachael asked.

'We are getting support and pulling out. We need more boots on the ground and air support,' he replied. 'Forberg, go check on the living room window, make sure that is secured.'

Private Forberg went without haste to the balcony and opened the door so that the candle lights inside the house wouldn't interfere with his night vision goggles.

All looked quiet for a moment then something caught his eye in the field. The private shouted to his captain to take a look. Larsen's night vision wasn't working since the display was cracked from the grenade hurled at him and instead used the scope on his rifle to look. People were running across the field in their direction. It was too difficult to see who they were at this distance.

Larsen called down for his men to be ready to engage. Each cover point of the house was manned and Larsen called for Rachael to take cover in the living room. Larsen continued to train his scope onto the figures in the field.

'Shit, stand down. It's Charlie. Forberg, come with me,' Larsen smiled.

They used the back door this time for ease. Ripping off the planks of wood Adrian had clumsily attached with recycled nails from other failed projects and went outside. Shouting and yelling for his team to see them and make it over. Larsen waved his arms in the air to make his presence visible to his men, racing towards the house. As they got closer Larsen saw they had their rifles but looked a little disorientated, stumbling around in the snow but managing to keep going. Not surprising since it was freezing. God knows what kind of mental state they were in. He would question them as to how they managed to escape later. But right now, he wanted them inside here and safe. Maybe they could shed some light as to when Evans ran away?

But something was amiss. He asked his private to hand him a flare. Twisting off the cap the flare burst into a brilliant white light. He threw it out far into the field and called for them to head for the light.

One of the disorientated privates raised his rifle and fired towards them. A single gunshot just missed Larsen and hit the house behind, splintering the wood.

'God sake, hold your fire,' Larsen ordered but the two men did not hear or perhaps did not follow the command.

Another shot and snow flurried in front of Forberg's feet. Larsen screamed for his privates to hold their fire. The order fell onto deaf ears. Another shot, better aimed, narrowly missed Larsen by a whisker.

Forberg grabbed his commanding officer by the scruff of his collar and hurled him to the ground, 'Sir, we have to fall back.'

'No, these are our men,' the captain stared into his subordinate's eyes like he was about to unleash hell from being hurled to the floor.

Another two shots whizzed past Larsen's ear and he knew his orders were not being followed. Either these men were completely disorientated and were now so frightened they fired at anyone, or something more insidious had taken their minds. Either way, the captain, and his private shuffled back into the house on all fours as more bullets whizzed past their heads. Slamming the door closed behind him Larsen ordered that under no circumstances were his men to return fire.

'God damn it, why aren't they answering?' Larsen questioned.

Bullets began to hit the side of the house. Wood splintered from the walls and glass shattered as bullets indiscriminately hit the back of the house.

Larsen screamed down the radio for team Charlie to stand down and make safe their weapons. They did not respond even though the order was clear and concise. Larsen used a small hole in the wall made by one of the bullets to peer through and saw his soldiers advancing passed the light of the flare. They now seemed to have retained their balance and their aim.

A loud bang hit the outside of the house. Unfortunately, Larsen was too close to the impact. He fell backwards, dropping his radio onto the hardwood floor. A sharp throbbing pain turned his attention to his left shoulder. Wood had splintered from the bullet's impact and the resulting fragment had punctured though the captain's clothes and had embedded itself deep into the muscle.

He examined his shoulder and saw the fragment was an inch long. Nipping the end he pulled it out. Blood began to seep out of the wound in an oily mess of crimson red. He tried his best to shrug off the pain – he could deal with that later. For now, he just pressed his hand to the wound in hopes that would be enough to clot. The wound was too big and too deep to clot by itself. He knew the injury was bad, but not life threatening. Even though his adrenalin was pumping, he could feel the dull pain begin to throb. He moved his arm to check the injury hadn't incapacitated him and was relieved to have full movement; even though it was painful.

Rachael shouted from upstairs that these men were firing at the house. She asked why Larsen had not returned fire? 'For God's sake, these men are trying to kill us,' she screamed. 'Fire back!'

Larsen positioned himself back to his observation point but by the time he had a view an eye was staring right back at him. Larsen backed off just in time as a knife was pushed through the spy hole narrowly missing him. Foreberg requested to engage but Larsen declined. The men out there were their brothers in arms, people they ate with, socialised with, and went on exercise and deployments with. But now these men were trying to kill them. At the very least they should wound them, nothing life threatening but maybe something to bring them to their senses. Maybe that would be enough?

Larsen shook his head, not in disagreement, but in disbelief. His next decision was one of the worse he had to make. But before he gave the order the wooden boards used to block up the window broke. A rifle butt was used to break down the boards and push some of the planks onto the floor.

One of the privates peered through the broken planks that had tried to keep out any attackers. He looked in and saw Larsen. A smile grew on his face but not a friendly one. This smile was sadistic and malicious with foul intent. Pulling back the rifle and bringing it up to a firing position he took aim in one smooth movement. Larsen rolled to his right just missing the first gun shot. The hardwood floor broke and the bullet ricocheted diagonally up and hit the ceiling. The private realised he had missed and trained his rifle back onto Larsen.

Forberg had sought shelter in the corner, away from the aim of the rifle. Now he had his rifle trained on his fellow private. Forberg closed his eyes in disbelief of what he was about to do and fired two shots. The first bullet missed and hit the wall. The second shot was dead on. The private's head jerked back with the impact of the bullet. He was shot in the eye and the rear of his head blew out with the impact. Splintered bone along with blood and brain fragments sprayed the snow red outside. The private dropped his rifle and fell backwards onto the snow. Forberg, in a complete delusional state of what he had just done ran to the window. He tried to rip the boards away to get to his comrade.

'Get back you idiot,' Larsen ordered.

'I killed him, I killed him,' Forberg now in tears refused to listen.

Larsen pulled but private's grip and determination to see the dead man made it difficult to move him.

Then his body fell limp and his grip relinquished. Larsen fell back with Forberg on top of him. He pushed him off and saw a knife embedded deep in the private's chest. The aim was precise and looked to have punctured his heart. Blood erupted out of the wound like lava from a volcano. His face was frozen with the sheer horror of both fright and disbelief. His mouth twitched but no words came out.

A hand reached in from outside to collect the knife, but Larsen was quick to rip his own knife from his webbing and slash the hand away. The hand withdrew, not from pain, but to raise a rifle and open fire into the room.

Bullets hit Forberg's body with spatters of blood painting the walls in bright red. Larsen screamed for help as the demented private tried to push his way through the broken in the window.

Larsen stood and hit him with his own rifle butt. The man fell back but did not go down. Instead, he stared directly into Larsen's eyes and grinned. He tried to get in again but was stopped by another blow to his head only harder. Larsen hit him again and again, but the man refused to stop even after his nose bent to the left and began to drip blood.

Pulling out his knife from his webbing, Larsen slashed the left hand of the soldier and gave an order hoping this would stop him. The soldier allowed the knife to slice the back of his hand but did not move or grimace. Larsen tried again but did not get the response he wanted or should have got. Larsen now realised this man was insane and did not feel pain. There was no other option but to put the poor bastard down.

Any other situation Larsen would have used the knife and punctured a major artery in the neck. But this was his man, one of his finest. He deserved a painless – even though the man didn't respond to pain – send off.

Larsen drew his side arm, placed it between the soldier's unblinking eyes. He whispered something in Norwegian and pulled the trigger. The lifeless body fell back, and Larsen tried to barricade the window with whatever he could find. Evans ran in holding a kitchen knife and saw the blood and body on the floor.

'Oh Jesus Christ,' he exclaimed.

'Don't just stand there help me get this window blocked,' Larsen had no time to think about what had just happened. He needed to act fast and stay focused. 'Where's that doctor?' Then he screamed as loud as he could, 'MEDIC!'

Evans did as he was told. They tried to block the hole with boxes and anything they could find. Larsen told Evans to stand guard over the window and instructed him to fire on anything that tried to get in.

Rachael was still upstairs doing her best to keep it together, to keep Adrian in one piece. The gun shots had scared her, the screams, the creatures, everything was now just too much; but she held it together. She wanted to run and escape, but quickly suppressed those thoughts as suicidal. The only thing she could do was to put her trust in these soldiers.

A small candle served as the only source of light. The dim orange flame danced and reflected the look on Adrian's face. There was a macabre in those eyes of the doctor. A blank stare that stretched out into the blackness of the night from a face Rachael hardly recognised. She tried to bring him back to the present. 'Adrian? Adrian, come back to me.'

Adrian took a moment before blinking, 'I'm okay, Rachael. I can deal with this. Are you okay?'

Rachael nodded and shot Adrian a smile. He smiled back and slowly his eyes became his own.

Larsen shouted upstairs asking if anyone saw other movements from outside?

The reply came, 'Things look quiet, sir.'

Where in the hell was that helicopter? Larsen said as Adrian appeared in the basement's spare room.

'Adrian, was it?' Larsen said, humped against the wall. He pointed to the soldier on the floor.

Adrian looked down and saw the soldier lying in a pool of his own blood. Upon seeing the man Adrian could hear the screams of the soldier back in Basra; blood oozing from a severed leg that trailed across the sand. Even when he took a breath, he could smell the burning flesh and scorched carbon from rifles being fired. Upon instinct he bent down and felt for a pulse even though he could clearly see the man was dead.

Adrian shook his head. Larsen nodded and said nothing at first. He glanced back up from the body and looked at Adrian. There was something strange in this doctor's face. It was blank and lifeless. He had seen this look before, on the faces of soldiers returning from conflict. But this was a doctor, surely to God he must have seen injuries and death before.

'Is this your first dead body, doctor?' Larsen said, somewhat feeling more masculine trying to put Adrian down.

Adrian turned his attention to the captain. Parts of his green uniform showed through the tear in the white overalls. All that Adrian could think of was the same army officers barking out orders in Iraq. The same men that sent our boys to war while they sat in air-conditioned buildings some two hundred miles away. Safely drinking port and casually talking about the day's events.

Adrian felt his pulse race, his mind cloud of all judgement. He could no longer control himself. He swung at the captain with a balled fist and cracked the side of his cheek.

The punch was clumsy, and Adrian instantly felt his knuckles swell with fluid from the impact. The captain fell to one side but was conscious. Shocked by the strike, and angry at himself for allowing this civilian to strike him, he reached for his rifle and aimed at Adrian. The barrel of the rifle just inches away from his face.

'You do that again and I'll put a bullet right in your fucking face,' the captain snarled.

Adrian stood there for a moment while his anger began to subside. He didn't care about the rifle and instead turned around and sat down in the corner to check on his hand.

Larsen kept the gun trained on Adrian and said to Evans, 'Evans, you stay in the basement. Get some lights down here and for God's sake move Forberg and get a bunker built from anything you can find,' Larsen tapped Evans hard on the shoulder. 'Take the rifle and keep watch. Nothing comes in, you understand! Nothing!'

Evans was shaking but nodded in response. Larsen rose to his feet and examined his cheek. A bruise was forming and felt like a large lump that was tender but not serious. He took a few steps to Adrian and kicked his foot, 'You, upstairs now!'

36

Becker grabbed Karlsson hard by his suit collar, dragging him onto his feet and knocking off his headset with a slap of his hand. Other team members of NIS just looked on in shock by the sudden act of aggression that they didn't have time to intervene; nor did they really want to. Becker's own officers and staff were present, and none would allow anyone to intervene with this scuffle. Instead, they just sheepishly looked back at their monitors or maps.

'You,' the colonel said as he pushed the NIS agent onto his back across the desk. 'You knew about these things; you knew we would make contact. And you didn't think to tell me?' the colonel was practically spitting at the NIS agent.

'Colonel, I...'

'Don't you fucking colonel me, boy. Because of your secrecy some of my men are dead and the rest left defenceless out there. Now I suggest you start talking, or by God, I will gut you like a fish right here, right now,' Becker reached into his pocket and produced a small flick knife. A swift flamboyant flick of the catch the blade flung out.

The agent didn't need to think twice that this man was ready to use this. In a quivering voice he replied, 'We... we knew, the

CIA knew; the FBI, MI6, all governments across the world know. We just didn't know how severe it was here.'

Here? Just what was this man jabbering on about?

'What do you mean *here?*' the colonel demanded slightly relinquishing his grip on the man's collar.

'Outside Tromsø, Narvik, places near Bergen, those *things* have been seen all over.'

'And you didn't think to consult me once?'

'We had orders from the defence minister.'

'Get him on the line right now.'

'I can't do that.'

'You fucking well can, you answer to him and now he will damn well answer to me.'

He let go of the man and pointed at the phone on the desk, 'Call him!'

The agent did as he was told and picked up the phone pressing just one speed dial key. The colonel waited impatiently, never once relinquishing the pocketknife. He looked around the room and nodded for his officers and blonde secretary to watch the other five members of NIS in case one tried to be heroic to their secrecy. None of the NIS members moved, no doubt too scared to make any movement; even a shuffle in their chairs might incite a fist to the face.

The agent spoke down the line, 'Sir, Agent Karlsonn, I have Colonel Becker here and he demands to speak with you.'

Silence.

'I understand, Sir, but he has a knife.'

A pause then the Agent handed the colonel the phone.

Becker snatched it from Karlsonn's hand, and straightened himself up, 'Defence minister? This is Colonel Becker. Sir, just what the hell is going on? I have lost men out there tonight, good men; men that have served our country. Just what did they die for?'

A small voice came from the other end, 'Colonel, calm yourself.

We don't have much intelligence to go on, but this is an isolated incident.'

'Is it fuck. Your man here has just informed me this has been going off all around Norway and the world. Now either you tell me everything or by God we are going to have a military coup. I kid you not. Now speak.'

The minister muffled something to someone else in the room then replied, 'Okay colonel, the PM has given me authorisation to explain what we know. Yes, this is happening all over and no it is not a well-devised terrorist plot, and certainly not the Russians. What we, and when I say we I mean the world is experiencing is indeed an extra-terrestrial invasion. The prime minister is being relocated to a safe place along with other world officials. The King and other state heads are on their way to safe location. It appears the source of the virus is also extra-terrestrial. We are now sharing intelligence with our allies, and when I say allies, I mean everyone, Russia, America, China and even states in the Middle East. Everyone has been attacked.'

'Just what are their tactics? Why haven't they gone for the big cities?'

'Ah, now that is the interesting part. Global intelligence thinks this is their plan. Take the smaller towns and villages forcing us back to the cities. Seems logical, I mean you need small areas to gain a foothold.'

Becker immediately recognised the tactic. Gain the surrounding land and chokehold the remaining population, 'And when were you going to tell me this? How many more men do we need to lose before you realise, we need a new plan?'

'Colonel, we are doing everything we can. But these things have taken us all by surprise. They were fast, sneaky and are using us against one another. Do you understand how hard it is to know who is who now? Not only are we trying to find and fight these creatures, but they have turned our own people against us,' The defence minister huffed. 'Colonel, you are granted all powers of authority. Get your men out and pull back to Oslo international Airport. We are setting up an airbase there and pulling all serving and reserve military in as we can. Do whatever you can.' The line went dead.

Full powers? Becker was quick to address the room, 'I am now in full charge of operations, and you will *all* answer to me. First get me full air support over Røyken right now. Get jets into the air. I want heavy armoured divisions on route to Røyken; give my men as much fire power as you can. And for God's sake get me on comms to Larsen. Make this happen right now.'

37

The cut to Larsen's shoulder was superficial but none-the-less needed stitches. Deep crimson blood seeped through his white overalls and stained his clothes. Rachael saw the injury was about to ask why he hadn't had it cleaned up when she saw the large bruise on the side of his face highlighted by the candles.

'You pushed him too far, didn't you?' she said. Her tone was that of disappointment.

'He attacked me. I should have shot him,' Larsen snapped.

'No,' Rachael's voice grew stern. 'He didn't attack you; he attacked the situation. You were just an enemy from his past.'

'What do you mean?' Larsen asked, looking up from fiddling with his radio.

'He has post traumatic syndrome. Before Adrian was a GP, he served in the RAF and was deployed to Iraq back in 2003. We came to Norway in the hope he could get better; be good at his job and help others. Until all of this he was doing fine. You have to understand what it is like to have PTSD. Gun shots, helicopters, and even smells can trigger something. The fire at the school and those bodies triggered it. I did try to warn you. You were lucky it was just a punch. People with this respond in different ways. You're a military man; this should be something even you must understand.'

Larsen lowered his head; partly from the shame but also failing to read the situation. But then how was he supposed to know? He was under fire, attacked by creatures that belonged in a child's nightmare and not reality. He found the courage to finally speak, 'I didn't know. I am sorry. But you also need to understand I could not have read the situation. We were fleeing from an attack. I have also had to see three of my men die tonight, with another three out there.'

Rachael placed a hand on his shoulder and smiled. Neither had to say anything but she saw the human side to the captain. He cared about his men, he shouted and was abrupt, but he cared. He tried to smile back but could only raise the side of his mouth. If it wasn't for his short ginger hair he could have passed for Harrison Ford with that smile.

She looked at his shoulder and then to his cheek, 'We need to address this wound before it goes septic. We can just use some ice for the bruise. I am going to check on Adrian and make sure he is okay. Then he will come up and treat your injuries. Just please be gentle. I will also have a word with him, and we can start functioning as a team and get the hell away before those creatures come back.'

'It's just a scratch, I think it will be fine,' Larsen tried to hide his shoulder by turning his body.

'No, it's deep. Adrian is the physician; I am the psychologist. There is no need to hide the pain. I have dealt with men that have tried to hide the horrors and pain before and it never ended well for them. You just sit tight. I am sure your men have the place secure now. Let them do their job and once we get you fixed up, you can get back to them.'

Rachael left the captain on the sofa with a towel to stem the bleeding. She went to the basement and found Adrian sitting in the work room staring at the wall. The room was lit by a small stubby candle that was about to go out. The orange glow illuminated a blank expression on his face. In his hand she saw a knife used for trimming wood. At first, she thought he was going to do the unthinkable. But then the knife was blunt and useless at cutting flesh. She saw he had been trying to trim a piece of wood so that the end was pointed.

'Adrian, how do you feel?' she asked calmly.

Adrian gave no response.

'Come on, you've been through a lot today. Can you just nod if you can hear my voice?'

Adrian nodded his head slightly to Rachael's relief.

'Good, Now I want you to think back to those therapy meetings we had back at Headley Court. Do you remember those? You would sit and I guided you through meditation. Do you remember where you went on those meditation sessions?'

'A forest by the lake,' he replied in a monotone voice.

'That's right. You would tell me how much you loved both the lush green forest and freshness of the lake. I want you to see those images again. Feel the tranquillity of the wind moving through the trees. Go towards the bank and turn around. See the stillness of the lake reflecting the sun and trees on its surface. Smell the air. What does it smell like?'

'Damp leaves,' Adrian closed his eyes and took a deep breath.

'Yes, leaves. Put your hand into the water. How does it feel?

'Cold.'

'Can you see anything in the water?'

Adrian nodded, 'I can see salmon swimming around my hand.'

'Do you remember fishing in the fjord when we first arrived here? It was such a lovely day. You told me it was just like those sessions.'

Adrian smiled.

'I think you are going to be okay, Adrian. Now I need you to do something for me. We have a patient upstairs that needs a doctor to repair him.'

Adrian opened his eyes and blew out the candle. He held his breath until far enough not to smell the burning wick. He walked past the soldiers who gave him a smile, stepping past one who was squatting on the stairs fiddling with his radio. Getting to the top he saw Larsen sitting on the sofa holding a rag that was now stained red with blood. Both men gave one another a long stare.

Rachael broke the uncomfortable silence, 'Doctor Hope, your patient is waiting. Captain Larsen, Doctor Hope will be tending to your injuries.'

Adrian knelt besides the captain and removed the cloth. The wound had not stopped bleeding and was in need of a few stitches.

'It will need stitching back together. I can close it up and apply some antibiotic cream. That should be fine. Have you had a tetanus shot?'

The captain smiled, 'I am all up to date with my vaccinations.'

Adrian asked Rachael to go into the kitchen and fetch the medical bag he had put together from the surgery. She left the two men.

There was a moment of silence again. Adrian never once took his eyes from the captain's wound; afraid of looking the man in the face.

Larsen decided to speak first and break the silence. 'Your fiancée tells me you served in the air force.'

'A long time ago now,' Adrian replied, never taking his eyes from the wound.

'Where did you serve?'

'Usual detachments, Falklands, Kuwait… Iraq.'

'You did Iraq? When were you there?'

'Back when we invaded, in 2003.'

'So, you saw action? Takes some balls to do that. I have done my time in areas of conflict; Africa mostly. I did a spell out in

Afghanistan. These places change a man, don't they?'

'They certainly do.'

'Yeah. We have to be thankful, though. Some of our changes are up here,' Larsen pointed to the side of his temple. 'To think of those poor bastards who are physically altered. I've seen them. Sometimes we take a moment to ourselves and just think what it is all about. Why we do what we do. Seems the human race cannot just get along. We always seem to need to build better war machines and more advanced ways of killing people. In a sense, we're not so different to those *things* out there. The only thing we have right now is being us, being human.'

Adrian looked at Larsen in the face.

Larsen cleared his throat, 'What I am trying to say is that I am sorry. I am sorry for your injuries and sorry for my actions. I deserved this,' he pointed to the bruise on his cheek.

Adrian broke a shy laugh, 'You know, that is the first time I have hit a man.'

Larsen laughed, 'Well, you did it right. It bloody hurts.'

Adrian laughed a little, 'So does my hand. You have a hard head.'

'Just don't be doing it too often. It can cause some long-term problems of the knuckles. Look,' Larsen straightened his right hand. The fingers couldn't extend all the way due to severe bruising and fractures of the knuckles. 'This is your future if you keep doing that. And as a doctor you will want full use of your fingers.'

Rachael came back in and was delighted to see both men had now begun to get along. She handed the bag to Adrian, and he took out some sterile cloths and some hydrogen peroxide. He told the captain this was going to sting a bit while he cleaned up the area. The pain wasn't that bad, not until Adrian swabbed the area with some iodine solution for good measure; maybe trying to have one last dig at the captain. Then Larsen succumbed to the stinging sensation. Adrian let the solution dry for a moment before producing a small bottle of glue.

'I don't have a sutra kit with me, but this is the next best thing. I am going to glue the skin back together and then apply some strips and a bandage. This will close the wound and keep it clean. You may not need stitches but will have a lovely scar to talk about.'

Adrian pinched the skin together and applied the glue to one side. Pushing the skin together and holding it for a few minutes allowed the skin to bond. A few sticky strips kept the wound closed before applying some thick field bandages to the area. Larsen tapped Adrian on the shoulder in a gesture of thanks.

'You okay to go back onto watch?' Adrian asked.

'Certainly am. We're all getting out of this tonight. Now, to put my military hat back on we need that helicopter and infantry here now so we can begin our pull out,' he paused. 'You keep close to me. If you start to feel like you are having a flash back or anything you tell me. But if you are feeling up to this, I really could use your military skills. Do you think you could be my second officer?'

Adrian's eyes opened, 'I really don't know how much I have to give. I was air force and not army. But in the circumstances, I think we all have limited options tonight. I can do my best, but my military skills are limited. I am a doctor after all.'

Larsen held out his hand and Adrian shook it.

'I will be grateful for any additional support. Right,' Larsen straightened himself, 'let's find out what is going on with our transport.'

Olsen came up the stairs with his radio buzzing and handed it to his captain

'Alpha, go ahead,' the captain said.

'Delta to Alpha, sir we are in the vicinity, which house are you in?'

Larsen smiled with relief, 'Wait, we are coming outside. Look for a torch flashing.'

Larsen shouted for Evans to join him outside and asked Adrian to wait just inside. Opening the door Larsen flicked on his night vision scope and glanced to the left and then to the right of the main road before dropping to a kneeling position. Evans came out next and ran to the road before turning back to the house so he could cover the sides of the house in case something wanted to make an attack. He signalled for the torch to be lit. Larsen switched on the torch and began to wave it, moving the light from left to right in large elaborate movements.

It was deadly quiet out here and dark. A small fog had begun to creep in as if to remind everyone why this place was called *The Smoke*. Through the night vision Larsen saw three figures stand from behind a snowbank and wave. Larsen waved the torch in their direction. The three men picked up the pace and ran towards them, the two privates on either side ran first to provide cover while the Baxter ran on ahead. Larsen provided cover by scanning the road from left to right, while Evans maintained visual on the house and made sure nothing was going to come from around the sides. They had a pretty secure path for Delta to get back to them. Corporal Baxter ran towards Evans and tapped him on his back to get up and fall to the house. Larsen beckoned them inside and closed the door after the last private got in.

'Thank God you guys made it. Is anyone hurt? Are you all okay?' Larsen asked tapping each man on his shoulder.

'All good here, sir. Where's the other teams?' Baxter asked taking off his Bergen and pulling out some frozen packets of food, laying them down in a heap on the floor to warm up.

'This is all that's left I'm afraid. Charlie was compromised and… well we have a lot to catch up on. We lost a member of Alpha and two from Charlie are gone. We are in a shit state, but we can hold up here until we get reinforcements. Is all of your equipment working?'

Baxter nodded.

'Great. Did you see anything or make contact while on observation?'

'No, sir. But we have picked up a lot of activity in the area. Explosions and then some weird shit happened during our way over,' Baxter looked at Adrian.

'It's okay, corporal, he knows enough of what's going on first-hand. I don't think we need to hide what we know any longer. Spit it out,' Larsen demanded.

Baxter looked back at his captain then said, 'All of these flashes started appearing around the town. Isolated at first then before we knew it all of Røyken was being illuminated with these flashes.'

'Flash grenades perhaps or police?' Larsen asked.

'I don't think so, sir. We heard no bangs, no sirens. The police station has been petrol bombed. We managed to avoid contact but we came close a few times.'

'Contact with whom?'

'Just regular people doing some very fucked up things. They bombed the police station; some were dragging people out from the building and beating them to death. We couldn't engage as there were far too many of them.'

'We saw those flashes too. Does that mean what I think it does, captain?' Adrian asked.

'Let's not jump to conclusion here. We have already been compromised twice. We need to maintain a low exposure level now. I want all fires and all lights out right now,' Larsen sounded slightly chilled by the notion of being attacked a third time, and if the numbers of attackers were growing then this was almost suicidal. He went to the bathroom and pulled out the monitor from the lynx helicopter. The monitor was distorted but Larsen could see the house with bright white windows against dark grey through the thermal imager.

His team did what they needed to do, and all the candles were snuffed out, and the fire dowsed with water. The living room went cold within minutes of losing its only heat source. Rachael brought more blankets up from the basement. She was okay going down there now they had two soldiers guarding the window and doorway. They had made a sort of bunker from some boxes and bags. It wasn't going to stop a bullet or knife, but it would make getting to them difficult for anyone or anything that managed to break in.

Larsen radioed the helicopter, 'Alpha to Cat, request visual over Røyken and our location, over.'

'Cat to Alpha, glad to see you boys are holding up. We have your location on thermal but have lost visual with Røyken. Possible faulty thermal camera, no coverage over the south of your position, over.'

'What do you mean no visual? You can see us, right?' Larsen asked.

'That's a roger on your position. Not sure but Røyken cannot be observed through thermal viewer.'

Larsen asked for the camera to move to a different location and saw what seemed to be a blanket of grey moving slowly over the small town.

'You see something is probably wrong,' the pilot said.

'Can you identify the problem?' Larsen asked.

'Negative, like some large thermal blanket, but that is impossible,' came the reply from the lynx pilot.

'A freezing fog has crept in from the fjord. Maybe that has caused some malfunctions in the camera?' Larsen said.

'Negative, fog is creeping from the west. No fog sighted over the fjord,'

Something was causing a thermal and visual blackout. How the hell was this possible?

'Just so you know, Alpha, Thor has radioed and are ten miles out. Due to fog and visibility, they request you prepare a landing drop.'

This meant Larsen needed to get out the red flares and light up a landing zone for the helicopter. Going back out there was not something he was overly happy with but knew he had to secure the landing.

Again, this would be routine for him. But he had never done this under the cover of night and nor in such poor visibility. Adrian piped up explaining he had done this before with medical helicopters in similar conditions and perhaps he should be the one to coordinate the landing. Larsen was apprehensive knowing that if something were to happen could send the doctor into a state panic. But then he would have him covered and would make sure nothing was going to get him.

Packing the monitor away he went back upstairs. Everything seemed quiet now. He called his men from the basement up to the living room for a small brief. He explained how they would prepare for the helicopter landing and what would happen. Evans and Larsen would be out in the field providing ground cover for any attackers; Adrian would be in the field with the flares and would guide Thor down. Corporal Baxter would be on the balcony with Higgs, and two privates covering the rear of the house. It was a good plan, and Larsen was thankful he had the manpower to pull this off.

Evans was the first to hear the sound. To him it sounded like the fire crackling as wood split and burnt. But then the fire had been out for some time. This was a kind of scraping noise. He looked around for the source. Larsen saw Evans and was about to say something before he too began to hear the noise. Now everyone in the living room heard the scrapping and tapping sounds. Larsen called for everyone to stay still and keep quiet. Rachael stayed close to Adrian, who kept close to Larsen.

Gentle tapping sounds came from above and they instinctively knew something was on the roof. It sounded like a bird hopping from one side to the other, pecking at morsels it considered food. Larsen picked up his rifle and gestured for everyone to do the same. He pointed for Adrian to get into the middle of the room and kneel. Carefully Larsen walked towards the window and followed the sounds; constantly glancing up at the ceiling.

Then they stopped.

'It must have been a bird or something?' Rachael said hoping this was true.

Oh God, let it be true.

Then her hopes were extinguished, just like the fire earlier, as a small white hand reached down from the roof and touched the large living room window. Larsen held his ground and aimed his rifle at the small, almost child-like hand. Then a small face descended from the roof mere inches away from the glass.

A small oval face with large shiny black eyes descended upside down and peered into the room. The small creature squinted as though trying to adjust its eyes to the room.

To everyone inside the room that had seen the creatures before, they did not recognise the one that was looking at them. This one was different, much different to the others. It was small, similar in skin colour and eyes, but seemed more child-like, a dwarf of the much larger ones.

Larsen said in a low voice like he was trying to get close to a wild animal and did not want to scare it away, 'No one fires or makes a movement. Evans, get a camera on this thing right now.'

Evans picked up his head camera very slowly, switched it on, pointing it at the creature. The small grey creature hung from the roof like a curious monkey observing the occupants inside. It was if as though this smaller creature was checking out the occupants inside, getting a feel for the firepower it was up against.

Larsen was amazed of how different this smaller creature looked. It did not resemble those large things that had attacked his team earlier. This one seemed, well, passive, Larsen thought. Maybe this one did not belong with the much larger creatures. Their gnashing teeth, elongated arms and grotesquely hunched backs were nothing like the softer features of the one that was interested in the room.

They stood motionless watching this small creature observing them from outside like a monkey in a zoo watches people and children. It was hard to know who was studying whom. Rachael watched on as the creature relinquished one of its hands and began to feel the glass. It had almost child-like hands that caressed the cold glass, leaving a smear of dirt over the pane. It seemed fascinated with the window.

'It's studying us. It doesn't look like the others. This one is smaller,' Rachael said beginning to see a pattern.

'Studying us?' Larsen asked and then realised what was probably going on. 'Get back all of you.'

As he cried his warning three of the much taller creatures began to pull themselves up over the balcony railings. Rachael screamed out in terror. The small creature pulled itself back up onto the roof; small tapping sounds indicated it was running to the top. The larger creatures raised themselves up and stood tall. The middle giant stretched its arms out like a bat would stretch its wings that reached the length of the window to show some form of intimidation. It gnashed its teeth and gazed inside.

Click-click-click.

Larsen felt something inside him fire up; something primitive. He saw the creature standing tall looking as menacing as it could; it was calling Larson out. It was taunting him with its size. Larsen's fear declined almost as quickly as it had come. He pulled out his knife and walked confidently to the window, almost pressing himself against it. His Viking ancestry was riding high and proud. This was not a conscious movement. No. This was a Viking meeting with an aggressor. In New Zealand and the Pacific Islands, the Māori would confront their enemies in a similar manner, chanting a war dance to show strength and aggression.

The creature grinned; its skin had bumps and craters like a teen with acne over its face and body. It looked down at Larsen and Larsen looked up at it, staring at one another in a mutual stand-off. They were separated only by the glass that could have been broken easily if the creature wanted. Larsen was tall, around six feet. But this creature dwarfed him.

Larsen showed the creature the knife and gestured it towards its neck. The creature looked down at the knife and then back up at him. Larsen smiled almost as sadistically as those poor deranged bastards in Røyken.

The creatures snapped their heads around towards the field as if something had disturbed them, and then began to back away. The creatures pulled their thin gigantic bodies back over the balcony and descended to the ground below in loud thuds. Larsen watched them scuttle off into the fog that had begun to engulf the house and surrounding fields. The faint sounds of a helicopter came from the darkness and Larsen kicked the wall, 'Get your shit together, Thor inbound.'

Evans grabbed two red flares and handed them to Adrian. Adrian nodded and took a deep breath reassuring everyone he was up to the task. Rachael tried to intervene, but Adrian explained it was something that needed to be done and he was the man for the job. Baxter went out onto the balcony and used his scope to find those creatures almost forgetting about the one on the roof. He could not see those creatures anymore and shouted back all clear on the ground. If the smaller one was to have a go, he could take it out with a few well-placed punches and kicks

Larsen dragged his three soldiers down the stairs and outside.

The two privates took their positions guarding the front of the house while Evans and Larsen ran to the back; rifles cocked and ready to engage. Adrian followed holding the two flares.

The helicopter sounded close now and Adrian got as far as he could, or really wanted to go to the field. He could feel that same pressure he had felt in Iraq. Not knowing where those creatures were or if they were going to ambush him. But he absolutely had to get those flares out. His body tried to pull him back to the house, and he had to force himself to stay and light the flares. Ripping the cap from his flare he held one above his head and the other he threw as far as he could onto the field. The fog turned bright red with the burning phosphorous. Large plumes of smoke rose to meet the fog.

All the time Adrian was forcing himself to stay where he was. Even with armed men covering him, he felt vulnerable and naked. The flares made him stand out and a prime target for anything that was out to attack.

The helicopter was closer and must have seen the flares through the thickening fog. It had begun a rapid descent. The landing lights illuminated the fog above and Adrian felt a moment of relief. His hopes of getting the hell out of here rose like a warm feeling. The back was loaded with troops with firepower to take back Røyken quickly. The sea king helicopter brought itself into a hover and slowly descended pushing snow and ice in all directions under its huge rotors.

Adrian dropped the flare in front of him and ran back to Larsen. A moment of relief to get back into the house fell over him. Larsen shielded his eyes from the snow being kicked up by the rotors, missing the events that followed.

A flaming petrol bomb was hurled from the fog and hit the side of the helicopter. The bottle burst upon impact engulfing the rotors in flaming petrol turning the fog bright yellow. Another one was thrown from the mist and hit the windshield. The sea king shook as the pilot's view went from dark to bright orange. The helicopter tilted on its once perfect axis for landing and began to descend onto its rear.

The pilot fought to gain control, but the sudden impact of the improvised bombs had managed to damage the flight controls. The rear rotor hit the ground and broke sending parts whirling into the air. Larsen ducked for cover as the helicopter lost its yaw capability and twisted around before falling to the ground. The blades hit the ground with a metallic ping sending parts in all directions, some being flung far away and others hitting the house and shattering the wood; thankfully missing the windows and occupants inside.

Larsen and Evans fell back to the house and hid from the crash. The helicopter's rotors banged and clattered against the ground, twisting the aircraft around, and throwing the occupants inside. The blades snapped free, and the aircraft settled in the snow, flames rose from the sides. Screams came from the darkness as people advanced towards the burning helicopter.

Larsen was quick and fired off a few rounds. More shots from the balcony as Baxter tried to hit the people rushing the helicopter. A gunshot was heard from within the crowd and Evans felt the rush of air passed his ear. He fell to the ground and looked to the crowd silhouetted by the flames in the fog.

Twenty people of all ages stormed the helicopter. Some caught fire trying to open the doors while others smashed the windows to get to the pilots. Larsen fired and hit one reaching into the cockpit. Some of the town's people saw Larsen and made for his position. Evans tried his best to fire at them but there were too many, and more were emerging from the fog.

'Fall back, get inside now,' Larsen screamed.

Evans laid down as much cover fire as he could then ran with his captain, yelling at the two privates to get inside. The helicopter burst into flames and Baxter saw burning bodies being dragged out of the wreckage and onto the snow. The people kicked and tore at the bodies, some finding weapons and others finding explosives.

The helicopter's fuel tanks burst from the exterior heat and blew up with such force the windows in the house shattered sending splinters of glass onto the occupants. Baxter fell to the ground from the impact and crawled back into the house.

'Alpha to Ulysses, Thor down, send immediate evacuation now. Where's the armoured vehicles and troops?' Larsen screamed down the radio at his commanding officer.

'Troops entering Røyken and heading for your position. Evac helicopter is ascending once position is secured.'

'Did you see the damn video? What the hell are these things?' Larsen continued.

'Captain, get your men out of there. Is there any way you can meet up with support troops?' Becker ordered.

'No chance, we are surrounded. We don't have the supplies to engage these many hostiles.'

'Fuck, hold tight, support is almost there.'

'What's the plan, captain?' Rachael asked, clutching a poker for defence, shards of glass had sliced her cheeks, with some glittering her blonde hair.

Larsen just looked up at her with a blank expression. Tonight, he had killed one of his best soldiers and friend, lost soldiers and was now on his back foot trying to stay alive. This was the first time since the divorce he had truly felt naked and vulnerable. Rachael saw his face and knew what was going through his mind.

Amidst the rioting and explosions outside, Rachael said in a calm voice to Larsen, who had slumped onto the floor, 'What is happening here no one could have predicted. Whatever and wherever these things have come from is of no concern at this point. They have managed to do something to these people, this is clear. Captain, we are probably the only ones left in Røyken that haven't gone mad. We need you to pull yourself together right now and make an escape plan. If an evacuation has been called and more of your troops are coming, then we need to get them here. And we need to survive.'

Larsen looked up. She had addressed him by his rank and that by itself was enough to remind him of who he was… a soldier.

Larsen stood up and patted Rachael on the shoulder, 'Right, evac in one minute, support comes in and will no doubt draw these rioters away from the house. We land the helicopter and get the hell out. Evans, get on the radio and explain what is going to happen to the support so they are prepared to engage right away. Baxter, take your men and secure this level. If those bastards break in downstairs, then we bottleneck their ascent with the stairs and door. That will reduce rounds needed. Rachael and Adrian, we are getting you out of here,' Larsen handed Adrian a pair of night vision goggles. 'Flight lieutenant, I need you to go upstairs and be my observer. And Rachael,' Larsen handed her his pistol. 'This holds six bullets; you seem calm enough to handle this and I see trust in your eyes. Hold it at arm's length and bend the elbows before firing. None of those creatures get up here.'

Rachael took the pistol from Larsen. Even though she had never fired a gun in her life, she felt better having it. She went with Adrian and looked out of the window to the burning wreck of the sea king.

'It's madness. I'm half-expecting to wake up any moment,' Adrian said.

'I know, look at those people out there. They are lost souls now.

Adrian turned to Rachael, 'It is human nature to kill one another; to exterminate other races, other countries, for what reason?'

Rachael looked back at him, 'To exterminate the area for occupation?'

And that was when the pieces of the jigsaw came together. This was their plan all along, those creatures. They did not go for large cities, nor did they reveal themselves with fancy weapons, charging in with huge machines turning people to dust or blowing up the White House in a statement to the world. They simply found a way to force humans to kill themselves off while they just watched from the back; by attacking our own immune system with a simple virus that could not be identified or cured.

Then another fearful thought came, they were not going to the cities because it was easier to conquer the surrounding areas and all resources. They were pulling the military out of the cities to engage and then perhaps they could move in using human shields; or waiting for the cities to run dry of supplies?

Small hands descended from the roof once again as the small creature peered back into the house, possibly reassessing the occupants after the attack. Rachael did not jump at the sight this time, but her scientific mind, now piecing everything together, needed to understand. She walked towards the window and got as close as she could to the small creature.

It moved its head back as if uncomfortable with the having its space invaded like this. She examined it, its tiny body, its small hands, but large head. Why would such a creature be running with these giants? But then they weren't the same. The small one was a child? No, if it was then surely it would have some resemblance to the larger ones. The only feature it shared was the colour of its skin. The way it moved and its position on top of the house, this was not running with the pack. This was orchestrating them, guiding them, probably the one in charge. Rachael made a theory that the head being large housed a large brain, the giant creatures had smaller heads, smaller brains. She stepped close to the broken window.

'No, wait,' Adrian tried but Rachael ignored him.

The creature looked at her. It opened its mouth and made a high-pitched clicking sound, its small mouth vibrated with each click. Rachael identified the sound and knew this was indeed orchestrating the attack. She raised her gun and did as the captain had instructed her. She bent her elbows, relaxed her shoulders and…

… Bang-bang.

She fired two bullets through the creature's head. Blue blood and brain fragments blew out from the rear of its head as it fell back and over the balcony from the force of the bullets and hit the ground below.

Adrian saw grey arms ascend over the balcony and cried out for Rachael to back away. She did not. Four bullets left and she actually enjoyed the experience. She aimed the gun between the arms and fired one bullet as the giant creature raised its head. The impact was hard, and the creature fell back to the ground from which it came. A second creature was coming over the side and Rachael fired into its side cracking ribs and puncturing whatever organs it had. It fell but did not die right away. It screamed and Rachael decided to let it suffer. No more arms came over.

'Just call you Doctor Quick-Shot,' Adrian tried to joke and began to move her away from the window.

Rachael was shaking. The adrenalin of firing a gun combined with killing something was both exhilarating and frightening. Although, she didn't see this is as killing someone; she had killed *something*, a creature. That was very different.

Lights came from above as the evacuation helicopter ascended through the clouds and into the fog below. It hovered after seeing the burning sea king.

Larsen shouted upstairs for Adrian and Rachael to get moving and radioed the helicopter to move to the rear of the house and land on the road where a white flare would be used to mark the area.

Adrian took one last look outside to see people climbing onto the burning helicopter and leaping into the air trying to reach the new one. Some were engulfed by flames and looked like fireworks in the sky as they leapt towards it. Others curled up on the ground as their bodies burnt to a crisp. Even though the bodies were burning, Adrian couldn't smell the smoke.

More noises came from the outside as light armoured vehicles pulled up with thirty soldiers jumping out of two trucks behind. Shots were fired in all directions providing enough cover for the helicopter to land. Larsen got all his men together and pulled Rachael and Adrian into the middle of them, forming a circle around the two civilians. The helicopter broke through the fog and landed hard on the ground bursting a tyre. The side door of this magnificent contraption flung open, and the load master beckoned everyone to get in. Larsen sent the civilians in first then his men while he provided cover.

The trucks and armoured vehicles illuminated the road and house with bright lights. Hundreds of shadows moved in the fog. People from the village and some giant slender figures all trying to reach the soldiers and helicopter.

Larsen fired off into the fog hitting some of the shadows and watching them fall. He was ready to get in when a hand grabbed his ankle and yanked him from the door. The grip was strong and pulled him with such force that he dropped the rifle. He was being dragged away from the chopper by someone or something. He snapped his head around and saw one of the large creatures pulling him away.

The burring of the helicopter and gun fire muffled the screams of his men to get help. Larsen kicked at the creature hard to free his leg. The creature let go briefly and then reached for his neck. Its large fingers easily wrapping around his windpipe that began to squeeze hard. Larsen struck out and hit the creature's ribs. But there was no power in his thrust. He tried again with the same outcome. The creature leaned in. Its fowl breath reached his nostrils and for the first time he genuinely believed this was the end. He couldn't fight the creature on his back. And the grip around his neck was so strong he was beginning to choke and feel the blood restricted to the brain. Unable to inflict damage with his own fists, Larsen began to make peace with the situation. This creature was too strong.

As he began to snatch his final breaths, and the world became dark he saw something about his attacker. His eyes fell to the legs of the creature. It only had one foot. This was the same creature that had attacked Adrian, attacked a former military airman, a comrade, a brother in arms. His peace suddenly turned from demise to anger. This creature had attacked one of his comrades, and that simply would not go unanswered. If he was to die in combat, then he was to do it like his ancestors.

He kicked at the creature's stump, only this time getting the response he wanted and needed. The creature felt the pain and screamed out. Its grip loosened and allowed blood and gas to return to Larsen's brain. He reached to his webbing and ripped the hunting knife from his chest holder. The creature had left just enough time for Larsen to push the knife deep into the creature's stomach. The pop of flesh was a relief to Larsen. Bringing it back out he thrust it into the creature's bony concaved chest. The creature fell to the side as Larsen scrambled on top of it. Now Larsen leaned in close to the creature's face.

'All this way to die by my hand,' Larsen said and brought the knife high above his head and aiming the blade edge straight down.

The creature stared up at Larsen and was about to scream when the knife blade slashed its windpipe preventing anymore cat-like noises from its mouth. The creature reached for its throat. Larsen did not want the creature to have the satisfaction of stemming the flow of blue blood from its wound. He grabbed the large hand by the wrist and held it away with all his strength. Using his knee and almost sitting on the creature's face he held the other hand down. He watched as the life began to fade with the loss of blood from his attacker.

Click-click…click.

Finally, the teeth stopped chomping and the clicking subsided.

Now it was the human's turn to smile down at the creature. Revenge is a dish best served cold, and in the freezing temperature, the personification of such a phrase was never been truer.

A hand reached from behind taking Larsen by surprise that he brought the knife back up for another attack. He stopped himself when he saw the face of Adrian pulling him away from the dead creature and to helicopter. The load master called for the pilot to get up and get home. The chopper's blades raised, and the helicopter rose into the air in a flurry of snow. The fog was dense, but they could all see the fires around Røyken as bright orange and reds.

Larsen quickly got onto the radio to command, 'Alpha to Ulysses, inbound for command. Pull the troops out of Røyken before we lose any more men tonight.'

'Welcome home, captain. We're pulling troops out of Røyken now.'

The helicopter rose above the fog and into the night sky. The machine leaned forward and accelerated towards Oslo. The small town of Røyken, now consumed with creatures and people infected with the virus was illuminated only by the fires.

A few minutes later two F-35 Lightning's swooped passed to the right and deployed bombs when the army had got to a safe distance. The clouds below brightened white then yellow as the bombs detonated on the village behind them. Rachael felt a tear of both joy and sadness over the bombs demolishing everything; her home, her life and those people below gone with a simple push of a button.

38

'Captain, glad to see you back home safe,' Colonel Becker greeted Larsen with a handshake at Oslo Gardemoen airport.

Larsen looked around as he shook his colonel's hand. Tents had been erected all around the airport. F-16's and F-35 fighter jets were parked on ramps that were usually reserved for passenger aircraft, now moved to other areas of the airport.

'We have the airport to ourselves now. This was a plan back in the Cold War days. Ha, we never actually though we would do this for real,' Becker said.

Larsen just looked surprised, 'When did this happen?'

'Let's get you inside; we need to discuss things, captain. Bring your men and who are these two civilians?'

Larsen called Rachael and Adrian to the colonel, 'medical Doctor Adrian Hope, and Doctor Rachael Taylor. These two should be included at my request. Their expertise may be useful to us.'

Becker looked at them both, 'Fine, at this point there is no use in hiding information anymore. We've already been screwed by our own government. Happily, I am now in command.'

They went into the terminal where communications had been

set up. A large map of Norway lay on a table with red circles around Oslo, Bergen, Trondheim, and Tromsø. Thirty men and women were bent over computers, radars, and radios. Military personnel from all services ran to and from the airport's lounges and walkways.

'Take a seat people, we need to catch up,' Becker said. 'We were caught by surprise. It seems Røyken was not the only place these things have shown up,' he pointed to the large map of Norway and continued, 'and it's not just Norway that has been targeted. UK, USA, Europe, Russia, Australia, all over the word. And each target is just outside major cities. We have drafted in reserves and former military personal from all over Norway, but we are still desperately undermanned, and we do not have the resources. We are fighting these damn things and our own people. Our prime minister, senior members of parliament and Royal Family has been airlifted to a secure location in Svalbard to meet with other world leaders. Again, Norway has not seen this since the Second World War.'

Larsen spoke up, 'Sir, what is our next move?'

Two F-35s took off from runway nineteen-right causing the glass to shake in their frames. Bright yellow and blue flames extended from their engines as they climbed into the air.

Becker looked towards the window seeing two afterburners ascend into the black sky, 'We begin *our* attack.'

It was Rachael that went to the large window, formerly where holiday makers would go to watch the large passenger aircraft take off and land. She glanced out of the window onto the bright-lit runway. There were no passenger planes now and no passengers in the terminal. She had flown from here a few times, but now the place seemed as alien as those creatures.

Adrian joined his fiancée at the window and placed a hand around her shoulders. His words were soft yet sent an icy chill through Rachael's spine, 'I don't think we will ever look up at those stars again and wonder.'

Nothing else needed to be said.

The fight now was to take back the world, for governments to put aside their differences, petty rivalries to end, was all for the good of mankind. The only real question was…

… Could they work together as one?

THE END